Also by Sharon Ashwood

Ravenous

SCORCHED

The Dark Forgotten

SHARON ASHWOOD

A SIGNET ECLIPSE BOOK

SIGNET ECLIPSE
Published by New American Library, a division of
Penguin Group (USA) Inc., 375 Hudson Street,
New York, New York 10014, USA
Penguin Group (Canada), 90 Eglinton Avenue East, Suite 700, Toronto,
Ontario M4P 2Y3, Canada (a division of Pearson Penguin Canada Inc.)
Penguin Books Ltd., 80 Strand, London WC2R 0RL, England
Penguin Ireland, 25 St. Stephen's Green, Dublin 2,
Ireland (a division of Penguin Books Ltd.)
Penguin Group (Australia), 250 Camberwell Road, Camberwell, Victoria 3124,
Australia (a division of Pearson Australia Group Pty. Ltd.)
Penguin Books India Pvt. Ltd., 11 Community Centre, Panchsheel Park,
New Delhi - 110 017, India
Penguin Group (NZ), 67 Apollo Drive, Rosedale, North Shore 0632,
New Zealand (a division of Pearson New Zealand Ltd.)
Penguin Books (South Africa) (Pty.) Ltd., 24 Sturdee Avenue,
Rosebank, Johannesburg 2196, South Africa

Penguin Books Ltd., Registered Offices:
80 Strand, London WC2R 0RL, England

First published by Signet Eclipse, an imprint of New American Library,
a division of Penguin Group (USA) Inc.

First Printing, December 2009
10 9 8 7 6 5 4 3 2 1

Copyright © Naomi Lester, 2009
All rights reserved

SIGNET ECLIPSE and logo are trademarks of Penguin Group (USA) Inc.

Printed in the United States of America

PUBLISHER'S NOTE
This is a work of fiction. Names, characters, places, and incidents either are the
product of the author's imagination or are used fictitiously, and any resemblance
to actual persons, living or dead, business establishments, events, or locales is
entirely coincidental.
    The publisher does not have any control over and does not assume any re-
sponsibility for author or third-party Web sites or their content.

October 1, 7:15 p.m.
101.5 FM

"**G**ood evening to all you fanged and furry listeners out there in radio land. This is Errata, your hostess from CSUP, the FM station that *denies* and *defies* the normal in paranormal. It's October first and a crisp evening up here on the Fairview U campus. Looks like there'll be frost on the pumpkin tonight.

"We have our usual dark and dangerous lineup ahead, but first a special alert. It's come to our attention that a certain demon detective is back in town. Word has it he's been lying low for the past while, but my informants spotted this local bad boy out and about last night. Welcome back from the dark side, detective, but be careful of all those bridges you burned last year. I think the footing's a little treacherous.

"Oh, and by the way, I wouldn't count on running a tab at the local watering hole—I think a Thanksgiving turkey has a better chance of long-term credit."

Chapter 1

So, they buried her at a crossroads.
Some folks just bring that out in people.

Conall Macmillan shoved his hands into the pockets of his Windbreaker. Autumn dusk closed around him in shades of blue and charcoal, heavy with seaside moisture. It would be dark in minutes. He could hear the wash of waves in the silence. St. Andrew's Cemetery was empty, except for the dead. And him, of course, though where he fit on the whole dead/live continuum was open to debate.

The grave lay at the intersection of two white paved walkways, smack in the way of joggers and dog walkers. Not much of a crossroads, but enough to keep her down. It said something that the ones doing the burying had been vampires. They didn't scare easily, but the woman now resting beneath the earth had been a demon, a monster's monster, evil pure as ... What was the right comparison, anyway?

Mac looked up at the fading horizon, memories as black and sharp-edged as the cedars etched against the ocean. Sudden, cold nausea invaded his gut, riding a wave of remembrance at once intimate and brutal.

What could compare to the desperate, terrifying hunger that had flayed him until he shrugged off humanity like a tattered bathrobe? What could compare with the silver

sweetness of each human soul as it slid over his teeth and
down his throat like a delicate summer wine?

Each life was a drop of relief in a desert of desperate
need. That was the thirst of a demon, a soul eater. A mur-
derer. He knew, because the woman beneath the crossroads
had made Mac just like her. Walking evil.

The brass plaque on the headstone simply read: GENEVA.
It had been a year since she was placed, suddenly human
and instantly dead, beneath the dirt.

A breeze hushed through the leaves that littered the
lawn, an anticipatory sound. The wind was changing as the
sun bloodied the sea, carrying in the smell of brine. Mac
walked around Geneva's last home, viewing it from every
angle.

*What am I looking for? To reassure myself she's really
down there—human, deceased, and rotting the way she's
supposed to?* Not a good thought. Geneva had been beautiful, for all her wicked ways. The memory of her still brought
heat to his flesh.

He'd always gone for the wrong women, the kind who
weren't interested in forever. After years on the squad, his
heart was entombed in dead bodies and paperwork, insu-
lated against a cop's daily dose of carnage. A quick and
dirty grapple in the dark was all he had to give and those
mad, bad babes fit him to a T.

So when a pretty blonde had invited him for a drink,
he'd considered it lucky, but business as usual. Bad mistake.
Life-ending mistake.

Now the forever kind of woman was beyond his grasp.
Even if he dared to make her his own, one day he might
fall off the wagon and then it would be, "Sorry, darling. I
scarfed down the kids."

A short brick wall encircled Geneva's plot, holding in
the sod. The site was on a hill and had views of everything:
the ocean, the acres of yew trees and headstones, even
glimpses of the strip mall to the north. It was fitting. Geneva had loved to be in the center of things.

Dead center, ha-ha, Mac thought bitterly.

A desolate feeling stole over him. It was bad when you had to laugh at your own lousy puns. Fortunate that he wasn't a drinker. It would be far too nice to forget everything, even for just a little while.

Thunk!

A knife thrummed into the dirt at his foot, silver blade quivering as it struck. The dark steel hilt had the elegant simplicity of all vampire armaments.

Mac hunched, his spine itching at every spot where the knife might have struck. "What?" he snapped to the empty air.

The answer was dry with sarcasm. "You finally showed up. It's been a year."

Mac had forgotten how much he hated that low, smooth, arrogant voice. His teeth clenched so hard, pain shot up his left temple.

Between one blink and the next, Alessandro Caravelli appeared on the other side of the grave, his weight resting on one hip. Yes, it had been a year since they last met. Shrink-wrapped in leather, the vampire still had the rock 'n' roll biker vibe going on: boots, studs, and attitude. Curly wheat blond hair fell past his shoulders; his amber eyes were steady, unblinking, and not at all friendly.

"The sword's a nice touch," Mac said. "Very retro."

The vampire held the huge blade loosely at his side. "Special edition. It kills everything. Even demons."

Despite himself, Mac felt a sizzle of fear. "I'm not a demon anymore. I'm not evil. I'm cured."

Caravelli's chin lifted; he took a subtle sniff of the breeze. "Faint, but the demon stink is there."

Mac's lip curled at the insult. "Oh, yeah, and seeing you brings back all the good times, Caravelli. I've so missed your bad-assed sheriff-to-the-Undead routine."

"I still keep the law among the supernatural citizens in Fairview." Without a flicker of expression, Caravelli took a step closer. "And you're still a danger. You were Geneva's thrall. Our enemy."

"Yeah, well . . ." Mac trailed off. The events of a year

ago were confused in Mac's mind, but he remembered the
essential facts. Geneva picked a fight with Fairview's supernatural community—werebeast and vampire, demon
and fey—in a bid to control the territory. Yes, he had
fought with the black hats, being a demon and all at the
time.

His side lost. Holly Carver, a witch, had turned the
tide, blasting Geneva with a spell so powerful that it had
stripped away the demon's powers. The moment Geneva
became human, her own soldiers had killed her. Drained
her blood. Left her corpse to the mercy of her enemies.

It's hard to get good help when you're an archvillain. It's
even harder to change careers from henchdemon to harm-
less civilian.

Caravelli frowned, a slight movement of his foot signaling his impatience.

Oh, crap. Shifting his weight, Mac forced himself not
to bolt, though the urge burned along every nerve. *Never
show a vampire fear.* He couldn't take his eyes off Caravelli's sword. *How come I'm walking around unarmed?
Stupid!* He'd lost the habit of carrying weapons during his
demon days.

Mac played his only card. "Hear me out. I was caught by
the same spell as Geneva. If she was made human again,
so was I."

It worked. The vampire lowered the blade an inch or
two. "Then tell me this. You disappeared after the battle.
We looked for you. The queen offered a reward for your
return. Where have you been?"

"Out of my mind." Mac looked away. "Yeah, I feel
guilty. I was a cop, for God's sake. Geneva made me turn
against everything I stood for." Heat rushed up his face, but
he forced himself to meet Caravelli's gaze. "I didn't join
her willingly. She corrupted me. You know that. You were
there."

For the first time, Caravelli showed emotion. Damn him,
it was pity. "That would've been the point, with her."

Mac used a few pithy obscenities. "Yeah, ain't that the truth."

It had taken only one long, hot kiss to infect him with that craving for human life. A hunger he hadn't entirely lost. Not that he was going to mention that to Caravelli and his meat cleaver.

Now Mac let himself take a step back, then another. "I'm sorry for what I did. I've prayed for some means to atone. It's not enough, but there's nothing else I can offer."

"Not so fast." With a rush of wind and leather, Caravelli sprang into the air, sailing lightly over Geneva's grave. For a moment, he hung there like a biker bird of prey.

Mac scrambled backward, the instinct to run winning out. His legs felt clumsy, as if he were trying to run on bags of water. Caravelli's arms stretched out, the moonlight kissing the sword and the studs on his coat and boots. He had barely touched down when he bounded again, right over Mac's head. Mac spun. The vampire landed with a muffled thud, his boots sinking into soft grass as he turned to face him. The force of his landing stirred up the smell of dew-soaked grass and leaves.

Crouching, Caravelli lifted the sword in both hands, the tip level with Mac's chest. "You have to pay," he said softly. "Sorry or not, you broke the law. We can live among the humans only so long as we do not harm them. You drank them down like cheap beer. Perhaps it's not your fault, but demons destroy. It's their nature."

Caravelli said it with the tired cadence of a cop reading a criminal's rights. Mac wondered whether he'd sounded the same when making an arrest—utterly, remorselessly cold.

"Not anymore. I've lost the ability to feed," Mac replied carefully, keeping his own voice level. He would not beg to live. He would never beg Caravelli, the bloody-fanged poseur, but he had to set the record straight. "I eat spaghetti now. Bagels. Frosty Flakes. No souls. I'm corporeal. No magic tricks. I must be human."

The lie was ash on Mac's tongue. They both heard the falsehood.

"But you're *not* human, so what the hell are you?" asked the vampire.

I'm hungry. He might have lost the ability to feed, but not the desire. "I haven't a clue."

The statement hung between them, the deepening darkness giving a hazy aura of nightmare. "The spell didn't Turn you all the way back," Caravelli said neutrally. "It's not over."

An involuntary shiver made Mac cross his arms. The pain of the spell's blast had been surreal, almost beyond his perception. "I was at the edge of the spell's power."

"Too bad. I might have been able to pardon you if it had worked." His regret sounded real.

Mac's temper snapped like rotten elastic. Blood rushed to his face. "What the hell, Caravelli? Why bother? I'm already dead in any way that matters. Everyone I ever loved is terrified of me. I've lost my friends. I've lost my family. I've lost my job. The very essence of who I was has been twisted and perverted. Anything you do is plain overkill."

"And yet," said the vampire, "killing you is why I'm here."

Fright and anger narrowed Mac's vision until all he could see were Caravelli's burning amber eyes. He *hated* him. Why the *hell* did this bloodsucker get to pass judgment? Mac stabbed his finger in the air. "Go sit on a stake. Leave me alone. I came back here to figure this out."

Caravelli hoisted the sword, taking a slow, deliberate practice swing. He was toying with Mac, drawing out the kill. Stalling. "Figure what out?"

"Damn you! Isn't it obvious?"

Caravelli looked up, eyebrow raised. "What?"

"I want my old life back. I don't destroy. I'm the guy with the badge who saves people. That's who I need to be." Mac sucked in a deep breath. "I want to be human again."

To his utter fury, Caravelli laughed. He *laughed*.

That pushed Mac's misery one step too far. Faster than

a human eye could follow, his hand shot out, grabbing the vampire's sword arm by the wrist. The laughter jerked to silence. Caravelli tried to tear away, out of Mac's demon-strong grip. Not a budge. Caravelli swore in some other, antique language.

Satisfaction blossomed, an ugly bloom born of frustration. Mac tightened his fingers long enough to make a point, and then shoved Caravelli backward as if he were no more than a boy.

The vampire stumbled, but somehow made it look like a dance step. His look was sharp, as if he had just solved a puzzle. "You were holding back. I thought so. I needed to know."

"You pushed me till I fought back."

"Anger doesn't lie. Now you've told me just how dangerous you really are."

Mac cursed. He'd been trapped by the shreds of demon still festering inside. Brute strength to go with his brutish, voracious appetite.

The vampire slowly shook his head. "We're all Pinocchio, wishing we were real boys. If only we are good enough, save enough lives, perform the right rituals, sacrifice ourselves—or someone else—we can turn back into the humans we once were. I apologize. I laughed only because what you said was so familiar."

"Give me a chance."

"I died when men still thought the world was flat. I didn't survive by being charitable."

There was a moment's pause. Distant traffic merged with the rush of the ocean. The sharp autumn air carried a tang of wood smoke. It was finally cold enough for Fairview's residents to stoke up the fireplaces and curl up in the warmth and safety of their homes.

Caravelli passed the huge sword from hand to hand as if it weighed no more than a ballpoint pen—a not-so-subtle show of his own strength. Mac wouldn't count on surprising him twice.

The vampire seemed to be musing, taking Mac's measure. The air between them hummed with raw male will-power. Demon rage pulsed against the eggshell of Mac's human facade. It was hard, so hard, not to revel in it, lap it up and surrender to an orgy of fury.

And get chopped to pieces for his trouble. The silence sawed through Mac's nerves. "So, are you going to execute me or what?"

Chapter 2

The blade swept out of nowhere, too fast for the eye to track. Mac dodged, more by instinct than by any conscious decision. Caravelli swung again, using the impetus to wheel in an airborne circle of leather and steel. The follow-through would take Mac's head for sure.

Except Mac slammed to the ground, using the downward slope of the lawn in a quick roll-somersault-vault maneuver that took him over the low iron railing that enclosed a family plot. He heard the sword whoosh through the grass, the quick scrape of metal on gravestone. *Shit!* He bounded over a series of low fences and grave markers as if they were track-and-field hurdles.

I'll take that as a yes on the planning to kill me question.

Feet pounding the grass, Mac ran, not daring to turn to look. He knew Caravelli was behind him. Yeah, running looked weak. He could stand his ground—maybe even take Caravelli despite the sword—but the price was too high. If cornered, Mac's demon instincts would grab control. Those episodes gave new meaning to *mood swing*.

Breath came sharp, laced with the scent of his own sour sweat. He headed for the roadway north of the cemetery, where there was traffic. Even psycho vamps hesitated to slice and dice their victims in front of human witnesses.

Again, Mac ducked, a sixth sense saving him as a blow lanced out of the sky, perfectly silent. The wind in the trees had masked the rustle of air through Caravelli's clothes.

Frigging leech!

Mac zigzagged to make himself a harder target. He dodged angels and crosses, urns draped in stone veils and the virgin weeping granite tears. He knew he was running too fast for a human, saving himself through sheer speed.

From the corner of his eye, Mac saw Caravelli land on the branch of an oak, coat eddying around him, pausing before he leapt again. Mac veered beneath the hawthorn trees, hoping their twisting branches would shelter him. He could see the road now, make out individual cars and streetlights. The bus shelter glowed like a holy temple of safety.

Mac jumped another grave, almost stumbling over it before he saw the overgrown marker. It was a bad takeoff and he landed awkwardly, the lumpy ground wrenching his foot. *Crap!* He let himself roll into the fall and back onto his feet, pelting forward.

This time he heard Caravelli's approach, the vampire's boots on the grass, and he jerked aside. The tip of the sword kissed his ear, a nip meant to be a killing blow. *Shit!*

Gathering a last push of speed, he sprang over the low iron fence of the cemetery, thumping to the sidewalk just in time to see the city bus rumble around the corner. Mac sprinted toward the bus shelter, waving his arms for the driver to stop.

For God's sake, Caravelli, stay in the graveyard with the other dead things!

The bus loomed, its bright bulk slowing as Mac ran forward. The door wheezed open and Mac ran up the steps into a hot fog of humanity. At the smell, a sudden rush of soul hunger ached in his gut. He turned and looked, but the vampire was nowhere in sight.

Thank you, God.

He grabbed the sticky pole as the bus lurched forward, using his free hand to dig in his jeans pocket for coins. They clanked as they fell into the fare box.

"Nearly missed me," said the driver, steering back into traffic.

"Yeah," said Mac, still breathing hard. "Lucky I caught you." *Life-saving lucky*.

He picked his way over feet and backpacks until he found a sideways seat near the back exit. Advertising lined the bus walls.

PREGNANT AND NEED HELP?

WEREWOLF PACK SILVERTAIL VOTES FOR LEASH-FREE PARKS!

CHEAP PAYDAY LOANS!

ADDICTED TO VAMPIRE VENOM? YOU'RE NOT JUST ANOTHER JUNKIE. WE CAN HELP.

Mac read the bus number. The five. That route went downtown, which was where he lived, anyway. Not that he could go home. Caravelli would be waiting. *What the bloody hell am I going to do?*

He checked his watch. Just after eight. His arm felt heavy with spent adrenalin. All over his body, nerves pinged as they reset to a normal resting state.

So are all the vamps after me, or just the Fanged Avenger? Hard to say. Mac had been back in town a few weeks, but had only just started to venture outside his apartment for more than groceries. The places he'd been scouting for gossip didn't cater to vamps. Still, it was safest to assume the worst.

So what next? He couldn't think. He was too pumped on fear and outrage, his pounding pulse making all else seem bizarrely slow.

A droopy guy across the aisle was staring blankly at Mac, the wires from his earphones trailing like white brain-spaghetti to the pocket of his hoodie. The girl slumped next to him was chewing gum like a nervous sheep. Peppermint weighted the stuffy air.

Nothing special. Just humans. They had no idea how precious ordinary was. Once upon a time, Mac had been them.

The whole supernatural thing had started in Y2K, just after he'd made detective. The vamps had come into the public eye at the turn of the millennium, creating a ratings bonanza for more than one euphoric talk show mogul. The other supernatural species had followed. The reason for the big reveal: the shrinking, computerized world made it impossible to live in secret any longer. The supernaturals wanted integration. Citizenship. Credit cards. A piece of the economic pie.

Good luck. Humans were quick to give lip service to pan-species rights legislation, but slow to make real changes. Too many humans wanted the spooks and weirdoes gone. Others wanted to exploit them.

Meanwhile, as the humans bickered about what to do, the monsters were building houses, businesses, and communities. In ten years, few of the students riding this bus would remember a time when an ad for Zom-B-Gone perimeter fencing was anything but normal.

But Mac would. *And I remember when old friends would say hello, not cross themselves and run the other way.*

The vehicle took a corner too fast, forcing him to grab the stained vinyl seat for support. He could see the lights of the downtown now, with the dense sparkle of the Fairview University campus to his right.

The bus stopped, and a woman got on, towing a stroller, a toddler, and an armful of grocery bags. Mac got up and let her have his seat. He stood in the aisle, grabbing the overhead rail as the bus jolted back into motion.

Then Mac heard a footfall on the top of the bus, too soft for the humans to hear. His gaze automatically tracked the sound to a point above the exit door. He heard it again, and then again—the scraping scuff of boots. Annoyance needled him as he realized what was going on. Caravelli hadn't given up. He was on top of the bus, just waiting for Mac to get off.

Crap. Sure, he could call 911 on his cell to report that a homicidal vamp was bus surfing, but why bother? Even if the cops came pronto, Caravelli would be long gone. Human law enforcement just couldn't keep up anymore.

Silently cursing, Mac turned to get a better view out the

window. They'd reached the city center. As the bus trundled to a stop, half the passengers stood, gathering backpacks and newspapers.

Keeping his head down, Mac left the bus right behind sheep girl. The cold night air bit at his face, heavy with the greasy fog of the burger joint on the corner. Mac hustled, staying with the throng past the big-box bookstore, past the pharmacy, past the stereo shop. He could *feel* Caravelli looking for him, the weight of his predator's gaze sliding over Mac's skin. *This is getting old, fast.*

Frustration raked through Mac, a whip snap of rebellious temper. *Damn it!* He spun, searching the street, but could see nothing but humans hurrying about their lives. But he could hear—or was it his imagination?—the vampire's chuckle.

Temper leeched the color from Mac's sight. Knuckles cracked as he clenched his fists, aching soul hunger souring to an urge to rend and tear. *I'm going to kill him.*

No, you're not. He's goading you. Making you easier to kill. Making you a monster.

The demon inside him trembled with eagerness. It was a hairbreadth from grabbing his mental steering wheel. Mac drew in his breath. *I will not surrender. Not to him. Not to myself.*

Walk away. But where? His apartment was too obvious. He needed to hide. Where?

Mac had an idea, then wished he hadn't. But it made sense. Nanette's strap-'em-and-slap-'em funhouse was open around the clock, a place mostly for weres with liberal views on pain. Caravelli wouldn't think of looking for him there. It was a good place to lie low for a few hours. Very low. Like under the bed.

Mac dodged traffic across the busy main drag. He slid into the revolving door of the department store, passing through the stench of the perfume section—that should hide his scent—and then into the connecting shopping center. From there, he exited onto a side street.

He couldn't feel Caravelli's presence any longer. With

luck, he had lost him. In two more blocks, he turned the corner into an alley. The flashing neon from Nanette's Naughty Kitty Basket caught the metal of the iron gates that stood open at the alley entrance. The alley itself was dark and cramped, paved with the same crumbling cedar bricks laid down when the city was young.

And it was empty. Nanette's back door—the one Mac wanted—was far down the alleyway. There was another door he had to pass first, and it usually had at least two hellhounds keeping watch. Caravelli kept them on his payroll. Mac approached cautiously.

Tonight there were no guards. *Sloppy.*

Then again, the door hardly needed security. No one was ever, ever going to break in. There was nothing anyone wanted to do or witness across that threshold.

Hell has no atmosphere and the cafeteria sucks.

Mac's pulse pounded in his temples, quick and fast. He didn't like having to pass that doorway in the old brick wall, but he had to and he turned to look at it. It was about nine feet high, the vertical oak planks reinforced with black iron straps. A heavy bolt secured it from the outside. It looked like something out of Tolkien.

Behind it was a land of nightmares. He'd been there. It wasn't literal hell, but a place called the Castle, a prison for the supernatural. It might as well have been the real pit of fire, because he'd be damned if he ever went back inside.

"Macmillan."

Mac turned to see Caravelli wheel around the corner of the alley, sword in hand. The neon caught the aureole of his curly fair hair, turning it to a multihued halo. The iron gates framed him, a lattice silhouette around the dark, threatening form.

"Back off, fangster." Mac kept his voice level, but anger rose on a flood tide. He waited as Caravelli approached with the cautious grace of a matador.

"You deaf as well as dead?" Mac said, the words stumbling. The demon inside struggled for control. It would feel so good to let it loose, so easy, so free.

Mac fell back a few steps, bumping his shoulders against the wall. *I can still walk away. I don't have to be the thing I hate.*

The vampire was right in front of him now, all aggression. Caravelli's hand slammed against the bricks, barring Mac's path. Mac jerked away, but Caravelli leaned in. The vampire's face, with his strange golden eyes, was inches from Mac's. "You might have just spared me the trouble of cleaning my sword. There is the Castle door. Go inside and don't come back."

Nuh-uh. Mac's hand slammed into Caravelli's midriff, sending the vampire sailing across the alley to smack with a slap of leather and flesh into the ancient bricks. The sword fell with a clang, spiraling end over end before it skittered into the wall.

Mac didn't notice the half dozen hellhounds slouching out of Nanette's back door.

Chapter 3

The mountain of dark brown fur, high as a man at its shoulder, swung his head to growl at Constance, lips curling to reveal scythe-sharp teeth. Drool pattered from the werebeast's jaws to the floor; ruby eyes flared like coals of hellfire. The beast's—Viktor's—deepening rumble vibrated in her breastbone, warning thunder.

There was only one thing that would appease the horrifying monster.

His great, glowing eyes fastened on the spit-soaked, raggedy doll in her hand. Gingerly, Constance held up the toddler-sized toy, doing her best to avoid the damper sections. Viktor hunkered down on his front paws and slid the growl into an expressive whine. As a final plea, he gave a tongue-lolling head tilt.

"Ha!" Constance flung the tattered doll into the murk of the damp, stone corridor, vampire strength giving it distance. The stuffed doll sailed through the air, vanishing against the shadowy ceiling before landing with a faint thump in the dust. "Go, boy! Fetch!"

Viktor wheeled and plunged toward the toy. His jaws champed the air with ferocious glee, the banner of his tail thrashing as he gave a puppyish bounce. Constance lifted her long skirts and sprinted after. Her shoes were silent, drowned out by the scrabble of Viktor's nails on the stone floor of the corridor.

She kept poor, mad Viktor in sight. He might forget what he was chasing and go trotting off to parts unknown, stuck in his beast-form, dangerous, doomed, and dim-witted as a loaf of bread.

They had been chasing the wretched doll for hours, and her feet were starting to hurt. Still, a game of fetch was about Viktor's only pleasure. She wasn't going to deny him. Besides, it wasn't like she could rule her loved ones from the kitchen, the way her mother had. First, she didn't have a kitchen. Second, vampires were notoriously bad cooks. She had to come up with something besides mealtimes to keep the household together—so she threw the doll.

Giving what we can is what families do. What does it matter if we're not blood relations?

Mind you, not every family had a senile werebeast on its hands—though she did dimly remember a human uncle who'd come close after one too many pints of ale.

Constance stopped running long enough to push her hair out of her eyes. She watched as Viktor scooped up the doll and shook it with nightmare fury. The sheer savagery in Viktor's growl scuttled over her skin, raising gooseflesh.

Some creature of the night you are, Constance. Scared of a dog.

She would have been happier by a bright fire, or anyplace with light. It was always dark in the Castle's windowless, cavernous halls. The maze of hallways and chambers, stairs and archways, audience rooms and lifeless grottos meandered into infinity around her. It was all stone—irregular, gray, damp, and mortared with magic a millennium old.

Torches dotted the corridors, set into black iron brackets in the walls. They wavered, but never went out, throwing smears of smoky light for a scant few feet beyond the flames. It was never enough to really see what was there, hiding in the shadows. The Castle liked its privacy.

Understandable. The Castle was a prison for foul things like her. There was no *outside*, just the endless, rambling interior. Prisoners roamed free to make alliances, to set up kingdoms and networks of spies, to make war, or to suffer as the slave of another.

Memories made Constance edgy. Her fingers brushed the knife she wore at her belt, the bone and steel hilt worn smooth with time. It was useful for a thousand daily tasks, but she'd fought with it, too. She passionately hated violence, but in the Castle weakness was an invitation to worse than death.

She had been trapped in this world between worlds as soon as she had been Turned—or at least mostly Turned—when she was barely seventeen. She'd been an ordinary servant girl on an Irish farm who had played with the dogs and her brothers and sisters and had gone to work as soon as she was strong enough to carry a pail of milk. *So long ago. So much change.*

But parts of her hadn't changed. She still played with dogs. Constance grabbed the leg of the doll, wrestling with it. Viktor whined, hanging on as she made a show of struggling. Finally, he wrenched it free and galloped into the darkness.

"Stop!" she called after him, breaking into a run again. "Get back here, you sorry lump of fur!"

Viktor ignored her, pausing midlope to chase his tail. He understood her well enough, but had lost the ability to return to human form. His brother, Josef, had escaped to the world outside. That desertion was hard to forgive, but still Constance loved them all: Viktor, Josef, and young Sylvius. *They are everything I have.*

That was true now more than ever since they had followed their master to this deserted corner of the Castle. Atreus of Muria, sorcerer and king, had been exiled. Constance had been his maidservant since she came to the Castle, so now she was in exile, too.

It was a relief. Finally, Constance had time to do more than dodge backstabbing courtiers eager for favor and power. She could dream. To her, exile was another word for peace, a calm that allowed for fantasies of her own home, with a big kitchen table and loved ones gathered around, telling stories, making music, sharing plenty. *Happiness*.

How she yearned for that home to be real.

Constance whistled around her fingers. Viktor came trotting on paws the size of platters. The toy drooped from his jowls, stuffing leaking like entrails.

"There's a good lad." She thumped his shoulder.

He wagged his tail all the way to his haunches, sporting the idiot grin of a happy dog.

Then Constance heard footsteps.

She froze.

Boots. Several pairs. Crossing the corridor up ahead. Viktor gave a low *whuff*, dropping the doll. She shrank against the wall, just in case the owner of one of those pairs of boots would turn and see her. *Oh, bollocks*.

Every prison has its jailers. The Castle, dungeon for all creatures possessed of magic, had the guardsmen. Once ordinary men, they had been taken from their homes and forced into service. The Castle gave them strength and immortality but took away the kernel of whatever made them human.

The guardsmen had snatched Constance, just risen from her grave, and put her in this terrible place. If Atreus hadn't taken her in as his serving girl, they would have broken her as they had so many others, one indignity at a time.

Her gut twisted at the memory, a sick feeling welling into her throat. She threw the doll again, farther this time, to trick Viktor into running safely out of sight of the marching men. For once doing what he was supposed to, the beast bounded after it.

Constance began walking backward, too nervous to take her eyes from the guardsmen for more than a moment. As she retreated, her fingers trailed along the stone wall, whispering over cold, rough stone punctuated by grit-filled seams. The solid feel of it reassured her.

A change in the air currents behind her said she was backing toward another hallway, somewhere she could vanish from sight. Then she would circle around and find out where the guards were going. What could they want in this deserted corner of the Castle? There was no one here but her family.

She spun on her heel, and then sprang back with a hiss. A dozen steps away stood the guardsmen's officer, his feet planted apart, his hands clasped behind his back.

"Captain Reynard!" Her hand was on the hilt of her knife.

"Constance," he replied. "Did I startle you? If so, I do apologize."

His accent spoke of wealth and education—all the advantages she'd never had. She pressed her lips together, saying nothing. *Why are you here?* she wondered.

"I thought a vampire's hearing would detect my approach," he went on. "You must have been distracted."

He walked toward her, tall, aristocratic, and darkly handsome. His captain's uniform—a faded remnant from his human life—was neatly mended, every bit of gold braid shining in its proper place. He might have been whisked out of his old life centuries ago and put in charge of this slice of hell, but he still had the discipline of a British officer.

He paused a few feet away, looking down at her. Next to him, she felt small as a child, pinned by his pale gray eyes. She swallowed, nervous. Reynard wasn't as brutal as his men, but he still held the keys to the jail. He might be friendly, but never a friend.

"You shouldn't wander alone, pretty Constance," he said. "That little knife of yours just isn't enough."

"Viktor's with me, sir."

Reynard folded his arms and looked around. "That would be more effective if he was actually visible. He comes to anyone's call, you know, even mine. He's too daft to know his own master."

"That doesn't worry me, Captain, sir. I have teeth of my own."

"Like a tiny little tabby cat, and about as fearsome." His mouth quirked, a hint of a sad smile.

There was no flirtation in it, but still she looked away,

flustered by an involuntary twinge of interest. She liked
a different kind of man, but the captain was a fine speci-
men nonetheless. It reminded her that hundreds of years
past, she'd been a young woman. Now she was a monster
that existed only because the magic of the Castle kept her
alive.

Reynard reached out, one fingertip touching the pendant that rested just below her collarbone. The slight pressure made her shiver.

"A skilled piece of work. Bronze, is it?"

"Yes, sir. Sylvius made it from an arrowhead. He said it
is a reminder to see the possibilities in what's around us."
She avoided the captain's eyes, instead watching the torchlight dance on the gold braid of his coat. "He's taken to
working with his hands."

"Not a natural warrior, then."

"He's just a boy, sir," she replied, her tone stiff.

Reynard retreated a little under the sting of her words.
"How is Atreus? Is his mind still wandering?"

"He is the same." It was a lie. Her master was failing, but
she wouldn't betray his dignity.

"Poor Constance. I'm sure the burden of his care falls
on you."

"There is little to do, sir, and it is my place to serve
him."

"But what about visitors?"

"No one bothers to come to this part of the Castle." *Except you. Why are you here? Why are your men here?*

"Isolation doesn't bring safety, especially when fear is
in the air."

She gave a sour laugh. "There's always fear, Captain.
There are always wars between the vampires and the werebeasts, or between one warlord and the next. To tell you the
plain truth, sir, I'm tired of worrying about it."

"This is different."

"How, sir?"

His shrug tried to be casual, but it showed tension.
"There are stories running like roaches through the halls.

Whispers and murmurs claim that in the darkest corners of the Castle, the corridors have collapsed. Rooms are vanishing. Creatures have been driven from the deeps and wander the halls at will."

Constance leaned against the cold stone wall, now a little amused. "But, sir, surely no one believes this? There're plenty of monsters here without adding fairy tales."

But the shadows in his eyes grew deeper.

Holy Mother, there's something to this. Her stomach grew hard and chill.

"Myths grow with the telling," he said. "Both guardsmen and prisoners teeter on the edge of panic. It gives new fuel to the wars, and you know the guards aren't invincible. No new recruits have come since my time. There aren't enough of us anymore to stop every skirmish."

Constance frowned, her mind scrambling to sort through the conversation. "Captain Reynard, why are you here? Why are you telling me this? Were you with the patrol? What has any of this to do with my family?"

"That was no patrol." Reynard lowered his eyes from her face. In that instant, he seemed to age a decade, the lines around his mouth and eyes falling into bitter grooves. "We're on a different errand. You know I will do what I can to keep peace here."

She nodded, not liking his tone.

"There is something they all desire—Prince Miru-kai, Shoshann, and all the other warlords and sorcerers of the Castle. This thing is a danger to both the prisoners and my men, and it is left carelessly unguarded. For a time, the warlords lost all knowledge of its location, but now their spies have found it. Precious secrets don't lie hidden forever."

His harsh expression, even more than his words, fanned her anxiety. "Then you must lock it safely away!"

He lifted his chin. "That's my intent."

"Why are you telling me this? What is it?"

"I want you—of all people—to understand." He said it quickly, the words clipped, and turned away.

Constance grabbed his sleeve. "Captain, wait! Why does it matter what I think? I'm no one."

He pulled himself free, his touch nearly as cold as her own. His eyes had gone flat, all sympathy between them ended. "You're still an innocent, Constance, despite all that you've seen. Maybe I'm looking for absolution for doing my duty."

Constance let her hand fall away. "What is this thing that everyone wants?" she demanded.

But Reynard strode away from her instead, stiff and silent. He moved as if the uniform alone kept him from crumbling to ash.

She slumped against the wall, bewildered. She didn't have patience for this sort of riddle. Captain Reynard should have just spit out what he had to say. Now he'd made her afraid.

Deeply afraid.

Up ahead, she could hear boots on the stone floor. Reynard had joined his men. Now four guardsmen were marching toward the part of the Castle where her family lived, and she had no idea what they wanted. Their mysterious treasure? *Why are they looking for it here?*

She whistled for Viktor. After a long moment, he came bounding out of the shadows with his doll. She dug her fingers into his heavy coat, grateful for his reassuring warmth.

"Come on, boyo," she whispered into his ear. "We have to go home. I don't know what we're going to do about our visitors, but Atreus isn't himself and Sylvius is too young to help him. You and I have to be the level heads."

Viktor looked doubtful.

"Best leave the talking to me," said Constance.

He woofed agreement, drooling around the doll.

With one hand clutching the werebeast's fur, she followed the guardsmen, keeping a long way back. Viktor padded at her side, possessively close. *What do they want with us?* she wondered. *We've already lost everything we had.* Constance turned hot, and then cold as anger and apprehension chased each other through her blood.

There were no gates or fences to define the borders of her family's home, but everyone in the Castle knew where their neighbor's territory lay. Atreus's corner of the dungeon was a handful of chambers clustered around a square hall.

The guardsmen strode directly into the hall and formed a semicircle, standing an equal distance apart. Constance lingered in the doorway like a half-remembered ghost, Viktor still at her side.

Despite the four visitors, the room felt bare. There was furniture, but it was plain wood pitted with centuries of use. At one end of the room was a high-backed armchair, sculpted like the throne of an ancient king. No subjects waited at its feet.

Atreus sat on it, one finger tapping his lips, watching but saying nothing. That stillness meant the calm before a storm of temper. Either Captain Reynard didn't know, or didn't care.

"Sorcerer," Reynard said, with the merest sliver of a bow—a show of courtesy, not subservience.

"Captain." Atreus nodded. He shifted on the great chair, light playing over the soft folds of his jeweled blue robe. A sleek circlet of gold bound his mass of ink-black hair. His face was strong, rough-hewn and swarthy, the visage of a prince. "You trespass here, you and your guardsmen. This is my place now."

Reynard gave the specter of a smile. "You cannot bar the door from us. You have no army."

"I have followers."

"You have a dog." Reynard's eyes slid toward the door, where Constance hovered. "And a vampire who's never tasted blood. Almost a human. Lovely to look at, but weak."

Constance felt hot shame crawling up her cheeks. A look of surprise flickered in Reynard's eyes, as if he hadn't expected his words to sting. He looked quickly away. "You must negotiate with us, Atreus of Muria, if you expect to live here in peace."

Atreus rose, taller than even the largest of the guardsmen. "I ruled a kingdom within this Castle. I kept order over the demons and werebeasts when you could not. Who are you to give or take permission? You are merely turnkeys, lackeys of the prison."

Reynard locked gazes. "It's no secret your magic has rotted away to nothing."

"Lies and rumors."

"Truth. Your subjects chose a new king and left you to scrape an existence out of dust. You're finished. A ghost with barely a chain to rattle."

As Reynard spoke, Atreus's face flushed dark with rage. He fingered the hem of his wide, draping cuff, kneading it as angry tension soaked the air.

"I speak the truth," Reynard repeated softly, almost in apology. "Think of the loyal few who stay with you. For the sake of their welfare, you must listen to what I have to say."

Atreus looked over Reynard's head, as if the guardsman were beneath notice. The seam of the cuff was starting to give, the ancient silk shredding between his hands. "I ruled. I held the power and wealth of the Castle's vampire clans, the prides and the packs, between my hands. I took tribute from those who came to me for refuge from your beatings and your shackles. Do not speak to me of sacrifice for the sake of my subjects. I have sheltered them for a hundred of your lifetimes."

Among the guardsmen, there were impatient shuffles of feet and shared glances. Constance heard tearing cloth, and winced. She was running out of thread to mend her master's robes.

Reynard shook his head. "Prince Miru-kai sends spies deep into your territory. Soon his warriors will take what little you have left. You need our help."

"You would help me as a jackal helps a wounded lion."

Constance slipped from the doorway into the room, past

Reynard, and took her place at her master's side. She gave the guardsman a hot glare.

Atreus glanced down, dark eyes barely focusing on her face before he turned back to Reynard. She put her hand over her master's, stilling his fingers, smoothing the hem of his sleeve.

The Captain rested his hand on the hilt of his sword. "We will keep you from harm, but first there is something that you must surrender. It tempts others."

"But you said yourself that I have nothing."

"You still hold one object of great value," said Reynard.

"Do I?" Atreus returned.

"Something others will try and take." Reynard gave Constance another of his sad looks.

"Oh!" She suddenly understood. *Holy Bridget, no.* She should have guessed. Should have known. Reynard had tried to prepare her—as if that were even possible.

Constance felt suddenly light-headed, as if a void had opened where her stomach should have been. *Reynard, you cold bastard. This is what you consider your duty?*

She looked up at her master. "No, don't let them!"

Atreus gave her a quelling glance, his fingers working at his robe again. "Whatever I have, I can defend."

Reynard narrowed his eyes. "I think not."

"Don't let them!"

"Be silent, girl!" Atreus warned, his voice sharp and dark as an obsidian blade. "You're not a fishwife bickering at the market. The wrong word at the wrong time is as fatal as a plague."

Constance nearly bit her tongue in her haste to close her mouth. Part of her wanted to die and turn to dust. The rest—the bigger part—wanted to explode with fury.

Atreus put one hand on her shoulder, gripping it tight. "Silence."

Constance squirmed, until he squeezed all the harder.

Reynard took a deep breath and let it out slowly. "Give us what we want, and we'll keep your enemies away."

"And if we do not?"

"If I were in your position that is a chance I would not care to take."

Atreus dropped his hand from Constance's shoulder. "What do you want?" he asked. "A spell book? A jewel?"

Reynard's eyes grew hard, skating past Constance as if she weren't there. "The incubus you call Sylvius."

My son.

Chapter 4

Outrage jolted Constance so hard that she gripped the arm of Atreus's chair to keep from staggering. Her one instinct was to stay upright. If she was standing, she could defend her child.

Something moved behind the guardsmen, gliding through the shadows.

Not something. Someone. *Oh, no.*

As if he had come at the mention of his name, Sylvius paused in the arch of the doorway, the gray stone framing him against the eternal dark beyond. He was as tall as Atreus, but pale as moonlight. He wore only loose trews of dark silk. Muscles rippled under his fair skin, but his was the lean body of a youth, not a seasoned warrior. Silver hair fell thick and straight to his hips. Startling dark eyes dominated a long, angular face that was softened only by a wide, expressive mouth.

Just sixteen, Sylvius had never set foot outside the Castle. A foundling, Constance had raised him from a babe.

His posture was drawn tight, like a bow about to fire, or a bird about to take flight. She could see from his face he'd heard every word. Her lips parted. Instinct made her want to call out—to warn Sylvius, to comfort him, to bring him to her side—but caution won out. Every second he remained unseen by the guardsmen, he remained safe. Constance dropped her eyes and forced her face into a neutral mask.

She wasn't a good enough actor. Reynard raised a brow and turned his head slowly toward the doorway. "And there he is."

Calm, almost casual, Atreus sat again, rearranging his robes with a careless flick. "Why do you want the boy?"

The question was a stall. Even Constance knew the nauseating answer. The Castle took away hunger, thirst, and lust—no doubt a safety spell to keep the inmates from reproducing or feeding on one other. The result was an eternity devoid of basic, pleasurable drives.

The antidote was the power of the incredibly rare incubi—like Sylvius. For an hour or two, their intimate touch—or blood—gave back passion. Not just the urge to mate, but gusto, energy, the gleeful frenzy of spring. This was the treasured drug the warlords were willing to kill for. With it, they could promise anything, bribe anyone.

At sixteen, Sylvius was just coming into his power. His newly adult blood was a treasure and a weapon. And it would take no time at all to bleed him dry.

Run! Constance willed the word with all her soul, but telepathy had always been beyond her talents.

"The incubus is a rarity. Too dangerous to leave unprotected," said Reynard. "My plan is to put Sylvius under lock and key. Now that he is grown, the Castle will go to war over your pet. He is the Holy Grail that could kill us all. I won't allow it."

That was too much for Constance. "No! Sylvius, listen to me!" She dodged out of the reach of Atreus's restraining hand. Every nerve in her body burst with angry excitement. "Get out of here! Run while you can!"

"But where would I go?" Sylvius looked at his master, confusion in his eyes. He had known only kindness in his short life. Constance had protected him too well.

Atreus cast a sideways look at Reynard, and then turned his gaze on the youth. "There is no place to run to. Do not listen to Constance, my boy. Your first duty is to obey me."

Atreus is taking the guardsmen's side! Constance gaped for a moment, shocked. It was as if the universe moved, the stars and planets spinning awry. *To blazes with that!* She bolted forward, grabbing Sylvius's arm, swinging him toward the door, but she was too slow. The guardsmen closed around them with the lethal swiftness of a well-tied noose.

"Constance!" Atreus snapped.

She ignored him and drew her knife. Centuries of obedience could not trump the instinct to protect her child.

"*Constance!*" Atreus bellowed. His voice bounced off her, meaningless sound.

"They always say it's the women who rule any household," said Reynard dryly.

"Let me give her a fight," put in a big, tattooed guardsman named Bran. "She looks energetic."

"Silence, Bran," said Reynard. "We're here as men of honor."

Bran closed his mouth, but his expression made Constance's skin shrink against her flesh. She tried to put her body between Sylvius and the men who threatened from all sides. There just wasn't enough of her, but she'd fight any way she could. No rules. This was her family, *her child*, at stake. Constance bared her teeth—her hated vampire fangs—in a snarl.

"She can't hurt you," said Reynard to his guards. "She's never tasted blood. Her powers are barely more than human."

But I'm a mother. Don't underestimate mothers.

A swarthy-faced guardsman tried to grab past her to get at Sylvius. She could hear Sylvius moving, feel his solid weight as he bumped against her. He was young and strong, but she doubted that he'd ever thrown a punch. *He needed to have brothers, like I did.*

The guard lunged again. Ruthlessly, she swiped at the soldier with the blade. His arm came away coated in blood that splashed down his long green tunic. "Fanged whore!"

Viktor growled, reacting to the blood or the angry

words. He ripped free of Bran's hold on his ruff and joined the fray, grabbing the guardsman in his jaws.

"Atreus, control your minions!" Reynard roared.

"*Constance!*" Atreus flicked his fingers, threads trailing from his cuff like wisps of smoke.

An invisible weight hurled into her, smashing her to the stone wall behind. Her spine took the impact, her arms and legs flopping like the limbs of Viktor's toy. The knife dropped from her hand. She barely noticed. Her ribs felt as if they were bending inward, crushing into her chest, squeezing the air from her lungs. She became one with the stone, sinking into it for a split second before she realized it was her own bones that gave.

A moment later, Constance crumpled to the floor like a rag, waiting for the waves of pain to come crashing home. If she were a human, she'd be dead. Instead, she felt the eerie crawling feeling through her flesh that said her body was already healing. Her mind was like a clean white page, empty, blank. Stunned.

When her senses returned, she had her first thoroughly disloyal thought, and it burned. *Atreus, you bastard.*

Reynard picked up her knife, carefully sliding it through his own belt. The captain paid attention to detail.

She smelled as much as heard Viktor bound to her side. The werebeast straddled her, as if sheltering her with his body. Then there was the rough wetness of his tongue, licking at her face. The blunt affection melted her resistance to the pain. It swamped her like bad whiskey, tides of nausea and dizziness and hot, brutal agony. She willed her eyes open and managed a sliver of vision.

They had Sylvius, bewildered and passive, a guardsman holding each arm. Reynard stood before the youth, a considering look on his face.

Sylvius looked from the captain, to Atreus, to where Constance lay. "What are you going to do with me?" His voice shook.

Reynard took a tiny red lacquered box from his pocket

and set it on the floor between them. He depressed a catch and the lid sprung open. "Do you understand what this is?"

Constance tried to scream, but couldn't draw enough breath.

Sylvius nodded, turning deathly pale. "It's a demon trap."

It's a prison, four inches square.

"No one can harm you inside there. Nor can your influence cause harm to others." Reynard spoke with the air of someone doing a difficult but honorable thing. Of course, he wasn't the one getting inside the torturously small box. *Evil, devious prig.*

Sylvius suddenly flung up his arms, surprising the guardsmen into letting him go. Through the haze of her injuries, Constance felt a stab of terror and fierce pride. *He's going to fight back.*

Instead, he unfurled the wings he kept folded tight against his back and leapt into the air. Sylvius landed on a ledge high above them, crouching so his hands and one knee touched the stone. His wings spread above him, boned and webbed like a bat's, but finer and more elegantly arched. Like all of him, they were pale and beautiful, a translucent white flushed with the heat of his blood.

Sylvius gave a polite smile that didn't reach his eyes. "My apologies, Captain Reynard, but I'd rather not spend the rest of eternity as a paperweight."

"That is not your decision," said Atreus. "You are mine to dispose of as I please."

"No," the youth said quietly. "Not about something like this."

Captain Reynard looked sad. "You are a prisoner here."

"But not in your box." Sylvius flew to a ledge closer to the door, landing with the grace of a hawk.

Reynard swore under his breath. Things were obviously not progressing according to his well-reasoned plans. "Atreus?"

Constance let her eyes drift closed, riding a cushion of

pain. Atreus was old, older than she had ways to measure. Time and the strange magic of the Castle were finally stealing his wits. Still, he had good moments. She prayed this would be one of them. She forced her eyes open again.

And was disappointed.

Atreus moved to face the ledge where Sylvius was perched. The sorcerer was pulling at his hair now, twining a few long, black strands around and around his fingers. "Captain Reynard is right. Your very existence is a danger to everyone. It would be better to surrender."

Sylvius's reply ached with reproach. "I thought you loved me, my king."

"It would not be love to let you roam free. Too many desire you."

"They desire what I could do for them. I do not think it's me they want."

The men stood like a tableau, staring up at the demon-angel perched on the stone ledge above.

"Do this out of love, Sylvius," said Atreus. "You see what damage you've caused already. Constance is hurt."

I have to move. Constance crawled on hands and knees from beneath Viktor's hairy belly. Every motion made her body scream, but she wasn't going to give them one scrap of ammunition to use against Sylvius. Her foot got tangled in the hem of her dress, but she got to her feet, raising her eyes to her boy.

"Sylvius."

They all turned.

"Don't listen to them. This isn't about you. They're afraid."

The look he gave her broke her heart. "I know that, little mother."

All eyes bore down on her, waiting to hear her answer. All eyes, except that of the captain. Reynard moved the box with his foot, sliding it forward an inch or two, wordlessly stating his insistence. The sound of the wood on the stone grated harshly in the sudden silence.

Pride more than strength kept Constance on her feet.

She wasn't used to speaking out, and the very audacity of it was adding to her dizziness. "Put that trinket away, Captain Reynard. You're not taking him."

Viktor whined, but she motioned him to stay. She walked toward the men, putting one foot gingerly before the other, but her attention was on Sylvius. He sat still and silent, his eyes fixed on her with the look of someone losing his world. *I'm all right. Don't let them use me to trap you.*

She heard the rustle of Atreus's robe as he raised his hand to strike her again. She wheeled on him, the sudden movement making her head swim. "Threaten me if you like but you can't kill me. I'm already dead."

He blinked, looking away. "You will be silent."

"Think!" she snapped. Insulting a sorcerer wasn't smart, but she was wild with fury. "You're letting the captain bully you into betraying the few people left who still love you."

Atreus raised his eyes and glared. "You know nothing of my reasons."

"Reasons? You're my master! You're supposed to protect me!"

Atreus stared at her a moment, but his eyes grew distant until he looked straight through her flesh.

Constance's voice grew low and hard. "I don't know how I'm going to stop this, but I will."

"You're a girl. A milkmaid, at that. A nothing."

"Be careful, Constance," Captain Reynard warned softly. "Your bravery does you credit, but you will not win this battle."

"I'll do whatever it takes."

Atreus blinked, seeming to awaken from a momentary trance.

There was no feint, no warning gesture. She was utterly unprepared.

The sorcerer slammed her into the wall again, this time holding her there with the brute force of his magic. She was pinned six feet above the floor, like a butterfly stuck in a shadow box. He held her hard. Insanely hard. She could feel the compression doing something inside her, something not even vampire bodies were supposed to endure.

Viktor howled his outrage, but Atreus used a second bolt of power to smash the huge werebeast to the floor. The sorcerer may not have had enough power left to rule a kingdom, but he had more than enough to wound those closest to him.

Captain Reynard looked up at Sylvius. The look was almost a plea. "You can end this."

There was no air in Constance to scream with. She watched, helpless, as Sylvius stood on the ledge, a look of utter devastation on his face. "I'm afraid," he said.

"I will protect you," said Reynard. "I give you my word."

"But will you protect them?" Sylvius pointed to Constance and Viktor.

Reynard nodded. "I will see to it. My men will come here every day to make sure they are well and to supply whatever they might need. That is my pledge in return for your freedom."

Sylvius said nothing more, but seemed to droop even as he poised on the balls of his feet, balancing on the very lip of the stone. Then he fell forward, wings half opened, arms loose at his sides. His long hair fanned behind him, his eyes closing with all the resignation of death. As he fell, his form thinned and lengthened, melting into an iridescent haze that shone from within. The cloud seemed to be made of dust particles swirling around and around, neither sparkling nor dull but gleaming with the sheen of pearls.

Hardened as they were, the guardsmen still gave a collective gasp of wonder. The spectacle was beautiful, the mere sight enough to revive some of the urge for life that the Castle had stolen away.

Like a glowing finger, the cloud that was Sylvius landed on the demon trap, making the red lacquer dazzle with intensity. The box seemed to inhale, dragging the billowing particles inside itself—more and impossibly more, fitting what seemed like a roomful of pearly cloud inside the tiny cube. At last the lid snapped shut, and the brilliance was snuffed out.

Once again, Constance slammed to the floor as Atreus released her. This time, she didn't open her eyes. She heard the guardsmen shuffle and talk in low voices. She heard their footsteps as they marched away. She heard Viktor's low whines. Finally, she heard the rustle of Atreus's robes as he wandered out of the chamber.

They took my boy.

She lay coiled into a painful ball. If only her mind could slide into the pain and dissolve, but she was a woman. As long as one of her own needed her—be it a stray calf or a foundling incubus—she couldn't rest. She had to save Sylvius, but how? She had needed a protector to survive in the Castle. How could she possibly save someone else?

Constance braced one hand against the floor, then the other. Experimentally, she pushed herself up enough to slump against the wall. Viktor butted his head against her thigh, letting her know he was there. She rested one hand on the beast's head, too weak yet to scratch his ears.

Despite Viktor, she felt horribly alone.

She touched the pendant Sylvius had made for her, pressing it against her skin. The feel of it was an anchor in a sea of nausea. A true vampire could heal much faster. A real vampire could fly and had astonishing speed and strength. Constance would need full vampire powers if she was going to rescue Sylvius.

Holy Bridget, what am I thinking?

She had never fully Turned, because she had never tasted human blood. The guardsmen had imprisoned her too fast. So, Constance needed to hunt.

Oh, bollocks.

She'd never considered giving up the last shreds of her humanity before. But then, no one had needed her help so very badly. Even so, could she bear to do it?

Drinking blood was beyond disgusting, and who was there to bite? The guardsmen were the closest thing to human, and they certainly didn't smell edible. Putting her lips on Bran's flesh would surely make her retch.

Her fingers stirred the thick fur of Viktor's ruff. He sighed. She sighed, and it was painful.

All right, maybe not Bran. But she had to be strong, like a warrior queen of old Eire. If she had to embrace her vampire nature to save Sylvius, so be it.

Her child was at stake.

She would find a victim.

She would become the necessary monster.

Chapter 5

October 1, 9:00 p.m.
101.5 FM

"Welcome back to CSUP. This is Errata, and we're speaking with demon expert Dr. Philip Elterland of our own Fairview U. So, Dr. Elterland, as a cryptozoologist, can you explain to us the difference between different kinds of demons? Are there, like, four-door and two-door models, or what?"

"Thank you, Errata, for such an interesting question. You are correct that there are a lot of different creatures we call demons. Calling one of these entities a demon is analogous to using the term 'bird.' There are chickadees and there are eagles."

"Tell us more."

"With pleasure. Keep in mind that some demons, like incubi, are born, and others are created from a human host."

"Dr. Elterland, isn't it true that species that are born as minor demons—like hellhounds and incubi—aren't particularly dangerous unless attacked?"

"That's true, but they are in the minority. Take, for instance, the species that most people have heard of, popularly called the soul eater. They are extremely aggressive.

These demons infect—some written sources use the verbs 'curse' or 'taint'—a human host with a parasitic condition popularly called the Dark Larceny."

"How does this happen?"

"All we have determined with any accuracy is that it takes person-to-person contact."

"You mean you can't get it from a toilet seat?"

"Um. No."

"So what happens once somebody's cursed, Dr. Elterland?"

"They are stricken with the urge to feed on human life essence. At some point, the host is entirely absorbed by the demon and acquires supernatural powers."

"How long does the process take?"

"A matter of days. It is interesting to note that although demons shape-shift, they can only make other demons when in human form, and they only attack humans."

"Is the demon a separate consciousness?"

"Not as far as we know. It's more like a cluster of driving biological imperatives the host cannot control. For the human, it is a painful, terrifying experience. The hunger. The loss of bodily control. The sudden realization that survival means feeding on other humans. Simply put, the human's civilized nature is no longer in the driver's seat. Eventually, those better instincts are extinguished and the human becomes a true monster."

"Huh. Sounds like the ultimate frat party experience."

"Well, it is about feeding and reproduction."

October 1, 9:00 p.m.
The alley outside the Castle

Mac was trapped in a solid circle of hellhound bodies. He lashed out, knuckles smashing against the hard metal snaps of a jean jacket. He heard an *oof* and then someone swept his legs out from under him.

Mac crashed to the brick pavement, his spine searing with pain as he landed on his tailbone. Then the toe of a heavy work boot drove into his kidney. Blind with pain, Mac tried to roll to his knees, but another foot thumped into his stomach. He flopped to his back, throwing his arms protectively over his face. He braced for an old-fashioned beat-down. There wasn't much even a quasi-demon could do against six hellhounds and a pissed-off vampire.

"Hold," snapped Caravelli.

They stopped midkick. Moving quickly, Mac tried to get his feet under him, but one of the hounds casually put a foot on his throat. Mac could feel the grit on the thick rubber treads scraping the flesh of his neck.

Shit. He was caught.

"Put him in the Castle. He was Geneva's thrall."

Everything in Mac tightened at the sound of the name. He hated that her mark still branded him like a Made in Hell sticker.

As one, the hounds bent, grabbing Mac's hair, his arms, his clothes. Their dark shadows blotted out the neon glow of the Kitty Basket's sign, leaving only an impression of shaggy hair and the glinting embers of their eyes.

Metal grated on metal, and the Castle door opened with a theatrical groan of iron hinges. Mac's feet left the ground as the hellhounds lifted him into the air. He squirmed, twisting in the hounds' stubborn grip.

"Caravelli, no! Please, no! I haven't done anything."

The hounds heaved him over the threshold like a sack of sand. Mac skidded on his stomach, his chin hitting the stone floor hard enough to clack his teeth together. He hit a jog in the floor and jolted into a sprawling log roll.

The bolt grated shut with a heavy, hard rasp. Mac tried to leap to his feet, but stumbled, his joints folding uselessly. The crash onto the hard stone floor had numbed every nerve.

"Caravelli! *Damn you!*"

He pushed himself up again, his palms flat against the gritty floor. His head spun, half from shock, half from the dim, flickering light but this time he made it to his feet. Pain flowed like hot oil as his flesh registered the fall. Mac dragged in a breath, then lurched to the door and gave it a single, furious blow.

"Damn you to the darkest hell!"

His demon could sense Caravelli on the other side of the door, a lurking presence. Caravelli, his judge and jailer. Mac gave the door a savage kick, putting all his force behind it. The heavy oak barely vibrated, adding insult to his fury. After a second's pause, he could feel Caravelli move off, the shadow of a passing storm. *He's leaving me here!*

Panic rolled up Mac's throat, cold and foul as a corpse's embrace. *I'm going to stake that walking mosquito. Slowly. With sharp toothpicks so it takes a long, painful while. Not to mention what I'm going to do to his hellhound henchmutts.*

Little by little, he turned to face his prison. The Castle was just as he remembered. There was no exterior, just miles and miles of dark, damp corridors that rambled outside of time and space. *And now I'm back in the joint.*

He took a few steps forward, shoving his hands into his pockets. Unease settled on him like thickly falling snow, palpable as the low hum of the Castle's magic.

The last time, that hum had nearly driven him mad. It was barely audible, a pressure just below hearing that made his sinuses ache all the way from his molars to the top of his head. It made the demon in him stretch and flex, suddenly restless. The Castle was supposed to damp demon hunger, but right now it was making it harder to control.

He had to do something. Move. Explore. He started walking, carefully noting each near-identical corner and hallway. The rubber soles of his track shoes were nearly silent, only the rustle of his clothes echoing in the cavernous space. He seemed to be alone. Where was everyone?

A year ago, after the battle where Geneva died and her armies were crushed, Mac had awakened somewhere in this maze. The force of the spell that had killed Geneva had blasted him deep into the Castle. He should have died.

Instead, Mac had made a half-dead crawl for the exit, like the survivor of a spectacular pub brawl—except there was no way out. As his injuries healed, the crawl had become a run, then a game of survival. Injured and confused, he didn't remember much, but his trek through the dungeon had given new meaning to the term "bad neighborhood." As far as he could tell, it had taken around six months to find a way out of the Castle. He'd stumbled on an open portal, a piece of pure dumb luck.

He'd escaped once. He could do it again. This time at least he knew the location of the door. The trick would be getting it open. *Then, a heartfelt discussion with the Vampire Caravelli.*

He stopped abruptly, his body reacting before he even knew why. Perfectly still, he listened. His ears strained to catch the sound again. Behind him. Faint, but growing. *Scuff scuff scuff.*

He turned. A man was running toward him—one that Mac knew all too well. *Good ol' Guardsman Bran.* A feeling of sour anger washed through Mac, adding old resentments to his already foul mood.

As if the day wasn't bad enough, an unholy grin of pleasure split Bran's face, the look of a bully finding new prey. Mac could run, maybe hide, but before he even reviewed his options, Bran was mere feet away and drawing a short sword.

Back in the Castle five friggin' minutes and I'm in the middle of an ass-kicking. Mac wiped a sudden sweat from his face. *Same old Club Dread.*

Mac circled his opponent, who mirrored his low, watchful crouch. Bran was a huge, bare-armed hulk covered with spiraling blue tattoos. He stank like old leather shut up in an attic trunk for far too long. A black braid swung past the man's hips as he moved, a dark slash against the scarlet and gold silk of his tunic.

Guardsman Bran was one scary, ugly mother.

Shadows ate at the ceiling and surrounding passageways, giving the illusion there was no reality beyond the circle of their combat. The solitary sound in the corridor was the shuffling of their feet on the stone floor. Torchlight played along Bran's short sword, reminding Mac the guardsman was armed and he wasn't.

Sharp objects mattered, but Mac's pulse roared in his head, drowning out fear with every heartbeat. He felt drunk, high, complete, even relieved. He was ready to pound this grunt and love every minute of it. *Kill or die.* The shredded remainder of his demon side had finally slipped its leash.

Mac lunged. Bran was quick, blocking him, slashing at Mac's ribs—but Mac was supernaturally fast, dancing aside before the blade could land.

They sprang apart, circling again.

"Nice to see you, too," Mac said with a taunting grin. Without warning, he changed direction, but Bran followed the sudden shift with the poise of a gymnast. Mac licked his lips, his mouth dry from breathing hard. "Interesting tatts. Still working the Bronze Age look?"

"Be silent." Bran curled his lip, his white teeth and pale skin making him look more like a vampire than a guardsman. "I found you, fugitive. No one escapes twice."

"C'mon, saying that's just tempting fate."

They closed again, grappling and snarling. Bran swept Mac's feet from under him, but they both fell, Mac on top. Mac's vision turned white, then red with bloodlust and rage. With his knee on Bran's throat, Mac smashed the guardsman's sword hand into the stone floor, pounding until Bran's fingers let go of the hilt.

Bran surged, tossing Mac off. Rolling to his back, Mac brought his feet up just in time to catch Bran in the chest with a satisfying thump. The guardsman stumbled, air whooshing from his lungs. Mac flipped to his feet, running two steps to sink a hard, knuckle-bruising shot to Bran's midriff. The man was solid as granite, but no match. Bran doubled over. Mac grabbed the sword and brought the hilt down with a smack, catching the guardsman behind his left ear. Bran dropped like a stone in a face-flat sprawl at Mac's feet.

The thump of his fall, like so much dirty laundry, echoed in the cavernous dark. Mac bent, feeling for a pulse. The guardsman was still alive but would be out for a good long time.

As he rose, Mac felt the surge of his own blood, the tingle and rush of human life in every limb. Behind it pulsed the demon, gleeful—lustful—at the prospect of even more violence. *Hunger*. The weight of the sword was a suggestion, the hilt hard and perfect in his greedy palm. There were so many ways to kill. A quick blade in the spine. The slow agony of a gut wound.

Gritting his teeth, Mac backed away. *I'm still too much a cop to kill a man when he's down. Even this one.* He clutched at that thought, holding it like a talisman that would preserve his slipping humanity.

But in the Castle, every moment was fight or die. Here, he needed his demon side to survive. Staying human would be a losing battle. *I have to get out of here, or lose my soul again.*

A flicker at the edge of his vision made him look up, reflexes poised.

Mac glimpsed a face, all wide eyes and pointed chin. It was a woman, barely more than a girl, with a thick fall of midnight hair long past her waist. Every line of her thin body looked startled.

All was silent but for the sound of Bran's faint, slow breathing. The woman just stared, her mouth pulled down at the corners.

She's afraid. He stepped over Bran and toward the woman. With a birdlike hop, she whisked around the corner. After a second's hesitation, Mac sprinted after her. Until he knew whether she was running from simple fear or running to get Bran's friends, he couldn't let her get away.

By the time he got to the corner, she was already out of sight, but he could smell a trace of sweet perfume. He followed it, mapping this new direction in his mind so he could retrace his steps.

She hadn't gone far, only down another turning. There she hovered, her back to Mac, peering anxiously around the far corner. He came up behind her, his movements utterly silent.

He hadn't realized how much noise a human made—breathing, rustling, swallowing—until, as a demon, he'd stopped. He'd made no sound, no scent, moved no air when he passed by. Now, partially human again, he could switch the ability on or off. Going stealth mode freaked him out a bit, but it came in handy.

He was close enough now to see the woman clearly. Her dress fell to the floor and was made of a heavy indigo fabric worn threadbare along the hem. She was small—barely five feet, small-boned, and almost frail. He could have picked her up in one hand. Most of her weight was surely in that thick, straight hair.

Just when he was close enough to notice a strip of dusty lace peeking out from beneath her skirt, her shoulders stiffened. She'd made him. Soundless or not, even demons couldn't hide from that sixth-sense survival instinct that makes a deer run before the cougar breaks cover.

She whipped around to face him, eyes wide with fear, white edging their deep blue centers. With the jerking motion of a cartoon character, she looked around the corner again, then back to him. *Caught between two bad choices.*

"What's there?" Mac asked in a quiet voice, wondering whether she spoke English. The Castle didn't have a universal language, unless one counted despair.

"More guardsmen," she answered, almost whispering. *Not going to warn Bran's friends, then.*

"Three of them, heading toward their quarters." Her words lilted. Irish, perhaps? She searched his face, clearly measuring the level of threat he presented. "Who are you?"

"Conall Macmillan, ma'am." Somehow it seemed right to use his best manners, as if the shade of his great-grandmother was cuffing him on the ear. "At your service."

"At my service, now, is it?" There was a flash of irony in her eyes. "And how is it that anyone who defeats a guardsman would serve the likes of me? Guardsmen are made stronger than us. We can't beat them, and yet there you were looming over Bran's broken body."

Uncertainty squeezed Mac's chest. He didn't want to hear from a pretty woman how he wasn't quite normal, much less that he loomed. "I'm just passing through. Maybe the rules don't apply to me."

Her gaze caught his, deadly serious. "No one just passes through here."

"I've done it before."

"You have a key, then." She said it naturally, as if it was no great marvel.

There's a key? Maybe more than one? Mac didn't answer, wondering what else she might reveal.

"Well, then." She was calming down, but still looked like she was expecting a dirty trick. "That would answer why I've never seen you before."

"I hope that means you wouldn't forget me if you had." He sneaked a glance at the neckline of her dress. Her low-cut gown was laced up the front, the tight crisscross of ribbons making the most of her slender shape. Besides a pendant on a leather lace, she wore a scarf of thin white fabric around her shoulders, the ends tucked modestly down her front and foiling any clear views of cleavage. *Damn.*

She caught the look. "And if I remembered you, would that be on account of your smooth tongue and practiced smile?"

"I have better souvenirs." *Careful, the last woman you thought was cute turned you into a demon.*

But she ignored his comment and looked around the corner instead, this time letting her spine sag with relief. "They're gone."

"Good." The sword, once so important, now felt cumbersome in his hand. He wanted an excuse to touch this woman. It was pure instinct. She was beautiful and achingly young. The fact that she was hiding from the guardsmen only added a protective urge to the mix. "What's your name?"

"Constance," she said, then added, "Moore," as if it was a piece of information she rarely needed.

"Were the guardsmen chasing you?" he asked.

"It's a long story."

"I'm a patient man."

"I've heard that one before." She gave him a bold look

that almost contradicted her earlier caution. "You men never make it to the climax of a tale."

Mac raised an eyebrow. "You must be one helluva storyteller."

She gave a sly, close-lipped smile that would have shamed the Mona Lisa. Her eyes dared him right up until they shifted away, a nervous tell. "I am. Ask any warm-blooded man."

Mac folded his arms, an awkward process when holding a sword. "Oh, yeah?"

She leaned against the stone wall, all fair skin, black hair, and cherry lips. Snow White in a reckless mood. "Indeed."

"But are you Scheherazade or Jane Austen?"

"I don't know those names. Which would I like to be?"

Despite the taunting jut of her chin, he could see the tremor in her fingers, the quick pant of her breath. His demon side licked up her fear like a cat lapped cream. He reached out with his free hand and cupped her jaw, tilting her face up to him. "What do you know about a key?"

Her eyes narrowed. "I know they exist. This place isn't as air-tight as one might think."

He dropped his hand, but didn't move away. "You got one?"

"No." She tried to hold his gaze, but failed. "You can trust my word on that."

"Worried that I might search you?"

"You'd probably like that."

"You think so, eh?"

"You're male, aren't you?" The words were more defeated than bitter, and somehow that made them worse.

"Yeah, but I'm not a ravening beast." *Not the human part, anyway.* "Trust me, undressing a woman is more fun when you're invited."

She laughed, but it wasn't mirthful. "And you're an expert, I suppose."

"Practice makes perfect."

"I'm sure it does." Again, the Mona Lisa smile. There was a history that went with that sweet, self-mocking sadness.

Definitely more temptation than he could handle. He bent and pressed his lips to hers, perhaps to taste that puzzling smile, perhaps to kiss it away. Or maybe just to prove his expertise.

Constance inhaled, a quick, light gasp ended by his capture of her mouth. Her lips were cool and soft, returning his kiss with surprised hesitation. That perfume he had smelled earlier, something flowery and old-fashioned, wafted up from her silken skin. He felt the tentative brush of her fingers in his hair, light as a moth's wings. Finally, her hand settled on his cheek, a girlish, uncertain touch so gentle that it tickled.

She was no practiced flirt, and he'd just called her bluff.

At a twinge from his conscience, he drew back. "I'm sorry. I didn't mean . . ."

She used both hands to pull his head down, bringing his mouth back to hers.

Okay. Mac wasn't about to argue. Heat surged through him, thick and electric. He drew his hand up her spine, over her ribs, up the side of her breast. Constance flinched, as if he'd touched a bruise, but then murmured in pleasure, rising onto her toes. Her body brushed against his. *Oh, yeah. Unexpected, but oh, yeah.*

He felt the tip of her tongue meet his, a shy inquiry. Constance tasted as sweet and wild as blackberries still hot from the sun. He couldn't drink down her soul as he could have in his demon days, but he could savor it, sad and pure, like her smile.

He already ached in his body, but that taste of her spirit made him ache in his heart. He caught the salty tang of loneliness. *That's just not right.* Was there no one to look after her? A tiny creature like Constance shouldn't be out wandering the halls of the Castle by herself. She was so small, he could nearly span her waist with his hands. The fabric of her dress felt rough, too coarse for such tiny perfection. And there was far, far too much clothing for satisfactory exploration.

Okay, whoa, buddy. In five seconds flat, you've gone

from sneaking a kiss to planning to get naked with someone you've just met. Get a grip.

Heedless, Mac's fingers slid beneath the flimsy fabric of her scarf, finding soft, cool skin and the gently rounded tops of her breasts. He kept his touch feather-light and was rewarded with a delicate shiver. Tracing his thumb over her collarbone, he caressed the satin flesh of her shoulder. *Nice.*

He deepened the kiss, but kept his beast tightly leashed. Whoever this girl was, she wasn't ready for his demon side. Hell, most of the time, neither was he.

So sweet. She knew about a key, a way for Mac to escape. It was almost a shame. This moment, so full of new promise, almost justified an eternity in the Castle.

And yet . . .

Yeah, okay, Macmillan, what's with the hearts and flowers? This isn't you.

Something was not right.

No shit, Sherlock. Nothing's been right for over a year. Was it the soul-sucking demon shtick or the eternal prison of darkness that tipped you off? As for the girl . . .

Mac winced, suddenly going very still. *Women. There's always something.*

Yeah, Constance was sweet. The teeth, however, were a surprise.

Gently, he pulled away. Her eyes were closed, her lips flushed and slightly parted to reveal tiny, perfect fangs. *A vampire.* But an innocent one that sent off none of the usual vampiric vibes. There was only one way that happened.

Constance had never tasted blood.

Pheromones. That answered why she had fascinated him so completely, sent him head over heels in less time than it took your average speed date.

But it raised still another interesting question.

A really good one.

Am I meant to be her first kiss or her first kill?

Chapter 6

Constance let her eyes drift shut, swamped by the absolute wonder of her changing luck. A human male, wandering alone in the Castle, beating the odious Bran into the very stones of the floor? And then kissing her? She couldn't have ordered up a fantasy more to her liking.

And to make it even better, he was the key to rescuing her son. She had to grab hold and make the most of this chance. And even through her sizzling fury with Atreus, Reynard, and the perverse curse that was her very Undead existence, she didn't mind the grabbing.

This Conall Macmillan was devouring her, his hands roving down her back with a strength that hurt her still-healing ribs. She didn't care about the pain. In all her days, no one had kissed her like this—all male and rising to the call of her feminine charms.

His fingers brushed her breasts. Such big hands, and yet he was so gentle.

You're not here for pleasure. You're here to hunt. To become a true, powerful vampire.

He fit her idea of a proper man—tall, strong, and square-jawed. His dark eyes were direct, his thick brown hair just long enough to curl. She liked the mischief that lurked around his mouth, showing itself in a darting grin.

Constance bet many a girl had made herself a fool over this fellow.

She would do no such thing. She would be sober and serious. All she had to do was bite him. The instinct was in her, made part of her when she was Turned.

At that thought, her fangs felt enormous, lethal and sharp. She tried to focus on that, instead of her aching breasts, the burn between her thighs. *Sober and serious*, she reminded herself. *Dour as a bloody nun. Just bite him.*

He cupped her backside, squeezing. A little mewing noise escaped her.

All right, if she had to sink her teeth into him, there was no reason not to enjoy the experience. She didn't want to hurt him any more than she had to. He seemed, well, nice. Warm. Hard in all the right places. His skin tasted hot and smoky, like an exotic spice. Most of all, she approved of his enthusiasm.

Get on with it, Constance! You can't afford to stall.

She felt his lips part from hers, cool air replacing the heat of his mouth. All her senses reached for him, clinging to his hard, male warmth. She let her eyes open a slit, just enough to make out his silhouette.

On second thought, he doesn't smell right. It had been a long time since she'd encountered a human, but there was something decidedly off.

Bite him! If he's not human, he's close enough. Bite him! Bite him for Sylvius.

Her head spun. She tried to focus on the hammering beat of his heart. It echoed along her every nerve. *Delicious.* She was ready. *I'm sorry, Conall Macmillan, but I need to do this for my boy.*

She moved in for the strike.

"Whoa, sweetheart," Mac said as Constance leaned into him again. "I never open a vein on the first date."

She reached up, stroking his cheek with dainty, cold fingers. "But I have to . . ."

He flinched and pushed her back, staying gentle but

firm. "That's what they all say. Y'know, I'm sure there's a support group for this sorta thing."

She pushed his hand aside as if he were no stronger than a kitten. "I need help."

"You have no idea."

"I need your blood." She was closing in again.

"Uh-huh, and I need a key out of this cozy piece of hell."

Less gently now, Mac shoved her out of his personal space. He had the sword in his hand, but he couldn't see himself using it. Constance was dangerous, but didn't exactly radiate evil—just desperation. That was odd, he thought. In the Castle, there was no reason she should be hungry. She closed the gap again, her eyes glinting in the uncertain light. "Forget leaving. I don't have a key."

"Then who does?" Mac felt the hair on his neck lifting. The animal part of him was fast heading into the fight or flight zone. She was spooking him far worse than either Caravelli or the hellhounds. No one that soft and pretty should have such a predatory look in her eyes.

She shrugged. "Right now? I don't know. No one ever admits it if they do. Not if they want to keep it for their own."

Mac backed away. "If you don't have a key and can't tell me how to get one, then I'm outta here."

"You can't go. We're not done."

She reached for him, but he dodged her fingers. A she-vamp's nails sliced as sharp as talons. Years in the supernatural crimes unit taught him that lesson fast, right along with just how well vamps could mess with their victims' heads. *Should've remembered that nugget of info five minutes ago.* Then again, Constance hadn't hit his radar as a bloodsucker, just a really pretty girl. Just his luck she had to embrace her inner Babe of Doom right when he came along.

He had to wind up this fiasco and move on. "Look, really, I'm flattered you want to drink my blood—"

She stamped her foot in frustration. "I don't want to, you great idiot. I *need* to. Stay still!"

"Oh, yeah. Sure. Right. Why?"

"That's a very personal question."

"Biting is a very personal act."

"Oh, be quiet! This is hard enough as it is."

"Look, I'm walking away. You stay. I go."

"No!"

He could feel her will pushing on his mind. Nothing he couldn't handle, but more than he would have expected. "Back off."

"Come *here*." She sprang like a cat, fingers crooked into claws.

Whoa!

In an instant, the demon took over. Pure reflex. There was a sudden flash of ice cold, like a freezer door had opened beneath his ribs, and every one of his senses cut out.

Black. Silent. Stifling.

The rush of blood in his veins just . . . vanished. The spaces where his pulse *should have been* beat in his mind, but not his body. The terrifying silence beat . . . and beat . . .

And he was back, as if a switch had tripped.

Constance was still leaping toward the spot he had been standing a moment ago. Somehow he had moved a good twenty feet down the corridor. He grabbed the wall, disoriented. *Huh, that hasn't happened in a while.*

She stumbled, grabbing nothing but thin air. "You turned to dust!"

Mac shook his head, although he knew it was true. Poofing to an insubstantial black cloud was a demon talent. He had done it fast, too, the way he had when he had been at the top of his game. A cold, greasy unease slithered in his gut.

Constance balled her hands in fury. "You're a liar; you're not human at all!"

The words hit with all the subtlety of a city bus. "Never said I was!"

He turned before a weird impulse to apologize could overtake him. *I'm sorry I turned out to be a less-than-tasty treat.*

"What are you? Vampires know a demon's stink, and you barely smell!"

He was walking now, not so fast as to excite the predator in her, but not wasting any time, either. He suddenly felt hot, as if he had spiked a fever. "Flattery still won't get you into my jugular, sweetheart."

Mac glanced over his shoulder, making sure she wasn't coming after him. She looked beside herself, eyes round with anger and disappointment, but she wasn't moving. Maybe that meant she'd given up. Maybe it was because he still clutched the sword. That was one of the bizarre things about the demon-dust-travel thing. Pretty much anything he was touching came with him. Handy, but strange.

Don't go there. If he was going to keep it together, thinking about what just happened was taboo. He wasn't supposed to have major demon mojo. That could only mean really bad news, and the last thing he could afford to do was work himself into a panic.

Think happy thoughts. Puppies. Kittens. Beer.

Doggedly, Mac kept striding. He focused on the immediate problem of getting out of the Castle. He worked his way back to the door without passing the spot where he'd flattened Bran—neither of them needed a rerun of that encounter.

The door looked as impenetrable as ever. Mute. Solid. A scar in the endless vista of stone walls. *What do I do now? Sit down and wait for someone with a key to come along?*

Mac folded his arms, leaning against the wall opposite the door, and settled in to wait. A cold draft slithered over his foot. As always, he wondered where the air currents came from in a world with no sky, no wind, and no weather. Nothing in the prison ever made sense.

Take the wars. The Castle dampened magic, so most of the fighting that went on was pure brute force. Swords. Fists. Guns, if someone had them. But the no-magic rule wasn't consistent. There were sorcerers that could still throw the odd zap of power. He'd seen werewolves shape-shift now and then. Odd things happened. Magic sometimes slid through the cracks.

He started to pace, walking a few feet to one side of the door, then the other. *Slid through the cracks?* The phrase nagged at him. There was something he needed to pay attention to. He could feel his cop brain struggling to find a connection.

Why had he been able to dust?

If I'm immune to the anti-magic rules here . . .

No, that wasn't right. He wasn't immune. He'd somehow *regained* power he'd lost. That part of the Castle mojo was working in reverse.

If the magic here doesn't affect me the same way . . .

In the world outside the Castle, demons didn't need no stinking keys. They came and they went as they pleased, drifting through tiny cracks and holes in their dust form.

The Castle was different. Here, demons smashed into the doorway portal like a bird into a glass window. But what if he could make it through? *Slide through the cracks.*

If this goes wrong . . .

The alternative was sitting by the door for the next millennium, like a dog waiting to go for a walk. Whatever magical blip was making him different might wear off. He could lose this chance.

If I get stuck in the portal or only half of me makes it . . .

Suck it up. Sometimes the only options available were bad.

Mac reached for the cold place where his rediscovered powers hid. He knew what he was doing. He knew he would regret it.

Cold shot through him with dizzying intensity, as if Jack Frost invaded his bones. The frozen sensation was stronger this time, but slower. In a fleeting glimpse, he saw his hand laced with veins of blackness, a latticework that melded and pooled as he disappeared into nothing. Bit by bit, his sensory awareness fell away as parts of him simply ceased to be.

Disintegration always followed the same sequence:

edges first, then his feet, his fingers, his limbs falling away
before the core of him blinked out into a smudge of darkness, an afterimage that faded away like errant smoke. This
time, he held onto a smidgen of consciousness to guide him
through the door. That's all he was—a thought.

He drifted to the door, then threaded himself into a
crack between two of the huge, upright planks of wood.
Then it occurred to him that this wasn't a real door at all. It
just looked like one. It was a portal made of earth magic.

He had no body, but he could still feel the buzzing energy of the portal, like ants crawling over flesh that wasn't
there. He roiled, the motes of himself spinning in the wild
energy, distracted, stirred to a frenzy. Pulling himself into a
hard knot of darkness, he willed himself through the force
field like a bullet, an image of the alley beyond like a bea-
con in his mind.

He popped out between two hellhounds, barely missing the elbow of one, and hurtled toward the neon sign of
Naughty Nanette's.

Mac's laugh whispered in the rustling breeze.

Then it died when he considered what he'd just done.

Chapter 7

October 1, 9:55 p.m.
101.5 FM

"Finally, Dr. Elterland, let's move on to talking about vampires."

"To be honest, Errata, I don't make them part of my study."

"Why not?"

"There's nothing there left to learn."

"I see. How many vampires have you actually met, Dr. Elterland?"

Alessandro Caravelli strode back to the graveyard where he'd parked his car. It was a long walk, but he didn't mind. He wanted time to unwind. Enforcing the peace among the supernatural population in Fairview was stressful, and he never took his work home with him if he could help it. Holly was a special woman and a powerful witch—the perfect mate for a vampire warrior—but even she had her limits. Decapitation and dismemberment did not make for good pillow talk.

A fitful wind blew garbage along the gutters, making a forlorn rustle. Pedestrians walked in twos and threes toward the parking garages, the early shows at the movie theater over. With his dark-adapted sight, Alessandro could see the street predators waiting in their lairs—an alley, a doorway, a patch of unlit street.

He silently dared one of the lowlifes to jump him, but that would never happen to a vampire with a broadsword. Undeath had its privileges. In fact, the part of town where the supernatural citizens had set up their businesses—some newspaper had called it Spookytown, and the name stuck—was remarkably free of crime. The merchants just ate the troublemakers, and the police rarely complained.

The thought of police took Alessandro back to Macmillan. Mac, as he preferred to be called. They'd never been friends, but there had been mutual respect. The detective had been out of his depth working preternatural crimes, but then, so were all the humans. He'd done better than most, up until the part where Geneva infected him with her demon taint.

And it still eats at him. He struggles, and he will lose.

Yes, magic might have blasted away most of the demon inside Mac, but the infection was like a virulent mold. If there was the tiniest remnant, it would spread and take over, reducing its host to a soul-eating machine, a monster's monster. It was just a matter of time.

Sad, but now he is a threat like any other. A task to be dealt with. Work.

He would have traded in his right fang for a better solution than a sword or a dungeon. Nevertheless, he couldn't stand around wringing his hands while Macmillan went evil and ate half the city. That just wasn't practical.

His cell phone rang, and he answered it.

"Hey," said Holly. Even that one word sounded tired.

"Hello, love," he replied, his outlook suddenly changing for the better, as if a projector had clicked to the next slide in the carousel. *Do people use those anymore?*

"Did you find Mac? Was the tip on the radio good?"

Alessandro sighed. "Yeah, I found him."

"Crap," she said softly. "Did you—"

"No. I put him in the Castle."

"Oh." Her tone was ambiguous. Holly had liked Mac. She had even dated him once.

There was a long silence. Alessandro kept walking, but his mind was with Holly, imagining her cradling the phone under her chin in that peculiar way. She was in the kitchen. He could hear the tick of the wall clock.

She finally spoke. "The Castle. Sweet Hecate, I don't know which is worse. That place or ... death." There was no criticism in her tone. It was an honest question.

"I don't know, either. He's still infected."

"Goddess." Another long pause while she digested that. "When're you coming home?"

"Now."

"Good. I need company."

With no more warning than that, she hung up. The night was suddenly emptier. Alessandro quickened his pace. He never liked leaving Holly home by herself, even if she was a powerful witch. She meant too much to him not to worry.

There was a lot to worry about. For one thing, the hellhounds had to stop wandering away from their post at the Castle door. He was going to call Lore, their alpha, and have a word. Alessandro didn't pay the Baskervilles to take kibble breaks whenever they felt like it.

Not with Holly home alone. Of course, all thoughts eventually led to her.

He finally reached the street beside the graveyard where his T-Bird was parked. The sight of her—the car was the other woman in his life—made his spirits rise. She was a sixties red two-door with custom chrome and smoked windows. He'd bought her new and kept her up himself. It was a point of pride that he never locked the doors. No one dared to mess with his car—except, of course, the occasional bird. Nature kept everyone humble, even vampires.

A cold wind whispered in the cedar trees as he threw the broadsword in the trunk and got behind the wheel. He wondered whether Holly had finished studying for the night, or if he'd have to coax her away from her books and over to the couch, where they could talk or watch television until other ideas pleasantly interfered. *The ugliness of the night is done, and I'm going home to the girl I love*, he thought, and he smiled. In all his long centuries of existence, this last year had been the first time he had been able to say that night after night.

He didn't mind. Holly had been worth the wait.

As he sped into the driveway, the first thing he saw was a strange motorcycle at the curb. He parked and got out of the T-Bird, looking first at the house. Holly's family home—where he lived now, too—was an 1880s painted lady with an ocean view. The usual lights were on in the kitchen and front room. He could see Kibs, the cat, staring out of the study window. Except for the motorcycle, everything looked normal.

But in the last few minutes, Holly had grown upset. He could feel it the way he could feel all of her strong emotions, as clearly as if she had spoken in his ear. Trouble had arrived.

He got the sword out of the trunk.

No doubt the trouble had ridden in on the bike. He turned and paused long enough to take in the red trellis design of a Ducati Monster. It was dirty, as if their visitor had ridden a long way.

Alessandro ran up the steps, mind scrambling for clues as to who this invader might be.

If this guy meant harm, he shouldn't have made it over the threshold. The house should have kept him out. Witch houses were semi-sentient and self-repairing, sustained by the ambient magic that surrounded their families. They were also able to work basic protection spells, so why hadn't it stopped this motorcycle-riding intruder?

The front door opened for Alessandro before he reached for the knob. He swept inside, noticing an unfamiliar red and white helmet on the front hall table. This guy had left it there like he owned the place. A sudden wave of territoriality made Alessandro clench his teeth.

He could sense Holly in the kitchen. She was always at

the table these days, studying for her university midterms. The last thing she needed was an outsider disrupting her work. Alessandro went to confront the stranger, letting his boots fall ominously on the polished oak floors. A sharp, bitter smell hung in the air, as if Holly had forgotten to turn off the coffeemaker.

When he reached the kitchen, his eyes went first to her. His Holly was dark-haired and beautiful, but slowly surrendering to the wild-eyed, disheveled look of a full-time student. She sat surrounded by textbooks, dirty mugs, a laptop, pencils, and two complicated calculators, neither of which Alessandro could figure out.

"Hi," he said. "What's going on?"

As she turned around to greet him, he could see Holly's huge green eyes were too wide, like she'd been shell-shocked. Frowning, he turned to the figure sitting in the chair next to Holly.

Then frowned some more. The motorcycle rider was not male.

The woman in riding gear was a bit taller than Holly, blonder, but had the same startling green eyes—which were riveted on him. She was grubby, her hair flat from the helmet and a hard set to her jaw. Alessandro knew the type—they swore hard, drank hard, and picked their teeth with a sharpened stake—just before they drove it through some unfortunate vampire's heart.

Which was just unhygienic.

No one said anything. The tap dripped in the kitchen sink. He held the scabbard of his broadsword casually, but doubted he was done with it for the night.

"Hey," said Holly.

"What's going on?" he repeated, looking pointedly at Kick-Ass Gal.

"This is my sister, Ashe."

"The vampire slayer," Ashe added in a voice like filthy snow.

Oh, great.

Holly's expression was projecting a version of don't-blame-me-I-didn't-invite-her. He tried to smile but could feel it sagging into a grimace. He liked Holly's grandmother. Holly's parents were dead. That had been the sum total of his thoughts about his *de facto* in-laws.

Except, I know this is the in-law who tried out major magic, destroyed her own power, almost destroyed her sister's power, accidentally killed both their parents, then ran away to live on the streets. Yeah, let's have her come and stay for a few weeks.

Then he remembered Ashe owned half the house. He was technically the guest here.

This just gets better.

Alessandro sank into a chair across from Ashe, setting the sword down close at hand. Her expression made him wonder whether that and the three knives he was carrying were defense enough.

"So, you're Alessandro Caravelli, the vampire queen's renowned champion warrior."

Ashe narrowed her eyes. He knew she was eight years older than Holly, which put her somewhere in her middle thirties. The hard lines in her face made her look older.

"I no longer work for the queen," he replied stiffly. "I work alone."

"I didn't think vampires did that."

"I'm hard to work with." The truth was, he worked with and for the entire supernatural community in Fairview, keeping order much as he had when he served the queen. That wasn't the point. "Why do you want to know?"

"You're with my baby sister. You're a vampire. What do you think?"

"I think you're leaping to conclusions."

"About what? The sex or the fangs?" She shoved one of the textbooks hard, sending it flying across the table toward a mug full of coffee.

With superhuman speed, he slammed his hand on the book, stopping it cold. With one simple act, she'd made him show his inhumanity. Show he was one of the Undead. Rough anger slid over him, scraping like coarse wool.

"Wait a damned minute," said Holly, clutching at one of the pencils and stabbing the notebook in front of her. "How'd you find out about us?"

"Grandma's letters finally caught up with me. I tried calling her from Calgary, but she'd already left for the family reunion in Waikiki. Maybe you should have taken lover boy there for some fun in the sun."

Holly gave Ashe an unfriendly look. "You said you were here to see me. What you really meant was you came all this way from . . . wherever to save me from Alessandro?"

"I was in Calgary," Ashe replied. "Doing a job."

"Killing vampires?" Alessandro asked, letting a little menace slide into his voice.

"Yep, and the guy paid me well. See the bike outside? That was just the bonus."

Alessandro stifled a laugh. Well, the sister had guts, saying that to his face. He had to give her that much.

Holly's face went white and she stopped staking her notes. "This is such BS. You walked out when I was a child You never wrote, you never phoned. Why the hell do you care now?"

Ashe folded her arms. "I had other problems back then."

Holly's mouth trembled for a moment and she bit it. Alessandro was half out of the chair, ready to solve this sister problem, before Holly held up her hand. "Stop. Just stop."

He stopped. He sat.

Ashe looked at her sister, her eyes narrowed. "Stop what?"

Holly's voice was hoarse. "Don't come in here and start threatening me and my partner."

"She doesn't frighten me," Alessandro put in.

Ashe's eyes focused on him like twin crossbows. "Consider it an intervention, Holly. For your own good."

Holly leaned forward, her words pounding like a nail gun. "You don't get to stake my boyfriend and don't *ever* tell me how to live my life. You have no right."

Alessandro forced himself not to grin. Ashe looked down at the table, her face like stone.

"Why a vampire slayer?" Holly asked. "What the hell are you trying to prove?"

Ashe answered without emotion. "I'm good at it. It's something even a broken witch can do."

"That's it?"

"I had to support my kid. Roberto was a bullfighter, and that's not steady work."

"Bullfighter?" It slipped out before Alessandro could stop himself. "Your—husband, I assume—is a toreador?"

Ashe kept her eyes on the table, but her reply had an edge. "Was. Beefburger one, Roberto zero. So much for hot Latin romance."

She looked up, but at Holly. Alessandro might have been invisible. "My kid's in boarding school. It's monster-proofed. Highest anti-magic tech money can buy. It's the best way to be safe these days."

Holly looked at her sister coldly. "For Goddessakes, Ashe."

Alessandro shifted back in his chair, an uncomfortable prickle running up his spine. He felt the air in the house grow heavy, as if the place itself was roused by the growing tension in the room. *But is it for me, or against me? I'm not one of the Carver family. Ashe is.*

Ashe folded her arms, mirroring Holly. "I didn't come here to look at home movies of our childhood. I've work to do here whether you like it or not. My concession to your *relationship* is that I'm giving fair warning. If fang-boy packs his bags, I'll let him leave in peace."

He'd had enough. Alessandro got up, reaching for the heaviest textbook to use as a blunt object. One whack with *Introduction to Business Law* would subdue most humans.

The moment he moved, Holly stood up, taking a step toward Ashe. "Alessandro, I'm sorry, but please go out for a while. My sister and I have to talk."

Their eyes met. Hers were apologetic, but resolute. Alessandro set the book down, silent and seething. A foul, acidic taste lay heavy on his tongue and coiled, burning hot, all the way down to his gut.

"Give us an hour," Holly said softly.

He was too angry to reply. Why would they need an hour? It had taken Ashe all of five minutes to get him out of the house.

He grabbed the sword, but the weight of it gave him no comfort.

Alessandro hated problems he couldn't kill.

Mac dragged himself through the door of his condominium. He closed the door, locked it, and listened, his eyes searching the near-blackness of the front hall. Nothing. He was alone. No vampires with swords. He might even be safe. At least, safe from things outside himself.

Dark, gritty panic backed up like the current in a storm drain. He swore, but no words were equal to the sick feeling in his gut.

I demoned out.

Twice.

Once he'd made the choice to grab at his demon powers, they had come back as naturally as reaching for a bottle opener. That was bad. That wasn't human. That had to make him less of a man and more of what he feared.

I'm backsliding.

Getting out of the Castle was important, but he'd done it by putting what was left of his humanity at risk. He'd tempted fate. *What if choosing to do the dust thing had pushed me over the edge?* Suddenly being a half-and-half freak in denial didn't sound so bad.

Mac didn't bother hitting the light switch. Time ticked by as he leaned against the door, too stunned to move. Something should happen—divine thunderbolts, perhaps—but nothing came. Just the queasiness of having made a wrong and irrevocable choice.

Hello, dark side. Where's Yoda when you need him?

He was still holding the sword. Slowly, he set it in the umbrella stand by the door and made his way to the living room. His condo was a corner suite, with floor to ceiling windows overlooking the harbor. Light from nearby buildings reflected from the white walls, washing everything in pale hues.

Like everything else, his condo—an inheritance from his investment-savvy mother—was in jeopardy. He'd been away for a year. Automatic withdrawals for utilities and all the other day-to-day expenses of keeping a residence had drained Mac's bank account. Now that he was unemployed, it would be a challenge to make ends meet.

Losing the place would be the last straw, the final break with his human life. *I can't let that happen. I'm not that guy who couldn't keep it together and ended up living out of a cardboard box.*

Suddenly conscious of his messy housekeeping, he picked up a newspaper that he had tossed on the floor earlier, then threw it onto the coffee table. It slid off again. *Damn.* Mac gave up and fell onto the couch, stretching out and draping his arm over his eyes. His jaw ached from clenching his teeth, but the pain kept him centered. *How do I pull the plug on this nightmare?*

Mac moved his arm and opened his eyes to the dark room. The low haze of the city lights brushed the edges of wall and chair, shelf and lamp. The room was silent but for the distant rush of water through the building's pipes. There was nothing to distract him from the one fact he didn't want to face.

Holly's magic turned me back—almost—into a human. Now it's wearing off.

The evidence was in front of him, bagged and tagged. No other entity *but* one of the demon species could poof into dust. Cold fear seemed to seep out of the couch cushions, chilling him through. Mac sat up and stared out the tall windows at the winking lights of the harbor, too shaken to absorb the sight.

All this because a demon kissed me once. It's worse than herpes.

Unbidden, the memory of Geneva's naked body rose

like Venus from the sea of his memories. The ride to perdition had almost been worth it. The souls she had fed him from her lips had been intoxicating. *She* had been terrifying. Insane. Cataclysmic. Sex, murder, power, and hunger had drowned his humanity in one murderous brew. The thought of it made him grow hard. Made his hunger rise, yearning for the taste of souls.

He yanked his mind away. Fantasizing about his demon mistress was like hankering for a shot glass of pure poison. Unfortunately, she'd set the erotic bar to Olympic heights.

He hadn't touched another woman until today.

Constance had been similar and yet different. She had looked so innocent, like the maiden from some fairy tale waiting for rescue. His inner caveman had approved. Still did. Caveman was not a great thinker.

Oh, yeah, Constance had roused every red-blooded yearning he had, and then some. His mouth would never forget the angle, the texture, the resisting, melting feel of hers. Deadly fruit was always the sweetest.

Remember the fangs. Unfortunately, they were kind of erotic, too.

God, I'm perverse. What is it with me and bad girls?

He wanted Constance even more than he'd ever wanted Geneva. Not good. Constance was far more dangerous because, once safe from her teeth, he wanted to know why she was alone, why she hadn't bitten anyone before, and why she'd picked him as her first. Curiosity meant getting involved.

Oh, right, as if I have time to get emotionally invested in a hungry vampire.

At moments, she'd seemed so heartbreakingly sad. And then there was that smile. That melancholy smile could slide under any guy's tough, manly man shell and go straight for the marshmallow center. Once he was vulnerable, he'd lose the edge of cool logic that made him a good detective. Then he'd make mistakes. Like getting his soul sucked out.

Forget it. The job came first. Dead bodies and paperwork . . .

But that wouldn't fly as an excuse this time.

I'm not a cop anymore.

The realization hit him afresh.

They'd fired him because he was a freak. Because he'd made that thinking-with-his-dick mistake once already.

Mac buried his face in his hands, an unruly mix of emotions digging a hot ache in his chest. Shame. Despair. Anger. Regret. Disgust. *Demons destroy. I used to be the guy with the badge who saved people.*

As his emotions raced, he could feel a restless throb of power growing inside him, pounding with every beat of his pulse. He lifted his head, instinctively bracing his hands on the edge of the couch. Heat swept through his body, a sudden, scorching fever. Sweat stung the cuts and scrapes Bran had left on his flesh.

Strong emotion made the demon infection flare up, as if it fed off the extra energy. He lifted one hand and examined it in the dim light. He was solid, not crumbling to demon dust. That was a good sign. It sucked when that happened at random moments, like standing in a supermarket checkout line.

Mac closed his eyes, taking a deep breath, fighting for calm. The throb spread through his blood, following the nerves like a tide. Not painful, not nauseous like it had been during his first infection. Now it was a flush of excitement, as if someone were running through the hallways of his body, flicking on all the lights as they went. As if all his cells were standing at attention.

Why is there no pain?

Last year, when Geneva had Turned him, every organ had hurt like hell. This felt completely different. Mac didn't know if that was good or bad. He sprang to his feet, pacing the room.

Maybe it's not the demon at all. Maybe you picked up a whole new monster flu in the Castle. For all he knew, he had giant squid disease and would start sprouting tentacles at any moment.

Crap. He needed a better supernatural immune system.

Geneva and her demon cooties should have been enough to inoculate him against anything else out there. *So then what is this? You're a detective. Detect, already.*

The problem was that he'd barely been able to think since the whole demon trip started. It was like his mind was a puddle, and some giant's boot had stomped in it, scattering his thoughts to the four winds. *Pathetic. Think like you're solving a case.*

That meant backing up, starting again from the basics and looking at the evidence with a cool, unemotional eye. A little hard, considering what was at stake. If his demon side got the upper hand, he'd be looking for someone's life and soul to eat. Many someones. He'd be his own worst nightmare, and he wouldn't care one little bit.

Grimly, Mac got up and went into the small second bedroom that served as his office. The desk was buried in paper, but he yanked open the drawer and rummaged until he found his notebook and a pen. He missed his partner. He missed the labs and computers and camaraderie that solved cases. He'd been reduced to the simplest tools: paper, pen, and brain. *Then make do.*

The notebook was black and hinged at the top, the same kind he'd used when he was working a case. Just holding it made him feel better. He walked back into the living room, now turning on a light. He sat on the couch again, flipping the notebook open to a fresh page. He started writing.

1. Return of demon symptoms when in company of hot vampire chick.
2. First instance of dusting was involuntary, under duress.
3. Castle a factor?
4. Not all symptoms same as previous. No pain. Much heat.

It was a halting, stumbling start, but it was something. As he wrote, the throbbing energy running through him sharpened his mind, seemed to help him take control of his ideas. For a moment, he felt like his old self.

5. Not enough data to conclusively determine cause and effect.

He didn't like the fifth item. It made the whole line of reasoning grind to a halt. Perversely, just because he'd been a demon, that didn't mean he was an expert—but he refused to believe that Destination: Demonville was inevitable. *Time to put on the research shoes.*

There was only one person who'd ever tried to help. She had books, resources, and a boatload of magical power. Feeling suddenly hopeful, Mac wrote:

6. Go see Holly Carver.

Then he frowned. It looked good on paper, but that idea sucked. Mac flipped the notebook shut. His stomach felt like a bag of nightcrawlers, writhing with uncertainty. Holly's stupid magic house had tried to bash him to pulp the last time he'd dropped by. And he really wished he hadn't tried to eat Holly's soul the last time they'd met. That made things so awkward. *Damn, damn, damn. Bad dates always come back to bite you in the ass.*

He sucked in a breath, clenching his teeth again. Once, there had been sparks between him and Holly. A sudden twinge of mirth disrupted his brooding. *Caravelli will absolutely hate it if she agrees to help me. Serves him right for chucking me in the Castle.*

He pictured the vampire's unhappy face. Now *there* was an upside to this whole fiasco.

Hey, if life hands you giant squid disease, make calamari.

Chapter 8

Ashe Carver scowled as the tall, fair-haired vampire stalked away. Slowly, her eyebrows lifted. The view was noteworthy. She could see why Holly was physically attracted, especially from the rear view. What she didn't get was how her own sister could be so stupid.

Ashe tore herself away from where she had no business looking and studied Holly instead. She hadn't been home for over fifteen years, and Holly wasn't a kid anymore. Ashe had been expecting someone weak, in the thrall of a vampire's venom. Instead, Holly was a perfect Carver: powerful, smart, and in charge.

Something, truth be told, Ashe was still working on.

They were two sides of the family genetic coin. Holly took after their mother: short and dark, with delicate features. Ashe was tall, fair, and athletic, like their father's family.

Holly would know that mostly from photographs. Ashe remembered her parents all too well. Dad standing right where Holly was now, talking to Mom, who'd be working at the counter, making sandwiches . . . the memory sunk into Ashe like the fangs of a steel trap. Or a vampire. For a moment, she wished she'd stayed away.

"You don't know a thing about Alessandro," Holly snapped the moment the front door banged shut.

Ashe jerked back to the present. "Fang-boy. What's there to know?"

"Alessandro's different." Holly held up her hand as Ashe drew a breath to protest. "He's my Chosen. It's an old legend. When a human loves a vampire completely and with free will, that vampire is freed from the blood thirst."

Oh, please. "Then what does he eat? Doughnuts?"

"Chosen vampires can feed energetically. From the bond with their human."

Nausea skewered Ashe. "They feed on hot sex?"

Holly blushed.

"Oh, ick." For a moment Ashe knew she sounded like the teenager she'd once been. Weird how a person reverted the moment they went back to the family home. "Gah!"

"We're . . ." Holly sat down again, clearly struggling for words. "We're happy. It's working. Alessandro's more human than other vampires. Humanish."

"Do you know how messed up that sounds?"

Holly's look turned sharp. "I'm trying to explain. You don't have to like it."

Ashe had heard enough. "Give your head a shake. Get real. Get rid of him."

"No."

"I'm speaking for Mom and Dad."

Holly stared at her for a long, hard moment. "They're dead. They don't get a vote."

The words were meant to be brutal. "I know," Ashe said quietly. "I killed them. I owe it to them to make sure you're all right."

Holly looked away, backing down. "They died in an accident."

"I cast an egotistical, idiotic spell to give Mom and Dad car trouble so that they didn't come home to find out I'd left you alone that night."

"You were sixteen. You wanted to go to a concert. That's normal teenage crap."

Surprise rung through Ashe, clear as the strike of a bell.

Holly had forgiven her. *She shouldn't. Maybe she was too young to really get what I did.*

Ashe hammered home her point. "I used powerful magic I had no business touching. I made their car crash. The aftermath nearly destroyed your powers."

"And it destroyed yours. You took off. I know the story. That's history. We both have to move on."

Ashe had been over and over this moment in her head. The one where she tried to make things right. She leaned forward, her mouth dry with the soot of burned-out emotion. "I screwed up back then. I'm sure as hell not going to screw up now. You're in trouble. I can do something about it."

The clock ticked. Ashe could hear the small house noises—pings in the radiator, a creak of the floorboards as the cat chased shadows. Those should have been comforting sounds, but they somehow wound the tension in the room even tighter.

"I'm not in trouble," said Holly. "And I'm not your redemption."

Ashe took a deep breath. She wanted to snatch Holly from her chair and shake sense into her, but this wasn't a problem she could solve with force. For starters, Holly was a powerful witch, whereas she was a husk with no active magic.

Ashe changed tactics. "What about a family? Surely you'll want kids?"

"Who knows?" Holly shrugged.

Oh, Goddess. "Surely you're not thinking of adopting?"

"Down the road, maybe."

"Crap, you're serious. A vampire baby daddy?"

Holly shrugged again. "Why not?"

Ashe felt a surge of panic, but stomped on it. Vampires couldn't father children, and no vampire male would tolerate someone else's young. Holly was tragically deluded. Delusions like that could destroy a woman. He might kill the kid.

"Damn it, Holly!" That was what Ashe hated most about

the monsters. They always looked like something familiar, until the mask slipped and showed the evil beneath.

As in the case of a sixteen-year-old girl who murdered her parents with a spell. She saw one of those masks in the mirror every day.

Brooding was an occupational hazard for a creature of the night. Alessandro disliked indulging the vampire stereotype, but there he was. He leaned against the T-Bird, smoked, and scowled into the darkness. At least he was wearing battle leathers and weapons. That gave the moment some cachet.

Ashe was still inside the house, talking to Holly. Sharp though his hearing was, Alessandro could only hear the rise and fall of voices—sometimes angry, sometimes not. A glance at his watch told him that almost an hour had passed.

He took a drag on the cigarette, watching the glow brighten as he inhaled. He'd started smoking to mask the scent of human blood when he walked in crowded places. Now it gave him an excuse to stand outside, staring at the front door Ashe had all but literally slammed in his face.

He was a hunter. He knew how to wait. Alessandro crushed out his cigarette, the sound of his boot on the driveway pavement a loud, gritty scrape. It was a quiet neighborhood this late at night, only the occasional rustle of a raccoon or cat breaking the silence.

At last the front door opened. Ashe clumped down the front steps, red and white helmet under her arm. Alessandro straightened, instinctively shifting his weight so that he could move quickly if needed. The urge to defend his territory burned fever-strong. It didn't matter that this was Ashe's house. He had put down emotional roots for the first time in hundreds of years. He would win this battle.

Their gazes locked with an almost audible clash.

Ashe gave a low laugh. "You look like the schoolyard bully, loitering in the dark." It was eerie how her voice had the same timbre as Holly's.

"If you leave now, I won't put that comparison to the test."

"Oh, I'm leaving—for tonight," she said coolly.

Alessandro remained dead still. *Nothing's ever that easy.*

"Don't rejoice yet. I'm staying in town. My sister and I have a lot of catching up to do." She yanked the zipper of her jacket closed another inch.

"Leave Holly in peace."

"I'm not the bloodsucker here." Ashe flicked her hair back over her shoulder. "Holly fed me a pile of crap about how you never bite her. I've heard that line before."

It was true. Holly's magic had released him from that burden, but Alessandro said nothing. Ashe would never believe him, so why waste his breath?

She went on, anger thick in her voice. "Last week I took out a nest of fifteen vamps that had kidnapped half the city council's children. That was Calgary. The week before that it was a horror show in Duluth. A dozen kills: six vamps, six werewolves terrorizing half the city."

Alessandro narrowed his eyes. "Am I supposed to be impressed?"

"I could take you out between breakfast and coffee."

"And I could kill you where you stand, but I'll take up sunbathing before I ask Holly to choose between her lover and her sister."

"Who says she gets to choose?"

"Don't push me."

"Yeah, yeah." Ashe let the helmet dangle from her hand, appearing to relax a degree. Above her, the stars were faint pinpricks, dimmed by the ambient city light. "Clear something up for me. Grandma wrote to me once that she knew you years ago. Is that true?"

"I've been in Fairview a long time."

"Then how come I never saw you around when I was growing up?"

"Vampires make parents and grandparents nervous."

"Now there's a shocker."

"I would never hurt a child. I do what I can to respect families, which is why you're still breathing."

Ashe laughed, and it hung in the air like a chemical accident. "Sure. Did you know there's a family reunion in Hawaii? That's where Grandma is right now, but Holly's not there."

"Why aren't you?"

"Because of you. I couldn't exactly play on the beach knowing my sister was sleeping with the dead."

"That's your decision."

"Yeah, before you blow this off, think a minute. If Holly went, she'd have to explain to the relatives that her main squeeze is an animated corpse. Like that's going to go down well with a bunch of witches hoping and praying for the next generation of magical babies. We're a dying people. Children mean a lot to us."

Alessandro stood silent and expressionless, letting the implication of her words turn him to stone. Holly hadn't said a thing about the reunion. "She's in school. She couldn't go anyway."

"We're her *family,* Caravelli. You say you respect the concept. Try and remember what it means."

"I would never stop her from going if she wanted to."

"Yeah, yeah, you love each other, blah blah blah."

Alessandro pressed his lips together. He wasn't sure what Ashe had in life besides attitude, but it wasn't making her a happy person. "Is there a point here besides the stake in your back pocket?"

"Just what the hell do you think you're doing to my sister? She's a warm-blooded young woman who deserves a real, live man. *You* leave her in peace."

Ouch.

Ashe walked toward her bike, cutting across the grass to give him a wide berth. "See you around, fang-boy."

Impassively, Alessandro watched her put on her helmet and mount the Ducati. The bike pulled away, the motor snarling through the still, dark streets. With a disgusted sigh, he headed up the front steps, trying to shake off the dirty feeling Ashe had left in her wake.

Surely if Holly was unhappy, she'd say something. . . .

So much for my first hunt. I am the most pathetic vampire ever to rise. After Constance's dismal attempt to bite Conall Macmillan, the Castle might as well crumble around her ears just as Reynard had feared. At least the rubble would hide her shame.

For a fleeting moment, she wondered whether there was any truth to Reynard's doomsday rumors, but she had far more immediate things to worry about, like rescuing her son. Keeping her family together. Anything else, however urgent, fell to a distant second.

Constance wandered slowly back toward Atreus's rooms, looking for Viktor. The beast had wandered off again. Like most canines, he'd come back to the last place he'd considered home. The question was always when.

She'd been searching for the werebeast when she'd seen Bran. She'd followed the guardsman, hoping he'd lead her to Reynard's headquarters. It was likely that's where they had taken Sylvius's box.

Constance stopped, twisting her long hair into a rope, a nervous habit from childhood. Then Conall Macmillan had come along. *And didn't he make a fine mess, knocking Bran unconscious so I couldn't follow him?* On top of that, after she had decided Macmillan would do for her first meal, he went and turned into a cloud of dust. *Blast him!*

She still felt Macmillan's touch on her flesh, a brand that marked her as a trusting fool. Men and demons were such expert liars. Then again, she had been planning to bite him. She couldn't exactly throw stones.

Resuming her path, she threaded her way through the maze of corridors. Her feet fell silently, only the rustle of her skirts marking her passage through the semidarkness. A cold draft told her she was getting close to her destination.

Too bad Macmillan had been so compelling. He had

good, capable hands. A deep voice. He had aroused a curiosity she'd all but forgotten, not just as a vampire, but as a woman. If she'd begun to dream of home and family, he'd sharpened that yearning, given it new details. A face with dark eyes and a fleeting smile.

It made her think of so many of her mother's songs, those ones sung around the table so long ago. *Come away, my lassie-o, come away, my bonny / Come away, my dearie-o, with rovin' soldier Johnny . . .*

That, more than anything, was a signal for caution. The last man who made her sing couldn't wait to put his hand up her skirts and his teeth in her neck.

She passed a large leather glove someone had dropped. One of the guardsmen? A spy of Prince Miru-kai? She stepped carefully around it, reluctant to touch it even with her shoe. It was too big for anything that was, or ever had been, human.

Well, any spies were wasting their time. Sylvius was gone.

Constance reached her destination. Viktor was nowhere in sight, but her master was there. Constance stood in the shadow of the door, trying to see without being seen. Atreus sat in the great, carved chair, but it seemed to engulf him, more a prison than a throne.

Atreus rocked back and forth, his face in his hands. She could guess what that meant. The strain of Reynard's visit had left his mind worse off than before. His slowly gathering madness took so many forms: Grandiose dreams. Forgetfulness. Hallucinations. Now, he had added violence and betrayal to his repertoire.

Did he grieve for Sylvius? She wondered whether he even remembered who Sylvius was.

Should I go to him? Instead, she lingered in the doorway, rubbing Sylvius's pendant between her thumb and fingers. In the past, she had reached out to Atreus, a flower tracking the light. She had hungered for his regard, his protection. Now, even her anger toward him felt muffled, wrapped in dull, colorless grief. What could she do for him? It wasn't a question of loyalty. It was a question of fact. She had nursed him for years, but he had nearly killed her and had given away her son.

Reynard had promised that his men would visit this part of the Castle daily to ensure all was well and to supply whatever goods might be needed. He would keep that promise. She need have no fears for Atreus's physical care.

For the moment, the only thing she could truly do for her master was to fix the damage he had done.

Constance crept along the edge of the room, hugging the wall. She turned when she got to a passageway on the right. It was a short hall that branched into individual bedrooms. Atreus had the largest. That door, a pointed arch of dark, polished wood, was to her right.

Atreus forbade anyone to set foot inside his chambers, always locking the door tight. That had always been quite fine with Constance. She had no wish to invade a sorcerer's private space—until now.

Anxiety shrilled with the urgency of an animal in an iron trap.

This had better be worth the risk.

It was a testament to Atreus's befuddled state that he'd begun to neglect his secrets. The door to his room was slightly ajar, just enough to see the faint glow of a lamp within. Cautiously, she gave a push, letting the door drift open with a faint creak.

The chamber was large, with a bed covered in dark furs. A terra-cotta oil lamp hung on chains from the ceiling. The far corner held a high table draped in black silk and littered with the accouterments of a sorcerer. At the foot of the bed was a trunk. Nothing looked actively threatening.

So far, so good. But with sorcerers, one could never tell.

She had heard that vampires could not enter where they were not invited. That didn't seem to apply within the Castle. Atreus's magic was another matter. It might do more than stop her. It might destroy her.

Her scalp prickling with nerves, she cautiously waved a hand in the archway of the chamber door, half expecting it to be blown off in a whoosh of flame.

Nothing.

She slid one foot inside the room like a swimmer testing the temperature of a pond.

Nothing.

With her heart in her mouth, she drifted inside Atreus's rooms like a guilty ghost, tiptoeing across the flagstones, every sense on the highest alert. What she wanted was in the trunk. At least, she was fairly sure it was. She might never have set foot inside this room, but that did not mean she had never spied on her master from time to time.

Constance nervously watched the table where Atreus did his magic. While the Castle interfered with so many supernatural energies, it had never stopped him from weaving spells. She had no idea what wild spirits lingered among his books and wands, ready to jump out at the unwary.

The guilty. Justified or not, what she was doing was wrong. She didn't like herself at all, but that didn't slow her down one bit. Sylvius needed her.

She knelt beside the trunk. At the height of Atreus's power, they had lived in splendor. Now all that wealth was gone, the remains of his kingdom whittled down to just the contents of the trunk. It was old and strapped in greening brass, the lid heavy as a coffin's. There was a padlock, but it was ancient. Constance broke it in seconds. The lid rose with a crackle of old leather hinges, releasing the scent of aromatic woods. Clothes, books, and a bundle of scrolls lay neatly piled inside—but she was looking for something else.

The jewel chest sat in one corner. She lifted it out and set it on the cold, gray stone of the floor. The chest was a cube of tooled leather the shade of old, dried blood. The handles on either side were ornate silver gone black with age, but there was no lock. No hasps. No hinges.

She turned the cube over and over, but couldn't figure out where the lid was fastened. Only the handles gave a clue as to which side of the cube was the top.

It was sealed by a spell. *Damnation.*

Frustrated, she ran her fingers over the surface of the

box, seeking any means of prying it open by sheer force. Her long nails found the crease where the lid closed and dug in, grabbing the silver handle with her other hand. She pulled, gritting her teeth and giving every ounce of anger to the task. Her fingers began to ache, the nails bending away from her flesh.

The only thing that gave was her grip on the handle. She slipped, cutting herself on the tarnished metal.

"Bollocks!"

Blood welled from her finger and dripped onto the tooled leather surface of the box. Constance hastily swiped it away, but left a dark smudge across the lid. *As if I needed to leave more evidence of my crime!*

The box made a noise like the pop of a latch. Startled, she pulled her hands away and it slithered from her lap to the floor, landing with a bump. Grabbing it again, she barely stopped it from tumbling over.

The top of the box sprang open in a corona of light. The only thing missing was a fanfare of trumpets.

Bloody hell!

Literally. The sacrifice of blood had opened it. *What's the point of that?*

Then she was distracted.

Rubies glinted in bracelets of beaten gold. Pearls snaked in endless ropes, winding in and around a glittering confusion of brooches, rings, and the crowns of long-forgotten kings. After years of the gray, drab monotony of the Castle, the glitter of light and color nearly burned her eyes.

She picked at the top of the pile, rattling the riches with impatient fingertips. And then she found it. There. That's what she was after: a circle of patterned gold no bigger than a cherry. She might have mistaken it for a coin. It was worth more than money.

A key.

Atreus had said there had only ever been nine, and four had been destroyed. One had been bound into a book of demon magic that was now lost. There were only four left, and Josef had already stolen one of those. He'd used it to escape to the outside world before he could succumb to his beast, like his brother, Viktor.

She'd never learned how he'd managed to steal it, but then, Josef was a daring warrior. She was a plain milkmaid. She had been used to enduring, keeping her head down, not thinking up grandiose and daring schemes, not risking her master's wrath—especially not once she had Sylvius to care for. Daring only came once Atreus had hurt someone she loved.

Well, she had it now.

She picked up the key. It looked exactly like the one Josef had shown her, a rich gold that held streaks of some darker, tawny metal. The design looked like a ragged sun.

Josef had said the keys would find a way out. Anyone could use them—but how?

A key will take me to the outside world, where there are many, many humans. I can hunt there. I can have my full vampire powers. Then she would come back strong, transformed, and rescue Sylvius.

For the first time since I was a girl, I will breathe free air.

A wave of dizziness overtook her.

Freedom.

A glove of ice fisted her heart. She hadn't walked outside the Castle for so long. Josef had helped her figure it out: she'd been here for two and a half centuries. The outside world had changed. She would be lost. Exposed. Confused.

She wanted to go. She *needed* to go, but the open skies would feel like the top of her skull was being lifted away. Fear of all that open space, of all those people . . .

A thick quiet sifted like dust in the Castle's shadows.

I've been here too long.

Don't think about it. Surely it's not so bad.

Constance dropped the key down the front of her tightly laced bodice. It slid, rough and cold, down the hollow between her breasts. The key was going to poke at her, a constant reminder of what she'd done. Just like her conscience. *Thief!*

Closing the jewel chest, Constance set it back in the trunk. Perhaps it would have been wise to take other jewels to sell or trade, but she wasn't going to compound the error of her ways. All the years spent in the Castle, in the violent courts of a sorcerer-king, hadn't clouded her sense of right and wrong. She'd fought to defend herself, but she'd never killed. She'd enjoyed luxuries, but never stolen. Until now.

She'd grown up poor, and had grown poor again as Atreus's power withered. She understood that when a person had very little, it mattered if someone took it away. For that reason, she never wanted anything she didn't have a right to. But then she did take a knife, sliding it into her sheath. She needed to replace the one Reynard had confiscated. Surely that was justified?

After she closed the lid of the trunk, Constance crept from the room, the key a hope held tight above her still heart.

She knew where there was a door.

It had appeared about a year ago after a great battle. It was clearly no ordinary door, for it was locked so securely that the guardsmen had never bothered to post a watch. Just the occasional patrol passed by it.

Still, its presence baffled Constance. Despite the keys, despite the odd portal that flickered open when a demon was summoned, the Castle was meant to be air-tight. A prison. So why was there suddenly a door? *Perhaps Reynard is right and the Castle's magic is falling to pieces. Like Atreus.*

She slowed her steps. The door was now within sight. Still walking, Constance took out the coin-shaped key. Unfortunately, Josef had neglected to mention how the wretched things worked.

She glanced over her shoulder, giving way to an involuntary shudder. A patrol could come, and she'd seen what they'd done to the last poor fool who'd earned their wrath. Bran had a taste for skinning his victims alive.

At a trot, she crossed the last few feet to the door and pressed her hand against the rough surface. Her fingers looked frail against the wood, except for the long, sharp nails. The possibility of liberty was delicious, but it was terrifying, too. She could taste fear on her tongue, bitter as a new penny.

Pay no attention. Keep moving. This is for Sylvius.

"Constance."

She gasped, wheeling. Then she recognized him. *Lore!*

"Where the bloody hell did you come from? What are you doing here?" she asked, every hair on her body tingling with shock. "I thought you'd gone. Escaped. You and your whole pack."

It was all she could do not to slap him for scaring her clear to her second death.

It had been a year since she had seen Sylvius's childhood friend, but Lore looked the same. His dark hair was still long and shaggy, his face still gypsy-dark, the prominent bones giving him the same rough-hewn look as all the hellhounds. The young alpha looked fit and healthy, his slim, tightly muscled body moving with vigor. His clothes were different, cleaner and better mended than she remembered.

He leaned against the wall, bending his tall frame so he could see her face. "Why are *you* waiting by the door, Grandmother?"

She grimaced at the name. It was a title of extreme respect, one he knew she hated. At her disgusted expression, a rare grin split his long face. Hellhounds, like any dog, were not above teasing those they liked.

"How did you get back in here?" She dropped her voice to a whisper, just in case.

"When we escaped the Castle, we regained our magic." He spoke slowly, his words slightly accented. The hounds had their own tongue, and rarely spoke with other species. "One of those talents is unlocking doors. As long as I do not stay long enough for the Castle's magic to affect my powers, I can come and go."

"Why by Saint Margaret's toenails would you want to come back?"

He gave her a long look, the torchlight deepening the hollows in his face.

She folded her arms, hugging herself. "I'm sorry. That was rude."

One never asked a hellhound too many questions. Unlike almost every other species in creation, they could not lie. It was even hard for them to evade a direct question.

"I don't like standing here in the open," she added.

He cupped her elbow and drew her around the corner and into the shadows. "You should not have asked me why I'm here."

She wasn't in the mood for more guilt. "I can keep your secret."

"Atreus—"

"Atreus is losing his mind. He grows worse each day, each hour."

Lore's face grew tense. "Even so—"

"Bloody hell, Lore, you know me. You were like Sylvius's big brother."

He licked his lips. She could see the moment he decided to trust her. "Most of my pack escaped, but some were left behind. They are slaves or soldiers for the warlords and sorcerers. One by one, I've been bartering for their freedom."

"Bartering?"

"You wear oil of roses. Where do you think it comes from?"

"Josef gave it to me before he left."

"And where did he get it?"

Constance blinked, putting the pieces together. Doors. Keys. "It came from the outside world."

"Like others before me, I've discovered the Castle residents have a taste for luxury goods."

"Smuggling!"

Lore gave a low laugh. "Clothes and books and tobacco. Goods are cheap and plentiful out there." He nodded toward the door. "So far, I've traded for a half dozen of my people. Shoes are popular. Cross-trainers."

Cross what? "And no one sees you come and go?"

"Bribery works. It is more the outside of the Castle that is a problem."

"Why?"

"Naturally enough, not everyone wants those in the Castle to escape, but I've arranged it so that my hounds guard the door. At certain times they leave. They can honestly say they haven't seen me go in with gifts and come out with another hound." He gave a sardonic smile. "It seems we are compelled to tell the truth in the outside world, the same as we must here."

Constance hugged herself, considering what he'd said, and what she needed. "Lore," she said, picking her words carefully. "Something has happened."

He put his big hands on her shoulders, solid and comforting. "What?"

"The guardsmen have taken Sylvius."

Shock blanched the hellhound's face. He swore, spitting something in the hounds' own tongue. Not sparing a single detail, Constance told him what had happened. Lore crouched to the floor, as if her news had robbed him of the strength to stand.

Constance knelt beside him. "I need your help."

Lore closed his eyes. "Constance, no one can help Sylvius now. I wouldn't pit my whole pack against Reynard and his men. They're as strong as the most powerful demons."

"I don't need your hounds. I'll do this myself. I just need your help leaving the Castle. Show me what to do when I get to the outside world. I'm sure it's changed since I saw it last."

Lore didn't answer.

Constance searched his face. "Will you take me with you when you go?"

He looked away. "No."

For a moment, she didn't comprehend his words. It was the opposite of what her ears wanted to hear. She stared at him, astonished. "Why not? It's such a little thing. A tiny favor!"

He shook his head. She gripped his arm until he turned back to her. "Why not?"

He stood, backing away.

She rose as well, refusing to let him avoid her. "Tell me."

He made a frustrated gesture. "Right now, you're still as much a human as a vampire. Would you throw that away?"

"If I have to."

His eyes grew dark with sorrow. "Didn't you say that you were captured as soon as you rose from the grave? That you never fed?"

"Yes. That's why I'm so weak."

"Did none of the other vampires talk to you about this?"

Constance flinched. "I'm not one of them. They call me a mistake and won't have anything to do with me. You know that."

Lore hung onto the words a long moment, but he finally, reluctantly let them go. "If you cross the threshold, the bloodlust will overtake you. There're humans everywhere out there."

Constance shrugged, doing her best not to picture the moment. "So I will feed. That's what vampires do, isn't it?"

"The newly Turned don't simply feed. They kill. They go mad with hunger. I've seen it. You'll attack someone. You'll tear them to shreds."

"No." Shaking her head, Constance struck him in the chest. The blow thumped, making Lore stagger back. "No, I won't. You don't understand. I have to get out."

"You'll be executed if you leave!"

"It's not fair. I shouldn't be a prisoner. I haven't done anything wrong! I'm not a monster!"

But hadn't becoming a monster been her plan? Constance trembled, angry and confused.

Lore took her hands in his. "It's against the law to harm a human. The punishment is death. And that doesn't even touch on how you will feel about what you've done."

"You mean I'm trapped in here forever?"

"Could you kill someone? Not a guardsman. Not someone intent on doing you harm. Just an ordinary person living their ordinary life. Could you do it?"

Doubt pooled in her gut. "I never thought I would kill them. I thought I would simply take some of their blood."

"You're such an innocent, Constance. And Atreus kept you that way. That was both good and bad."

"I'm on my own now. I have to learn to fight for myself. I need to finish Turning."

"Your life has been blameless, Constance. Would you give that up? The cost of power is always more than we expect. We pay with what's closest to our hearts."

She paused, turning over his words. "But I'm trying to *save* the one I love most."

"Be careful how you bargain with destiny. You risk destroying the good it brings."

"Spare me your cryptic hellhound prophecies!"

"It's not a prophecy. It's truth."

"But if I were free . . ."

"Freedom costs." He gave a bitter laugh. "I barter for my people every chance I get. Someday I'll pay with my life."

Constance sank to the floor, sitting down before her legs gave out. She felt suddenly hollow, an eggshell with nothing inside.

Freedom cost. Hope came at a high price, too.

She was really tired of being poor.

Chapter 9

October 2, 7:30 am
101.5 FM

"**G**ood morning, Fairview, this is—uh—CSUP, the super supernatural station on campus. Welcome to the morning show, brought to you by the Fairview Interspecies Cultural Association, proud sponsor of the new Fairview University and Community College Pan-Species Studies Department.

"Our regular host is off this morning, so this is, um, Dr. Perry Baker, your friendly resident computer professor. Is your laptop possessed? Eating your homework? Sending socially awkward e-mails? Give me a call, and I'll give you a diagnosis. I might even give you deniability. But first, a tune from my personal local fave songstress, Lupa Moon.... Hmm, okay, how was that, Dave? Am I talking too fast?"

"Turn the mic off, Perry."

The next morning brought cloudy October skies and a wind that smelled of frost. The atmosphere reminded Mac of endless hours spent doing sports drills before school—football, rugby, and whatever other team that would have him. Hockey outdoors if there was ice, after school on the streets if there wasn't. The memories of cold mud and bruises were sharp and precious. They gave the part of him that was still wholly human a source of strength.

Maybe that connection to his old self was what made it so easy to fall back into a man-with-a-plan routine. He had investigating to do, and he knew where he was going to begin.

As he got dressed, he looked inside the gun locker he kept in the closet. He'd had to surrender his police weapon, but his 9 mm Sig Sauer P229 semiautomatic was in good working order. He had plenty of clips of ammunition. Good to know. He'd never been the kind of cop who relied on firepower to solve his problems, but times they were a-changing. He wasn't going to need it in broad daylight when sword-toting vamps were safely in bed, but come sundown he was going armed to the teeth, silver bullets and all. One night of playing tag with Caravelli was enough.

And then it was time to go to work. The moment he took his raincoat out of the closet and slipped his notebook into its roomy pocket, Mac felt like himself again. His chest unknotted with relief, the same sensation as finding a long-lost set of keys.

His good luck held. His search for Holly on the Fairview University and Community College campus lasted less than half an hour. Like many early-morning students, she was walking, head down and eyes half shut, from the bus stop to the library. Mac came out of his lurking position beneath the spreading branches of a cedar tree.

"Hello, Holly."

She stopped dead in her tracks, turning the color of old cottage cheese. She was scared. "Oh, Goddess, what are you doing here?"

He held up his hands, palms out. "Okay, so I didn't leave a good impression the last time we met. I'm safe now. I'm on a strict diet of junk food and antacids."

Frowning, she shifted her overloaded backpack. It looked like she had half the bookstore in there. "How'd you get out of the Castle?"

"I walked out. The maid service sucked." He stretched out one hand, indicating a nearby bench. "Do you have a few minutes to talk?"

She didn't budge, but watched his every twitch. "You walked out, huh? How?"

"Luck and an absence of hellhounds."

"Goddess, Alessandro's going to be pissed."

"Can we talk? Anywhere you like." He kept standing, hands in the air, like a suspect under arrest.

She looked wary, then interested, and then checked her watch. "Yeah, okay. But this had better be good. And I want to talk someplace where there are lots of people around."

Mac wasn't going to argue. He'd have said the same thing. He lowered his hands slowly. "Coffee?"

"Okay." She turned and headed for the Student Union Building, but kept him a few paces away and within clear view. Her distrust bothered him, but it was no more than he deserved.

There were coffee wagons set up outside, releasing clouds of heavenly scent into the crisp air. Heavy plastic tables and chairs were ranged around them, the garish shades of green and pink almost luminous in the gray light. The outdoor eating area made more sense in the summer, but students seemed to use it all year around. Maybe they needed the cold air to wake up.

Holly kept marching until she joined the line outside the Zap Baby Espresso Bar. Her quick, graceful movements brought other things to mind, like the way she kissed.

And the way Connie kissed. Mac gave himself a mental head slap. *When did she become Connie instead of Constance?* For a moment he was lost, reliving the moment, the silken softness of her mouth, the wild berry taste of her. *She didn't know Jane Austen. What woman doesn't know* Pride and Prejudice? *That's just unnatural. The campus bookstore should have a copy. . . .*

Oh, come on! She tried to bite you, goof. Get a grip. No more Babes of Doom.

Mac blinked, rejoining the here and now with a guilty

jolt. He was daydreaming about a girl like he was in eighth grade. One with fangs and claws. Yup, he was one sick puppy.

He stood beside Holly. The tension between them felt like solid ice. "How's classes?"

She flicked her dark ponytail over her shoulder. "Hard. How'd you find me?"

"I was a cop, remember? Everyone knows you're taking a business degree. The rest was simple deduction."

"Who's everyone?"

"Everyone is everyone. You're a celebrity in the supernatural community after defeating my evil demon mistress in the smack-down of the decade. You sneeze and every vamp, fey, and werewolf wants to talk about it."

"Oh, great." Holly winced. The gesture emphasized the dark circles under her eyes. With her softly pointed features and the oversized sweater that hung almost to her knees—probably Caravelli's—she looked like a sleepy child. "So you listen to celebrity gossip, eh?"

He pointed to the Student Union Building. The CSUP call letters were mounted over a small door to the right, along with a large poster of the Gothed-up werecougar announcer, Errata.

"There's the radio station. They chatter on-air like it's the amateur stalker hour. And, you know, there are some bottom-dwellers in some of the motel bars who'll talk to demon trash like me. If I buy them drinks, that is."

Holly gave a lopsided smile, showing she was entertained despite herself. "So what do they say?"

"No one can figure out why you're bothering with school. You've got major magic."

That earned him an eye roll. "I was running my ghost-busting agency into the ground. I didn't know how to balance the books, or market effectively, and forget anything to do with payroll. Being a witch didn't make me a businesswoman. Get real. I beat Geneva. So what? It's not like I won the lottery and can retire. Life goes on."

By then they were at the front of the line. Mac ordered a

plain medium coffee, Holly a latte. They took their cups to a bright green table at the edge of the eating area. A scattering of crumbs on the pavement had attracted a flock of sparrows, and Mac had to walk carefully. They wanted the food more than they feared his feet.

Holly dumped her backpack and sat down. "So what do you want to talk about?"

"The demon thing," he started, but then stalled. It was going to be hard to put everything into words.

"What about it?"

He caught his breath and plunged in. "After you zapped me, I've been eating like a human."

"How long has it been?"

"I got out of the Castle about six months ago."

Her brow furrowed in surprise. "You've been back here all that time?"

"No." Mac smiled briefly. "I took a detour."

The corner of Holly's mouth turned up. "Is there a punch line to that?"

"Well, I got out of the Castle the first time by sheer accident. There were these New Agers in Sedona trying to summon an angel. They thought they were making a portal into the hereafter. They got me instead, poor bastards."

Holly gave a startled whoop of laughter.

Mac chuckled. "Anyway, to give them their due, these folks were terrific. I was a wreck, after everything that happened, everything I'd done. They let me stay with them out in the desert—and I mean literally just sit and look at the earth and sky—for as long as it took to put myself back together."

"So their angel had guardian angels of his own."

"Yeah, though I never did bond with the whole vegan idea. If that's heavenly food, I'm not pure enough yet to appreciate it. Anyway, I came back here about a month ago. I've been laying low, just picking up the pieces." He paused. "Quite a few of them are broken beyond repair."

Holly looked down at her hot pink travel mug, picking at the rubber grip. "You got a raw deal, Mac."

"Yeah, and it's going south on me again."

She looked up. "Alessandro said. The demon's still in you."

Damn Caravelli. "I have to stop it. I seem to be getting some of those demon-type powers back. And it's odd. It feels different this time."

One of the sparrows hopped onto the table, but Holly ignored it. She was staring at Mac. "How do you mean, different?"

"Not too bad. Not painful. Kind of hyped. It started up when I was in the Castle again."

She narrowed her eyes. "Tell me exactly what happened last night."

He did. There was no point in leaving anything out. He had no idea which details might be important.

As he talked, the clouds started to thin, allowing a wash of weak sunlight to dapple the trees and buildings. More busloads of students arrived, and the crowds began to increase. The coffee area was getting noisy.

When he finished, Holly set her coffee mug down, a faint smile in her large green eyes. "So do you know anything more about this vampiress?"

Holly's too-interested expression made him sit very still, just so he didn't squirm. "No. Not a thing." *Only that thinking about her makes me crazy.*

"Your ears are turning red. She was pretty, I take it?"

His reply shot out more gruffly than he intended. "Yeah, well, I think I might have just been the meal ticket without the ticket part. She damn near ripped out my throat. Okay, an exaggeration, but I'm just saying . . ."

"She roused strong emotions, which led to exercising your demon powers in a major way."

Mac nodded, unable to meet her eyes. They had reached the heart of the matter. "I always knew there were traces of the demon left in me. I've been a bit stronger, a bit faster all along, but I'd been controlling myself just fine for six months. Then suddenly I could dematerialize. What happened?"

Holly sat back, clearly pondering what he'd said. "The Castle is supposed to neuter magical creatures, not create them."

"Can we use a different word than 'neuter'?"

"All right. The Castle's magic *mutes* things. Desires. Special abilities."

"Yeah, and that's the weird part. Why did it jump-start this latest episode?" If the Castle was supposed to stop appetites—including lust—then why did Constance put his inner caveman on red alert?

Holly wasn't listening, but sat tapping her thumbnail against her bottom teeth. "And yet, I found a room in there once—a beautiful, amazing place. It was like a bedchamber, but much larger, with a waterfall and fireplace and tapestries."

She looked up, flushing. "Neither magic nor desires were dampened in there. The Castle isn't consistent. It was built by magic, like my house. It may have enough sentience to create what it needs."

He sat back, his mood clenching like a fist. "Then it's too bad I can't walk up and ask who ordered the fully functional demon."

"What did you have for breakfast?" she asked abruptly.

Mac blinked. "Cereal."

"Was it good?"

"Uh—yeah, I guess so."

Holly spread her hands. "You're not a fully functioning demon. If you were, you'd be eating everything in sight on the way to chowing down on somebody's soul. I remember how you were. You were obsessed with eating. It was incredibly scary."

"So? I'm still hungry. The desire to drink life never went away." He tugged at his cuffs, embarrassment making him irritable. He was getting hot. His coat felt tight in the arms. *Damned dry cleaners.*

"But you don't have to."

"No, thank God."

"So this time is different. I don't know why."

"Then how can I fix it?"

"I didn't say I was giving up. You deserve a chance."

Not a ringing endorsement, but he'd take it. "You really think it's something to do with the Castle?"

"If you were holding steady for six months, it's the only new variable in the equation."

Mac waved a hand. "Great. The cause of my latest medical crisis is an alternate dimension."

Holly grimaced. "Try being in charge of the entrance to the damned thing."

Mac nearly spilled his coffee. "You're in charge of the portal?" As he said that, he realized it kind of made sense. She'd made it. She was the only one with enough power to do anything with it. "So then why are the hellhounds always hanging around?"

"I'm supposed to be the guardian, but I'm in school. I can't watch it twenty-four/seven."

"So you hired them?"

"They were big and tough and unemployed. Alessandro hired them to help him do his law and order thing."

"I'd get his money back. They're useless." *Up until the part where they kicked my ass and threw me inside.*

Holly sighed. "Yeah, well, the X-Men were busy. The hounds are what we have."

"Uh-huh." Mac noticed again how tired she looked. "Do you want another coffee?"

"No, I've hardly made a dent in this one."

"Something to eat?'

"Ugh. No." She made a face.

"Not a breakfast person?"

"Definitely not. And I've got to get to class." She touched his arm lightly. "Are you at the same phone number?"

"Yeah."

"I've got to go. I'll see what I can find out and call you. Um, probably best if . . ."

"Don't worry. I won't call your house. Caravelli would freak if he knew we'd talked. That would be fun for me, but probably not so much for you."

Holly looked chagrined. "Sorry. And it's not just him. It's my sister. She's staying in town and she's, er, not like me."

"Not a witch?"

"Vampire hunter on a mission to save me from myself."

"That's gotta be awkward." He chuckled. He couldn't help it.

She made a face. "Maybe I'll sell ringside seats." With that, she rose and picked up her backpack, hefting it onto her shoulders. It looked so heavy, he thought if she fell on her back she'd be stuck there, like a turtle.

Mac grinned at the mental image. "Sure I can't carry your books to class?"

"No thanks. This saves me going to the gym. Gotta run." She grabbed her coffee mug and paused long enough to plant a kiss on Mac's cheek. "Hang in there. I'll be in touch."

She took a few steps, then looked back, the pale, clear sunlight highlighting the delicate structure of her face. "Stay out of the Castle, eh? No exploring until we know what we're dealing with."

"Right," Mac said. "Absolutely not."

Chapter 10

October 2, 2:00 p.m.
101.5 FM

"**G**reetings, Earthlings. It's *Oscar in the Afternoon*, your program about where to go, what you need, and where the savvy supernatural shopper will buy it. I'm your host, Oscar Ottwell of the Silvertail Wolf Pack.

"First, we have Dr. Ruby Yaga here to give us the low-down on safe sex and all that means for us supernatural types—plus, what products are on the market to make those moonlit nights a little less scary.

"We'll get started with a word from our sponsor, the Wily Wolf Delicatessen."

Mac seeped through the Castle door, pausing to spiral into a column before assuming his human shape. He had his eyes squeezed shut in concentration, so he didn't notice Constance until a moment later when he looked around to get his bearings.

Constance gave him a gimlet stare. "How did you do that, demon?"

"I went poof," he said, but wasn't really thinking about his answer. He was staring at her, trying to decide whether he was delighted to see her or disconcerted by what he saw.

She was sitting slumped against the wall opposite the door, her knees drawn up under her chin. He didn't need sensitive-guy training to see she'd been crying. She was a mess, her eyes red-rimmed and her hair mussed where she'd jammed her fingers through it.

Oh, crap. He could already feel the horns of a dilemma poking him in the backside. Beautiful, crying woman. Homicidal maniac who'd tried to bite him. Comfort or run like hell? His inner caveman was confused.

"Bitten anybody yet?" he asked.

She gave him a baleful glare. "It's not a joking matter."

"Um. No, I'd say not."

She crammed her fingers back into her hair. "Oh, off with you. What would a demon know about it?"

"Off with you," he mimicked, pinning the accent perfectly. "My gran used to say that. I'm too old to shoo away now."

"Well, I'm bloody old enough to be your gran's gran's gran. And a bloody lot of good all those years have done me. Just call me the bloody vampire queen."

Mac raised his eyebrows. That was a lot of bloody, even for a vamp. "I dunno. I met the queen once. She was a couple of millennia of bad-assed scary. I think you and I are still in the minor leagues."

"What league?" she asked crossly.

Apparently there was no baseball in hell. Figured.

She looked up, loops of hair standing on end where she'd been kneading her scalp. There were fresh tears on her cheeks. Clear, like a human's. Vampire tears were pink. She hadn't tasted blood yet. He'd never seen her eyes flash gold or silver the way a vampire's usually did, either. She was stuck in between two species. They were two of a kind.

Mac walked over to the wall where she was sitting. Despite her fangy performance the day before, he wasn't too worried. His gun was loaded with silver ammo, plus he had three stakes, two knives, his demon talents, and a werepartridge in a pear tree. Besides, he wanted to be close to her. Her presence gave him the same warm, smooth buzz as a good single malt. *Careful—you think she's way too cute.*

And he had a copy of *Pride and Prejudice* in his pocket. Now he just had to make up his mind to give it to her. Not the move of a clinical, detached cop. It was straight from his eighth-grade-crush self, the uncool kid who loved his mom and wrote thank-you notes after Christmas.

But the little vampire was so clearly unhappy, she obviously needed cheering up. "You look like you've been sitting here a while."

"I've come and gone." She looked sullen. "Does it matter?"

"Something about a dusty piece of hallway keep bringing you back?"

She didn't answer, but kept fiddling with a gold coin, turning it over and over, rubbing at the design. She saw him look at it, then dropped it down her front with a defiant glare.

He looked at her for a long time, considering that softly rounded hiding place. "Let's keep this simple," he finally said.

"Keep what simple? Who says I even want to talk to you?"

Her tone was hostile, with a go-away-I'm-feeling-sorry-for-myself chill. Mac's fingers hovered near the holster of his weapon, relaxed but ready just in case she was really serious about the go-away part. One never could tell with vampires. *So here I sit, gun in one hand, Mr. Darcy in my coat pocket. Romantic conflict, anyone?*

He could smell that old-fashioned perfume. It beckoned, soft and sweet. *Dangerous.* "You seem like a nice girl. Something's obviously bothering you. Maybe I can help."

"What makes you say that?"

Mac paused for a moment, pondering that. He didn't feel like explaining the whole cop-but-not story. Who knew if they even had police where she came from? "It's what I do. I interfere in people's lives for their own good."

Constance furrowed her brow. "Aren't you a demon?"

He shrugged. "Half. I've been this way for a while."

"Impossible. Either you're a demon or you're not. There's no two ways about it."

"Women frequently tell me I'm impossible." He slid down the wall until he was sitting next to her. He was still a head taller. "But I'm human enough to care about somebody in trouble."

She stared at him, obviously unsettled by his casual air. "You'll be riding to my rescue like Sir Galahad?"

"Nah, I'm not that good with horses. I'm better with dogs."

"My dog ran away."

"Is that why you've been crying?"

She blew out her breath, the sound bloated with sarcasm. "What are you doing here, half demon? What brings you back to a place you were so desperate to leave? Surely it's not just to make me feel better."

He hesitated, then decided to get to the point. "I have a problem. I need to speak to someone who's been in the Castle for a long time. Someone who knows its history and how it works."

The question caught her off guard, as if she hadn't expected him to say anything serious. Her lips parted slightly, reminding him how soft they were. Being so close to Constance was reminding him why he couldn't banish her from his mind. She was the type of woman you couldn't kiss just once.

"Let's make a deal," he said. "I help you, you help me."

Her eyes narrowed. "Why should I trust you?"

"You're the one who tried to bite me, sweetheart."

After giving him a speculative look, Constance ducked her head, hiding her face behind her long, dark hair. "All right. Atreus has been here longer than anyone else that I know of, but I don't know how much help he would be."

"Why not?" Mac knew Atreus's name from his previous stay in the Castle—one of the thugs who had muscled his way to a position of dominance. Gang leaders who called themselves kings. "He rules a lot of the prison, doesn't he?"

"Once." Constance pursed those full lips. "Not anymore. He's gone quite mad."

Mac looked around at the stone walls and lugubrious torchlight. "Yeah, this place could get to somebody after a while. How long has he been here?"

"He was here long before Viktor and Josef came. They were here before I came."

"When did, uh, Viktor and Josef arrive?"

"I'm not sure."

"Can we ask?"

"Josef is gone. Viktor can't tell you. He's gone mad, too."

Mac swore.

"It was Viktor's beast that made him that way. Eventually he gave in to his animal side." Constance hugged her knees with her slender arms. "It was too hard for him to stay human."

That sounded unpleasantly like Mac's first demon transformation. "What kind of creature is Viktor?"

"Viktor is my dog."

Mac stared.

"He's mostly wolf," Constance amended. "Part vampire. Human to begin with. It was a curse. They're not real werewolves. Atreus made Viktor and Josef into his personal guard back when he still walked the world."

"Before he came to the Castle?"

"Atreus had keys. He came and went at will. I think Atreus might be as old as the Castle."

Now we're getting somewhere. "Then I need to speak to him."

"I said, he's mad." Constance made an impatient gesture, flicking his words out of the air. The sudden movement made Mac jump and grab for his gun. Constance froze.

"Nervous?" she asked, dryly amused.

"Cautious."

"Good." She smiled grimly, an expression that looked

wrong on her elfin face. "Be afraid. Atreus doesn't give anything without a price."

"What kind of price?"

"I don't know. It could be anything. But I might convince him to help you."

"Who are you to him?"

"He took me in when I got here. I was his servant for hundreds of years. I kept a home for him and those close to the throne. He was my protector."

That made sense to Mac. Centuries ago, a person was either lord or servant without many options in between. A small, young female, vampire or not, would seek out someone powerful enough to keep her safe. Politically incorrect by modern standards, but a good survival policy in a hellhole like the Castle. That didn't mean Mac liked it. There was plenty of room for abuse in a system that traded service for safety.

"Before I take you to him, I need you to help me," she said.

"What do you want?" he said, more because he was curious than anything else. "And don't say blood."

"The saints above only know what sort of indigestion a half demon would give me," she said flatly, but there was still a flicker of speculation in her eyes.

She paused, a strand of her dark hair stirring in an air current. She smoothed her hair down, its dark length part of the shadows. The Castle felt even emptier and more cavernous than usual, the torchlight seeming to fade before it fully touched her features.

"You should realize that Atreus might kill you." She closed her eyes for a long moment. "But I'm the only one he has now. Maybe I can still make him listen. Maybe."

Her voice held a world of devastation. Mac fell into the spell of her soft lilt, past the fangs and the quick tongue and the pretty face, and wondered where all that unhappiness came from. *I really can't afford to get emotionally invested in a vampire.*

Mac ignored the warning. There was too much he needed

to know. "I thought Atreus had a big court with lots of soldiers and retainers. At least that's what I heard."

"That was long ago. As he lost his wits, he lost those who followed him. Now there is only me."

"King Lear and Cordelia," Mac said softly.

"Who are they?"

Things must be bad if I'm thinking Shakespeare. "Characters from a play."

"Ah." She lifted her chin, huffy. "I wasn't a fine lady, to go spending my time at the theater. There was always work to be done."

Mac couldn't stop a smile.

"What's so amusing?"

"Nothing. So, to get back to what we've agreed to so far, you will help me with Atreus. What do you want from me?"

She nodded, looking even more pale than the usual vampire white-on-white. He wasn't sure why, but interceding with Atreus wasn't going to be easy for her.

She pressed her lips into a flat line, her gaze shifting away. "First let me say I'm sorry I tried to bite you. I thought you were human. I need to bite a human to get my—well, like you, there is still a bit of human in me."

A faint flush rose to her cheeks.

A bashful vampire. Who'da thunk. Mac helped her out. "You need to hunt to fully Turn."

She nodded, averting her face from him. "Yes. I've escaped that fate for a long time. I can't any longer." She looked like she was about to start crying again, her lower lip tucking in.

Mac put his hand on her shoulder, the cloth of her dress soft from long wear. He could feel the bones beneath. "Why not?"

Her head jerked, her tear-starred gaze going from his hand to his face, but she didn't shake him off. "The guardsmen took my son by force—I mean the foundling child I raised. I have no one to help me get him back."

Mac caught his breath. He was suddenly and unexpectedly on familiar ground. A crime had been committed, and he had a witness. "They kidnapped him."

The skin around her eyes tightened, as if she were pulling him into focus for the first time. "Yes, you could call it that."

"How old is he?"

She touched a bronze pendant that hung at her throat. "Sixteen."

He had to make a mental shift to envision her child as a young adult. She looked so young. "What do the guardsmen want with your son?"

"Sylvius is an incubus."

"Oh, shit."

Mac dropped his hand from her shoulder, his fingers unconsciously seeking the shape of his weapon beneath his coat. An incubus added a whole new layer of complication. They were the so-called angels of lust, sought after like a drug.

"Atreus protected my son until now, but he's lost too much of his power, and Sylvius is just coming into his. The guardsmen said taking him was for the safety of everyone in the Castle, but I think it was for their own pleasure. I trust the captain to keep his word, but not the rest."

Angels of lust, Mac thought again. This one was going to be angel puree. Incubi were not fighters. The guardsmen would make mincemeat out of the kid. *What a train wreck.*

"Was there a demand for ransom?"

"No. They have Sylvius, and that's what they wanted."

Constance studied his every expression, as if she were trying to find hope. "They put him in a demon trap. The only good part is that Captain Reynard led the guardsmen. He is not as cruel as the others."

Mac knew who Reynard was. "But Bran is his second-in-command."

Constance bit her lip. "I—"

"Sh!" Mac held up a hand. He could hear the distant sound of voices and tramping feet, the clank of weapons against armor.

Constance lifted her head, suddenly alert. "It's the patrol. We have to leave here. We can't be caught near the door."

Swiftly, they got to their feet. Then Mac caught a glimpse of the approaching men. It was dark and they were distant, but their shapes looked wrong. *Not human.* He pushed Constance further into the shadows. "That's not the patrol."

"Come this way," she said, grabbing his hand. Her fingers were so cool that Mac felt like he had a fever. "Reynard said Miru-kai's spies are in these parts. The warlords want Sylvius, too, and they probably don't know he's gone."

"Oh, great."

She started to run, a quick, effortless glide through the shadows. He followed her down the corridor, sliding the Sig Sauer out of its holster as they moved. The cop in him was on high. For the first time in ages, he felt completely alive. Useful.

Her touch alerted every male cell in his body.

She was beautiful and in trouble. A double threat. *Oh, baby.*

"Where are we going?" he asked.

"I know a secret place."

An arrow hummed by his head, the wind brushing his ear. *Crap!*

It skittered harmlessly to the stone floor, but Mac and Constance jolted into a sprint. Someone shouted. It wasn't any language Mac knew, but the guttural, angry tone was clear.

If she's not fully a vampire, how badly could an arrow hurt her?

Constance darted around a corner, leading them into a nearly identical hall. Mac risked a glance at their pursuers. They were closer now. He could see four. All wore what looked to him like medieval battle gear. One had tusks.

Mac had a fleeting thought about werebacon.

He turned and scrambled after Constance. She led him through the maze, going deep into an area where Mac hadn't been before. Except for their pursuers, this part of the Castle looked deserted. This was not at all like the busy, thronging territories Mac had been in before, each with its own ruling bully. This was a wasteland.

Someone could make a fortune with a GPS system in here.

"Hurry!" Constance waved him forward, heading for a path that inclined gently downward. The rigid crisscross of corridors was breaking into longer, curving paths, the stonework ragged and natural. Drips of stone hung from the ceiling, frozen in time. It was like the masons of old had gone for coffee and never returned to finish the job.

For a moment, Mac could feel the magic of the Castle like a breathing presence, watching, considering. Then it was gone, the random bump of a shoulder in a crowd, but the vastness of that consciousness was enough to make Mac stumble, grab the wall for support.

What the hell was that for?

No time to think about it. Constance flitted down the path, pulling a small but efficient-looking knife out of a belt sheath. Mac trailed after her, listening for their pursuers. They were getting closer, heavy footfalls echoing in the gloom. The air was cold and damp. Mist clung to the floor, long fingers swirling over Mac's feet as he moved.

Then the ceiling rose, the corridor widening until it formed a huge cavern ringed with torches. It could have held a gymnasium with room to spare. Ropes of fog floated in the air, twisting like something alive.

Mac stopped cold, grabbing Constance's arm. "There's no cover here. We can't cross open ground. They'll shoot us." He could dust and float across, but that wouldn't do her any good. *Crap!*

"We have to get over there." Constance pointed. Ahead was a stairway. The light barely touched it, showing only a few horizontal edges highlighted against the prevailing murk.

Another arrow whirred over their heads, slicing into the mist. In a single motion, Mac crouched, pulling Constance down with him, turned, and fired two shots in the direction of their pursuers.

Someone—something—screamed. *A hit.*

Mac's heart hammered, adrenaline raging through his veins. His demon flared, sharpening sight and hearing, burning through muscle and nerve.

Was that it? Were they gone?

Darkness. Footfalls.

The thing with tusks burst out of the darkness with a feral roar, brandishing a spear over its head. *Shit!*

Images flew at Mac, sharp and lurid. Torchlight lit the creature's metal-studded tunic. Tiny eyes under a massive brow. Tusks jutting from the lower jaw, ringed with heavy bands of gold. It was huge, twice as big as a man, looming like a truck.

The spear left its hand, flying with ferocious speed toward Mac's chest.

Training kicked in. Mac dove to the side, rolled, and emptied three roaring blasts into the thing's chest. It flew backward, chest shattering to gore, spraying the darkness with a ruddy mist. The spear smashed into the stone where Mac had been a moment before, showering a fountain of sparks into the air.

Constance yelped, scrambling backward, knife ready to stab.

"You okay?" Mac bellowed.

"Bloody Bridgit's toenails!"

If she could curse, she was okay. Mac scrambled to his feet and down the tunnel, weapon at the ready. Hot demon rage warred with a cooler demand for caution. *Damned if another one of those things is going to get the drop on us.*

He stepped around the creature he'd shot, feet skidding on things he didn't want to name. It reeked, an unfamiliar putrid stench worse even than a dead werewolf. Mac held his breath as long as he could. The passageway flickered with torchlight, the irregular stonework casting gnarled shadows.

I shot this one. I hit another. There should at least be blood.

Mac slowed. A second body sprawled on the ground,

limbs at random angles. The body was melting to a puddle of slime, rotting in fast-forward. He'd seen that before.

Changelings—the twisted, malformed children of the vampire world. Those that hadn't Turned right. They made the Hollywood *nosferatu* look cuddly.

It wasn't easy to kill a vamp, but he'd hit it in the head.

Mac looked around. There was no sign of the other two. He finally took a deep breath but instantly gagged at the stink of foul blood. *Goddamned* Lord of the Rings *wannabes*.

Mac wiped the sweat from his palms, then his face. A tremor passed through him as the adrenaline left his system, leaving him hot and queasy. The Castle offered far too many chances to die.

He turned, looking again at the body of the first creature he'd shot. *What the hell is that thing?* He tried to remember if he'd seen anything like it the last time he was in the Castle.

"They were Prince Miru-kai's followers. I'm sure of it."

He looked up. Constance was standing nearby, the knife still in her hand.

"It was a goblin," she said. "They're fierce, but they're not very brave if you put up a fight."

"The others were changelings."

"I know. Turned wrong. Like me, but I was luckier." She held out a hand. "Come. They won't be back today."

Mac stared at her. She was solemn, but far from terrified. "You sure we're safe?"

Some of her poise faded. "What they really wanted was Sylvius, and we don't have him."

"Right." He still kept his grip on the Sig Sauer. He wasn't putting it away quite yet. "Attacks like this happen much around here?"

"Not here. There are many in the courts, of course."

"Were there many goblins in the courts?" He didn't really care, but it was something to distract them from what had just happened.

She lifted one shoulder. "A few. I spent plenty of time hiding behind the throne. It was good, sturdy oak."

Mac met her gaze. Her eyes were steady, but he thought he caught a slight curve of the lower lip.

"The werecats were the worst. If they got in a temper, you could say goodbye to the upholstery." She turned and beckoned him to follow.

Mac complied, his heartbeat almost back to normal. They were out of the corridor before she slid the knife back into its sheath. Mac watched her. "You're a vampire. Surely you're strong enough to use a sword?"

"And what would I do with a great blade, like a Highland clansman? I'm too small. Besides, it's hardly ladylike."

"Even a small sword would give you greater reach."

"Stealth and accuracy are just as important. You men are all about size. Sadly predictable creatures."

"Guilty."

She smirked, then took a glance at the Sig Sauer. "Mind you, something like that would come in handy."

"Women always like the big explosions. Delightfully predictable creatures."

She tossed her head. "Now you sound like you're boasting."

"I'm flattered that you think I have cause to boast."

"I think you have a smooth tongue."

"So I've been told."

"I wonder how often you've whispered that in a maiden's ear?"

"I'm not sure I've known that many maidens."

"And next you'll tell me that was your doing."

As they retraced their steps, Mac couldn't help but look down at the goblin he had shot, or the spear that lay across their path. Constance skirted the carnage, lifting her skirts to keep them clean. *How can she live in this place, with so much violence, and still seem so innocent?*

Because she's not. She's a vampire. You're playing with fire.

As they crossed the cavern, the ropes of fog clung like spiderwebs, dewing Constance's hair like a mantilla of jewels. Then they started up the uneven steps, ascending into a mass of shadows that billowed where the ceiling should have been. The soles of Mac's ankle boots slid on someting slippery.

"What is this crap?"

"Moss," Constance replied. "Be careful."

"I didn't think anything grew in here."

"The tales say once there were gardens."

Mac gave her a disbelieving look.

She shrugged. "There are dead trees in one of the great halls. The stories might be true."

He reserved judgment on that one.

When they reached the top of the stairs, they started down a corridor that looked different from the others, the walls polished to a dull sheen. It opened into a vast space ringed with balconies. In the center was a dark pool, the sparkling black surface rippled by a faint wind. White marble rimmed the water, the carved lip fluted and curving outward. The overall shape of the pool was geometric, squares overlapping squares, reminding Mac of a Chinese design. Rather than torches, fires burned in four braziers that ringed the space. Beautiful though it was, the hall echoed strangely, making Mac think of people and places he had lost.

"Where are we?" Mac asked, looking over his shoulder. Something about the open space put all his senses on alert, as if the lightless corners had eyes.

"This place doesn't have a name that I know of," she said. "Atreus used to come here to meditate."

No wonder he's nuts.

Constance looked around. "I was hoping Viktor would be here. He always finds his way home, but he likes this place. With Miru-kai's soldiers around, I'd rest easier if I knew where he was."

Mac started to follow her gaze, searching the inky shadows, but she grabbed his hand and pulled him along like a child. He allowed himself to be led, his eyes following the way her skirts swirled around her knees. All those layers of cloth made a swishing rhythm that had a seductive music all its own.

They crossed out of the open space of the hall and entered a long corridor mottled with patches of torchlight. The passageway angled, then branched into three. Constance went to the left. Finally she stopped at the entrance to a large room. Mac reached around her, opening the door. She nodded, accepting the courtesy, and walked in. Mac followed.

A waft of sweet-scented air greeted him. Mac looked around in wonder. It was like walking from Frankenstein's castle into the *Arabian Nights*. "This is called the Summer Room," she said. "I don't think anyone knows it's here."

It didn't look particularly summery, but it was extraordinary. The space was gently lit by a scatter of pillar candles. Tapestries hung on the walls, strange-looking birds and animals glittering with silver thread. Swaths of silk draped the high ceiling, giving the impression of a tent. There were couches and chairs and a canopied bed in the corner, piled with a mountain of gold and black velvet cushions. Books were scattered everywhere. A violin case on one shelf. A waterfall ran down one corner of the stone wall, splashing into an enormous marble basin that drained away below. Expectation hung in the air, like words formed but not yet spoken.

"This isn't like anything else I've seen in the Castle," Mac said, his voice hoarse. He turned around, and around again, trying to take it all in. "This is the *opposite* of the Castle. It's beautiful."

Then he remembered Holly's description of the room she had found, and wondered whether this was the same place. The one place in the Castle where natural appetites were not repressed. *This could be interesting.*

Constance trailed her fingers down one of the tapestries, making the silver threads glitter in the candlelight. "There are a few havens like this. Remnants, I think, of another time. I found this place not long ago. It belonged to Atreus's household once, but he doesn't come here anymore. He left everything under a spell so that it wouldn't decay."

Mac touched the arm of one of the chairs, feeling a faint

ants-over-the-skin vibration of magic. It went straight for the gut. Growing more and more curious, he looked around again, taking in additional details this time. A wardrobe, the door ajar to reveal feminine clothes hung on hooks. Soap, towels, a silver-backed hairbrush. Everything had a careful neatness.

"Do you live here?"

"I've always come here as much as I could, but now I . . . Yes, I live here now. I needed a new place to stay." Her eyes seemed to go dark, as if she was retreating from him. Whatever Constance was thinking, it was painful.

Mac's gaze fell on a stack of women's magazines—*Vogue* and *Chatelaine*—that looked like they dated from between the two World Wars. A few were later, perhaps from the early sixties. "Do you read these?"

An inane question, but as he'd intended, it snapped her out of her thoughts.

Constance looked momentarily sheepish. "Oh, um. I found them. Sometimes people smuggle things into the Castle. I like to read them to see what people wear now. How they talk, what words they use. I don't like to feel like I'm old-fashioned."

Never mind her clothes look like they came from Colonial times. And her pronunciation was sometimes off—though some of that might have been the Irish lilt. It didn't matter. He could understand her well enough.

Now she was busy as a model homemaker, straightening the ornaments on a dainty side table. There was a fleck of goblin on her skirt, which she cleaned off with a fussy little grumble. *No, I can't say I've met anyone quite like her before.*

Mac picked up one of the magazines. It had been read so often it was nearly in shreds. "What do you think of the new styles?"

"Oh, they're lovely, but clothes that fine would be wasted on this place. What I have is good enough for me." Constance turned away and rearranged the cushions on the couch.

Mac set the magazine down. At least by his standards, Constance had been too young to begin living when she was trapped in the Castle. Now she was trying to catch up vicariously with magazines a good seventy years out of date. That was just wrong.

He slid the Jane Austen out of his jacket pocket and beneath the top *Chatelaine*. The gesture felt good, especially after blasting the goblin to chunky soup. Not that he had a big choice when Tusky came yodeling out of the shadows, but his karma still felt like a twelve-car pile-up.

Constance turned to face Mac, extending a hand to the chair where she'd just fluffed the cushions. "Please, sit."

Mac sat down in the chair. The Castle's magic felt thick in this room, almost touchable. Conscious. The vibes—or maybe it was the aftermath of the fight—were making him feel light-headed, as if he'd had one too many shots on an empty stomach. Which reminded him he'd skipped lunch.

Wait a minute. If he was hungry, that meant the lid was indeed coming off his appetites. This must be the same room Holly'd been talking about, the one that let a person's natural desires run free. *Keep an eye on your impulses. Keep an eye on the pretty little vampire.*

His gaze traveled to Constance, who was pacing back and forth, her slim, straight back a fierce exclamation. Her hips swayed when she walked, twitching her skirts like a cat's tail. Mac blinked, fascinated by her curves. It was getting hard to think.

Reynard. Incubus. Bran. Right.

At least where the guardsmen were concerned, it didn't take a genius to figure out what would happen next. The captain might be an okay guy, but there was only one Reynard and a whole Castle full of Brans. With a prize like an incubus at stake, it was only a matter of time before the guardsmen's already shaky discipline came tumbling down like a house of cards.

So not good.

Mac leaned his head against the back of the chair. Con-

stance took the seat facing him, her expression intense.
"What can we do?" she asked, fingering her necklace again.

It was an odd moment, but in many ways the situation
was familiar. He had a missing youth, a grieving mother,
and a gang of bad guys. Not exactly a no-brainer, but he
knew how this stuff worked. It was a problem he could
wrap his head around and, with so much in his life that
made no sense at all, that was good.

I'll take kidnapping for two hundred.

"Tell me more about this demon trap. It will catch a
demon in cloud form, right?"

"Yes. The traps are usually about this big," she said,
describing a small cube with her hands. "A demon can be
forced to enter by a command, or they can enter of their
own free will."

"Sylvius?"

"He went in on his own."

Mac heard her ragged, sawing drag of breath. He could
almost feel her composure crumbling with the same inex
orable collapse as his own body giving way to dust. He'd
seen this with victims and witnesses so many times, and still
it hurt him to watch.

No emotional investment. Keep a clear head. But that
warning had lost all its teeth. He'd saved her from the bad
guys. She'd offered him a case. There was mutual need.

Constance was still trying to talk. She gestured with her
hands, but no words came out. She did it again, a strangled
sound choking whatever it was she was going to say.

She covered her face with her hands.

Mac froze. "Constance, what happened?"

"Sylvius did it to protect me," she said, pulling her hands
away. She gulped back a sob. "He gave himself up to save
me. And Atreus just watched."

Fury hit Mac like a hook to the jaw.

Constance drew in another breath, the air dragging past
the ache in her chest. Mac was kneeling by her chair now,

looking at her with that worried expression men got, as if she were about to catch fire or foam at the mouth. In her experience, not one male could stand tears.

Mac was holding one of her hands in his. She wiped her eyes with the sleeve of her free hand. "So what should we do?" she asked. "Where do we start?"

The muscles in his jaw bunched, as if he were grinding his teeth. "You tell me everything again. Every detail."

Bitter disappointment caked her tongue. She pulled her hand away from his. "I don't want to talk anymore. I want to *do* something. They've got my boy."

There was sympathy in the strong, square lines of his face. If it was sympathy for anyone else, it would have melted her heart. Because it was for her, she felt exposed.

He took her hand again, engulfing it in his own. "Slow down. No one thinks clearly when they're upset."

Upset? How could he describe the grief and fear she was feeling as *upset*? She nearly slapped him. "There's no time to slow down!"

She knew that sounded childish, but his patient expression didn't flicker.

"Stealth will count more than strength," he said gently. "Stealth takes planning. Do you know where the guardsmen keep their prisoners?"

"I was following Bran when you interrupted and beat him to a pulp."

He showed an instant of surprise, then chagrin that slid into humor. "Ah. My bad." His momentary smile showed slightly crooked teeth.

"Indeed." Constance pulled her hand from his and stood. She was too nervous to sit any more.

He stood, folding his arms. He was wearing a soft sweater the color of mulberries. It brought out the darker undertones in his skin. Next to him, her skin was as pale as bone.

These were details she shouldn't have noticed. There wasn't time except—oh, he smelled deliciously human. That had fooled her the first time they'd met. The demon scent was there, but right then the human overpowered it.

She could feel his heat like a lamp, drawing her in as if it could ease the furious pain of loss. She wanted him to hold her. No one ever held her. She remembered his salty skin, that delicious musk of man. Those thoughts had flitted past, dark butterflies of desire, when she got the idea to come to this room, where there was no spell to keep passion buried.

And the urgency of passion was exactly what she needed. Whether Mac was half demon or not, Constance was willing to gamble that his blood was still human enough to Turn her. She had led him to believe he was safe, but she hadn't given up on the idea of taking his blood. The room, with all its sensuality, was her trap.

People believed she was so innocent, but up until now Constance had chosen to stay that way. That didn't mean she was oblivious to the ways of deceit. She'd just never thought anything worth the sacrifice of her morals. Not until she'd lost her son.

Now she was faced with a choice of evils. Surely taking her first drink of human blood inside the Castle—even in the permissive confines of the Summer Room—meant that she could avoid turning into a ravening beast. Didn't it? Wouldn't that excuse deceiving Mac?

He had been wary earlier, but no man was all that careful in the throes of lovemaking. At least, that's what other girls had said. Her own experience was woefully sparse. She had to play her hand with great care.

But was it right to bite him now, after he'd just saved her? Been so kind? Promised his aid? A sense of fair play shouldn't hamper her, but it did. She was terrible at this biting business. *Just get on with it, for heaven's sake!*

Mac was looking at her curiously, as if he'd caught her daydreaming. Constance realized she couldn't remember what she'd been saying.

He touched her cheek with the back of his fingers, an intimate familiarity. His skin felt rough and warm. "Our first task is reconnaissance. We can't make any other choices until we know what we're dealing with."

He looked down, his pupils reflecting the image of her face. Constance felt a chill of need and dread course over her limbs.

"Don't worry," he said. "Kidnapping is exactly the kind of thing I was trained to handle. This is going to be a bit different with, y'know, the monster factor, but I'm seeing the possibilities here."

He gave a dry smile. "It'll be fun. Really."

Swept along by his magnetic warmth, Constance put one hand on each of Mac's shoulders. Almost automatically, his hands grasped her waist. She wasn't sure what she was feeling. Attraction? Certainly. Hunger? Yes, but many kinds. Drumming like thunder inside her veins, those hungers called to places deep in her belly.

Mac's nostrils flared, his dark eyes growing darker. He was feeling it, too. She pushed against him, her body aching, itching to be free of the laces of her garments. They confined and teased, pressing against the soft flesh of her aching breasts. The throbbing beneath her teeth made her part her lips, easing the burning sensation that only feeding would cure.

Mac seemed to hesitate, teetering on some knife-edge of decision. She watched him fall, the surrender in his eyes and in the sudden quickening of his breath. He was aroused, hers for the taking. On shaking breath, Constance murmured a prayer to whatever saint guided untried lovers and beginning vampires.

Mac caressed her, a low growl rumbling through his chest and into her bones. His lips crushed hers, pricking against her fangs, a burst of blood radiating across her tongue. Constance stood on her toes, leaning into the hard, bruising grasp, lapping at the strange, demon-spiced blood. It wasn't enough, not nearly enough, and it only sharpened her need.

Strong hands ran up her body, making her twitch as they pressed against a sore place left from Atreus's punishment. The scent of him was exotic, drawing her face to his skin. His hands were on her bodice, peeling away the thin scarf she wore. He bent, his lips, his tongue finding the arch of her collarbone and following the valley between her breasts. His breath was hot, electrifying, sizzling against the wet trails his tongue had left.

Mac's dark, wavy hair brushed against her cheek, the springy texture of it begging to be touched. Her fingers fell against his neck, feeling the pulse that called to her through her belly, her nipples, through the painful clenching of her sex. Her knees quivered with it. She could feel the hard evidence of his desire pressing against her flesh.

Take him. Take him now.

But her senses were swimming. Her body wouldn't obey, only react.

With a groan, he lifted his head. The irises of his eyes glittered with a scarlet fire. There was nothing there but pure, primitive possession. His scent was changing, the human smell fading as they stood there.

No. Oh, no.

What have I done? I've called forth his demon.

She'd missed her chance to feed, but here was something else. Fear and desire was a potent combination. Savage delight rose in her, ready to fight. Ready to grapple, however he chose to do it. This was even more exciting.

Demon or not, she still wanted him. Maybe she wanted him even more. She couldn't really hurt a demon. They couldn't be accidentally Turned. There would be no guilt.

Mac—or the thing that had been Mac—held her by the upper arms, his grip beyond even vampire-strong. He put his lips to her ear. "If I take you, I'll hurt you."

He pushed her away, leaving every nerve in her body shrieking with rage.

"No!" she said, grabbing the front of his sweater to reel him back in.

"I'm not human anymore," he said, the mirror of her own emotions in his face. "I won't play by the rules. I won't be any good to eat, sweetheart."

"I know that. I don't care." There were more needs than food. She pushed forward, her lips finding the hollow of his throat, salty-sweet with the taste of him. He was hot to the touch, almost burning. For the first time since she had been bitten, she felt truly warm.

He grabbed her arms, setting her back once more with that insane strength. "If you don't back away, I won't be able to stop myself."

"Is that a bad thing?"

"Only if you're willing to take a demon for a lover. I have no idea what my demon might do, but it wants you."

And then she felt it, a pressing wave of need that rolled off him and sent her skittering backward. He took a step forward, the very proximity of his energy nearly bringing her to her knees. Her jaws burned with the need to taste him. Her body felt like it was breaking apart in its haste to surrender.

Constance panted, hugging herself, shivering with frustration. Now she wanted him for so much more than a first meal. A door had just cracked open, and there were all kinds of temptation on the other side. Everything she had missed since she was seventeen. Everything for herself.

But could she put her desires first, when there was a rescue at stake? Could she be that selfish?

He saw her hesitation. His jaws bunched, and the red light in his eyes flared, but he let her go. *Damnation.* She almost wished he wasn't so honorable.

"The demon changes things, doesn't it? It's different when I don't smell like dinner." Mac gave her a long, narrow-eyed look, the burning glow lurking in his gaze. "I hope you didn't bring me here thinking you could get your teeth into me."

Constance drew herself up, trying to summon enough anger to wash away the lust burning up her body. It didn't work. "What does it matter?"

"Sweetheart, if you have to ask that, you've been here too long."

"Maybe." She felt herself drooping, but pulled her head up again, refusing to look as defeated as she felt.

He gave her another look that said he was weighing and judging her soul.

Constance felt like she would burst into tears. "I'm sorry. Don't walk away. Please don't make Sylvius pay for my mistakes!"

She closed her eyes, wishing she could tell him about the kitchen table, the family she wanted, how he had blown into her existence and made that dream almost touchable because it was his face she saw there. Someone real.

All he could see was how she'd tried to trick him. Again.

"Please," she said again, forcing herself to look at him.

He stared at her for a long time, thoughts chasing themselves across his face. The foremost was a sexual heat scorching in its frankness.

"Please," she repeated, softer this time.

"There are some things I need to find out. Promise me you'll stay here until I get back."

"I can't."

"*Promise me!*" Mac grabbed her by her arms, his grip hard and hot through the fabric of her sleeves. He shook her a little, his strength lifting her to her toes.

She set her jaw. "Let go of me." Her voice was quiet.

He flexed his arms, pulling her to him. She could feel his breath on her face, warm and urgent. "I need your word. I won't help you if I'm going to come back to find you torn to pieces by the changelings or staked by the guards. I'm not that selfless."

His demon's energy was as palpable as rushing surf. His hands shook as he relaxed his fingers until he stopped crushing her. But he still held her, barely banked need alive in his touch.

Fear warred with the urge to cling to him, but she had her pride. "I've lived here for a long time, Conall Macmillan. I'm not easy prey."

He swallowed, clearly forcing himself under control. "I don't care."

Constance thought about resisting, dragging out her surrender because something about it was delicious. *This isn't a game. This is serious.*

She cursed inwardly, but did the reasonable thing. "Very well, but I won't wait long."

"Good enough." Mac released her arms and folded his own, as if to keep them out of mischief.

The air in the room changed, taking on the same final feeling as the moment someone closes a book. The heat slipped away like water draining through a sieve. "Later, then."

Cool. Businesslike. In charge.

He was holding back, being what Constance needed.

The mother in her approved, but the young woman that never got to live began to silently weep. "No, wait . . ."

He was already dust.

Bollocks!

Chapter 11

Alessandro was hoping for a perfect couple of hours, which meant old jeans, no sword, and no sister-in-law. Ashe hadn't come back since last night. Even Holly wasn't at home. She'd stayed late in the reading room in the university library. She'd left a note saying she would call when it was time to drive there and pick her up.

Seizing the moment, Alessandro retreated to the third floor of Holly's house, where he'd turned a corner bedroom into a studio. There, he kept those things that were uniquely his.

The room was filled with instruments in stands, in cases, hanging on the wall—guitars, lutes, citterns, and other members of the long-necked, plucked family. Some had fat, pumpkin bellies; others were sleek. There was a solid-bodied Gibson and pieces of a French lute he meant to rebuild someday. Alessandro had owned hundreds of instruments over the centuries, but these were the voices he could not bear to part with.

When he had moved in with Holly, those had arrived first. The rest of his things—mostly books and an armory's worth of weapons—had taken more time to put away. Piles of car magazines still tottered on the old desk, their pages stirred by the draft from the double-hung window. Truth be told, he liked things a little messy. He didn't mind at all that Holly was a haphazard housekeeper, because he was the same way.

From where he sat, he could see outside, across the street and down the brush-covered cliff, the moon trailing a silver scarf across the calm water. It was a clear, cold night. Holly's huge cat curled into a ball at one end of the lumpy Victorian sofa. Alessandro was sprawled with his favorite Martin acoustic at the other. He'd built a small fire, the pitchy scent of the wood blending with the must of damp wool carpet. The house felt content, the sort of drowsing quietude he associated with nesting chickens.

Alessandro switched on the radio, keeping the volume low enough that he could still hear himself running over and over the finger exercises he practiced every day, up and down the frets of the Martin's glossy neck. Vampire speed was great, but that meant twice as much work to achieve perfect precision. Of course he would do better if he sat up straight, but he was too lazy to move.

The Kibble-ator—Kibs—uncurled and rolled onto his back in a full-body stretch, claws extended. Without breaking rhythm, Alessandro rubbed the cat's stomach with one stockinged foot, listening to his passagework and the radio at the same time.

"This is Errata and you're listening to CSUP at FM 101.5 in Fairview. That was the Happy Dead People with their latest release, *Afterlife, After You.* It's ten o'clock and time for *Unnatural Enquiry,* the current issues portion of our show. I have with me a very special guest, George de Winter of the Clan Albion vampires. Welcome, George."

"Good evening, Errata."

Clan Albion? Who gave those villains airtime? Suddenly annoyed, Alessandro rolled off the couch, walking a few steps to put the guitar safely in its stand by the wall. Kibs flopped over, a boneless heap of stripes, and yawned.

On his way back to the couch, Alessandro turned up the volume of the old plug-in radio. The werecougar announcer was in fine form, her sultry voice making the patter sound like a come-on. "We're here tonight to talk about nothing less than the state of the paranormal nation. Are we monsters or are we citizens of the world at large? Should we obey the same laws as our human neighbors? Scrap that, kiddies, and let's ask why we should obey any laws at all besides the call of the wild?"

This can't be good. Alessandro sat, absently petting Kibs as the cat waded onto his lap.

Errata went on. "Let's begin with the basics. There's no argument that humans and the human economy have the upper hand. Those in favor of integration say we should live, work, and pay taxes just like everybody else. They say we have to fit in and earn the trust of human law makers, and that means following a strict code of peaceful behavior."

"That illustrates the whole problem with this new integration philosophy." The vampire's retort was so sharp, Kibs's ears went back. "The laws of my people are not democratic. The strongest predators rule. We are not 'everybody else.' We are the *nosferatu.*"

"All right!" said Errata, nearly purring at the prospect of an on-air dust-up. "I think we know where our guest stands. Now how about our listeners? The phone lines are open. The question of the night: should we be monsters or model citizens?"

Alessandro sighed. *Should I call in and state the obvious?* Humans might be a food group, but they were by no means helpless. The invention of the computer and its many databases had made the whole swirl-the-cape-and-scuttle-off-to-the-next-village method of hiding a joke. Even if you could afford to change your identity every time the Van Helsing brigade got busy, reinventing yourself wasn't as easy as the movies made it appear.

"I'd like to add something, Errata," said George de Winter, sounding almost reasonable now. "Many people believe the nonhuman separatists are just dinosaurs unwilling to relinquish their glory days."

Yeah, that's about right. Alessandro leaned on the arm of the couch, propping up his head. *And while you win your point, you'll frighten the human majority into staking us all in our beds.* Maybe it was time to remind Clan Albion to keep their heads down and their mouths shut. They seemed to need it about once a year.

De Winter continued. "I don't think it's a secret the humans don't want us here. We don't have equal rights. We pay taxes, but we can't vote. We aren't tried by a jury of our peers, but are subject to summary execution. I could go on, but simply put we're second-class citizens. We want that to end."

"By civil disobedience?" Errata asked.

"Rebels are simply oppressed individuals demanding their rights."

De Winters had a valid point, but the chill in the vampire's voice was worse than a snarl. Kibs jumped to the floor with a heavy thud and waddled under the couch to hide. His own instincts roused, Alessandro inched to the edge of his seat.

A knock came at the study door. Alessandro jumped, so absorbed in the radio he hadn't heard anyone come in. He looked up to see Holly open the door a few feet and peer in. "You busy?" she asked.

At the exhausted look on her face, he reached over and turned off the radio. "Not at all. I thought you were going to call for a ride. Are you done studying for tonight?"

"Yeah."

She crossed the room, her fuzzy slippers silent on the carpet. Sinking onto the old sofa, she curled her feet up beside her and leaned against his shoulder. The warm weight of her body, the scent of her skin, was intoxicating. The scent of the night air clung in her hair, as if she'd just come in from outside. He circled her shoulder with his arm, the soft fuzz of her hoodie tickling his fingers. She closed her eyes.

"Why don't you just go to bed?" he asked, amused. "You were up early."

"I will in a minute. I just wanted to be here with you a while. I'm tired, but my brain won't slow down. It's all spazzed out like a werepuppy digging holes." She tilted her face up to his. Her green eyes looked a little glazed.

"When's your first exam again?"

She rested her head on his arm. "A week from tomorrow. Today. What time is it?"

"It's only just after ten."

She yawned. "Tomorrow, then. Crumb. I shouldn't have taken a full course load. I should have eased into it."

He hugged her closer. He was no scholar and there was nothing else he could do to help. "Just remember you've got eternity to finish the degree."

He felt her silent chuckle. "You mean I can't even die to get out of my exams?"

"Sorry, you're stuck."

Few witches were immortal; it took good genes and an ability to handle huge amounts of power. Holly had both. She had also been able to turn myth into reality by Choosing Alessandro. For the first time since he was Turned, he could love without addicting his partner to the venom of his bite. She had given him a gift beyond any price.

Holly curled under his arm like a rescued waif. It was only at times like these that she allowed him to be utterly in charge, as protective and possessive as he wanted to be. They both surrendered sometimes, and that made the balance between them not only possible, but perfect.

The fire had nearly died out, leaving only a smear of glowing embers and the light of a single floor lamp. Holly's eyes had drifted closed again, her lips parting as she collapsed against his side. Alessandro felt a moment of pure peace.

At last, Holly blinked, licking her lips before she spoke. "I heard the radio when I walked in. What were you listening to?"

"CSUP. The debate over living in peace or terrorizing the humans."

"Oh, brother." Her voice held the same dismay that was lodged in his chest.

He kissed the top of her head, wishing he knew the right

thing to say. Any politics could prove explosive; nonhuman debates could get uglier than most.

Holly was silent for a long moment, her fingers tight on his arm. "I wasn't exactly studying tonight."

He looked down on her in surprise. "No?"

She gave her head a tiny shake. "There's too much going on. I can't concentrate. I keep worrying about the door to the Castle."

He shifted his head to look down at her. "I've already called the wolves to help with guard duty. They won't wander off like the hellhounds."

"Good, because I went and looked at the doorway tonight. Not a hound in sight. I don't know what Lore's doing, but he's not keeping his guard under control."

He felt his jaw drift open. "You went yourself? Into that neighborhood?"

"Hey, I can blast a hole to an interdimensional prison. I can handle a mugger." She sounded annoyed.

With an act of will, he let the point go and moved on. "What made you go look?"

"I saw Mac today."

"*What?*" He stiffened, and the sudden tension made her sit up.

She pushed her long, dark hair out of her eyes. "I ran into him at the university. Rather, he was looking for me. He said he walked right out the Castle door. No one stopped him."

Alessandro swore. *How dare he set foot in my town yet again!* "What did he want?"

Holly was watching him, her gaze on his face. "Help. Something in the Castle gave him back at least part of his demon powers. He's not happy about the implications."

Neither am I. Alessandro gripped the arm of the sofa hard enough the wood squeaked. "I thought the Castle was supposed to tamp down magic powers."

"Well, it's not working for him. I spent the evening researching. I can't find anything that sheds light on what's happening."

Alessandro tried for a reasonable tone. "I suppose it would do no good to tell you to stay away from Mac. After all, I was trying to execute him just last night."

She looked away. "Yeah, well, I . . . uh. I know we talked about what would happen if you found him, but he seemed okay. I mean . . . I have to help him, right? He didn't ask for any of this."

"You don't have to do a damned thing." He looked at her squarely. "He could Turn at any moment. He's dangerous."

"That's not fair." Her eyes were hot with anger. "So are you."

He flinched. "I'm in control."

Her mouth went flat. "So is he. If I can help him, he'll stay that way."

"You didn't have a problem with his execution yesterday."

"I hadn't talked to him then." Her face softened. "It stopped being theoretical."

Alessandro felt his stomach chill. Doing his job was always harder when it meant killing someone he knew. That was probably why Mac was still alive. "So you saw Mac and went to the Castle door without me. Anything else I should know?"

"What's that supposed to mean?" Holly had on her don't-push-me face.

"Why didn't you go to the reunion?"

She took a short, sharp breath, almost a hiccup of distress. "You talked to Ashe last night, didn't you?"

He nodded.

Holly bit a fingernail. "I didn't tell you about the reunion because I didn't want to go. I didn't want you to think I wasn't going because of you. I didn't want to have a stupid conversation going in circles because it's not an issue. Ignore Ashe. She doesn't know what she's talking about."

But now he was feeling stubborn. "Why didn't you want to go?"

"The timing was just wrong. I'm overloaded as it is. I don't even have time for exams. I can't stay in school. Not with Mac, the Castle, the hellhounds, and a bunch of fanged and furry anarchists to cope with. What do midterms matter?" She laughed bitterly. "And then comes Ashe, blowing into town like the Terminator."

Alessandro was listening to her words, but he also heard the tone in her voice. It was pure panic. *Exam nerves.* The problems were real but, with the exception of Mac and Ashe, none of them were new. Her emotions were skating on too much algebra and a slick of black coffee.

But there was something she wasn't saying. Perhaps most would miss it, but he was a hunter. Changes in scent, in mood were signals, and he sensed something was wrong. Something extreme enough to make her dreams of going back to school waver. Something solemn enough she didn't want to share.

Women have secrets. He was old enough to know that a hundred times over.

Therefore men have worries.

"Let's not anticipate the worst quite yet. We're dealing with a lot of what-ifs. You worry about the tests." He gave a confident smile. "I'll deal with the rest."

"What about Mac?"

To hell with Mac. But he knew when to take a strategic step back.

He picked up her hand and kissed it. "Do your research for Mac. I'll go with you if you need to talk to him in person. But don't let yourself get distracted from your exams. You've worked too hard to get sidetracked now."

She ducked her head. "Thank you."

"I'll look after everything." *I am vampire. I am invincible.*

She gave him a long, searching look, her green eyes clear and warm. "I know you will."

After she'd turned his existence from nightmare to joy, what wouldn't he do? He took her face in his hands, tipping it up to give her a kiss. As their lips met, he felt the familiar electric sizzle that was part sex, part magic, and pure emotion. It filled him with sudden heat, the same delirious rush that used to come from feeding on a victim's blood, but now it came from love.

She gave that special little sound low in her throat. He kissed her again, this time parting her soft lips, teasing her with a prelude to something more.

Holly drew back her head, looking into his eyes. "This sofa sucks. Let's go to bed."

This time his smile was genuine. "That's more like it."

Whatever it was that was causing her stress, he'd do his humble best to make her forget all about it. True warriors knew how to fight with more weapons than a sword.

October 3, 7:15 p.m.
101.5 FM

". . . and to those animal control officers who put my main man in the pound, a big hello from the Fairview University and Community College, good old F-U-C-C U.

"It's seven-thirty and this is Errata, your nighttime guide until the witching hour. Speaking of rules and regulations, I have an e-mail from a listener responding to our interview with Lore, the local leader of the hellhound pack. Tail2-Scale@islandweb.net writes: 'Dear Errata, I love your show but I hate the way you're always dropping hints about a place called the Castle. What is it and why won't you talk openly about it?'

"Well, my furred and fanged ones, if I was to start talking about a world of trouble behind a mysterious door in a local alley, I would get my pretty paws fired right off this station. That's why I really wish someone would come on down, grab this mic, and spill the beans. I may be a naughty kitty, but I might be just too weak to stop you from blowing the lid off the worst-kept secret in town. The truth is out there, my friends.

"Why the muzzle? Hey, if you think freedom of the press and independent investigative reporting is alive and well in any community, much less the supernatural community, go look up the phrase 'advertising sponsors.' And that's your final answer.

"Okay, movin' on with a number from our favorite zydeco zombie dudes with 'Babe, You've Got My Arms (so give 'em back)' . . ."

Ashe Carver twisted in her seat and pondered the coffee shop—Brownie's Bistro—over her shoulder. Although she'd picked a seat at the counter to chat up the waitstaff, she hated sitting with her back to the room. Vigilance was the first thing a slayer learned. The second was to know the quarry.

Ashe was in Spookytown, where humans—even hereditary witches—were clearly in the minority. She'd come into the café hoping to round out the information she'd already gathered on Alessandro Caravelli, including his routine, history, and associates. As it turned out, she was the sole customer in the joint.

It was a nice, quiet place for a conversation. The only sounds were the radio and the whoosh of traffic outside. The building was old and comfortable, clearly from the turn of the last century. The walls were covered with abstract oil paintings. A dark wooden counter with barstools stood opposite the door to Johnson Street, leaving the remaining space to a scatter of café tables.

A clatter caught her attention. She swiveled around on her stool. The guy who'd served her—probably the owner, from his in-charge bustle—shouldered through the kitchen door. He was carrying a rubber bin of silverware, which he stowed under the counter with a clash.

"It's getting busy out there," Ashe commented with a nod toward the window. Night was falling. The streets were filling up.

The guy looked up. About forty, he was wearing jeans and a Harley Davidson T-shirt that strained across his chest like a barrel. He had shaggy, dark hair and small, shrewd eyes. Almost visibly, he switched from busboy to host, putting on a smile and wiping his hands on an already-rumpled apron.

Werebear, she thought. Low threat, as long as she was polite.

"We get the after-movie crowd, mostly," he rumbled. "You new in town?"

"Just came back. Grew up here." Ashe leaned her chin in her hand. "This area used to be derelict. It's really improved."

"Coming along. Hard work pays off."

"Looks pretty peaceful around here."

"We feed those that want feeding and discourage the rest." The bear gave her a narrow look. "We don't want trouble."

Which is great, except vamps are vamps and werewolves will happily chew your leg off if the pretzel bowl's empty.
"Good for you. I was on the prairies when they had that big problem with the pro-human vigilantes ..."

The bear waved her words away with one huge hand. "Don't even go there. We all get along fine. Anyone hassles anyone else in this neighborhood, and the sheriff gives them a talking to."

She'd heard the same thing twice already that day. "Sheriff? That this guy Caravelli I keep hearing about?"

The bear leaned on the counter. "Yeah. What's your interest?"

"I need to talk to him. Where does he hang out?" She wanted to confront him alone, away from Holly.

"Why?"

Ashe took her inspiration from the radio program she'd heard on the café's sound system. "I'm writing a story. I'm an independent investigative journalist."

The bear gave a slight smile. "I'd think again if I were you."

Ashe returned his look, carefully neutral. "What do you mean?"

"You're no reporter. You move like a fighter." He pushed away from the counter, folding his arms. "I know your type. You want to be a bad-ass. If you're looking to prove something, try another city."

"This is my city." She kept her voice flat and gray as a steel blade.

"No." The bear leaned across the counter, moving quickly enough to make Ashe spring off her stool. "It's *our* city. You have to share it now. And I'm damned if I'm going to end up as a scatter rug because you don't think I'm good enough to hold a business license."

"I'm not interested in you."

He heaved a noisy breath. "Fine. But mess with Caravelli or his woman, you'll answer to half this town."

"We'll see about that," Ashe said quietly, but the bear had turned away, pointedly giving her his back. *Brave bear.*

Ashe threw a five on the counter, not bothering to ask for change. No point in wasting her time with Pooh here, however much she would have liked to pick a fight. She allowed herself an angry glare at the point between the bear's slablike shoulders.

The Caravelli fan club she'd uncovered in Fairview was definitely getting on her nerves.

So was the fact that fang-boy and Holly seemed to be glued at the hip. *Move over Brangelina, here comes Hollesandro.* The one thing she hadn't heard was that Holly was his venom-addicted thrall. According to gossip, she seemed to wrap the deadly warrior around her pinkie. Could it be that Alessandro really was a vamp with a heart of gold? Chosen by his lover to live off the power of their passion?

Yeah, right. And I'm the tooth fairy. She turned to leave.

The bell over the door chimed. A young, attractive couple came in, smelling of the early evening rain. They had a fluid way of moving, almost like they walked on springs— something wild beneath the velvet and denim. The man laughed, the full-throated joy of someone just falling into lust. *Werewolves.*

They were beautiful. Ashe walked past them, invisible because they only had eyes for one another. She'd been in love like that. With her husband, that passion had never dimmed. *Has he really been gone four whole years?*

Rain greased the pavement, leaving it slick and shining. Neon signs reflected back from the wetness, smears of random color. Ashe could smell the ocean mixed with exhaust. She stopped, zipping up her jacket, wondering what to do next. It was too early to go back to the motel where she was staying.

What if Holly's really and truly as happy as I was?

That thought led to a treacherous, slippery slope. Sure, a slayer's job showed her the worst side of the monsters. That didn't mean the only good monster was a dead one, but Ashe couldn't second-guess herself in the middle of a job. That could put her six feet under. Or get her turned into the walking dead. Thinking in black and white was safer.

Moreover, she wasn't willing to bet her sister's life on the slim chance that Caravelli was the one vegetarian vampire in history. Ashe had already killed her parents, lost her husband, and had to send her daughter to boarding school to keep her safe from the vengeful relations of past targets. She couldn't afford to screw up.

Ashe started walking, taking the long way back to the place where she'd left her Ducati.

If she had to get busy with a stake to keep her sister fang-free, she'd do it. Still, there was due diligence. She'd at least talk to the bloodsucker before sending him straight to hell—for Holly's sake.

I'm not a hard-assed bitch 24/7. More like 23.75/7.

As if in answer to her thoughts, she saw Caravelli's T-Bird parked in a puddle of streetlight.

Bingo.

Chapter 12

Mad humping disease. That's what he had.

Mac hadn't felt the drive to *own* a female this way since he was a teenager. As an adult, other things came into play. Career choices. Mutual goals. Educational compatibility. Family dynamics. Certainly being the same species fit in there somewhere.

The driving, dirty, have-her-at-all-costs impulse might not exactly fade with maturity, but it got diluted. It got weighed in the balance. Cooler heads prevailed.

Then he'd met Constance and somehow all that rationality had turned to ash, just like a staked vampire. *Great. Whoever said they wanted their teenage years back was lying or brain-damaged*. For one thing, all that cooler-heads stuff was for safety's sake. In a world populated with divorce lawyers and other monsters, impulse control was key.

Which only part of him cared about. The rest just *wanted*. It wanted Constance. Naked. It was as acute as the soul hunger, a killing thirst he simply had to slake.

Was this the demon talking? The room she'd taken him to? More of her pheromones at work? He didn't care, and that's what scared him.

He'd forced himself to be cautious. He'd spent the day doing research, trying to figure out how best to outwit the

Castle guards. He'd kept an appointment to update his will, just in case. Mostly, he was counting on Holly to come up with anti-demon mojo—and waiting.

The Empire Hotel had been beautiful once, respectable for longer, and derelict for the past forty years. It was in the heart of Spookytown, right around the corner from the Castle door. Recently, it had reopened to serve the supernatural community. Human customers were giving it a wide berth. If the werebeast clientele didn't finish off the patrons, the food certainly would.

Mac gave up on the hunter stew—possibly made from organic hunters, safety vests and all—and turned his attention to the beer. It came from a bottle, so it was presumably safe.

The pub area reminded Mac of an old Western saloon, with wooden floors, a double swinging door, and an enormous bar decked out with marble and brass rails. He wasn't sure who had bought the old place, but there was plenty of work to be done before the hotel would be fully restored. The rooms upstairs were still under repair.

Despite the construction dust and the dangerous cuisine, the place was hopping. About forty patrons were scattered around the tables or leaning on the bar. Someone was playing an old piano in the back corner, pounding out upbeat jazz standards. The atmosphere was feel-good rather than a serious drinker's bar.

Mac picked up his spoon and poked at the stew again, wishing it was nontoxic. He was hungry, but he still had internal organs to think of. Plus, he hadn't felt well since coming back from the Castle. Achy, headachy, and running a bear of a fever. In any other circumstances—like being human—he'd say he was coming down with old-fashioned flu. As it was, he could only ignore the symptoms and hope for the best.

Work was the best antidote, and this business with the Castle was as absorbing as any case. Heck, there was even a complimentary kidnapping. When Holly had called to give a report, he'd had the old thrill-of-the-chase shivers down the back of his neck. Taking it as a sign from the universe, he'd asked to meet.

On cue, the doors swung inward and Holly walked in, Caravelli at her side. Mac felt an instant dump of adrenaline hit his veins. *Great. She brought the guard dog.* Mac pushed his chair back, jumping to his feet. He'd run or poof to dust before he started firing silver ammo—or any other ammo—in a crowded room.

The quick move was a mistake. Caravelli leaped forward, sailing over one table and darting between the rest. Mac spun backward, putting the table between him and the vampire. He would have run farther, but the wall was in the way.

Every head in the place turned to stare, the piano music trailing off as if the tune had ripped in two. A couple of the werewolf patrons lumbered off the barstools, hitching up their pants and adjusting their baseball caps. The floor show was about to begin.

"Alessandro, what the *hell* are you doing?" Holly asked in the voice of a woman pushed to the edges of her patience.

Caravelli was half-across the table, poised to close the distance between him and Mac. The vampire gripped a long silver knife, the casual dress version of the broadsword. Just as deadly for stabbing, much messier and slower for beheading.

Mac held up his hands, showing they were empty of weapons. "I come in peace."

He said it loudly enough the whole room could hear, and with an edge of sarcasm. His heart was pounding like he'd just run the four-minute mile. And to think he'd been looking forward to a quiet social drink where the only weapons were the little plastic swords that went through the olives. *Like I'd ever do anything to Holly.*

But he had. Mac had done her serious harm when the demon had been in control. Beneath his disappointment, he couldn't blame Caravelli for protecting her as best he knew how.

He stole a quick glance away from the vampire, who was still poised like a macabre centerpiece. Holly was furious, her hands on her hips, glaring at the two of them. She was wearing a belted tunic and leggings that reminded Mac of Robin Hood or Peter Pan. The thought of Caravelli as Tinker Bell nearly made him laugh out loud.

Holly pointed to the chairs, her expression no-nonsense. "Sit. Both of you."

Caravelli slowly backed off the table, sliding the knife into a sheath hidden by his jacket. Once the weapon vanished, the patrons started returning to their seats. The piano man struck up "Skylark."

Holly threw herself into a chair, her lips compressed. "I said, sit."

Mac complied, inching his chair back a little. Caravelli was too close for comfort, but he tried for a carefree tone. "Word of warning: stick to the drinks. The menu needs work."

Obviously reluctant, Caravelli folded himself onto a chair, every inch the graceful predator. His gaze traveled from Holly to Mac, the vampire's amber eyes glinting in the low lights. He leaned forward, raking his yellow stare over Mac. "I don't agree with this meeting. You have no right to walk these streets. If you give me any excuse, I'll finish what I started on Wednesday."

By way of reply, Mac took a slug of his Bigfoot and stifled a belch.

"Since we're all such good friends, I think we can skip the small talk," said Holly, squashing the testosterone fest with a glare.

Caravelli put his hand on Holly's. "Good. Say your piece and then we'll leave."

"Relax." She looked up into his face. "Have a drink or something. You drive me crazy when you're like this."

Caravelli's expression closed, as if someone had pulled the shutters tight.

Interesting. He's going all protective, and she's just annoyed. Vampire men were prone to territorial behavior, but what about the women? He wondered about Constance.

Holly turned back to Mac. "You look kind of ragged. Are you feeling okay?"

"I'm okay," he said, which wasn't entirely true. "I think I'm just fighting a cold."

"Demons don't get colds," Caravelli said flatly.

"Then I'm only getting half a cold. I'm so relieved."

Holly gave them both a disgusted glare. "I looked for anything to do with the Castle creating or changing the inhabitants. There's so little written, it didn't take that long. The only references I found just covered the usual stuff— no need to feed, no need to drink, and so on. So I tried some other books on demonology."

Mac sat back, crossing his arms, trying to listen to her and ignore Caravelli's death-ray stare.

She went on. "There was one unusual reference to the Castle. It said something about an avatar being stolen, but the manuscript was in Bulgarian and so I tried running the text through translation software, but that never works all that well. I'm trying to get a line on someone at the university who can put it into proper English."

"Avatar?" Mac asked. "As in the incarnation of a god? A concept?" He didn't think an ancient manuscript would be referring to chat-room icons.

"I don't know. As I said, the translation was garbled. All I got for certain was that the Castle is decaying somehow."

"Yeah, well, I heard the place had gardens once," Mac replied. "I don't know what could grow there. There's no sunlight."

Caravelli narrowed his eyes. He hadn't stopped watching Mac's every breath. "Queen Omara reported rumors that the magic of the Castle is fading."

Mac trusted very little that came out of the vampire queen's mouth, but this once she could be telling the truth. Dying magic usually meant magic going wonky. Could it be that the remnants of his demon infection were reacting to that?

Holly shook her head. "Unfortunately, theories and rumors are all we've got. I'm sorry, Mac, but nothing I found was all that helpful."

Shit. It was all he could do to control his face and hide his disappointment. It wasn't her fault.

A waiter stopped, a young weresomething with a name tag that said JOE. Both Mac and Caravelli shifted in their seats, dialing down the glare fest for the benefit of the staff.

Joe was oblivious. "What can I get you?" He cleared away the remains of the stew, then picked up Mac's empty beer bottle and added it to his tray. "Another drink?"

Mac nodded. Caravelli ordered red wine. Holly asked for mineral water. Joe left with the order. For a split second, everyone seemed comfortable. It was a good act. Too bad Mac had to put a wrinkle in it by asking for more favors. If Holly didn't have the answer to one problem, he had to move on to the next.

"Holly, I'm really grateful to you for helping me out, but there's something else."

Predictably, Caravelli tensed, but Mac forged ahead. "What do you know about demon boxes?"

Holly lifted her eyebrows. "They're kissing cousins to genie bottles. Sorcerers use them. Y'know, the whole make-the-demon-do-your-bidding shtick."

"How interesting." Caravelli looked like he was getting ideas.

Mac grimaced. "What kind of protection does a demon have from getting sucked into one? I don't suppose they have, like, safety latches on the inside?"

The drinks came, Joe setting out little napkins before placing the glasses on the table.

"Do you think there's a box with your name on it?" Caravelli asked, his hostile stare veering to the waiter for a moment.

"Don't sound so hopeful." Mac picked up his brew, wiping the condensation from the label. He didn't really want another beer. He was feeling worse as the evening progressed. "There's a case I'm working."

Holly blinked. "You've gone private eye?"

"Yeah, right. Every ex-cop's dream job. Nah, this is personal. There's that vampire chick in the Castle—the one I was telling you about—who is trying to rescue an incubus from the guardsmen who kidnapped him. She has an in with a mad sorcerer who might be able to help me with my demon problem. Did I just say that?"

Caravelli took a long swallow of the wine, then set the glass down, looking almost amused. "It took six hundred years, but I think just now I finally heard everything."

The piano player started another tune, the old one about a wonderful life.

Holly squeezed the lime perched on the edge of her mineral water. "It won't be as hard to find out something about the boxes. I think there's even stuff in a language I can read."

Mac toasted her with his bottle. "I'd appreciate that. If the guardsman trapped the incubus in a box, I'd rather play it safe. I'm not eager to end up on somebody's shelf."

"So you're really working a case?" Caravelli said, sounding skeptical. "Inside the Castle?"

Holly gave him an exasperated look, but held her tongue. There was a lot of fondness mixed with her frustration, and it made Mac smile. *Caravelli's one lucky bloodsucker.*

He met the vampire's eyes. "Yeah, well, crime happens everywhere. I believe in keeping order as much as you do."

Caravelli picked up his wine. "Then why aren't you in the Castle doing your job?"

Because Constance is there, and I had to get my head on straight before facing her again. "The answers I need are out here."

"And when you have them?"

"I'll work the case. Just because I'm part hellspawn, that doesn't make me a bad person."

"Strange as it may seem, I might be starting to believe you. Just starting, mind you."

Glory Hallelujah, break out the fireworks.

People had been coming and going, the swinging doors

letting in blasts of cool night air. This time, something compelled Mac to look up. A woman with dark blond hair walked toward them, dangling a motorcycle helmet in one hand.

All the male heads in the room turned, taking in the show. Just as quickly, they carefully looked away. She was a bad kind of dangerous.

She was tall and lean, dressed in dark jeans, dark jacket, heavy boots, and a long-sleeved T-shirt made of some elastic, sparkly fabric. The jacket was open and the shirt left nothing to the imagination. Neither did the hard lines around her mouth. She was ready for a fight.

Her gaze lit on Caravelli, then on Holly. Something crossed her face—disappointment, maybe, then speculation. Caravelli's hand was resting on the table. It started to curl into a fist.

Interesting, thought Mac. The woman came straight up to Holly. Mac pushed back his chair again, this time ready to intervene.

Caravelli shot him a glance and a slight shake of the head.

The woman draped an arm around Holly's shoulder. "Hey, sis."

Mac nearly fell off his chair. *Sis? Ah, so this is the vampire-hunting in-law.*

Holly's face went dark, then carefully blank. "Ashe. What brings you here?"

"I saw the T-Bird outside. Thought I'd come say hello."

Ashe set the helmet in the middle of the table, claiming all the available space. No one spoke as she pulled up a chair between Holly and Mac. Alessandro stared into the bottom of his glass.

"Hi," she said, turning to Mac. He got a better look at her face. Now he could see the family resemblance. She wasn't bad-looking. If she smiled, she could be a beauty.

"Mac," he said, offering a hand. *Friendly neighborhood demon.*

He thought he saw Caravelli smirk.

She took Mac's hand in a grip meant to wrestle gators, then turned to the table in general. "Hope you don't mind if I join you?"

Mac noticed she asked after she'd made herself at home.

"We're having a quiet, *private* drink among friends," Caravelli said with his special mix of sarcasm and Bela Lugosi.

Ashe snorted. "You know how to make a girl feel welcome."

Caravelli shrugged and Holly winced. Mac felt sorry for Holly. She was the one caught in the middle. He looked for a diversion.

"What do you ride?" he said, nodding at the helmet.

"Ducati Monster 1100S."

"Nice. I'm more of a Harley man myself."

She looked him up and down. "How many strokes is your engine?"

Unfazed, Mac gave Ashe his most charming smile. "Trust me, the ride's smooth, and the mileage is great." *And the scorching finish is a hair-raiser*.

She stretched, sinuous as a cat, the jacket falling open to show off anything the see-through shirt hadn't already disclosed. "I'm just tire-kicking tonight, or I might take a test drive."

Mac wasn't sure he was flattered. He sure as hell wasn't interested, but it kept the conversation on a lighter note.

"Any reason you're here besides hello?" Holly asked, her tone cool.

"We got off on the wrong foot, Hol." Ashe looked at her sister, who was finishing the mineral water. "Is it okay if we try again?"

"Of course," Holly said, more cheerfully. "We can do that. Do you want to meet for lunch tomorrow?"

"What's wrong with here and now?"

"I was in the middle of something." Holly pushed her glass away, looking weary.

Ashe's fingers twitched, as if she'd been stung. "I'm family."

A flash of temper lit up Holly's face. "The world doesn't stop because you decided to drop by and stake my boyfriend."

Caravelli sat forward, his gaze on Ashe. "Perhaps it's time to go."

"You stay out of this, fang-boy." Ashe turned on the vampire, and Mac saw the face of a predator every bit as dangerous as Caravelli.

I hate domestic disputes. "Is there something that can't wait?" Mac asked tentatively.

"She wants to stake me," Caravelli said, his tone mocking. "I tremble."

Ashe leaned across the table, all but snarling at the vampire. "Sure, I want to. Why wouldn't I? Swear to me you've never, ever bitten her," she grated out, her voice barely audible above the noise of the other patrons.

"Ashe!" Holly snapped.

Caravelli sat like stone, his expression saying that he was guilty as charged.

Ashe gave a cold smile. "Thought so."

She slowly got to her feet and picked up her helmet. Caravelli stood, tracking her every move. Her body said more of rage than any curse. Then she turned to Mac, her expression venomous. "And where do you fit in?"

Mac took in the violence in her eyes. Carefully, he resurrected the charming smile. "I'm a nice, quiet guy, but if I find out you're going all Van Helsing on my friends, then I'm your worst nightmare."

Ashe gave a lopsided smile. "I'll look forward to it." She turned, recoiling when she nearly bumped into Caravelli. "Get the hell out of my way."

He fell back a step and she swept toward the door. For the second time that night, the whole pub turned to stare.

Holly looked shell-shocked. "Oh, Goddess, what just happened?"

"We tried to reason with a madwoman," Caravelli said, dropping to one knee beside her chair and raising a hand to her cheek. "I'm sorry, *cara*, but she won't be happy until I'm dust."

"She's my sister," Holly said quietly. "I want her to be the way she was when I was little. I want that Ashe, not this one."

Caravelli hushed her.

It was time for Mac to go. He was a third wheel. He put money on the table for his dinner and got up. He touched Holly's shoulder lightly, but he addressed Caravelli. "I'm going to make sure Buffy isn't hanging around outside."

The vampire nodded. "A sound idea." His face was unreadable.

Mac headed for the door, pushing aside the headache bashing the inside of his skull. With all the angry energy flying around, his demon should have been straining against its leash, but instead it lay queasy and still.

The fresh night air felt delicious against his baking skin. It was doing the raining-but-not-quite routine, tiny droplets stinging the skin with icy pinpricks. Mac ducked into the pool of shadow beside the Empire's door and scanned the street. A Ducati would be easy to spot. He didn't see it, but it wouldn't hurt to take a tour of the block to be sure. He'd been listening and hadn't heard a motorcycle.

Hunching against the dark, he walked to the corner, turned left, and went as far as the alley that led past the Castle door. The iron gate stood open and Nanette's neon sign blinked an antiseptic blue from the other end of the passage. The flashing light made the dark corners of the alley even blacker. He could smell the damp bricks and the heavy pall of age that seemed to rise out of the ground—or maybe that was his imagination adding color to the scene. He'd heard once that the old town gallows had stood nearby.

They knew how to get rid of troublemakers back then.

Mac nearly passed by, but he took one last, closer look into the alley. Ashe was standing in front of the Castle door. He'd nearly missed her, except the faint light had caught the sparkles on the front of her shirt. He started walking toward her, the old cedar bricks sounding hollow under his feet.

"You really don't want to mess with that," he said, using the firm-but-friendly community cop voice.

Ashe didn't look up, but laid one hand against the door. "What do you want?"

She didn't wait for an answer, but moved her hand over the surface of the door. "There's power here. Even I can feel it."

"If you snuggled up to a nuclear reactor core, maybe you could feel that, too." Mac jammed his hands into his pockets. "It's about as dangerous."

She trailed one hand down the wood like a lover's caress. "What's behind the door?" she asked. "It feels amazing."

He suddenly realized the hellhounds were absent. *Don't those guys ever work?* "It's the back entrance to Nanette's," he lied. "She had a sorcerer put a spell on the door so no one walks in to see the bondage shows for free."

Ashe pulled away from the door with a disgusted noise.

"I'd thought maybe you'd like that sort of thing."

"It's no fun unless I get to hold the whip. Besides . . . werecats? That would be like watching a kitten play with duct tape."

That surprised a laugh out of Mac. Ashe gave a warped smile.

"Speaking of werecats, I heard something on the radio," she said. "I think it was the university station. Something about a door in an alley leading to a big secret called the Castle."

"Leave it alone."

"You shouldn't lie. It doesn't suit you," she said, and walked toward the other end of the alley.

Crap.

Mac watched her go past the kitchen exit of a Chinese restaurant, the door propped open with a big white pail. In the brief pool of light, her slim back and fall of blond hair looked like a teenager's. The swing of her hips did not.

Mac had no reason to stay, but he lingered for a moment in front of the door, suddenly tired. It was time to go home and sleep off his headache, but he hesitated. What was Constance doing? Was she still in the Summer Room, thinking up new ways to bite him?

A twisted corner of his soul hoped so. It was a very *stupid*, twisted corner.

Mac bowed his head. He *couldn't* need her. He *shouldn't* want her. But he did. It wasn't as simple as falling in lust with a set of fangs. There was also a woman there, just like he was still a man. He had looked into that woman's eyes, and been smitten.

The same way, he was sure, Caravelli had once looked at Holly. They'd made it work, hadn't they? He'd just seen them stand united against Ashe.

I so don't need this. Even as he thought it, he felt a thread of resignation in his soul. Constance might not have gotten her teeth into him, but she was firmly on his radar, and she was in trouble beyond even the guardsmen-stole-my-baby problem. *Crap.*

It wasn't in Mac to stand by and watch her flounder. Not that he was in favor of the whole Turning thing, but there had to be an easier way to go about it than jumping and biting a stranger. Unfortunately, Mac knew squat about the whole vampirization process. If she did manage to drink from a living victim, what exactly would happen? How would she change? Would her personality stay the same? Weren't vampires supposed to have a sponsor, or a team leader, or whatever they called them? He should ask Caravelli. Maybe he could help.

He heard a motorcycle start up about a block away, the engine revving to life.

Would it work if Constance drank from a guy who was only part human? *And that part is getting smaller and smaller.* Mac pushed away the memory of his demon rising, trying to claim her. *It won't happen again. It can't. I don't trust myself with that dark side riding me.*

He put his hand on the door, feeling the swirling energy of the magic all the way to the bottom of his uneasy stomach. *Maybe I can make a difference. Maybe I can save the incubus and kiss the girl, but what will be left of me by then?*

Every time he went into the Castle, he came out less human. There was no denying it.

But there was work to be done. The kind he was good at and thrived on. If he didn't go in and help Constance get Sylvius back, kick guardsman ass, and undo the crime that had been committed, Mac was denying the part of himself he valued most. The thing that made him human in the first place. The part that cared enough to become a cop.

Demoned if you do, damned if you don't.

Lost in thought, he almost felt the velocity of the Ducati before he heard it. Mac spun around to see the bike barreling down the alley, Ashe perched on it like a Valkyrie on her steed. Mac's headache cost him a split second of reaction time. He sprang aside.

He wasn't even sure if she hit him, but it sure as hell felt like it. He bounced against the brick of the alley wall, smacking the back of his head.

Oh, God. Mac slid down the wall, his vision exploding in blasts of white. He heard the Ducati tearing away, the motor a distant snarl.

Now he finally had something in common with Caravelli. He hated that bitch.

Chapter 13

"**G**ood morning! This is CSUP at seven o'clock for your local and world paranormal news bulletins. . . ."

Mac's hand slammed down on the radio button before he opened his eyes. Blessed silence rang like the aftertones of a bell. He did a quick inventory. His stomach had settled and his headache was gone. Whatever bug he'd had yesterday had shoved off. Sleep had done the trick.

Good, because he had a lot to do. He wasn't awake enough to remember everything, but the list ended with—if he could get it together—rescuing an incubus from the bad guys.

Mac threw the covers off, stifling. He sat up and nearly fell to the floor. Obviously, he was still half asleep. He caught the edge of the mattress, steadying himself. *Need coffee.*

For a moment, he thought the light-headedness came from smacking his head on the wall when Ashe had buzzed him with the Ducati. Then he realized it was hunger. He hadn't eaten a lot of that god-awful stew, but he had made himself a sandwich when he got home. That should have been enough to hold him until morning, but he felt like he hadn't eaten for a week.

Time for breakfast, then.

He stood up, feeling thick-headed and oddly clumsy, and padded into the kitchen wearing nothing but his pajama bottoms. The condo felt too warm. Still groggy and feeling all thumbs, he switched on the coffeemaker—he always prepped it the night before—and shoved bread in the toaster, eating another piece untoasted because he was too starved to wait. While he waited for the appliances to do their thing, he shuffled into the bathroom.

When he went to wash his face, he noticed the problem. Mac froze, the water gurgling down the drain as his brain groped with what he was seeing in the mirror.

What the fuck?

His brain backed up and tried again. His reflection wasn't exactly *him*. For one thing, he had to duck to a new angle to reach the sink. Not much. Just enough to realize that he was slightly taller than when he'd gone to bed. And he had put on pounds of hard muscle.

Huh?

His mind went absolutely blank. He blinked, the confusion on the Mac-but-not-Mac's reflected face multiplying his alarm. *Aw, c'mon, what the hell am I supposed to do with this? I look like a fucking action figure.*

Mac reached under the stream of water with trembling hands—hands that now felt too large—and splashed his face. His basic features, at least, hadn't changed, though he looked like he hadn't shaved for three days. Well, he probably hadn't—and with dark wavy hair that had gotten far too long, all he needed was a loincloth and he'd be good to go for Mac the Barbarian. He sluiced water over his face again, and again, stalling while his brain scrambled for footing. *No. No. No. I don't need this!*

Finally, he turned off the taps, grabbed a towel, and blotted the water from his eyes. Then he looked down at himself, shivering with delayed panic. *Oh, God.* There was too much leg sticking out of the pajama bottoms he wore.

The lightweight pants showed that whatever had happened to his body had left him much more than anatomically correct.

Oh, God. No wonder he'd felt so horny last night.

Not enough air.

He stumbled out of the bathroom, throwing open the sliding balcony door. The force of his shove made the glass all but jump the track. *Shit.*

He stepped outside, the concrete cold under his feet. He sucked in lungful after lungful of the October chill, grabbing the painted iron of the railing to steady himself against the swimming sensation in his head. *What's going on?*

Disorientation didn't cover what he was feeling. It was like going through adolescence all over again, and in eight hours. The big body, clumsy and unfamiliar. The raging hormones. *It makes no sense. Why did this happen?*

His brain stalled again, crashing under a wave of panic and outrage. *What is this? More demon crap? A curse?*

All he'd wanted was to be human again. Instead, he got Mac 3.0, manly man edition. He made a fist, watching the play of extra muscle in his forearm. He'd been strong already, fit, in perfect shape, but his demon strength had been limited by his human frame. This body could do so much more. He'd grown into that demonic power.

Maybe that was the point. The demon infection had been stalled by Holly's magic, so now it had taken a new direction. Under the Castle's influence, it was still Turning him, just a different way. *That makes no sense. People are supposed to renovate houses, not the other way around.*

Mac let the fist go, feeling blood flow into the relaxing flesh. Every time he went into the Castle, something bizarre happened. He sucked another lungful of air, now noticing the stronger swell of his chest. He'd been a big-enough man before. This was—well, like he'd spent his life chasing woolly mammoths instead of felons. Most guys would like this. He should be feeling jubilant. Potent. Powerful. What he felt was pissed off. He'd had enough of magic messing around with him.

Anger steadied him. Plus, the cold air had cleared his head a little. Straightening, he looked out over Fairview. At least it looked the same as it always did. The pale morning light showed patches of russet and gold in the trees. The distant strip of ocean gleamed pewter gray. Life woke in the town, pulsing.

It pulsed through him, too. That strange, electric feeling he'd felt before rushed through his blood at full tilt. He was insanely *alive*. Every muscle and thew of this body wanted to run, fight, and burn off this fierce, hot energy.

Beneath it all, his demon powers hummed like a dark, Gothic chorus. They had gained ground, leaving him feeling far less civilized. *I'm so screwed. How the hell am I going to come back from this one? Am I even a little bit human anymore?*

Well, the upgrade would make fighting idiots like Bran that much easier.

He noticed the curtain of a neighboring condo twitch. The place had a clear view of Mac's balcony, which was why he seldom used it. *Great.* He looked around and noticed a few other female faces in other windows, one with a camera phone.

He thought of a few fresh obscenities, but a corner of his ego did the happy dance. He stomped on it. Mac stalked back inside, feeling the confinement of the apartment like an assault. Hunger was moving on to nausea. He was going to pass out if he didn't eat something.

He grabbed the cold toast out of the toaster and shoved one piece in his mouth. He put two more slices of bread in the slots and punched the button down. With a sigh of relief, he chewed the dry toast, washing it down with black coffee. Then he felt patient enough to actually butter the second piece. He rummaged in the fridge for a block of cheese, ripped open the pack, and broke off a piece with his hands, not bothering with a knife. By then the next round had toasted, and he started the ritual over again. Mindlessly, Mac kept going until he ate nearly every damned thing in the fridge. Then he checked the freezer. Nothing there but frozen peas. He could go to a restaurant, but he wasn't sure he was up to facing the world as SuperMac just yet.

Still, more groceries were an urgent priority. Mac refilled his coffee cup. He'd always taken it black before, but now he piled in the milk and sugar, still craving fuel to burn. His bones ached, as though they'd been stretched and pulled. *It must hurt to be a werebeast. Never thought about it before.*

He slurped the coffee, stalling.

What are you doing? Going through the motions of coping doesn't mean a damn thing. But that was all he had, outside of running through the streets screaming at the top of his lungs.

Admit it. Who doesn't want to wake up in a better body? And it's not like you haven't switched species before.

But this isn't me.

Well, it is now.

That's not exactly a bonus.

He sat down, the wooden kitchen chair creaking beneath his unaccustomed weight. He felt healthy but insanely hot, like the fever he'd had last night had become permanent.

Hunger raged, the same way it had the last time he'd been transformed into a demon. The only positive was that this body didn't seem interested in eating souls. It definitely preferred meat. Lots and lots of it.

It wanted a fight, the exertion of all this power against another. It wanted to dominate.

It wanted sex, and not the pretty kind.

His mind went to Constance, sleek and small and aching for his touch. He had smelled the desire on her, the musk beneath her perfume. He itched to get to her, to claim her the way her hungry lips had said she wanted to be claimed.

And the vampire hickey? This body could take it. *Bring it on, sweetheart. Bite me if you dare.* He swam in that thought for a moment, remembering how eager she had been to seduce him. *Oh, yeah.*

Oh. Hmm.

Dragging his thoughts from the mental home theater,

Mac set down the coffee cup, careful of the fragile ceramic handle. *Maybe the first thing this new body needs is a cold shower.* It had all the rampant enthusiasm of a seventeen-year-old. *Great. I'm never going to ask anyone to supersize me again.*

Already his stomach was cramping with hunger once more, his enormous breakfast forgotten. *This is ridiculous.*

The phone rang. Thankful to connect with the normal world, he picked it up, holding the receiver gingerly. He had visions of squishing it by accident.

"Macmillan." He nearly dropped the phone. His voice resonated differently, bouncing around in a larger rib cage. It was also shaking with stress.

"Hello? Mac?" It was Holly.

"Hey," he said, clearing his throat, trying to shrink his voice back to normal.

"Sorry to call so early. Have you got a cold?"

He rumbled again, feeling like a sports coupe that woke up as a monster truck. "What do you know about the Castle making superwarriors?"

"Guardsmen? Mac, are you all right? You sound strange."

Guardsmen. Was that what he'd become? But they were originally human, not demon. They were bound by oaths and spells and trapped against their will, sent to the prison by some whacked-out secret society in charge of supplying Castle guards. Nothing to do with him.

"Mac? What's going on?"

How much did he want to say this minute? He was too hungry to think, too impatient to explain himself. Too scared. Too embarrassed. "I'm okay," he said.

"I found something on the demon boxes. I figured you'd want the information as soon as possible."

His cop side jumped to attention. Good to know it still worked. "Hit me."

"They're not exactly common, but they're not rare, either. I popped into my grandma's place and had a look through some of her books. Sure enough, I found something. I made up a charm that should stop you from being sucked inside."

"Great!"

"Lore was over here about something else. I'm sending him to you with the charm. He should be there in about fifteen minutes."

"Great," he said again, inwardly cursing. He wasn't ready for visitors, but after the effort Holly had gone to, there was no way he was going to complain about timing. "I owe you big time."

"No problem, Mac. Take care." She hung up.

He hung up, grappling with the jumble of problems he had to solve, starting with the most basic. *Crap, what am I going to wear?* Nothing was going to fit.

Mac paused, remembering his raincoat. He'd noticed the sleeves felt short a couple of days ago, when he had been talking to Holly. Had the first signs of this change already started then?

What if it wasn't over?

His stomach growled. He ached. He got up to head to the shower and knocked over the hallway lamp. Everything was too close, too cramped.

I hate this. He was an alien in his own landscape. *Just call me Ogg, cousin of Tarzan.*

After the shower, he grabbed his largest pair of sweat pants and a muscle shirt. The shirt, straining across his chest, made him look like something from a cheesecake boy-toy calendar.

Great. Just great.

The door buzzer rang. Mac walked to the hall and pressed the button for the outside door, not bothering with a greeting. As he moved, he could feel muscle shirt pulling tight across his back. Prowling back to the kitchen, he rummaged in the cupboard until he found some soda crackers. He tore the package open as Lore walked in.

The hellhound reached the kitchen, stopped in his tracks, and looked Mac up and down, the only change in his expression a slight lift of his dark brows. "You've been working out."

Mac chewed a cracker. "I had a makeover."

Lore narrowed his eyes, considering. Hounds seldom showed emotion to outsiders. The merest flicker was like anyone else having a spazz attack. "Did you mean to do this?"

"No."

"Then it's not an illusion."

"Nope."

"Huh." Lore was silent for a moment, and then held out a brown paper bag. His hands were large, the type that would deliver a bruising blow in a fight. Mac could have crushed them in his.

"Holly asked me to give you this," Lore said.

Mac stuffed another two crackers in his mouth and took the bag, unrolling the top. It held a small cloth pouch pulled shut by a drawstring long enough to hang around his neck. Mac pulled it out of the bag slowly, cautious just in case it didn't mix well with whatever transforming spell he was packing. When it seemed safe, he slipped the string over his head and tossed the bag on the counter. The pouch looked primitive, filled with who-knew-what witchy herbs and rocks, but it was small enough to stuff under his shirt and out of the way.

Lore watched him silently, dark eyes following Mac's every movement. "Holly said that charm protects against demon boxes. You're going after Sylvius."

Mac looked at Lore sharply. The hellhound's expression was guarded. It was like looking into the gaze of a street-tough stray. Which, in a way, he was.

"How do you know about Sylvius?" Mac asked.

"He's a friend." Lore folded his arms and leaned his shoulder against the refrigerator. "I would have said it was sure death to attempt to rescue any prisoner of the guards-men, but you can do it. The gods have obviously prepared you."

For a moment, Mac forgot about refueling. He had no idea what hellhounds believed in, but he didn't like the idea of being prepared by some entity. That smacked of being the anointed one, or inflated one, or whatever. More crap he'd never signed off on.

"How do you know what I can do?" he asked. "How do you know what goes on in the Castle? You haven't been there for a year."

For the briefest instant, Lore looked smug. "Hounds are good with locks."

"What does that mean?"

"We're half demons. We have power over doorways and thresholds. Things between one realm and the next. Prophecy. Now that I'm free, the Castle door is no problem for me."

Mac choked on a cracker crumb. He poured a glass of water and drank it down. Then he started back in on the crackers.

Lore watched him with steady eyes. "We've been watching you."

"That's creepy." The hellhounds in general were pretty weird—not harmful, but too silent, too watchful for comfort.

As if reading Mac's mind, Lore lowered his gaze, studying the kitchen floor. "When you returned to Fairview, some thought it was a miracle. You had fallen into the dark, but came back in defiance of your curse. Our elders thought the gods had called you here for a purpose."

Mac made a dismissive noise. If the gods were calling, they could leave a voice mail.

Thoughts chased across the hound's strong-boned features, whole arguments Mac would never hear because he didn't belong to their closed, silent community. Finally, Lore said, "You don't believe me. Hounds don't lie. We can't."

"Whatever." Mac reached for another cracker, and realized the box was empty. He crumpled it in disgust.

The hound stiffened, pulling away from the fridge to stand straight, his hands half clenched at his sides. "Events are moving quickly. You need to listen."

Mac threw the box back on the counter, a white haze of frustration flooding his mind. "Screw all that. I need to eat. You wouldn't like me when I'm hungry."

The words came out between clenched teeth. The alternative was roaring like a wounded bear. He didn't want to deal with gods and legends. He had more immediate problems.

Lore edged back, cautious now.

Mac steadied his breath. "Whatever you're selling, I don't want it. I'm done with being special. I don't do destiny."

"That's your decision."

"Damned straight."

Lore held on to the ensuing silence until Mac met his eyes. Then he carried on as if Mac had been listening intently all along. "Nothing happens without reason. If you've been brought back and changed, there's something you need to do. Something even bigger than rescuing my friend."

Mac felt irritation bunching his shoulders. "Like what?"

"If the task is yours, you already know."

"That's crazy."

"That's the way it works."

"I don't want to play."

The hound's expression went from neutral to icy. "Destiny doesn't make you special. It's simply more responsibility."

"I just want my life back."

The words, however true, suddenly sounded childish in Mac's ears. That just made him more annoyed. "Get out of here."

Disappointment flickered in Lore's eyes, then vanished as he shuttered his expression. "When you need help, call us."

He left without another word. From the kitchen, Mac heard the door click shut.

Crap. That was stupid.

Mac had never asked Lore why he had brought up the prophecy in the first place. Or why he had offered the hounds' help.

Hellhounds never involved themselves in other people's business. What was their interest in whatever it was the Sparkly One was supposed to do? Was there trouble in the hellhound kennel?

He'd been so wrapped up in his own shit, he'd missed all that. Motivation was something a cop should never overlook. He'd be damned if that would happen twice.

There was something going on there. He could smell it.

God, I'm hungry.

Chapter 14

October 5, 2:00 p.m.
101.5 FM

"That's what I mean, Oscar. What *can* the supernatural community do about humans who believe they have the right to kill us on sight? We all know there're even tribes of so-called Hunters that have existed for centuries in Eastern Europe. Some say they've even evolved into a species of their own. Their whole culture is based on exterminating vampires. What have I, George de Winter, ever done to them? And yet they would still kill me at a moment's notice and the law protects them from retaliation. How do we shield ourselves from something like that?"

"But really, isn't there a greater threat from random violence against supernaturals, the vampire slayers who appoint themselves vigilantes?"

"Most of them are rank amateurs, but you're right. Every so often they do get in a lucky stake."

Alessandro slept. For vampires, dreams were usually lost in the deep, deep sleep of the Undead, slipping away during the long climb back to consciousness.

The odd quality of this one stuck with him, though.

There was a magpie the size of city hall trying to carry off the T-Bird, and he was trying to stop it with a garden hose.

Why the hell am I spraying it with water? The hose is long enough to wrap around its neck. This is a stupid dream.

The image blanked as absolutely as if someone had pulled the power cord.

Merda!

His hand shot out from beneath the covers, grabbing the stake inches from his chest. It was pure vampire survival reflex. His eyes squinted open a moment later, tears forming in reaction to the daylight peeking from beneath the blinds.

Through the haze, he saw Ashe's rage-mottled face. His other hand shot up, snatching her throat. Delicate rings of cartilage tempted him to squeeze and crush.

He really wasn't a morning person.

Ashe wasn't letting go of the stake, but was yanking on it with rabid persistence. Alessandro started to sit up. She tried to poke her thumb in his eye. That did it. With a snarl, he flipped her over onto the bed, knocking the stake from her hand. It hit the wall and skidded under the bed.

"Agh!" she yelped, clawing at the hand he still had wrapped around her throat.

He snarled, letting her see the fangs. "I've had it with you, hunter. I've held back for Holly's sake. You crossed the line."

She brought her knee up sharply, catching him in the ribs. He grabbed her hair, using the leverage to tip her head back and sniff her throat. Her eyes went perfectly round in a moment of pure abject terror. The stink of it roused the predator in him. In the single tick of the clock, Ashe wiped the look from her face, but she couldn't hide the slight trembling of her chin.

Fear was spice. Saliva pooled in his mouth. As Holly's Chosen, blessed by her magic, he didn't need to feed on blood any more than a human needed a candy bar. That didn't mean the temptation wasn't there. Just ask a chocoholic.

"You aren't supposed to be awake," she said, her voice shaking just on the last syllable. She cleared her throat.

"Really?" The light was making his head pound.

"You can't move in daylight." She squeezed her eyes closed, for a moment looking so much like Holly it made him loosen his grip on her hair.

"Of course I can."

He was kneeling beside her on the soft mattress, bracing with one hand while he held her down with the other around her throat. Ashe was strong enough to break the grip of a human male. Against him, she didn't stand a chance. Both her hands clutched his wrist. Any moment she'd start trying to pry herself free because survival instinct demanded it.

She wouldn't win.

He gave a deadly leer. "Trade secret. Any vampire that is old enough can wake during the day. It just makes us very, very cranky."

At the moment, he felt like he had the mother of all hangovers.

"What's Holly going to say when she finds me dead?"

A low growl slipped out. "What's to say she'll ever find you?"

Ashe made a tiny, rebellious noise. "You're a monster."

"Your point?"

The floor shook, a brief rumble. The tension between them was waking the house's sentient magic.

Ashe hauled on his wrist, her fight coming back. "You won't win. I've never lost yet!"

She bit him.

Alessandro ripped his hand away, swearing as the blood welled up. "Son of a whore!"

Ashe sprang off the other side of the bed and whipped a second stake out of her boot. "Hurts, doesn't it, asshole? How do you think Holly felt when you bit her?"

Alessandro reached the end of his rope. With vampire speed, he hurled a pillow straight at her face. Reflexively, she stabbed, releasing a snowstorm of feathers. He used the moment to sail over the bed and grab her from behind, twisting her arms behind her back.

The house trembled again, this time rattling the blinds on the window. Soon it would become dangerous, but to which one of them? Both?

Ashe gave a bitter laugh. "You can kill me if you want, but that doesn't make you a living man. You can't be part of my sister's *life*. You're death."

Her words sliced so deep, he didn't feel the sting until a second had passed. Then it seared him to the marrow, too deep for any real response. He twisted the second stake out of her fingers, not caring if he hurt her. "I'm still better than the family she has. I wouldn't send my child away to be raised by strangers."

"I'm keeping my daughter safe from the likes of you."

Alessandro bit back a profane retort. He had few options. He could kill Ashe, lock her in the basement, or toss her down the front steps. He dropped his voice to his coldest, cruelest tones. "How do you feel about family counseling?"

"Fuck you."

His conscience was clear enough to introduce a final option.

"Then I have a very special place for you to go where you can kill all the monsters you want."

"Pissed" didn't begin to cover Mac's mood.

He'd bought groceries, stuffed himself to bursting, and, suddenly exhausted, fallen asleep on the couch. He remembered getting up for a midnight snack that had involved another normal day's supply of food. When he woke up midmorning, he was sure he'd changed even more. He felt like an ox. Maybe somebody out of *Alice in Wonderland*. It would have been funny if it had been happening to anybody else.

He was not amused.

That was just the physical stuff. The demon had put his aggression on high, something he'd noticed the second time he'd been forced out of the apartment to find clothes and food. He'd nearly attacked a guy who'd cut him off in the beef aisle in the supermarket. Yeah, Mac was pissed, and there was fear underneath the anger. At moments, he was hanging on to his self-control by the fingernails. The demon was taking over.

He tried to call Holly, but she wasn't home. He'd hung up without leaving a message. He had a sixth sense that this was his problem to solve, anyway. Or maybe he'd listened to Lore too long and all that prophecy crap was curdling his brain.

He was hungry again. Mac piled sliced ham onto a bun, feeling like he spent his life at the fridge door.

There were only two things keeping him focused. One, he'd made a promise to Constance to rescue her son. Two, he needed answers—all kinds of them. He was determined not to let his brain slack off just because his body had gone into overdrive. The slip with Lore had been warning enough.

Mac bit into the sandwich and chewed while he split and buttered a second bun. Ham or beef on this one? Why not both?

His plan was simple: Get Sylvius. Interrogate Atreus. After that he'd find out what Lore was really up to. If the hounds had a clue about what was going on, he needed to know. The Castle had done something to him, and he needed it undone just as soon as he'd rescued Connie's son. There had to be a way to get back to his life as a human. For one thing, he couldn't afford his demon's insane grocery bill.

After eating his third sandwich, Mac slung the charm Holly had sent him around his neck. The shirt he'd just bought already felt tight through the shoulders and chest.

Whatever was happening to him, it wasn't over. The simple truth was, if he didn't do something—take charge, act, focus—he would give in to the panic bubbling up inside him. It was hard to hide from the monster when it was the very flesh you lived in.

But turning into a monster didn't mean he would go back on his word. He'd let the demon infection distract him long enough. It was time to go back to work.

He grabbed the sword he had taken from Bran from the umbrella rack, testing its balance. This body would know how to use it in a way his old one hadn't, but he still took his semiautomatic—the holster's seven-way comfort adjustments worked to their XXL limits—and all the ammo he had. No point in giving up the tried and true.

He dusted from his condo to the door of the Castle. The first challenge was finding out where the guardsmen kept their special prisoners. Constance's advice might cut hours off his search. She'd been following Bran before. She would at least have an idea which corner of this cavernous Goth-o-rama to start with.

No doubt he could find her in the Summer Room, like a tiny, dark pearl in the safety of its oyster shell. He'd made her promise to stay out of trouble, but that didn't cover the trouble she represented to him. Just the memory of the place—and what had nearly happened there—was intoxicating. That much temptation should have been a warning in itself to stay away, but his body remembered the feel of her pressing against him. It made the decision.

Finding the room involved only a few wrong turns. It was exactly as Mac had left it. The candlelight was soft, glittering in the silver light of the tapestries, casting misty shadows on swooping fabric that draped the ceiling and swathed the great canopied bed.

He lingered for a moment in the doorway, and then closed the door behind him and slid the bolt that locked it home. It was true he had all but fled from the room— and Constance—only days before, fearing what his demon might do to her, what her blood thirst and the room's lust-filled magic might do to him.

This time would be different. He was in control. He had come for her.

But I didn't come here for her. Not that way. I came here for information on how to find her son.

Think again.

She had tried to seduce him. By some übermale libido logic, she had offered herself, so now she was his. His dark side applauded. *Teach her a lesson for tricking you.*

Whoa, there, demon dude. Keep your head on straight. Remember you're a cop first, even if you don't have a badge anymore. You have a job to do. No time for anything but dead bodies and paperwork.

But that argument wasn't working anymore. The cold comfort of human logic was losing ground. He simply *wanted.*

He should never have come. His demon crumpled that thought like a beer can and tossed it aside.

Like a sentimental memory, Constance's perfume hung in the air. There she was, stretched out on the dark velvet spread, the wealth of her long, dark hair nearly invisible against the inky background. Mac stood at the foot of the bed, looking down on her through the sheer silk of the draperies. She looked as pale as the dead, her faded dress shabby against the opulence of the gold-tasseled pillows.

Don't you have to save the kid? Figure out how to be human again? Remember what always happens when you get involved with Babes of Doom?

She was so vulnerable. A wave of possessiveness swamped him, heating his already-pounding blood. Human or demon, Mac was all male. Beneath the pull of her beauty, the two sides of his soul were starting to blur. They both ignited with desire.

Mac set the sword down on a nearby table, then removed his shoulder holster and heavy boots, careful to make no noise. He crept to the side of the bed, and parted the curtain with his hands. The clearer view didn't disappoint. When she had been bitten, her face still had the soft perfection of extreme youth. He had looked at enough women to know how much Constance stood out.

Intense satisfaction rippled through his gut. She was his for the plucking. She had already asked for what he wanted to give her. There was nothing to stop him.

Except himself. Mac was frozen by the tender innocence of her face. His conquering impulses gentled. If he was going to make her his, there would be no victory without surrender. For that, more than brute lust had to come into play. He needed persuasion, too.

He leaned forward, one knee on the bed, and balanced himself above her. She was so small, he was going to have to be careful. Slowly, savoring the moment, he lowered himself, touching her lips with his. Her mouth was cool, slightly parted, showing the tips of her fangs. He found them even more erotic than before. He drew himself fully onto the bed, then kissed her again, harder. He propped himself on one hand now, using the other to slowly draw away the thin scarf she wore. The ends were tucked demurely between her breasts, a puritanical tease. The fabric slid away with a whisper that shivered along his nerves. The scarf smelled of her perfume.

"Constance," he whispered in her ear. There was no response. The Undead rested deeply, falling into sleep so deep it was often mistaken for true death. He had no idea how long one would rest in a place that had no sun to hide from, but it could be a while.

Ah, well, that just gave him more time to play.

Skimming a finger along the top of her dress, he admired the whiteness of her skin, the soft way her breasts fell as she slept. The laces that held the front tightly closed tempted him. The tips were frayed, the ribbon soft from time and use. Carefully, he pulled one end, loosening the knot. As it gave, the lacing relaxed, the blue cloth parting to give a glimpse of more layers of clothing beneath. What he thought was a dress was actually a skirt and kind of jacket, petticoats and other cottony bits beneath, and then a stiff vest-thing that laced up the front. He guessed it was some type of corset, except it didn't look like those he'd seen in men's magazines.

How the hell could anyone move in all this stuff? Getting her out of it was going to take some determination, not to mention an engineering degree.

"Constance," he whispered again, but louder.

Her eyes snapped open, her expression one of confusion deepening to desire and then absolute shock. "You came back!"

"I said I'd come back."

She sat up, amazement filling her eyes. "What happened to you?"

Mac sealed her mouth with his before she could say another word. Her hands gripped his shoulders, trying to keep some distance between them. That wasn't what he wanted. He worked the kiss, using every trick in his repertoire to prolong it, to make her forget whatever fear was slipping between them. Bit by bit, the tension in her fingers eased. He pushed her back down to the pillows.

Eventually, he let her break away. He left tiny kisses on her nose and eyes and brow before he retreated.

"It's fortunate that I don't need to breathe," she said tartly, but her tone was shaken.

Her eyes had drifted shut, and now she opened them again. For a moment, she looked blind before she pulled him back into focus. Slowly, her brow furrowed, and she pushed him away, one hand against his chest.

This time, he let her.

Her head crooked back, trying to get a fuller view. Fear had faded to caution. "Conall Macmillan, what happened to you?"

He cocked an eyebrow. "Do you like what you see?"

"By the sweet saints, what have you done?" Though she spoke barely above a whisper, her tone was whip-sharp. "And you're burning up. Are you sick? What magic have you got yourself into?"

He thought he might have heard concern somewhere in there. He swallowed, the taste of her still clinging to his tongue. "It just happened. I feel fine."

She raised herself up on her elbows, nearly bumping noses with him. Her gaze slowly slid down his front. She tensed, then flushed a faint, faint bloom of pink against her white, white skin. "I can see that."

He couldn't stop a grin as curiosity widened her eyes. He leaned forward, using his body to force her back to the bed again. He leaned on one elbow, supporting his head on his hand. He used the other hand to tug at the ribbon that held her jacket shut, quickly working it free.

She closed her hand over his, stilling his fingers. "You know you don't smell the least bit human anymore? You smell *other*."

Her words jolted Mac. "What does that mean?"

"You've changed through and through. You're a demon now, no 'half' about it!"

The words stung, pulling his mood into darkness. Rolling away from her, he sat up. "I didn't ask for what happened."

Not human. He'd already lost his job, his relations, and his friends. It shouldn't have made any difference. It was the last flicker of a dying bulb winking out, nothing more.

But he had prayed so hard for a road back.

Driven by the hot burn of emotion, his demon stirred, shadows sliding through his thoughts. He could sense the demon was adapting, deciding how it could use this new form, savoring its strength and gargantuan appetites. No, the only human part left in him was his reason and what remained of his conscience. The rest lay scattered like flotsam from a shipwreck.

Demons destroy.

Constance sat up behind him, her hands resting on his shoulders. Her touch was tentative, but he could tell it was meant to comfort. "You didn't want to hear that, did you?"

"No."

"I'm sorry." She paused. "Why did you come?"

"I said I would." *Badge or no badge, I'm still the guy who helps people*.

"I wasn't sure I'd see you again. I kept looking for Viktor and the guardsmen's quarters."

As he turned, her hands fell away from his shoulders. She was sitting on her heels, her black hair in a tumble around her, the laces of her clothes dangling free. His breath caught, swamped by the burning in his blood. "I said I would help you find Sylvius."

"But that's not the only reason you came back, is it?" she asked uneasily.

"No. I came here to take you."

"What?"

Caveman alert! "Um. I mean, make love to you." *Look, bud, you can rule little Mac, but leave my mouth out of it.*

Pale though she was, she turned even whiter; then red spots showed on her cheekbones. Fear, excitement, anger all chased through her eyes.

"You want me to lift my skirts for the likes of you?" She tossed her hair back over her shoulder, her dark blue eyes narrowing. "Why should I want that? Your blood's no good to me now. The smell of it doesn't tempt me to bite nearly so much as before."

It was more a challenge than an outright refusal.

"I have other uses."

"And what might those be?" She crawled backward a foot. Her voice teased, but underneath he could hear a tremor of fear. It didn't matter that she had kissed him back a moment ago. The balance between them had shifted.

The ancient pursuit of male and mate had been declared.

Chapter 15

His limbs heavy with need, Mac swung himself back onto the bed. "Come here and I'll show you."

She was panting. Not that she normally needed air, but adrenaline was taking its toll. His stomach tightened, gripped by blazing heat. "Come here," he repeated in a thick voice. He moved forward, prowling across the counterpane.

She feinted left, vampire fast, but his enhanced reflexes were quicker. He had her caged under him in a second, his limbs trapping her as surely as iron bars. He stripped the ribbon through the last holes of her jacket in a series of efficient jerks. It went spiraling to the floor.

One obstacle down.

She tried to twist away as he pulled the jacket aside, but he held her firm. The corset beneath her top was nothing but stiff cloth laced tight. He was tempted to simply rip it in two. His hands felt clumsy, his brain too consumed with heat to manage another fiddly unpackaging job.

"Get it off," he demanded. It came out in a growl.

"To hell with you," she said, writhing like a cat about to be bathed. "I'm no alehouse whore."

"How else do you expect this to happen unless you untie that bloody thing?"

"Let me up!"

Her wiggling was making things all the more urgent. He had her pinned between his thighs, balancing so as not to actually sit on her. He caught her chin, turning her face to him. His demon was aroused, but his better nature urged caution.

"Am I frightening you?"

She scalded him with a look full of bravado. "You?"

"Or do you like this?"

"Lout!"

"Uh-huh."

He was stifling, his skin burning with the exertion of holding his demon in check. Without letting her escape, he stripped off his plaid shirt, then the charm Holly had given him, putting it in the pocket of his jeans. Last, he pulled off his T-shirt, welcoming the cool air of the room against his hot skin.

With an intake of breath, Constance stopped her squirming. Mac sensed her interest like a heat lamp. She was transfixed.

A low laugh rumbled out of his chest.

"Holy Mother of God," Constance whispered as Mac tossed his shirt to the floor. She was utterly out of her depth. She'd never seen a man like that, not even a blacksmith. Not even the guardsmen who, to a man, were physical perfection.

Mac was a fantasy on a grand scale. Every muscle was visible and alive as he moved. The candlelight loved him, washing the landscape of his body with licks of gold. He looked like a giant killer from one of the old tales her grandfather used to tell: *He loomed like a thundercloud, heavy with storms.*

She felt suddenly limp, as though all her bones had been melted from her limbs. Her arms were trapped at her sides, or at least she thought they were. She couldn't tell anymore.

With one finger, he scooped up the ends of the lace that tied her stays, then pulled the tail of the knot until it let go with an audible slide of fabric. The sound seemed to catch on her insides, tugging at things with no name.

If I do as he wishes, will he rescue my boy? It was an old bargain—a woman's body for a man's strength. Would a creature like him understand the trade? She wasn't sure. She wasn't even sure that was why she was doing this.

He kissed her again, leaving her breathless. *That's why.*

Their previous encounter had wakened desire, brought her to an unfamiliar peak of need. Even though he couldn't Turn her anymore, even though he didn't smell like prey, that didn't dampen her urgency. She wanted more than blood. She wanted the sensual womanhood too long denied her. *It's the magic of the room. The loss of control. It's making me want him.*

But she knew it couldn't give her appetites. Only free them. The desires were in herself.

Centuries ago, Constance had prayed for a passionate lover, one who wanted her for more than just blood. Her wish had finally been granted. Overabundantly. He was unlacing her underthings right then and there, his big, square fingers as careful and efficient as a watchmaker adjusting a spring.

Without warning, desire flipped back to apprehension. He was too big, too *male*, and he was touching her in places no man had ever been. *Holy Mother, how do I get out of here?*

She couldn't do this. She'd *never* done this, not really, and it terrified her—even worse than the door to the outside world. This was a door to someplace even more fraught with danger.

Vertigo seized her, dragging her down some hellish drain.

"Let me go," she ordered again, putting a waspish sting to the words. She started worming her hands free, only to realize they weren't trapped at all.

"No," he replied, giving her one of his fleeting smiles. "If you really wanted me gone, you would have poked me in the eye by now."

"Are you sure you want to give me ideas?"

He bent and kissed her. Gently. Reassuringly. Confused by his tenderness, she nearly burst into tears. "You don't understand," she said.

"I think I might. Don't worry. I'll make everything all right."

"But . . ."

"*Shh.*" He put a finger on her lips. "Your son. Your dog. Everything. My word on it."

Kissing her again before she could reply, he gently dragged the second lace away and sunk his hands beneath the layers of cloth to caress her through the thin fabric of her shift. Trembling, she dragged in a breath. She was unarmored, helpless, her defenses gone. Traitor that it was, her body arched to meet him.

He was a demon. The fact didn't matter. Or that he was magnificently, bizarrely changed. Mac had reached the core of her yearning the way no one else ever had.

He'd been so gentle with her clothes. No man had ever taken that much care of what was hers. No man had ever wanted her enough to peel back the layers around her. Not in any sense of the words. And his kiss . . .

"You're so beautiful," he said, in a thick, husky voice.

Tentatively, she lifted her hands to his face, digging her fingers into his thick, wavy hair. "Liar," she said, and pulled his mouth down to hers.

"Far from it," he murmured just before their lips collided.

The kiss was long and leisurely, and they barely moved apart when it was finally done. For a long moment they stayed, noses almost touching, sharing the same breath. The bones behind her fangs began to ache, waking her own sleeping beast. She had been too shy, too shocked by this unexpected tryst for her own hungers to fully rise before this. He didn't smell like food, but desire and biting went hand-in-hand. Still, Constance held back, swallowing the saliva pooling in her mouth. She didn't want anything to spoil the moment.

Slowly, he sank down beside her, stroking her hair back from her face. Stroking her arms. Drawing the long tendrils of her hair through his fingers. Loving her. For all the impatience she could feel radiating from his big body, he was going at a cautious pace. His dark eyes hadn't changed—outside of a slight smolder of demon fire—and for that she was glad. His gaze was what had called to her when they first met. Despite the wildness of his demon nature, those eyes were still wise and mischievous and kind. The look of someone who had seen more than they should have, but had survived to jest about it.

Feeling less intimidated, she rose and shed the garments he had unlaced, leaving nothing but the flimsy, shabby shift. She unhooked her skirt and pushed it off, but left her petticoats. She wasn't ready to part with them yet.

As she shed her layers, he stripped down to his skin, but slid under the covers before she could get more than a glimpse of his male parts. They were like the rest of him. Distressingly large.

Bloody hell.

He sat up and pulled her under the covers, steering her into the circle of his arms. He smelled like spice. Resin. Dark, fragrant woods. Musk. This new form of his was exotic and unfamiliar. Hot to the touch.

Kissing her again, he plundered her mouth with the gusto of a pirate. Her resistance melted in all that heat. She ran her hands over his chest, feeling the play of strength beneath his skin. That weak feeling swamped her once more, followed by a wave of her own slick fire.

"Connie?"

Connie? No one had ever called her that. "What?"

"Have you . . ." He gave a little lift of the eyebrows.

One thing hadn't changed over the centuries. Men still had problems with some words.

"No."

"Do you want to?"

"Yes."

She would have said more, but that was all the information he seemed to need. He had given her the chance to back away from this encounter, but now he was back in control. One hand reached around her waist, untying the tapes of her petticoats. She kicked them free.

She lay half on top of him, captured by his strong arm. His mouth quested down her neck, his hands circling her breasts. His teeth dragged against their peaks, teasing through the thin fabric of her shift. She felt them harden, aching and tight. He suckled through the cloth, sending a stab of pleasure right down to her belly. She gasped, her back arching, pushing her farther into his embrace.

As they moved, Constance slid her hands down the ridges of his stomach, around his hips, over the cresting arch of his backside. Her mouth found his flesh, tasting, savoring, but keeping her fangs from seeking the sweetness below the skin. Her teeth ached, but the discomfort only made her more eager. She tentatively ran her fingers over the hair that curled low on him, and the hard, long, thick evidence of his pleasure. It was unexpectedly smooth, in places soft.

As she fondled it, a sound came from him, half rumble, half moan. She filed that information away, and slipped off her shift.

A soft gasp came from Mac, and his hands were on her breasts. Then his mouth. Then his fingers reached between her legs, finding the hot, wet secrets there. Instinctively, her knees drew up, parting to give him access. A restless pressure built in her stomach as he stroked her, finding places no one but she had ever touched. Pleasure coiled through her, pooling like oil in her belly, in the hard nubs of her nipples. She began to feel like she might burst, all her desire leaking from her, sweet and sticky.

A convulsive stab of wanting wracked her. And again. He kept up the questing, teasing, pushing, caressing until the stabs became a single, uncontrollable gasp of pleasure that ground her pelvis beneath his hand. Her vision blurred and meaningless, the candlelight melted into a single sunburst as waves of heat seared her.

She came out of it panting like she'd run a race.

"Holy Mother," she murmured.

"That's just the beginning," he murmured in her ear. The demon was in his eyes, sparking scarlet. She was starting to like that demon.

He poised himself above her, the muscles in his chest and arms bunching under his weight. "I'll try not to hurt you."

Her mouth went utterly dry. "I'm a vampire. I'm not easy to hurt."

He lowered himself to one elbow, using his free hand to move her leg, move himself until he was poised at her hot, wet entrance. Slowly, slowly he pushed his tip inside. The sensation seemed to flow, full and delicious, all the way to her throat.

It was too much. She reared to strike, to taste him, but the urge to bite was swept aside by a completely new and wondrous sensation. There was no way she was going to distract him now. But it was so hard to not bite, so hard, so hard. . . .

. . . Oh, and yes, he was. He slid out and slid back in, farther this time, stretching and filling her more than felt possible. She moved to ease him in, instinct telling her when and where to push. The sensation blazed all conscious thought to ash. She pushed again, finding his rhythm.

A longer thrust pierced her, took the maidenhead that had been frozen in time along with the rest of her. She let out a rough cry but kept pushing, yearning, doing everything to engulf him inside her.

Her heart, long still, shuddered out a beat, and then another. Keeping time with his thrusts. It was a brief, temporary tryst with life, driven by extremes of emotion. He was bringing her back to life.

She hurtled toward the next crest. She tried to hold herself back, but the momentum was too huge, too urgent.

She clung to Mac, digging her fingers into his back. His skin was burning hot, shining in the candlelight. His scent rocked her senses, the sound of his lungs, his driving pulse loud in the Castle's silence. It was too much.

He thrust again and her body clenched around him. He let out a sound that said as much as he had conquered her, she had conquered him. The power of it staggered her. At that moment, she ruled this massive demon-beast.

She felt a scream rising inside her, tickling between her aching breasts, then low in her throat. When Mac gave a last heave, the thrust drove her into the soft bed, hot, hot life spilling inside her. He shuddered, his face a mask of lust, the dark smell of him swamping her. She lost control, pleasure brutally slaking a thirst buried for the whole of her long, dry existence.

At last, the scream ripped out of her, a sound of raw triumph.

By the time Mac slept off the sex-induced-haze, he was ready to begin again. Apparently if he wasn't stuffing his face, his body moved on to Plan B with equal drive.

Constance was curled against him, her cheek pressed against his chest. It was odd, because she was so still. No stirring. No breathing. No way to tell if she was awake or not. One hand was hooked around his waist, holding him as tightly as he was holding her.

It felt good to have her there. It had been far too long since he'd woken up with a woman. The night had given him even more pleasure than he'd expected. Snow White had hidden depths.

He looked down without moving his head. The view gave him a slice of her face: one brow, the bridge of her nose, a scoop of dark lashes. Constance was right where she ought to be, where he could keep her safe.

He'd lost his humanity, but he'd gotten laid. There had to be some cosmic meaning there. Or not. He didn't feel like picking holes in the first good thing that had happened to him in a long, long time. *Talk about a silver lining.* Thinking about it was making him horny.

Constance lifted her head, her gaze tentative. "Hello."

He grinned. She looked sleepy and tousled and terribly cute. "Hello."

She folded her arms on his chest, resting her chin on the prop they made. Her bare arms were slender, but he could see the muscles in them. She'd worked hard when she'd been a human woman.

They looked at each other for a long moment. He could see all the usual post-lovemaking questions written on her face, and for some reason it made him happy. If she cared enough for all the usual womanly fretting, that made what they'd shared real. "You belong to me now," he said, figuring that covered all the important points.

"I do?"

The way she said it, both relieved and resigned, made him stop and think. She came from a time of slaves and servants. "I don't mean that I literally own you."

She looked perplexed.

Caveman was messing with his words again, making them come out like he was some knuckle dragger fresh from the How to Discover Fire seminar. He tried again. "I mean anything you want, anytime you're in trouble, I'm here." He wound a finger into her hair. It ran over his skin like dark, heavy silk. She was the sort of beauty anyone would be happy to have on his arm. The sort that would stop a room cold.

Her gaze searched his features. "You'll rescue Sylvius?"

"I keep my promises."

"Good." The word was heavy with more nuances than he could guess at. Maybe she wasn't used to people keeping their word.

"Once that's over with, you really should come see my world sometime," he said. "You'd have fun."

She hesitated, objections, then uncertainty, filling her eyes. "I'm sure that would be nice."

"I'd make sure you had a good time."

The look she gave him was pure female. Her thigh shifted against his, severely distracting him. "It couldn't have been better than what we just did. I never imagined . . ."

He put his finger on her lips. "There's more ahead."

She blinked at that. "What I meant to say is that you were kinder than I deserved. I did try to bite you before."

Mac laughed at that. "True, but you didn't this time."

"I was busy. I'm only half a vampire. I think that made it easier to hold back. Plus, you're not really food anymore."

"Maybe." He wound another piece of her hair around his fingers, using it to draw her in for a kiss.

"You were good to me," she said.

"You were good to me."

They kissed, taking their time over it.

"You left me that book about Elizabeth and Mr. Darcy," she said.

"Did you like it?"

"I did. I liked everything about it."

"Like what?"

"It wasn't just about one or two people; all the folk fit together. It reminded me of so much of my old life. There was the wise sister and the foolish sister, the pretty one and the one you just knew would never make a match. And the men had fine families, too, although they weren't altogether what I would call easy sorts to get along with."

Mac was enchanted. "And were you the pretty sister, or the wise one, or both?"

"I was the baby straggling behind the rest." She smiled ruefully. "All my sisters were wed. Only the last of the boys were still at home. I wished I would've been older, when there were more of my family in the house. Still, it was grand at celebrations when everyone came home. That's what I've always wanted—everyone around the table, eating and laughing."

Such talk of domestic bliss was enough to make most men bolt. Mac was too comfortable to move.

"What about you?" She blinked away a strand of hair that was hanging in her eyes, tangling in her lashes.

He brushed the hair away. "There was just me and my mom."

"Just you? No one to share the chores?"

"It's not so bad when you live in the city."

"All the same, lucky for your mother you were there!"

"So she liked to remind me. She's gone now." He paused. "But say, I brought you another book. I'm not sure what it'll be like because I picked it up in the grocery store. It has a pirate on the cover."

"A pirate?"

"With no shirt. He's going to get a sunburn."

She gave him an incredulous look. "He's daft! Even a sailor can afford a shirt. I'm not sure about your pirate."

"But you'll give him a try?"

She gave him a wicked look. "If you insist. Although he'll have to cut a fine figure to shoulder past Mr. Darcy."

Mac rewarded that look with a kiss.

"Do you know . . ." she said, trailing off into an uncertain sigh.

"What?" He touched his finger to her chin.

"I want you to know there's a place you can always lay your head." She shimmied up his torso until her face was poised above his. "Wherever I am. Sometimes it helps to know where you can go when everything else turns upside down. I'll always take you in."

"Would you?"

She hesitated. "You don't have a family standing behind you. Everyone needs a family. You'll get lost if you're all alone." Her eyes were serious.

Just like that, she had turned the tables on him. He had promised her protection. Now she had just done the same. The solemn look on her face said she meant it.

Mac felt a pang of tenderness in his chest. She'd found his soft, marshmallow center and sunk her dainty fangs right in. *Crap, I am lost.* But he didn't care. Not one little bit. A dark yearning stirred inside, but it was dark and sweet at once, like melting chocolate.

Constance survived in a violent world. She might be small, but she had to be tough to have made it this far. Clever and stubborn enough to keep her values in one piece. That moved him.

Logic said the bond they had formed was instant and intense, the kind that happened during wars and disasters. Perhaps there was something supernatural to it, too—the result of the room, or his new body, or her vampire nature.

None of that mattered. He knew one thing with conviction, something that no sorcery could ever change. He wasn't letting Constance Moore slip out of his life. In the most unlikely place of all, he'd found a forever kind of woman.

Chapter 16

"You did *what* to my sister?" It was the closest Holly had ever come to a shriek.

Alessandro was fairly sure he'd made a tactical blunder. "She'll like it in the Castle. There's lots there to kill."

"When did you put her there?"

"Right after she tried to stake me. And bit me."

Holly's angry eyes seemed to fill her face. "What. Time. Did. It. Happen."

Alessandro balked. The housekeeping spell Holly had laid on the vacuum cleaner suddenly wound down. The motor died with a sickly wheeze.

"Um. This afternoon."

Holly clenched her teeth. "She's only human, Alessandro. She doesn't even have her witch's powers anymore. She's my big sister. She used to read me stories."

He sighed, but it was an angry sound. "What should I have done, Holly? She tried to kill me in my bed. She damned near succeeded."

Holly dropped into the nearest chair, covering her face with her hands for a moment. He knelt in front of her, sorry that he'd snapped, and captured her hands, one by one, and drew them from her cheeks.

Her eyes were moist, catching the lamplight like stars. "She's my sister. How could you do that?"

Oh, no. He'd made her cry. It was the first time. A heavy, bleak feeling threatened to crush him to the carpet. "I'm so sorry."

He could have torn out his own heart then and there. *How could I be so stupid? Vampire logic isn't human logic.*

"I don't know what you should've done," Holly said, her voice thick with tears. "I don't blame you. You had to do something, and I don't have any answers. I could kill her myself."

Confusion washed over him. How could he fix this? "I can go look for her. Bring her home. Right now."

"No!" She squeezed his hands. "If she doesn't get you, the guardsmen will!"

Alessandro blinked, his male pride flattened to road kill. "I can look after myself," he said gently. "I was the queen's champion swordsman. I'm still pretty good with a blade."

"Of course you are."

"I'm in and out of there all the time." Long enough to toss someone in, at least.

"I know." Holly closed her eyes, and fell silent.

The house was silent but for the ticking clock. A car whooshed by outside. From the kitchen, the cat was crunching kibble. They were home sounds. Sounds Alessandro had begun to treasure.

Holly swallowed. "I can't bear to risk you right now."

"But Ashe . . ."

She shook her head. "I don't know what to do about her. She's not the same person I remember, the one I want her to be so badly. It's like I keep trying to fix her in my mind, fit the old Ashe over the new one, but it doesn't work."

"Do you think the sister you remember is inside her somewhere?"

"Goddess knows. I think an awful lot has happened to her over the years, and I know she blames herself for our parents' deaths."

"I think she's angry," he offered. *Was the stake the first clue?*

"Whatever. I don't want her back in this house. Who knows what she'd do next." Holly let go of his hands and wiped her face dry with her fingers, clearly exhausted. "But we can't leave her there. Sweet Hecate, I can't believe my family is fighting like this."

Alessandro put his hand to her cheek. As always, she felt warm to him, hot and vital. "I'm part of your family?"

She looked at him, her brows drawn together. "Absolutely. The most important part."

"Thank you." *Then are you really afraid to introduce me at the reunion? Does it bother you that I can't give you children? Will you still love me when you realize the cost of living with a man who is so different? Who has no family of his own?*

He knew some of his doubts were Ashe's poison at work. Alessandro forced himself to let them go. "What do you want me to do?"

"Just—let Mac deal with it."

"*Mac?*" That was the last thing he expected her to say. "What can he do that I can't?"

Holly shrugged, trying to look casual and missing by a mile. "Finding a missing person is kind of, y'know, cop stuff. He's trained to talk to crazy people, and Lore said Mac's going into the Castle, anyway. Plus, Mac owes me."

"And he's expendable if Ashe decides to take him out?"

"Of course not!"

"Then why is it okay to risk him?"

"Have you talked to Lore today?"

"No." He intended to tear the alpha a new one about the hounds' poor guard duty performance. He had a feeling the hound, like any smart dog with a mess to its name, was making himself scarce.

Holly seemed to slump even more. "Mac's . . . well, from the sound of it, the demon caught up with him in this other weird way."

Alessandro's eyes narrowed. "How weird? In what way?"

"Physically." Holly told him what Lore had told her.

Unable to sit still any longer, Alessandro got to his feet and started to pace. "I was just beginning to trust Mac. It seems I was wrong."

"I'm not sure about that. He didn't sound, y'know, evil."

For how long? If the demon taint was on a roll, who knew what else might change? "I should have asked this before. Is there any way you can reverse what's happening to him? Your magic made him half human before."

Holly shook her head. "That was a complete accident. The only thing I know how to do with demons is fry them to cinders. Pure blunt force. I'd kill him."

"Then is he powerful enough to deal with your sister? She's a good fighter."

"Sounds like he is."

Alessandro wasn't sure he liked that answer. He took a few more steps, then stopped. "It isn't that I want Ashe dead. I hoped putting her in the Castle would teach her a lesson. Show her there are worse things than a vampire trying to keep the town safe. That we're not . . ." He trailed off, unable to find the right words.

Holly's expression was sad. "You're not all evil."

"Not as long as I have options."

Alessandro reached down, rubbing away a stray tear from her chin. He was so grateful for her. She made him, if not human, much less of a monster. "You're sure you don't want me to handle your sister?"

"No, I'm sure Mac will help, and Ashe doesn't have a beef with him. It'll be easier this way."

"But . . ."

"I'm right about this."

Alessandro wasn't so sure. *On the positive side, if Ashe and Mac kill each other, that's two of my problems solved.* But he didn't mean it.

He should have been happy to wash his hands of an annoying situation. He should have liked the blade-clean logic of two dangerous individuals annihilating each other. He didn't.

He wanted it all to work out, for everyone's sake. Bloodshed wasn't the answer.

Novel thought, for a vampire.

Maybe Mac isn't the only one changing.

Mac ran through the corridors of the Castle at an easy, gliding pace, sword drawn. Dusting through the maze was faster, but that only worked if he knew where he was going. Connie had given him some useful information, but to conduct a search he needed solid contact with his surroundings.

He'd left Connie asleep. After she'd told him what she knew about the guardsmen's lair, they'd made love again. Twice.

It had sated them both and exhausted her, sending her into a deep, comalike slumber. He'd held Connie for a long time, studying the soft curves of her face and body. There was no inch of her skin that he hadn't touched that night, and he knew without doubt he would touch, taste, and claim it again.

His inner caveman beat his chest and roared with jubilation. Today it was good to be Mac the Barbarian.

He stopped at a crossing of corridors. The wavering torchlight showed one hallway curved away to the right. To the left, the stonework had crumbled like a giant fist had punched through the wall. A vast cavern loomed beyond.

Connie had mentioned this place. He hopped up the rubble, using the fallen stones as a stairway to the gaping hole a dozen feet above. The section of missing wall was more than man-height, the thickness of the stones uneven and treacherous. He balanced there, looking into the darkness. A hot, sour wind seemed to rise from below, flowing up the chimneylike cavern. His hair floated away from his face, caught by the breeze. There were fires far, far below, flickering like the stars of an upside-down sky. They called to him, blinking like mysterious eyes. No one, Connie'd said, had ever ventured into those depths.

Maybe he would someday, just to find out what or who

lived there. *Maybe dragons?* A tingle of excitement rippled through him. *That would be cool.*

He could almost feel the Castle agree. It wanted to be explored. Everything about it spoke of neglect, but who was to say it had to be that way?

Connie had told him Reynard's tales of collapsing corridors and disappearing rooms. Was there a specific cause, Mac wondered, or was the magic that made the place simply winding down? Were the rumors true at all? He knew how fast a lie could travel around a lockup. Who was to say the Castle was any different?

Still, it was a good reminder to stay alert.

Mac jumped down, landing easily, and kept on walking, following the left-hand corridor. Truth be told, he was enjoying this new body's stamina. The more he used it, the better it felt. Plus, it seemed to be settling down. His clothes were too tight again, but the change was not as dramatic as before.

Just as well. There was a limit to how much size was actually useful.

He started to run, covering ground in a relaxed lope. The punched-out-wall phenomenon repeated itself a few more times, and then the wall between him and the cavern gave up altogether. Mac ran for about another half hour, barely breathing hard.

In the distance, he could hear the sound of voices. Probably one of the settlements that drifted around the Castle, moving as the warlords claimed and lost territory, established their courts and then surrendered to rivals. Politics in the Castle was an endless chess game, one Mac had been too insignificant to play. Not that he'd wanted to. He'd just wanted out.

The noise grew more distinct, coming from his left across a vast, wild space of crumbled granite. Curiosity tempted him to look. He climbed up an easy slope of rock, pushing higher and higher until he could see the source of the babble.

Not a town, but an encampment. Campfires glimmered, backlighting figures who moved through a forest of tents. Most inhabitants of the Castle lived in its rooms, but a few preferred the open places, living like nomads. By their size and the way they moved, these were werecats. Lions or one of the more exotic species.

Cats tended to roam on the fringes of the main populations, which meant the town proper would be just beyond what he could see. *And it can stay there*. He'd flown beneath the radar so far. He meant to keep things that way. If this Prince Miru-kai was setting up shop in the area, he had to be careful not to attract attention.

So far he hadn't run into any other wandering goblins or changelings. The area leading from the Summer Room was as deserted and secret as Connie had claimed. Still, he worried about leaving her alone. He added home security to his mental to-do list. Maybe once she had her son back, she would want to leave the Castle altogether.

Mac resumed his course. Eventually, the Castle grew darker, the torches farther apart, the slope in the floor descending. At the same time, across the floor of the cavern to his right, he saw a honeycomb of caves emerge from the black rock. Scatters of torches appeared here and there, showing signs of habitation.

Mac slowed to a walk. The air was warmer here, drying the light sweat on his body. There were no corridors to his left now, and the path he was on narrowed to a mere walkway, an iron rail guarding against the sheer drop into the cavern. The pit was still deep, but he could see the cavern floor clearly now. This arrangement went on for another fifteen minutes of brisk walking. The light below steadily increased, the torches supplemented with fire pits. Up where he was, there were no torches at all, providing him with a wash of convenient shadow.

A good thing. This part of the cavern was inhabited. Most of the figures walking below were guardsmen, recognizable by their weapons, their size, and the blue tattoos painting their bodies.

Mac allowed himself a wolfish grin. He'd found their headquarters, or at least their clubhouse. The large area directly
below was scattered with tables and benches where guards
lounged, read, diced, or talked. Rooms opened onto the area,
guards coming and going. One in the far corner looked larger
and had more traffic, as if it served an official purpose.

Mac finished scanning the scene below, and began examining the rocky expanse higher up. Above the rooms,
caves dotted the raw stone face of the wall. Some had bars
or gates. Were those cages? Storerooms? From where he
was, it was impossible to tell, but either explanation would
make sense. Now that he looked closely, networks of open
stairways were chipped into the rock, zigzagging up from
the floor.

And that was as much as he was going to find out from
his present vantage point. He had to get closer.

Mac picked an empty-looking cave that overlooked the
busy room below. He took a deep breath and melted to
dust, flowing through the shadows and down, down to land
in the heart of the enemy's home.

What have I done? Constance wondered.

It was a simple question. There should have been an
easy answer, but like the lady in the song, her demon lover
had carried her away with fine promises. The difference
was, Mac used a bed rather than a ship.

> *When they reached the shore again*
> *On the far side of the sea,*
> *Then she spied his cloven hoof*
> *And wept most plaintively.*
> *"What is that mountain yon," she cried,*
> *"With fire and ice and snow?"*
> *"It is the peaks of hell," he cried,*
> *"Where you and I must go."*

Mac, however, didn't seem the seafaring type, and he
definitely didn't have cloven hooves. They were already in

hell. The only question that remained was whether he was a trickster.

She had awakened alone, and that worried her. He had asked how to find the guardsmen, but how could she be sure he had gone to keep his promise to bring back her son?

Candles bathed the room in a topaz glow. Constance stared at the ceiling, curling into the warmth left by Mac's body. He could not have been gone long. His heat still bathed the sheets, and she nestled down like a chick in the nest. She was utterly, thoroughly satisfied in ways she hadn't known existed. But being awake meant facing the future. Emotions crowded in like street hawkers, all shouting for attention. *What should I feel?*

During her life, she would have known fear. Girls who gambled their maidenheads away on love risked losing everything: their good name, their employment, their futures. No work meant no food. An unwanted baby all too often meant utter ruin. But that wouldn't happen now. For one thing, she was Undead, already about as fallen as a woman could get.

He's a demon. Yes, but she was a vampire, more or less. They were on even footing there.

He's a stranger. That had more meaning. Some might accuse her of naïveté, of falling prey to temptations of the Summer Room. Her appetites had been muted for far too long, only to burst forth like some unseasonal hothouse blossom.

It was true, she had been quick to surrender, but it had felt perfect. It had been the right combination of gentleness and need, wild demon dominance and pleasure. Conall Macmillan suited her through and through, better than any romantic fantasy she had spun for her own amusement.

But would he keep his promise to find Sylvius? Constance dangled one hand over the edge to pick up the Castle key tangled in the mess of garments she had tossed to the floor. It felt cold, hard-edged, the opposite of the fine, soft sheets that still bore Mac's imprint. She turned it over and over, watching the glint of gold in her palm.

She could tell he was in trouble. His demon had taken hold, and there was no telling where that transformation would lead. What had been a mere streak of danger was now barely in check. He needed an anchor, a home. Something to tip the balance between beast and man. Someone with a claim on him.

In the course of their lovemaking, she had made up her mind about one thing. Love was far more important than innocence. The bonds to her dear ones meant more than anything else.

She prayed Mac felt the same. She'd surrendered to their mutual pleasures that night, falling under the spell of his expert caresses. In the most primal ways, he'd made a gift of the womanhood so long denied her. *My demon lover.*

And yet, as much as she wanted to drown in the languorous haze of lust, her next thoughts had to be of her boy. Whatever Lore said, abandoning Sylvius would make her more of a monster than any blood hunger. If Mac failed her, she would have to find the courage to save her son all on her own. She wasn't a servant anymore. She didn't have the luxury of someone else's protection, nor could she wait for someone to tell her what to do. It was up to her.

She rolled onto her back, holding the key up to the candlelight. If she left the Castle, would she truly become the ravening beast Lore feared? She could not wait long to put her fate to the test.

Please, oh, please, keep your promise.

When Mac rematerialized, he whipped around, sword ready, but saw the cave he was standing in was a storeroom. He was alone.

The first thing he noticed was that it was noisy, sound pouring up from the plateau below. After the silence of Connie's corner of the Castle, the clamor felt like a physical blow. Most of it was male voices, booming and loud, and the occasional clank of weapons and armor. The context was different, but the mood was a lot like a busy squad room.

Mac looked around the cave. There were piles of old armor, shields, and breastplates emblazoned with the six-pointed sun that was the guardsman's symbol. A rough wooden rack held ranks of spears. A trunk with no top overflowed with dusty uniforms. The place smelled like leather and oil.

Mac thought about changing into some of the clothes, but decided it was pointless. After hundreds of years of serving together, these guys all knew each other too well to count on a disguise. Besides, his plans were too vague. He had no idea what he needed yet.

On the other hand, he did poke around until he found a scabbard and shoulder belt for his sword. His hand was getting stiff from carrying it around. He'd even considered ditching it now that he had his Sig Sauer with him, but there were some critters a bullet wouldn't stop.

It took a while until he found a rig that didn't interfere with the gun holster, but finally he found something that did the job. Surveillance was the next step.

Mac settled near the mouth of the cave, burying himself in shadow and pulling the dark plaid shirt closed over the white of his T-shirt. From this angle, he could watch the tops of the heads of people coming and going from the busy room below. A dozen feet from the doorway, four guardsmen sprawled around a table. One, he saw with a flicker of annoyance, was Bran. He didn't know the other three, but he could see the round, ruddy face of the man sitting next to Bran. There was enough firelight that it was almost bright.

Idly, he calculated the position and angle of each man, estimating their vulnerabilities and strengths. If he jumped from here to there, landing in the center of the table, he could probably take all four in eight sword thrusts or less.

That's the demon talking, and it's an optimist. There were at least forty other guardsmen to consider, and a major bloodletting got him no closer to finding Connie's boy. Mac gave a quiet sigh, resigned to pursuing his mission the hard, dull, *smart* way.

The fair-haired man sitting across from Bran was talking. "... got there and the passageway was collapsed. We're cut off from the north quadrant. It's bad. We've lost communication with Captain O'Shea, and he's got the trolls on his hands. We can't send reinforcements. He'll have to battle it out for himself."

"What about Sharp?" Bran asked.

"He can't get through, either. The bridge is down."

Bran swore. "This whole damned place is coming apart. I'd hoped it was nothing but tall tales."

Mac stiffened in surprise. So it was true. Something was wrong with the Castle.

The red-faced guardsman spoke up. "O'Shea said that's why the trolls were coming up from down below. The places they made their dens are gone."

"Fine for the trolls," said blondie. "We're stuck here. We can't leave. We're cursed."

"We know what we have to do," said red face. "It's not pretty but it's the only way."

"Enough," growled Bran.

"You said so yourself!"

"The captain doesn't want to hear that kind of talk."

But I do. Mac leaned forward a little, taking a better look at the guardmen's rooms. From here, he could see into a few. About half looked like dormitories, each with a number of beds. The others were empty. Had they once been filled? If so, what happened to the men who'd slept there?

The fourth guardsman spoke up. "You're too young to remember, but once the Avatar brought rain and sun. Nothing's the same now."

Avatars again. Holly'd said the Avatar had been stolen.

The others groaned and shuffled, as if this was a story they'd heard a thousand times. Blondie stood. "I'm off to patrol. Coming, Hans? Edward?"

The two others got up and joined him, walking away to leave Bran on his own. In the distance, another group of three guardsmen were wrestling a huge, misshapen creature up one of the staircases carved into the stone wall. *What the heck is that? A troll?*

All Mac could see from that distance was that it wore a tunic of some kind and was bald. Shackles around its wrists, ankles, and waist made climbing the stairs awkward. It lurched, nearly falling. One of the guards poked it with the butt of his spear, saving it from tumbling down the cliff face, but clearly hurting it at the same time. Mac scowled. He hated guys who took advantage of their authority that way. It wasn't like the prisoner had been trying to escape.

The guards opened the barred door to one of the caves and shoved the creature inside. *Well, that answers that question. Some of these caves are indeed cells.*

Fuming, Mac returned his attention to the table below. Bran sat like a disgruntled lump. The only thing lacking was a beer to cry in.

The Castle didn't have beer. Or bratwurst sausages. It truly was hell.

Reynard appeared, walking out from the room below.

"I'm tired to death of writing up the log," said the captain in his la-di-da accent. He'd always sounded to Mac like he'd just quit his job as an announcer for the BBC. All he needed was a Rolex and a polo pony to complete the *GQ* picture.

The captain slid onto the bench, his back to Mac. "There are times I'd give anything for another one of those perpetual pens. We need to catch another smuggler and confiscate his wares."

Perpetual pens? Was he talking about a ballpoint?

"Why not simply do business with the rats?" Bran asked with what came close to a sneer. "Then you could have all the pens and log books you want."

Reynard's answer bit the air. "Because smugglers also bring in weapons for the warlords to use against us. I won't tolerate their presence."

Bran shrugged. "As you say."

Mac's mind skipped away from the conversation. If Reynard had been doing paperwork, the room below was the captain's office. That would be well worth a look. There might be some indication of where Sylvius was being held—

like in the log book. Most officers would record anything of significance, and capturing an incubus surely counted.

If Reynard was sitting outside, that meant the room was probably empty. It was a risk. There might be others there, or supernatural traps he couldn't anticipate. Still, he'd walked into equally dangerous places as a mere human.

Mere human? His demon was getting carried away again. If there was the slightest chance, he would strive to be human again.

Was that the best thing?

This wasn't the time to think about it.

Mac dusted and trickled down the rock face, stretching himself out to be as inconspicuous as possible. He reassembled in a crouching position, hiding in the corner.

He got an immediate case of the creeps. Nerves tightened his shoulders to the point of pain. *I wish I had backup. Or a warrant.* Standard operating procedures. A nice jail cell to pop the bad guy into when the day's work was done. *Dream on. Suck it up.*

Staying perfectly still for a long moment, he listened, felt for any movement in the air. Nothing. He could find no reason for his sudden case of nerves, but he knew enough to trust his gut. Cautiously, an inch at a time, he rose from his crouch.

Again, he was in luck. He was alone. The room was dark, all the lights extinguished. Despite good night vision, Mac found himself straining to see detail.

The space was average, about the size of a large bedroom. Two walls were floor-to-ceiling shelves crammed with thick, leather-bound tomes, each bearing a number. Were these old log books? For how many years? Were they all Reynard's work? If so, the guy'd been in the Castle a long, long time.

Anxious, Mac turned to the other side of the room. A comfortable-looking armchair filled one corner, but it was the only sign of rest and relaxation. Beside it was a drab green metal filing cabinet, dinged and scraped in a way that said office surplus. *More smuggler's wares?*

At last, his gaze lit on a desk that stood at a right angle to the door. Its surface was cluttered, a candle lamp and inkstand framing an open book the size of a jumbo cereal box. *Yes!*

Mac inched toward the desk, bracing his sword to his side. It would be just his luck to knock something over and give himself away.

Then he froze. It was so dark, he'd almost missed them. On the bookshelf, poised like knickknacks, was a series of three boxes. He leaned closer, trying to see by the trickle of firelight that found its way through the open door.

The middle box was red lacquer, exactly matching Connie's description of the demon-catcher. Instinctively, Mac's fingers sought out Holly's charm. It was still there, safe beneath his shirt. With every sense peeled, he reached out, sweeping the air above the boxes.

C'mon, demon, if you're listening, how about some help here? It answered instantly. There were indeed sentient beings inside those tiny cubes.

Yes! Mac snatched the red one and stuffed it into the pocket of his plaid shirt. The fit was tight, but at least that would keep it from falling out.

"Helping yourself?"

Mac wheeled. Reynard stood in the doorway.

Whoops!

Wasting no time, Mac willed himself to dust.

Nothing happend.

He tried again.

He was trapped.

Inside, the demon yowled in panic, but Mac's will held on, doggedly trying to put two and two together. *Why won't it work?*

He tried yet again with the same result.

Calmly, Reynard struck a match and lit the candle lantern. The whiff of sulphur seemed almost comically appropriate. The candle flared up, highlighting the captain's face from below. "Macmillan, isn't it?" he asked pleasantly.

"Yeah."

Reynard turned, closing the door. Despite the heat in this part of the Castle, his dark hair was neatly tied back, his uniform buttoned, boots polished, and neck cloth perfectly tied. He was either crazy or had steely self-discipline.

"You were a soul eater, if memory serves." Reynard's voice didn't stray from the pleasant, gentleman-to-gentleman tone. "You've changed your appearance. Interesting. Well, you'll find your demon powers don't work in this room. You can enter in any form you please, but I'm afraid the only way out is on your own two feet."

"A trap." *Damn*. If his dust-engines were down, Mac would try to talk his way out of this. If that failed, he'd just have to fight all forty-odd guardsmen and hoof it back to Connie with the box.

"A trap?" Reynard shrugged. "A precaution, though I have to say you're the first to ever dare enter here."

"Call me precocious."

"I'll call you prodigal. I thought you had escaped us. But you're back, I see, and it seems your demon symbiont finally got the upper hand. Opportunistic creatures."

Mac felt a flicker of something like embarrassment. His muscular body was evidence of how much ground the demon had gained. "Can you tell me how it happened?"

"Ah, took you by surprise, did it?" Reynard clasped his hands behind his back, a faint smile on his lips. "Demon infections are infinitely adaptable. If you encounter strong magic, one strain can mutate to another, taking advantage of the forces around it. You change to better serve your demon's needs. You grow into its strengths, if you like."

Mac leaped at the scrap of information. This wasn't the time to play twenty questions, but he'd take what info he could get. Plus, he needed time to think about an escape.

"I thought the Castle did this," he said.

Reynard's smile faded. "Perhaps. The Castle has grown unpredictable, though what it would want with a fire demon is beyond me."

"Fire demon?"

"I can feel your heat from here."

"But why . . . ?"

"You won't have a pretty end, I'm afraid. Its appetites—fed by your emotions—will eventually get the upper hand. Then, whatever you touch will be scorched to ashes."

"Bullshit!" Mac growled. *That can't be true. I'm not that out of control.* But fear and anger blazed inside, bringing his skin to a slippery sweat.

The captain watched him, his expression neutral. "I don't need to argue the point. I'll wager you already know the truth of it."

As he spoke, Reynard reached beside the door, picking up a long, wicked-looking firearm at least as old as Reynard himself. *You gotta be kidding me. A musket?*

Mac reached for his Sig Sauer just as the muzzle of Reynard's weapon swung his way. Reynard beat him to the draw. "I'm using silver shot."

Mac paused, his hand hovering above his holster, eyeing the big, ugly bore aimed at his head. Those old firearms were never as accurate as a modern weapon, but at this range it was impossible not to blow Mac to smithereens.

Mac feinted, grabbing another one of the demon boxes.

"No!" Reynard barked. "Don't touch that one!"

"Why not?" Mac said, suddenly feeling his chances improve. "Was this one a bad boy? How about this one?" He picked up the last box and tapped the two together just hard enough to make a clacking sound. He felt vaguely foolish, but Reynard looked terrified.

"Why don't you put down the musket and we'll talk."

Clearly reluctant, Reynard lowered the weapon, his eyes deadly. "You fool. Either one of those two demons would tear us all apart. The incubus is a temptation. The creatures in the other two boxes are holocausts."

Mac looked from one box to the other. "Just the thing to keep around as paperweights. Buy a safe, dumb ass."

"They need to be seen by the men. They need to be reminded of our victories."

"Right. Good thinking. Whatever. All I want is the incubus."

"He's dangerous."

"He's a kid."

Reynard gave a dry smile. "He's a monster, just like you. Worse, he'll make monsters of the rest of us with his seductive powers. The Castle's hold over our base instincts is slipping already. The influence of an incubus is all that would be needed to turn us into a den of savages."

The guardsman had been holding his musket in one hand, but the other had reached to the desk behind him, pressing a catch beside one of the drawers. A compartment sprang open.

Mac held up one of the boxes, a black cube of heavy, dense wood. "Don't try anything stupid. You know, monster that I am, I could crush this in one hand."

"You would die as quickly as I."

"So what? If what you say about my future is true, I'm already as good as dead."

Reynard had withdrawn another box from his desk, this one painted green. He pressed a catch, and the lid sprang open. "It's a little hard to threaten me from inside here."

Mac's heart cartwheeled in alarm.

"I command you to enter!" Reynard barked, just like he would to a wayward private.

Crap!

Mac felt a yank of gravity, as if a dozen vacuums were sucking at his skin. The air around the box flared with cold, brilliant light, vibrations humming just beyond what Mac could truly hear. It rattled his teeth, crushed his temples like someone grinding their knuckles into his skull. He squeezed his watering eyes shut against the light and leaned away from the fierce pull, roaring a protest. Where it lay against his bare chest, the charm bag burned like acid.

But Holly's magic held. Mac felt the light wink out before he even opened his eyes. Gradually, the pull on his flesh faded. He stumbled a little, adjusting as he no longer needed to dig in his heels.

Reynard had one arm lifted to shield his eyes. As he lowered it, his jaw dropped a little as he saw Mac still standing there, a box in either hand and the red one in his pocket.

"Surprise, Merlin. The mojo ain't working," Mac said in a low, warning voice. "Now stop fooling around and let me go. That incubus has someone waiting for him at home."

"Did Atreus send you?" Reynard hissed.

"No way. I sent me, because it was the right thing to do. But let's not get sidetracked."

The door flung open. Bran hulked in the doorway. "You!"

"Don't come any closer. I'm armed," Mac waggled one of the little boxes, and felt ridiculous.

"Obey him, Bran," said Reynard, not taking his eyes off Mac. "He's taken hostages."

Great. I'm in an armed standoff with demonic gift boxes. He held the black box in the palm of his hand, curling his fingers around it. "What's the magic password out of here?"

Bran looked at his captain sharply. Reynard's eyes were on the box.

"Don't make me do this, Reynard. I just want to correct a mistake."

"Demons lie," said Reynard.

"So do humans."

"Demons have no honor."

"You broke a heart when you took this boy. I'm setting that right."

Reynard gave him a long look. "You won't smash those boxes."

"So you're willing to gamble that I'm a good monster? You can't have it both ways. I'm evil or I'm not."

"You argue like an attorney."

"Low blow, Captain, but I'll tell you one thing. I'm no coward. Call my bluff and I'll play my cards."

A beat passed.

Reynard said a word in a strange tongue. Mac felt the atmosphere in the room lift, as if someone had thrown open a window. Whatever spell had kept him from dusting away was gone.

"Captain!" Bran roared, and launched himself at Mac.

The guardsman was too quick. Mac went sprawling, the boxes flying from his hands. His head cracked against the bookcase, but he rolled Bran over, smashing a fist into Bran's jaw. Roaring to the surface, his demon flooded his mind with a need for scalding, red violence. Mac's skin flared, fiery-hot. Seizing Bran like an overpacked gym bag, he tossed him across the room with a snarl.

Reynard's musket went off with a boom. Mac twisted, dancing away from the silver shot that slammed into the filing cabinet. A plume of acrid smoke clogged the air. Reckless with rage, Mac grabbed the musket by the barrel, ripping it from Reynard's hand and flinging it behind him. Then he grabbed the captain by the arm, wrenching him closer.

Reynard was a strong man in his own right, but his feet left the floor with the force of Mac's one-handed tug. Mac slammed him against the bookcase, holding him by the throat, forcing him to teeter on his toes. The buttons on the captain's coat had come undone, and his shirt gaped open to reveal the blue tattoos beneath. The mark of the guardsmen. It looked incongruous against the oh-so-civilized officer's skin.

Anger was as surf in Mac's ears, and he rode it, savoring the power of his muscles, the giddy sensation of his own strength. These men were as feeble as toys

He'd taken what he came for. He hadn't even drawn a weapon. Why should he? With his brain, brawn, and the willing violence of the demon, he *was* the perfect weapon.

Reynard was choking, his breath coming in rasping gasps. His skin was turning red from the heat of Mac's hand.

With all his force of spirit, Mac fought for control. As good as it felt, he would not surrender to his darker side. Slowly, he let Reynard ease back to the ground.

He heard Bran rushing him from behind. Just as the guardsman leaped, Mac dusted out.

The last thing he heard was the two men smacking together.

He'd always liked Wile E. Coyote cartoons.

Chapter 17

Mac materialized without a sound, bypassing the heavy bolts that kept the Summer Room safe. Or should keep it safe. Once again, he worried whether those bolts would be enough to keep the place secure. What if Reynard made a return trip to retrieve Sylvius?

More locks. There should be warding spells, too. Doorway magic sounded like Lore's department. If the hounds were willing to help him, this was something they could do besides making useless prophecies.

Stop fretting.

He looked around. *It's good to be back.* He couldn't help thinking it, even if he had only been gone a few hours. Constance was curled up in an armchair, her feet tucked under her. She was deep into the pirate book, chewing one thumbnail as she read.

Everything about her was at once innocent and unabashedly sensual. Mac's thoughts were stalled by a hot flood of memory, of the night they'd spent together. *Oh, yeah.*

"Connie," he said.

She started violently, snapping the paperback shut. "Mac!"

"Sorry!"

She ran to him, giving a little bound so that she could

reach to fling her arms around his neck. "I woke up and you were gone!"

For a moment, he was lost in the soft feel of her—the silky hair, the strong, lithe arms, the soft scent of her perfume. He held her tightly to his chest, not even wanting to release her long enough to kiss her. "You knew where I was going."

"I was worried."

That was nice. Nobody had done that for him for a long time.

"Hey," he said. "It's all right. I'm back." He kissed her, long and thoroughly, and then summoned the discipline to let her go.

"Did you find the guardsmen?" she asked.

"Yup." He pulled the red box from his shirt pocket with some effort. He'd really jammed it in there. The empty pocket gaped oddly; the soft flannel had stretched.

When he looked up, Constance's expression was marvelous to see. Her eyes had gone wide, her mouth open. Her hands reached forward in slow motion, taking the box from his fingers and cradling it against her breast.

"You brought him home," she said in a hushed voice. "You brought him back!"

It wasn't the first time Mac had returned a lost child, but it was definitely the strangest. He grinned. "Sweetheart, I keep my promises."

Still holding the box, she gave him a wordless, one-armed embrace. After a moment, he realized she was crying, sobbing silently against him. A relieved mother thing. It was normal. He'd seen it before. He'd tried to take it in stride, not let it touch him too much, but, oh, it was always wonderful.

"*Shh*." He stroked her hair. "It's all good."

God, she smells great. He could feel heat rising to his skin, prickling like electricity. *Reynard was right. Emotion drives the heat.*

"Did the captain have him?" she said at last, pulling away.

"Uh-huh. Y'know, I don't think he likes me much."

She smiled, her eyes shining with fresh tears. "But he kept him safe from the other guardsmen. He did that much."

That was true. *And I nearly strangled Reynard.* Or the demon had. *Gotta watch that.*

Mac sobered, his mood plummeting. The adventure had taught him much, some stuff he didn't want to face. He'd come within a hairbreadth of carnage. Worse, he'd liked it. The violence had been a whole new high.

His gaze caressed Constance, who was setting the box on the floor.

I'm in danger of turning into a killing machine. Again.

Constance was probing the box, her slim fingers stroking every surface.

That can't be me. I'm the guy who does what needs doing I fix things. I save people. I can't lose that. It's all that's left of me. Not even a demon can take that away.

I hope.

The box clicked, the lid springing open. Constance stepped back. Mac watched, curious despite himself. He'd heard of incubi, but he'd never seen one.

Soft light fountained from the box, coalescing into an iridescent haze that shone from within—dust, but different from the smoky black of Mac's incorporeal form. This cloud was beautiful, neither sparkling nor dull but gleaming with the sheen of pearls.

Mac watched as it grew and blossomed into a solid form of a tall young male. He was pale, his skin almost truly white, with dark eyes and long silver hair that fell to his hips. But what caught Mac's attention were the wings, beautifully arched, shot with delicate pink veins.

Holy crap. The kid has bat wings. And to think parents complain about piercings.

What happened next was a silent dance. The young demon—Sylvius—reached for Connie, grasping her hand in his. She turned into him, clutching him to her in a movement made smooth by long years of practice. There was no doubt that, in every way that counted, this was her child.

"It's so good to see you," said the incubus, and folded his wings around her. It was the oddest and most tender gesture Mac had ever seen. The two, mother and child, were still for a long moment, the candlelight fluttering against the shadows that draped around the pair. A profound silence thickened, making Mac's breath come loud in his ears.

Let them have their moment.

He was an outsider. This was Connie's time. Connie's and her son's.

Like a dark dream, Mac willed himself away.

October 6, 7:05 p.m.
101.5 FM

"In more news, Fairview's ad-hoc council of supernatural leaders raised the question of unauthorized immigration, requesting that any undocumented supernatural residents of the area be brought to their attention immediately."

All right. In the last forty-eight hours, I've been transformed to a bloodthirsty barbarian, had hot sex with a vampire, and rescued a bat-winged junior sex demon from a nasty little box.

Time for a beer.

As Mac re-formed from dust to demon in his condo, the answering machine was flashing. After weeks with barely a phone call, he had a half dozen messages. Mac ignored them for a moment, pausing to look at the city lights outside his balcony door. The moon's reflection pooled in the waters of the harbor, a golden, shimmering disk. After watching Connie's reunion with her son, he felt content. Sated. Masterful.

There were problems, but he'd saved the day and gotten the girl. In the wrong order, but heck, eat dessert first.

A plane flew over, adding its blinking lights to the bejeweled skyline. *Connie's never seen any of this.* She hadn't seen anything except that gloom-fest Castle for centuries. He would do something about that. There had to be a way for her to escape.

The answering machine's insistent light finally triggered his curiosity. But, when he reached down to push the playback button, there was a knock on the door.

Can't a guy even take his sword off before somebody wants something?

Mac opened the door. It was Lore.

"A nice old lady let me in the building," said the hellhound, barging in. Then he looked closely at Mac. "You're bigger. Again."

"And you're still creepy."

Lore handed him two huge brown bags. "I hope you like chow mein."

The smell hit Mac like a hockey stick between the eyes, but in a good way. It drove the question of what Lore was doing there into the boards. "Oh, yeah."

The Castle had turned off his need for food, and now the hunger came stampeding back. He carried the bags to the kitchen and set them on the table. "I'm going to wash up. There's plates in the cupboard and silverware in the drawer."

Lore watched him with dark, cautious eyes. "You're asking me to eat with you?"

Mac scratched the back of his neck, a dozen smart remarks making a log jam in his head. "Do hellhounds eat Chinese?"

The hound seemed to consider his response far too long. "Yes. The food they prepare, that is."

Riiight. "Then grab a fork."

Abandoning Lore in the kitchen, Mac took off his weapons and washed his hands and face. When he got back to the table, Lore was arranging a mountain of cardboard containers.

Mac had an urge to laugh. He had a nice dining room. He was a first-class cook with a drawerful of gourmet recipes. Yet, here he was, sharing a greasy takeout meal in his dirty kitchen with a hellhound—and loving the fact that he had a guest.

"I've got beer," he said. "That's about it."

Lore looked up from wrestling the top off a Styrofoam container of rice. "That's okay. I'm happy with water."

Mac settled himself and picked up a serving spoon. *Almond chicken. Mm.*

Mac observed as Lore followed his example. The hound watched every move Mac made, mimicking until he caught on to the routine of dishing and eating and what to do with the soy sauce. *He's not had takeout before. But he's picking it up damned quick.*

And apparently enjoying it. Lore had a good appetite. Mac noticed his own hunger was calming down as he ate, a normal, healthy need for food being restored. That was a relief.

Remembering his manners, Mac got up and filled glasses with water. "So, this is great but, uh, what brings you here?" He set a glass in front of Lore.

"I thought if your stomach was full, you would listen to what I need to say."

"Okay." *That's kind of embarrassing.*

"I want to explain to you about the hounds."

"Okay." Mac tore off some paper towels to use as napkins, and sat back down.

"Of all the species, we are the only ones to age and die, mate and have families within the Castle walls. The love of our pack gives us the strength to survive, but it also makes us vulnerable. When we escaped a year ago, we had to leave many of our number behind."

Mac put down his fork, giving Lore his full attention.

The hound looked up, examining Mac all over again from head to toe and gauging his reaction. "As I said before, now that I am free, I can use magic to come and go from the Castle. I smuggle goods to buy back those of my people who have been captured for slaves."

"What?" Then Mac connected the dots, veering around the fact that what Lore did was insanely dangerous on many levels. "Is that why the hounds aren't on guard duty half the time? You're running your operation at the same time you're supposed to be guarding the Castle door?"

"Yes."

Mac just shook his head, the security-minded cop in him scandalized in about six different ways, but he was beginning to see a bigger picture.

Lore went on. "The Vampire Caravelli has also hired wolves for guard duty. Many have helped us, but some have complained to their leaders. They do not agree with releasing more prisoners from the Castle. Soon, the council will meet, and it will punish me. I need your help."

"*My* help?" Mac said.

"I need an advocate with the council of supernatural leaders."

Mac busied himself with more fried rice. He needed a moment to think. "I'm no lawyer. Plus, the council hates me. I was a bad guy, remember?"

Lore leaned forward, his body language saying now that he had come to the point he wanted to make. "The hellhounds rank very low among the supernatural species. We survive however we can by staying humble, keeping to ourselves. We have not made powerful friends."

That was true.

"So I brought Chinese food. You need to help."

So Mac's estimated street price was an extra-large order of fast food. Good to know. "Why me?"

"You are—blessed. The gods have appointed you. But you don't want to hear that."

"No, I don't."

"Then you must find your own reasons."

"And if the task is mine, I'll already know what those are," Mac said, remembering Lore's line from their earlier conversation.

"Exactly." The hellhound looked down at his plate. "Convince the council to give me permission to set my people free. And there are others trapped there, too, not just us. In times when all magic was considered evil, anyone with power was shut up in there—even beasts and birds. The Castle holds many who shouldn't be imprisoned."

Like Constance.

"You must make those in power understand that the Castle is the responsibility of all the paranormal species. We will only survive in a human world if we work together. That is why I sit and eat with you. Someone must begin bringing us together. It may as well start with me."

Mac had a vision of Count Dracula leading a rousing chorus of "We Shall Overcome."

The hound stopped, looking exhausted by the effort of speaking for so long. Shadows from the overhead light showed the strong bones in his face. "Will you help me?"

How the heck he was going to pull this one off? But the job needed doing, and Mac couldn't think of anyone else who'd seen the side of the Castle he had—the part with innocent people who would like nothing better than to lead ordinary lives. Someone had to speak for the everyday main-street monsters, and he'd been hardwired to help folks in need.

"Sure."

October 6, 11:00 p.m.
The Castle

Ashe crept down yet another Castle corridor, a stake clutched in one hand, her boot knife in the other. Not nearly weapons enough, but she'd run out of bullets a thousand susurrating caverns ago.

She'd never seen anything like it—corridor after corridor, each gaping entrance like the last. Magic hung like a fog, sending the tattered remains of her witch-born senses into dust devils. When the spell she'd cast as a teenager blew up in her face, Ashe had lost the ability to manipulate energy—but she could feel power. Here, it pounded in her head like a migraine.

The flickering torches didn't help. For a while they'd seemed kind of funky, like being sucked into a bad horror film. Now she'd had more than enough of the mood lighting, and—ugh!—the Goddess-knew-what creatures she'd blown to smithereens. Four of them, so far. Ashe had seen a lot of monsters in her day, and she wasn't sure these even had a species—just bad tempers and worse breath.

She'd needed her gun and her hand-to-hand fighting skills to get rid of them. Tough beggars, with tusks. She'd pulled a muscle in the back of one knee.

It was a good fight, though. She'd liked that part. The rush never got old.

Needing to rest a moment, Ashe stopped at a corner. Every route away from this spot looked the same. She was lost. Time and direction had lost meaning back when ... well, she had no idea. How long did it take to get chased away from the door, bag your pursuers, and then figure out you were completely turned around? But after that, time had passed. How much, she couldn't say. She wasn't hungry or thirsty, but she was getting incredibly tired.

How on earth was she going to find her way out?

I'll get out. I always land on my feet.

And when I get out, I'm going to kill Caravelli for sure.

When I get out.

Doubt sloshed in her stomach like bad plonk. She started to think about her daughter and stopped. Eden was her joy and her weakness, and she couldn't afford either right then. Now was time for the hard-assed attitude, because that would get her home.

This shouldn't be happening. I'm a good person. I kill monsters to make the world a better place. It's a valuable job.

She savagely clung to her last shreds of calm. Raiding a house full of bad guys was so different. For one thing, there were doors. *Where the hell is that door?*

Something howled. Ashe jolted in fright. The sound echoed, pounding off the walls with ululations of such poignant despair that her knees turned to water. The cry rang in the stones, wave after wave, the aftershocks humming even when the sound itself had died away.

She hauled in her breath, sweat trickling down her ribs. Then she heard the scrape of nails on stone, the drag-flop of enormous paws, and panting like the bellows of hell's own blacksmith. Worse, there was wet, thick snuffling.

An animal of some kind.

Close.

Just around the corner.

No doubt she stunk of fear, like a nice, juicy, PreyBurger. *And if I run, I'll be a fun-filled meal.* She barely worked up enough spit to swallow. Ashe was no coward, but she was no fool, either. Gripping her weapons, she prayed whatever it was would just go away.

A nose came around the corner, wet, black, and huge. It was followed by a head caked in matted brown fur. Drool trailed from its jowls in strings of slimy pearls. *Oh. My. Goddess*. It looked like a mastiff had mated with a prehistoric bear. And the mother of all dust bunnies.

"Viktor!" cried a young man's voice.

The rest of the mountainous beast came around the corner, nearly brushing Ashe with its reeking fur. Reflexively, Ashe ducked. The beast gave a deep *whuff* and thumped her on the shoulder with a whack from its tail. Nerves tingled from the force of the blow, nearly making her drop the stake. Ashe danced to the side, taking up a defensive crouch, prepared to sell her life dearly.

A white shape swooped from the ceiling, too quick to make out. Ashe jerked back, one arm flung up to protect her face. The thing went past, air rushing with the snap of a kite in April breezes. The beast barked again, bounding into the air. The flying creature seemed to nearly collide with the beast's head, then did a somersault midflight.

"There you are, old boy! You're lucky we heard you! Why'd you come wandering back here? So what if it was home; don't you know this isn't a good place anymore?"

Ashe slowly came out of her crouch, her mouth open in raw amazement. A bat-winged angel was roughhousing with the huge, monstrous dog-thing. The angel? Boy? No, youth was a better word—had the thing by the ears and was half flying, half wrestling with it, laughing like a maniac.

It was one of the oddest sights Ashe had ever seen. She had an irrational urge to ditch her weapons and start taking pictures with her cell phone.

"Who are you?" said someone behind her.

Ashe whirled, stake poised. Her mind blanked, cold and ready to kill.

A small woman, barely more than a girl, stared back at her. She was dainty, with long, thick hair the midnight shade of Chinese ink. Pale as a ghost. Ashe's heart started to pound. *Vampire.*

The little vamp looked puzzled, and sniffed the air delicately. "You shouldn't be here. It's too dangerous for a human."

"Said the cat to the mouse," Ashe said in a voice of ice water. "Well, news flash, girlie, this mouse bites back."

The vampire raised one fine dark brow. "Well, I'll be the first to admit that I'm not the most powerful of my kind, but if I really wanted to make a meal of you, I'd have caught you already."

Her voice was light, her accent all Irish charm. Her eyes, though, were full of irony. "But I've learned my lesson. My last catch turned out to be a demon. Quite a disappointment." The vampire gave an enigmatic smile. "But only in the culinary sense."

Okay, why do vamps always insist on sharing too much information? Ashe held her position, every sense on full alert.

The vampire tilted her head. "But you do smell very, very tasty."

Ashe felt every hair on her head standing up to do the wave. *Goddess, get me out of here.* She could jump the vamp, but the dog thing was behind Ashe. Bat-boy was blocking the entrance to the corridor. She was pinned against the stone wall without even a mouse hole in sight.

The youth was approaching, his hands on his hips, silver hair falling loose around him. He wore nothing but what looked like silky pajama bottoms, his chest all bare, pale, lean muscle. The perfect picture of a Goth teen heartthrob. He would have been locker door material except for the huge beast shuffling along in his wake, drooling like Niagara Falls.

"Is the slayer bothering you, little mother?" he asked.

Mother?

The vampire tilted her head, eyeing Ashe as if she might make a meal of her yet. "Nothing to worry about, but I think it's past time she left. She seems very fond of that stake in her hand."

Leave? I'd love to leave. Ashe remained still and silent, too wary to admit she was lost.

The vamp lifted her chin. "Get away from my son. Go. I don't care where."

Bat-boy, on the other hand, gave Ashe a cocky smile. "Don't think for a minute you could catch me, anyway."

Good Goddess. It was the same everywhere. Mothers protected their young. Teenage boys were idiots. "You go. I'm not turning my back on you."

"Very well." The vampire pulled at her son's hand. "Then you don't move. Not a hair. Not until we're out of sight."

Ashe was confused. This was too easy, too *reasonable* for monsters.

But the youth nervously scanned the halls. "Be kind, little mother. No one can stay here. Not even her. We're too near Atreus's halls."

The dog let out another soul-splitting howl—not the lonely keen of earlier, but something new. An alarm. They all cringed away from the sound, the little vampire covering her ears.

No dog made a sound like that unless it sensed trouble.

"What's wrong?" Ashe demanded. Her pulse was kicking up even further, primitive instincts telling her to fight or flee *right now*.

The vampire lifted her head, sniffing the air. "Atreus is near."

"Atreus?"

"Sylvius is right; beware of him. He's unpredictable. Quite mad." The vampire's eyes had gone wary, just one step away from outright fear. She had one hand on the youth's arm, as if her touch alone was a shield. "We need to go. All of us. You, too."

Reflexively, Ashe tightened her fingers around the stake. The look in the female's eyes dug into her gut. *This is a mother and child. Okay, so they're not human, but they're afraid of something worse. What kind of creep would frighten a mom and her kid and dog?*

Whoever that was, Ashe didn't like that person one little bit.

"Where does this guy Atreus live?"

Mac rolled out of bed the next morning wondering whether he'd lost his mind. Somewhere in the course of the evening's conversation, he'd actually agreed to let Lore rent his spare bedroom. He valued his privacy, but he needed cash more.

Heck, he was one-stop shopping: Get your superhero and landlord in one giant package. He'd be in the Castle much of the time, anyway, given his growing to-do list. As long as the Castle was still there.

It turned out the hellhounds knew the place was falling apart, whole chunks at a time simply disappearing. There were warning signs, so for the most part the residents simply moved to another location. Any that didn't disappeared along with the stones.

Mac filed away one important footnote: The guardsmen's magical marching orders said that they could only leave the prison for short periods of time. Naturally, they had the most to lose if the place went poof altogether. Lore speculated they'd probably die.

It was a testament to Reynard's discipline that they weren't all rioting in panic.

It made Mac grateful to be waking up in a soft, safe bed. It would have been perfect if only Connie were there, too. *I wonder if she would want to leave the Castle?* It seemed like the obvious choice to him, but he hadn't lived there for centuries. She might be unaccountably attached to it. Then again, if the Castle kept crumbling, she had no choice.

He stretched, an enormous bone-popping roll of the shoulders.

Coffee. Must have coffee.

He eyed the bedside clock. Ten. *Crap.* He'd overslept. Opening the bedroom blinds, he squinted out at the sun. It was another beautiful autumn day. *Good to be alive.*

The demon was present, flowing through every fiber and bone, but it felt natural. Rather than two adversaries in the same body, it felt simply like the darker side of himself: dangerous, wild, and full of heat.

How dangerous? *Demons destroy. It's their nature.*

He sensed his own potential for savagery with every breath, every movement of his new muscles. It was tempting—a corked bottle of the finest vintage, just waiting to be poured out and savored. The demon thirsted for it like a drunk in the gutter.

But I'm staying stone-cold sober.

Bold words, but it wasn't going to be easy. He had begun by thinking that the clues to regaining his humanity lay in the Castle. That was why he had gone back in the first place, after his conversation with Holly at the U. Ironically, every time he went inside the Castle, he came out a little—or a lot—less human. This last time was no exception. Now his demon was making itself comfortable in its upgraded home.

But he hadn't exactly lost. He could not have rescued Sylvius without his demonic powers. If he rejected his demon side, he would be turning his back on the Castle residents who needed a protector, such as the hellhounds and their stranded family members. And what about the missing Avatar? What about Connie?

If demons destroyed, how come he was being so darned helpful? Caveman and all, Mac was confused on levels he never knew existed.

He switched on the coffeepot and went to take a shower. It was only after he dressed that he remembered the answering machine. Holly had left all the messages. He phoned her back.

"Oh, Mac, thank the Goddess you called. Were you inside in the Castle?"

"Yeah."

"Did you see Ashe?"

"No."

"Damn it!"

Mac remembered Ashe's reaction to the door. With everything else that was going on, he'd forgotten about that. "How'd she break in?"

"She didn't. Alessandro threw her in there."

"Heh."

"Mac, it's not funny."

He cleared his throat. "Of course not. Any particular reason he, uh, sent her on vacation?"

While Holly talked, Mac wandered out onto the balcony. Traffic was hopping below. A corner of his mind wandered back to Connie, wondering what she'd make of it. She'd probably never seen cars.

I'm going to fix that. His demon flexed, heating his flesh, firing his imagination. *Oh, yeah.*

"After we couldn't reach you, Alessandro went into the Castle himself," Holly was saying. "He had to come out this morning. He ran out of ammunition. He couldn't find her."

"Don't worry," Mac replied. "I'll look for your sister. I probably know the lay of the land a bit better. I might have more luck." *So Caravelli didn't kill Ashe, even though she tried to stake him. Isn't he getting all mellow in his domestic bliss?* "When I find her, I'll tell her to play nice. I don't want her running around with pointy objects inside the Castle, either. Someone might lose an eye. If she says please, I'll even let her out."

Holly sighed. "Thanks. I owe you one."

"Nah, I owe you several. And I'm about to owe you another. I know this sounds a bit, uh, trivial given what you've said about your sister, but where do women buy nice, y'know, date clothes?"

"Um. That depends on what they like. Mac, what are you up to?"

"A gift." With Lore moving in, he suddenly had a modest amount of free money. Enough for one night of fun, anyway.

"Uh-huh. What kind of gift for what kind of person?"

"The lady in question has retro tastes."

And a taste for blood. Would that be a problem? Nah. After all, she would be with him. If things got bad, he could always whisk her off to one of the freaky bars where vampires fed on the willing and stupid. Those joints would know how to handle a newbie vamp, right?

"How retro?" Holly's curiosity oozed from the receiver. "Is this for your fair lady in the Castle?"

Mac grinned, enjoying the moment. "She's into these old fashion magazines from the thirties and forties. Kinda Greta Garbo. If I could find something up to date but with that feel . . ."

"Do you know her size?"

"Not the manufacturer's size, but I could figure it out."

"That's what all men say, and they can't. Their fantasy lives interfere."

"I have a good memory for spatial relationships."

"Mac!"

"I'm just saying . . ."

"Put yourself in my hands."

"Caravelli would have my head."

"Let me rephrase. Put your shopping experience in my hands. I'm a woman, and I'm a witch. When do you need this for?"

"I'll let you know. Right now I have to go see a sorcerer about a Castle."

Chapter 18

Lore had given Mac directions to Atreus's chambers.

Mac peered around the corner into a big square hall. He was still hoping for a polite Q and A, but didn't have high hopes. He'd left the sword at home—if Atreus was unbalanced, showing up armed could cause more problems than it solved—but he wasn't about to wander into the lion's den completely helpless. He had a well-hidden boot knife, and he'd worn the flannel shirt like a jacket to cover his gun.

He'd come alone. He wasn't going to risk Connie. Not with so much chance of ugliness.

Mac slipped into the room, concealing himself behind one of the massive, fluted pillars dotting the room. He did a quick visual sweep. It was a huge space with upward-thrusting stone ribs, and he found his gaze drawn higher and higher. Banners hung from the vaulted ceiling like falling leaves, the jagged, rotting edges of the bright silk trailing cobwebs fringed with dust. A breeze made them stir, like they were eerily alive.

He circled the pillar to the right, trying to get a better view of the room itself. There wasn't much furniture. Chests and chairs, mostly. In the middle of the hall was a carved wooden throne. It was empty.

He was about to give up when he heard a noise, the barest shudder of an indrawn breath. Instinct made him draw the Sig Sauer and cock it, the harsh sound echoing like a bouncing ball. He paused, wondering whom it would alert.

Nothing stirred. Had he imagined that breath?

The noise had come from the far corner, behind the throne. Mac crouched and glided with demon silence to the next pillar, getting closer. And waited.

Nothing.

He straightened and turned, holding his weapon lightly, focusing on everything and nothing, every sense peeled. In an instant, he found what he was looking for. There was a tall man standing with his back to Mac, so still that it would have been easy to mistake him for part of the room.

Mac barely got an impression of blue robes and dark hair before his attention swerved to the thing the man seemed to be staring at: Ashe Carver, in all her biker-leather glory, hanging on the wall like a weird modern sculpture.

Holy crap! A jolt of adrenaline thumped his pulse into high gear. Mac stared for a long moment, not sure if she was even alive. Arms spread above her head, legs dangling, she was utterly still. There was no blood, no weapon poking out of her. What was keeping her up there?

Then her eyes slowly moved to meet his. Cold filled him from the bottom up, rising like a foul tide. He could see her breathing now, short, shallow pants, sucking in mere mouthfuls of air. She was choking to death.

Her bright green eyes glittered with knife-edged terror.

"You," Mac barked, raising the gun. "Back away from her."

The robed man took a step backward, turning just enough that Mac could see his face. Not an old guy with a big white beard and magic wand, but a much younger-looking man—hooked nose, high cheekbones, and long raven hair. The man held one hand up, fingers spread, like he was holding an invisible sheet of paper against an invisible wall.

He had to be holding Ashe by magic. *The sorcerer.*

"Identify yourself."

The man looked mildly surprised. "I am Atreus of Muria, of course."

That figured. This so wasn't the way Mac had wanted this conversation to go. He needed information from this guy. He couldn't just blow his head off. What had Ashe done to put this disaster into action?

Still, he couldn't let Atreus squish her to death. He'd made a promise to Holly.

"Let her go."

The man dropped his arm. Ashe fell to the floor with an unceremonious thud, rolling once to land on her side. Mac let his eyes flicker away from Atreus for only a second. *How am I going to get her out of here?*

"She's very rude," Atreus said. "She tried to poke me with a stick."

So you tried to stake a sorcerer. Good job, Ashe. "That *is* rude."

"I assume that's a weapon you're holding."

"Yup."

"That's also rude."

Before Mac could react, the semi slipped from his hand and sailed across the room, landing at Atreus's feet. It spun, miring itself in the hem of the sorcerer's robes. Atreus bent and picked it up, studying it with obvious curiosity. "Such toys humans invent."

He closed his hand around the gun, fondling the smooth finish a moment before a twitch of his fingers crushed it to dust. There was no muttering of spells, no flash of spectral light. This was sorcery so smooth it was damn near invisible.

Mac felt his jaw fall open, surprise clearing a path for fear.

The sorcerer's black gaze speared him. "You're like her, demon. You lack respect."

Atreus's gesture seemed to fold the air around Mac, hard pressure forcing him to his knees. "Bow before me!"

Mac was flattened until his forehead bumped the cold, gritty floor. He bit his tongue, the sudden tangy taste of blood filling his mouth.

Mac turned his head just enough to see Ashe's face. She was deathly pale, eyes closed, her skin shining with sweat. She was still breathing in quick, sharp pants. Ashe needed doctors and an ambulance. She wasn't going to get that here.

Mac couldn't dust out and leave her. He couldn't move, period. Claustrophobia prowled through him, almost exotic in its intensity.

Atreus was pacing the room in long strides. His robes followed him like something alive, twisting and flowing with Cecil B. DeMille dramatics. He picked up a long staff, adding to the effect. "My territories stretched through entire city-states. This was all my land. You have all forgotten the nine that made this place."

Keep it together, Mac. One breath at a time.

"Were you one of the nine?" Mac asked. He was in so much trouble, asking a question wasn't likely to make it any worse.

"I was. I put the sun in this sky."

And had he noticed it was missing? "When was that?"

Atreus took three long strides and thumped the staff down on Mac's back, pushing the end hard between his shoulder blades. "Before the light went from the world, you fool. And now the world itself falls away. The Castle has crumbled for sixteen years."

An electric, tingling flood spewed from the staff, shooting through Mac's nerves in white-hot jolts. *Pain. Pain. Pain.*

And then blessed numbness. Mac collapsed like melting rubber; Gumby left too long in the sun. Atreus wandered away, taking the staff with him.

"All my subjects turned on me. All they cared for was my power."

Connie was right. The guy was a few quarts short of a cauldron. Mac tried to move his hand, but couldn't. Ashe was starting to turn fish-belly white, but her eyes were flickering open.

C'mon, demon, let's get a move on. Help me out.

But he was talking to himself. There wasn't a separate being inside anymore. He was it. All there was. The realization startled him, but he shoved it aside. He could think about that later.

He could feel his skin burning, demon heat washing over his limbs. The smell of hot fabric hovered, like his clothes were going to ignite. *That could be embarrassing and painful.*

Finally, movement. His finger twitched. *You're going to have to do better than that.*

Atreus was ranting. "First Viktor turned on me, retreating to his beast form. Then Josef stole away. Even my little girl has left me."

Mac's mind raced. Okay. Back to saving the hostage. If he went to his demon form holding an object, it traveled with him. Would that work with another living creature? Or would it go horribly wrong?

Atreus thumped him in the back again. "What did you come to steal from me? What?"

Mac stayed in his facedown position, doing his best to look cowed and helpless. He had come seeking his humanity. Now his priority was saving Ashe. Still, he might grab something from this fiasco. He moved a foot and an arm. The paralysis was wearing off. *Thank God.*

"I came to ask questions."

Atreus's zigzagging path stopped in front of Mac, mere inches from his face. Mac could see the sorcerer's embroidered shoes, the threadbare toes padded and curled upward to gentle points. There were stray threads on both points, as if some of the glass beads that dotted the design had fallen off.

"What did you come here to ask?" Atreus demanded. "I will only grant one question. I am busy with matters of state."

One question. There were so many, and they all led back to the Castle.

"Who was the Avatar?"

Atreus went utterly still. "She was the mother of my

child. I made her from the sun and the rain, and then I killed her." The regret in his voice was gray and cold as the winter ocean.

Huh?

Was that madness, metaphor, or domestic homicide?

Atreus turned and walked to the throne, and mounted it. He settled, spreading the skirts of his robes over his knees so that the folds hung perfectly. He rested his hands on the heavily carved arms of the throne, and looked down on the room as if it were crowded with his subjects begging for favors. He nodded, gesturing graciously to people who weren't there.

"Alas," he mumbled. "Only real life makes more life. My creations can but hold the limited strength of my sorcery."

A forensic psychologist would have a field day with this one. If Atreus hadn't been so bloody dangerous, Mac would have felt pity.

There wasn't time for that. Ashe's breathing was getting raspy. Mac tried to estimate if he and Ashe were in the sorcerer's peripheral vision. He couldn't tell. He would have to gamble. His skin prickled with heat as he gathered strength.

He dusted, re-forming almost on top of her. Ashe's eyes were huge, staring into his with blind panic. She was trying to push him off, but all the strength had left her limbs. "What happened to you? You're burning hot!"

"Why, thank you."

"You're a demon!"

"And a Sagittarius. It's your lucky day."

Atreus was wheeling out of his throne, arms raised like Zeus about to chuck a thunderbolt. Mac wrapped his arms around Ashe, and willed them both to dust.

It was a weirdly intimate sensation. He felt them dissolve, felt the crack of force as power snapped against the stones where they'd been. *Just in time.*

Mac slithered ponderously through the Castle, mere inches from the ground. It was hard to carry another person, achingly difficult. Mac didn't bother with following any proper path. He cut through floors and walls in a beeline for the door.

Once outside, he let his passenger materialize first, carefully re-forming all things that were Ashe into Ashe before he solidified himself. The last thing he wanted was to end up as Mashe.

They were sitting on the cedar-block surface of the alley, Ashe's back against the old, stained bricks of the wall. Mac was kneeling, facing her, his jeans soaking up moisture from the ragged grass poking through the blocks. It had rained while they were inside.

"Oh, Goddess." Ashe clutched her side, her face pulling into a rictus of pain.

The hellhounds were back and crowding around, one talking on his cell.

"Call an ambulance," Mac ordered the one with the phone. Mac grabbed Ashe's shoulders. She was slowly falling over, slumping to the ground. He helped her down, cushioning her head on his hand until one of the hounds offered his jacket as a pillow.

Ashe watched him with pain-hazed eyes. "You saved my ass in there," she said.

"Please tell me I didn't waste my time," he replied.

"You gonna lecture me now?"

"Your sister would like me to." He didn't really have the energy.

Ashe pulled her mouth in what might have been a grin. "Holly doesn't get a vote. She's in bed with a monster."

Mac sighed wearily, "So who likes their brother-in-law? Get over it."

"She's my baby sister," Ashe whispered.

He could already hear sirens. Help was on the way.

Mac gently turned Ashe's chin so he could look into her eyes. She was fading in and out of consciousness, but he had to get his point across. "Let me tell you about Alessandro Caravelli. He gave up everything—his queen, his job, his rank—to be with her. He nearly gave his life to rescue her. He's a special guy. Holly's a special woman. Don't mess with them."

Ashe closed her eyes.

"Just think about this," Mac said more gently. "I don't have a problem with you being a hunter and taking out the real villains, but don't turn into the thing you hate."

"Or you'll kick my ass."

"Damned straight."

The ambulance pulled up at the mouth of the alley, the doors flinging open. The hellhounds were just as rapidly making themselves scarce. *Great. Leave me with the mess.*

Two paramedics were pounding down the alley, a tall blond man in the front. "What happened?" the leader asked.

Mac's mind went blank for an instant. "Uh—she was hit by a motorcycle."

He heard a small noise from Ashe. He fixed her with a glare. "A Ducati. Came whizzing right down the alley. Could've killed her."

Standing back, he let the ambulance guys do their thing. One started back to the ambulance almost immediately, calling for the stretcher.

"Sir, are you a relative?" asked the other.

"No. You tell me where you're taking her and I'll call her family. They'll meet you there."

"Are you sure it was a motorcycle accident?"

"Yeah," muttered Ashe, her voice gone thready. "Didn't catch the license."

The stretcher was rattling down the alley on wheels, pushed by the second attendant. She'd be gone soon, taken away and patched up to fight another day. That was the problem.

Mac knelt beside her one last time. "Ashe. Behave yourself. Don't come back here."

The paramedic gave him a curious look. Ashe took in a couple of short breaths, saving up enough air to speak. She grabbed Mac's hand.

"Thank you," she said. "I won't forget it."

Mac got out of the way while they loaded Ashe onto the stretcher. He watched them go as he took out his phone to call Holly. All he could see of Ashe now were the soles of her boots.

She was brave. He had to give her that.

Unfortunately, now his slim hope of learning anything from Atreus was lost.

Chapter 19

October 7, 1:00 p.m.
101.5 FM

"**T**ired of visiting the same old haunts? Adventures await with Wallachia Vacations! We travel to all the prime destinations for supernatural dream holidays. Visit your old home in Transylvania or yuck it up in the Yucatan with a full-moon blood ritual. We cover it all with comprehensive service package tours and specially prepared airline comfort. Friendly assistance with customs and immigration. Book now for the holiday rush!"

I'm revoltingly smitten.

Constance sat in the hall with the black lake, curled up on one of the hard stone benches with her arms wrapped around her knees.

Mac! The name brought a sweet tightness to her stomach, like she was about to leap down, down from a dizzying height. Girlish emotions to go with her girlish form.

Revoltingly, hopelessly smitten. For shame, Constance! You're not a child anymore.

But why not indulge? She was imagining herself opening the door of her dream house, wearing one of the elegant dresses from her magazines—the later ones, when skirts shamefully revealed the knees. She imagined the shoes, too. They had beautiful thin, tall heels that proved the woman who wore them never worked a day in her life. Truly, no one wearing those blade-thin stilts could lift a pail or scrub a floor.

She would be opening the door to well-dressed guests, who would all tell her she was beautiful. Mac would be at her side, looking on, proud of her and the way she kept their home.

What a glorious life. Nothing like mine.

If she walked into the world of beautiful houses and pretty shoes, she would become a killing nightmare. Nothing was worth that—not unless it was a crisis of life and death.

And Sylvius was safe now. She had no moral right to hunt. Even if the guardsmen stole her child away again, Mac was ready to help her. Why would she need full vampire powers? Now she could remain as she was with no blood on her conscience.

She'd faced that truth when she'd let the female warrior go—and, as if to prove that the decision had been right, that strange woman had stood guard as Constance led her family out of harm's way.

No, Constance did not need to change.

Ever.

She could stay as she was, eternally.

She was beginning to feel like a jar of preserves slowly going off. She wanted to taste the magazine world—Mac's world—with him. Maybe standing at night in some city scene, the artificial lights winking like earthbound stars, and she would be wearing pretty shoes.

Since when did the world hand you what you wanted? Remember what Lore said: Be careful how you barter with destiny.

That had to be wrong. She was tired of living like a ghost, of relying on other people to order her life for her—be it the lord of her childhood home, or Atreus, or even Mac.

Even if he wanted the best for her, it seemed unwise to rely on him completely for the safety of herself and her son. Shouldn't a vampire, even half a vampire, have some power of her own?

Those were rebellious thoughts for a peasant girl who had started out milking cows and then spent centuries as Atreus's servant, but they wouldn't leave her alone. She could feel her life changing, and her courage waxed and waned like the moon—now strong and bright, now all but disappearing. That change felt out of control, like a horse gone wild. There was no telling what path it would take.

Wishing had to count for something, and Constance wished with all her might for that moment with Mac, the romance of the city streets all around her. Romance in their hearts. That beautiful scene. If she could will her life one way, that was it.

Sylvius sat down on the bench beside her, quiet as falling snow. "You're thinking of him," he said.

"What makes you say that?"

With one finger, he touched the pendant she wore, and which he had made. "Macmillan makes you happy. That's good."

She looked into Sylvius's face. The time he had spent in the demon box had left its mark. His black eyes, so startling against his pale complexion, seemed older in ways she couldn't name.

"Should I worry that Mac is a demon now?"

"So am I," Sylvius said calmly. His smile was teasing.

How he's growing up. He's truly not a child anymore. "You're an incubus. Your strength is love, not violence."

"Your Macmillan is a protector. The world needs both. And besides, you like him."

"How do you know?"

"I'm not blind."

"Children shouldn't think of their mothers that way."

"I'm not stupid, either. And besides, I'm old enough now to find my own way. You'll need a new project." He kissed her forehead. "I'm a young incubus about town."

He'd been reading her magazines. "So your mother is that easy to shrug off?"

He laughed. "Never. You'll always be my mother, but I can't always be a boy."

Sylvius folded his wings tight against his back, making them all but invisible. He nonetheless looked no more human. Though strong and lean as any handsome youth, there was no mistaking him for one of the farm lads back home. It would be like comparing a fledgling eagle to a flock of geese.

I raised this beautiful, wise young creature. Fancy that. "I don't know what I would have done if Mac hadn't brought you back." She felt the tingle of tears.

"You would have come for me." He kissed her forehead. "You're as much a warrior as your man."

She looked away. "I'm not Turned."

"You could be."

"Lore says if I leave the Castle, I will turn into some savage beast."

Sylvius laughed. "I can't see that."

She pushed her hair out of her eyes. "Lore's people have the gift of prophecy."

"And sometimes Lore lives like he is holding a broken cup in his two hands, afraid to let go in case the pieces fall."

"What does that mean?"

"Maybe the pieces need to fall, so that our hands can be free."

Constance leaned against him. "It's not that simple, and you just like to argue."

He squeezed her. "Leap toward happiness."

Easy for a love demon to say. Constance laughed softly, afraid of the temptations brewing in her soul. Whether he knew it or not, Sylvius was telling her what she wanted to hear.

"I gave you this to open your heart." He touched the pendant again. "It worked. Don't undo the good it's brought you. You can live in fear or be the person you dream yourself to be."

"The good it brought me? Sylvius, is this really a love charm?" She clutched the pendant. "I raised you better than that!"

"It can't make you fall in love. It just shows you possibilities. Apparently, you liked the possibility you saw."

Constance was speechless; then she swallowed hard. "That's . . . that's . . ."

Sylvius looked smug. "Your Mac is here to see you."

"Here? Now?" she rose, rounding the edge of the stone bench, more than ready to go.

Sylvius got to his feet, jumped to the top of the bench, then off again, spreading his wings to float down beside her. "He made Lore come and put wards of protection all over the Summer Room door. He did the rooms next door, too, so I can sleep there."

Sylvius looked a little defiant, but Constance said nothing. It was only right he had a private space of his own, even if she was still fretting whenever he was out of sight. It was going to take her a while to get over their recent scare. To come up with a better plan than hiding behind locked doors, whatever wards the hellhounds put on them.

She wished she could leave the Castle. Maybe Sylvius should.

He watched her expression carefully. "Nothing stays the same forever, little mother. All things change. It's up to us to make them better."

Constance found a smile and forced it to her lips. He touched her cheek. His hand was warm, the gesture full of the soft, gentle magic of the incubus. Soft as the sunlight she'd almost forgotten. Soothing. Calming.

Her smile started to bloom of its own accord. Mac was waiting for her. Everything was going to be wonderful.

She wished it with all her heart.

Sylvius took Viktor to his newly warded chambers, leaving Constance and Mac alone in the Summer Room.

She looked up, falling into the rich brown of Mac's gaze. He looked tired, but happy to see her. They kissed, and she felt the inevitable need to draw him closer, search the kiss for more secrets and pleasures. To give him comfort.

"Did you talk to Atreus?" she asked when they broke apart. There was a lingering grimness about him. She wanted to know why.

Mac brushed the hair back from her forehead. "I did. Sort of. It's a long story. Let's talk about that later. I need something else right now. Just for a few minutes."

"What would that be?"

"You. I need you to make me forget the day."

He kissed her again, letting his hands slide up her ribs, caressing her waist, her breasts, finally cupping her face with exquisite tenderness.

"Do women in the outside world kiss the same way?" Constance asked when they finally allowed air to come between them. Part of her was afraid to ask. The rest of her couldn't resist.

"Not nearly so well," he said with a quick grin. "But d'you know what men and women do, when they want to get to know each other better?"

"What might that be?" Constance twined her arms around his neck, allowing him to sit on the massive, heavy sofa and draw her onto his knee. His strong, broad chest made the best cushion in the world.

"They go out someplace nice and spend time with each other."

"On a date?" She'd seen the word in the magazines.

"Yeah. A date."

"In my time we called it courting."

"Remember I said you should come see my world sometime?"

Constance felt her stomach drop like a bucket down a well. She remembered. He'd said it in the haze after lovemaking. She didn't think he'd remember. "I remember."

Mac gave another grin. "Miss Moore, would you go on a date with me tomorrow night?"

She opened her mouth to say no, but he looked too hopeful. He wasn't like Lore, telling her she'd turn to a rav-

ening, murderous beast the moment she set foot outside
the Castle door. *Which is the truth?*

She looked away in confusion, her gaze dropping to the
shining, lovely magazines he had brought. New ones, still
smelling of fresh ink. They were better than jewels. They
were filled with fuel for a thousand dreams. "I don't have
anything to wear."

"I've already thought of that," he said. "I'll bring you
something nice."

"You will?" The words came out like a prayer and a confession both. She sounded like a drowning waif, clutching
at the reeds of a riverbank. "But how will I get out of the
Castle?"

"Don't worry about that. I've got that figured out, too."
He touched his finger to the end of her nose. "Nothing's
ever perfect, but I'll make our night as close to absolutely
wonderful as I can."

Lore had to be wrong. Mac wasn't worried about what
she'd do. Still . . .

"What if I bite someone?" She had to say it. She still had
a conscience.

Mac cocked an eyebrow. "Do you want to?"

"No!" she said. "But what if I decide I do?"

He shifted his hands, holding her as gently as he would a
bird. "Why would you?"

"What if I can't help myself? It could happen. I'm a
monster, you know."

He gave a sly smile. "Tell me if you feel the urge. Then
we'll decide what to do. There are people who are happy to
let you bite them."

Constance was stunned. "Bloody hell! Why would they
want that?"

Mac looked confused, then considering. "How often
were you bitten?"

"Just the once."

He looked even more perplexed. "Your, um, boyfriend
tried to Turn you on, like, the first time?"

"Yes."

She flushed, remembering that vampire venom was supposed to possess erotic effects. She'd felt none of that. Though she did remember he slobbered. "He wasn't much for getting a girl in the mood."

Chuckling, Mac pulled her close. He was warm, his laugh a pleasant rumble. "Say yes, Connie. Come out with me. I'll show you how a girl is meant to be treated."

She let him wrap her in his strong, strong arms, imagining herself walking in the open air, the city folding around her like a sequined cloak. How could she deny him, after all he'd done for her? "Where will we go? What will we do? Tell me what it will be like."

He chuckled again, obviously enjoying himself, and it warmed her through to her spine. "What do you want to do?"

She knew the answer to that. It was in the magazines. "What every other man and woman does. Dinner and a movie."

"Dinner?"

"I'll watch you eat."

He frowned. "Are you sure? That won't be very exciting."

"I want to do what everyone else does. I want a proper *date*."

"Whatever you want."

"Really?"

"This will be your night."

Can I take this risk? She thought of the brave woman she had met, a mere human ready to take on the whole Castle. "You'll make sure I don't do anything I shouldn't? You promise?"

Mac's eyes were serious. "I promise, sweetheart."

Mac kept his promises. "Then, yes."

He grinned, that quick flash of mischief, and the last of her resistance melted. She wanted whatever he could show her. She leaned into him, turning on his knee so that she almost faced him.

He reached down, his fingers brushing against her ankle

as they crept up her stocking, following the curve of her calf. The fabric of her petticoats rustled, the old, soft cloth falling in languid folds over his arm. New garments would have been stiffer, but these lent themselves to furtive play.

Constance twitched when his fingers reached her knee. The undercover touch seemed somehow more illicit than flagrant display. Mac's hand crossed the barrier of her ribbon garter and found bare flesh to stroke. He ran his hand under her chemise, cupping her rump in a gentle squeeze.

"You're not wearing anything under here," he said in a very male tone.

"Only men wear drawers. No proper girl wears men's underthings."

He chuckled. "I need to introduce you to Victoria's Secret."

"Why would I need her secrets? Haven't I got plenty?"

"Oh, yeah."

His caress made her restless. She braced against his shoulders and hitched herself up until she could turn completely, straddling his lap, her knees on either side of his hips. Mac shifted, carrying her along as he found a comfortable position.

"Now what are you going to do?" he teased.

She noticed he'd kept a possessive grip on her hip. She wordlessly gathered her skirts up in front, working them until nothing was trapped beneath her legs. He slipped his other hand beneath the pool of cloth until both were holding her bare hips, steadying her as she hooked her fingers into his waistband and began working the buttons of his jeans.

He was wearing nothing beneath, either. Sliding away, she let him free himself of the thick denim, find a better angle on the heavy sofa. Settling again, she sketched the hard, sharp tip of her nail—one of the more dangerous attributes of the female vampire—around the base of him, then gently dragged it up the shaft, watching it quiver and blossom under her touch. Another stroke, and another, and she had him, plump and full, between her hands.

Constance felt wanton, an explorer in an exotic land.
She was starting to ache in all the right places, her breasts
feeling tight in the confines of her stays. She rose up, balancing like an equestrian for the best angle to kiss. Their
lips met, her hands gripping his shoulders, tongues teasing
each other. He was demon-hot, his skin warm as that of
someone who had been standing before a fire. She luxuri-
ated in it, pressing herself against him, drinking in that heat
with every pore.

And then she let her tongue slide down his strong, long
neck, torturing herself with the spicy taste of him. Her jaws
throbbed with the urge to bite, but she held back. If she was
going to walk in the outside world, she had to prove she
had self-control. Tears started to course down her cheeks,
the effort almost too much to bear.

And then she moaned as his clever fingers found the private territory between her thighs. He stroked her in small,
tight circles, filling her and then making her cry out as he
withdrew, exploring until he found the perfect nub that
made her gasp her surprise. She rocked against him, quivering as he wound her tighter and tighter. She dug her nails
into his shirt, crushing the cloth in her grip as he finally
brought her with a last skillful touch. She bucked against
him in frantic, pulsing waves, her mind white as a snowstorm, free of anything but blind sensation.

She was there, floating free, when she felt the press of
him. She opened, her body generous now, taking him in a
bit at a time, stroke after stroke, mourning a little every
time she had to let that fullness go. Mac had her by the hips
again, guiding them both, his teeth gritted. His hardness
stretched her —uncomfortable, exquisite pleasure. Her immortal body could take it, glorying in his size and strength,
gorging on him. Every angle, every glide unfolded new sen-
sations. New pleasures. New gratification.

Blood hunger raged through her, growing ever sharper
as she denied it, becoming part of the exquisite torture. The
pain of it was almost erotic in its own right.

Mac's eyes glittered red, his skin gone from warm to

burning with demon heat. Their surging rhythm quickened. Tension was building, layering, growing like something crystalline and bright. Then it shattered, a thousand shards of pleasure slicing at her flesh, drawing a piercing cry from her lips. She heard Mac roar and felt his rush of heat inside her.

Oh yes, wherever he led, she would follow.

Ashe woke. She wasn't sure how long she'd been out, but it was light now, sun peeping through the hospital room's curtains. She looked around, moving only her eyes because her head felt like a balloon. *Drugs.*

A page turned to the right of her. She jerked toward the sound, feeling her medicated senses swirl with the sudden motion. Holly was slumped in a chair, her stockinged feet propped on the edge of the metal bed frame. She was reading a textbook—the same one Ashe had shoved at Caravelli, tricking him into revealing his vampire speed.

Now Ashe regretted the act, sort of. It had been a cheap shot. "Hey."

Holly looked up. "You're awake."

"Yup." Ashe took in the monitors, the ugly fluorescent lights, the other two patients in the room. Both looked asleep or unconscious, but it was hard to tell. All she could see from this angle was lumps under thin hospital blankets.

The place smelled of disinfectant and death.

Holly closed the text, setting it on the floor beside her. "How are you feeling?"

They put me in a pink hospital gown! Pink? Do they think I'm twelve? "Like I've been in a garbage compactor."

"You need more painkillers?"

Ashe tried to sit up but abandoned the plan. "Nah, I'm woozy enough as it is."

Holly fussed with the covers, doing the pillow-plumping thing. Ashe swatted her away.

Holly sat down again, clearly uncomfortable. "I'm sorry Alessandro put you in the Castle. He's sorry, too."

Yeah, right. Ashe rubbed her eyes. They felt gummy. A

wave of fatigue swamped her, followed by a mood the same color as the sickly green bed curtains. "I didn't give him much choice."

Holly looked puzzled. "Are you saying you're going to back off about him?"

Ashe heard the hope in her voice. It cut her quick-deep. "I didn't want you to get hurt. I don't."

"Has it ever occurred to you that I'm an incredibly powerful witch?"

"I know. That doesn't make me worry about you any less."

Holly folded her arms. "Why not worry about Eden instead? It's not that I don't want you around, but she needs you more."

Eden was a tender place she'd rather leave alone. "She's fine. I've already made sure of that. I wasn't sure about you."

"I have Alessandro. Whether you believe it or not, he does a good job of looking after me."

Ashe could tell Holly believed it. She sighed as much as her sore ribs allowed.

A doctor came by, but went to the patient across the room. A cart clattered along the hall. Ashe wondered whether they were going to feed her. She was starving. Not that hospital food was anything to look forward to.

Holly leaned in closer. "How did you meet your husband? You never told me."

Oh, Goddess. Sharing time. "In a bar. He picked me up. It worked out."

"That's it?"

Not by a long shot. "We both loved action—mountain climbing, dirt bikes. He taught me a lot of fighting moves. He didn't care where I'd been or what I'd done. He was a here-and-now kind of guy. Brilliant. Energetic." *Dead.*

Ashe felt her throat closing up with unshed tears. *Damned medication is making me weepy.* "We called our daughter Eden because we were in Paradise when we had her."

"That's sweet," said Holly.

More like ironic. A hot tear escaped, sliding over her temple into the pillow. *Damned, damned medication.* "Roberto died when she was six. Then I was on my own. I didn't have any job skills. I couldn't afford to give her a good life. The couple of years after that were a huge struggle."

"So you went into—your current job?"

"Uh-huh." Ashe heard the quaver in her voice, hated it, but kept talking. For some reason, Holly needed to hear this. Best to get it over with. "I started out finding missing children. The cases just got stranger, more dangerous, and paid better. Now Eden is in the best, most secure school I could find. She lost her father. It was the least I could do for her. She has a future. I'm not saying I'm a great mother, but she's got absolutely everything I can give her."

Holly looked stunned. A silence fell between them, fading into the constant clatter and hum of the hospital. Ashe put her arm over her eyes, blocking out the light. Raising her arm pulled at her ribs, but she gripped the pain to her like a shield. "And now you know everything there is to know about me."

"Sure I do," said Holly, her voice denying it. "Ashe, you're incredible. In a good way. Mostly."

Ashe allowed herself a half smile. "That's me."

"What are you going to do now?"

"I'm going to make sure you're all right."

"Time to update the data, sis. I think *I'm* looking after *you* right now."

Ashe lowered her arm. "We're still sisters, aren't we? Looking after each other is what they do."

They stared at each other a long moment.

"Will you leave Alessandro alone?"

"Okay. Unless he screws up. Then I'll kill him twice over."

"Okay." Holly laced her fingers together, almost like she was praying. "Y'know, I want to meet Eden and she'd love Grandma. You should bring her here for a visit."

Ashe stared at the grimy acoustic tiles on the ceiling. They seemed to press down, pinning her to the lumpy bed.

"That would be nice. But, y'know, Eden's going to ask questions."

"About her witch heritage?"

"About where Mom and Dad are."

Holly sank back into her chair, deflating. "Ashe . . ."

Ashe sighed. She was broken, inside and out, and she so wanted to hand the jagged bits of herself to some other responsible party to figure out. Sadly, it wasn't anyone's job but hers. "I know. I'll bring her around. Someday."

Ashe turned her head, studying Holly's face. There was still the echo of that sweet—though sometimes bratty—kid inside the woman. Not everything was lost in the passage of time. Ashe relaxed a tiny degree. "I love you, Holly. I hope you get that."

"Yeah." A slow, sly smile stole over Holly's face. "And you always kept a secret better than anyone. I remember that about you."

Ashe narrowed her eyes. "What?"

October 8, 1:00 p.m.
Tiger Lily Vintage Clothes

"I thought for sure your sister'd punctured a lung," Mac said.

"She didn't, but that was sheer luck. You saved her life."

Holly flipped through the rack of dresses at Tiger Lily Vintage, Fairview's raging-hot boutique for recycled fashion.

"But Ashe is doing okay, right?" Mac asked.

The sun fell through the dirty window like weak tea. The place was decorated in basic Victorian Bordello, with a lot of worn velvet and faded purple fringes.

"Sure. Witches heal fast. Even if Ashe doesn't have active magic, she's still one of us. Lucky for her." There was a frustrated edge in Holly's voice. "I think she's coming around about Alessandro—I mean not killing him—but I don't think they'll ever be BFFs, y'know?"

"Uh, no," he said. "She's trying to protect you."

Holly flipped another hanger. "So why am I the one doing bedside duty?"

"When are visiting hours?"

"I was up there this morning. I'll drop by again later. They've got her so doped up she sleeps most of the time. It's great for hitting the books." Holly sighed. "Poor Ashe."

"Hmm, yeah, aren't you supposed to be studying and not shopping?"

"I'm in denial. Aren't you supposed to be figuring out why you're a demon again?"

"My best source of information tried to turn your sister and me into liverwurst." Bored with watching her flip through the procession of garments, Mac started to look for himself. He wasn't one of those antishopping guys, but this was moving too slowly.

"Aren't you chock-a-block with demon strength?"

"That guy, Atreus, is packing a whole lot more. How about this?" He held up a red dress with a poofy skirt that rustled. Mac liked it, but he wasn't sure whether that shade of red was the thing.

"Hmm, no," she said. "That looks like Shirley Temple meets *Saw*."

He put it back with an exasperated grunt. He never had this much trouble buying clothes for himself. "Okay, I admit defeat. What does every girl want for her first date?"

Holly gave him one of her squinty looks that said he was being an idiot. It was kind of comforting, because it meant nothing between them had changed. He was a normal-sized human idiot. He was an extra-large demon idiot. It was all the same to Holly.

"Little black dress," she said. "Every woman needs one."

"Okay," said Mac. *A plan. We have a plan.* "Do they have those in vintage shops?"

"Haven't you ever heard of Audrey Hepburn? Look, this is perfect" Holly pulled out another dress. This one was black and so plain, it looked almost severe.

Boring. "Isn't that kind of basic?"

"That's the point. It's all about the accessories. Strappy shoes. Evening bag. I bet you haven't even thought about lingerie."

"Ha-ha. Not touching that one."

"Beast."

"You bet."

"But a sweetie." She held up another dress, plain black with a neckline that plunged almost to the waist. "Whoa, that one makes a statement."

His inner caveman went on alert, definitely feeling more beastly than sweet. "We'll take it."

Chapter 20

October 8, 7:55 p.m.
101.5 F.M.

"Baba Yaga's Restaurant offers fine dining in the old world tradition in the heart of historic Fairview. With a wide and varied menu, we guarantee an unforgettable dining experience. Although we specialize in poultry, all dietary requirements are discreetly supplied. Please reserve in advance."

Constance clung to Mac's arm, unsteady on her beautiful, damnably dangerous shoes. Everything about the clothes he had given her made her feel exposed, from her ankles all the way up to her neck. Her upswept hair left her nape bared to chance breezes, shivering not from cold but from the sensuality of the promiscuous air.

She might as well have gone walking abroad in her shift. Except her shift wasn't silky and black as sin. This was a woman's dress. Not a girl's. His eyes had told her so.

He'd brought her flowers. Red and white roses. She hadn't seen, or smelled, or touched the velvet petals of real flowers for hundreds of years. They still ravished her senses, the scent of them clinging to her hands.

And he looked so handsome. Like the men in the magazines but better because it was him, Conall Macmillan, dressed like a prince but with a devil's twinkle in his eyes.

He took her out of the Castle in a cloud of dust. The first sensation on becoming solid again was the wash of rain-fresh space around her. The next was Mac sliding her arm over his, as if she was worthy of the finest courtesy. For that night, she would believe she was. He had promised to look after her. To make this night her own.

Her memory of his promise quieted the butterflies in her stomach. She felt awestruck, intimidated and giddily happy—but no hint of monstrous hunger.

Oh, the bliss! There were lights everywhere as they strolled around the corner and a street or two away to a building with BABA YAGA'S hung in bright, glowing pink letters above the door. She tried not to stare open-mouthed at the fiery sign—so strange and pretty!—just as she tried not to gape at the cars or the tall buildings or the other people striding so confidently past. She didn't want to look like a baby bird stretching its beak for worms. She had to look like she belonged on Mac's arm. Oh, the bliss!

Once they had passed beneath the pink sign, a man dressed in black and white, his clothes every bit as fine and formal as Mac's, greeted them with, "This way, please." He shepherded them through a maze of tables draped in white. Constance allowed herself one look around, telling herself not to stare.

"What do you think?" Mac whispered in her ear.

The high-ceilinged room was filled with people in fine clothes, and there were flowers and candles everywhere. Serving men and women hovered nearby, just as they had in her day in houses of the rich. Or so she'd been told. What did she know? She'd lived her life in the barn with the cows. "It's beautiful."

He smiled down at her, giving her hand a squeeze. She would have died of joy if she wasn't dead already. They settled at a table by the far wall, and the servant disappeared.

Constance glanced around again. Some of the other diners were human, some weren't. She could smell werewolf.

Her attention settled on Mac. His hair was freshly trimmed. Every other female was turning to stare at him, and so they should. He was good to look at but, more than that, he had a dark, electric presence that turned heads.

And his gaze was on her, his eyes both hungry and soft. His expression promised, well, everything. Constance was eager to see where that slight curve of his lips might lead.

Another servant arrived and asked about wine. Mac gave his order and turned back to her, his focus like a physical weight.

They had barely spoken a word. It was as if they were both tongue-tied, talking only with glances and the occasional squeeze of the hand. None of the magazine articles—not even the new, modern magazines—had made a date sound this good. None of those silly writers had ever been with Mac—though they had invaluable advice about many things, like how to shave her legs. It was a good thing she healed fast.

The man came back with the wine. At the end of the ritual of tasting and label reading, he poured some into Constance's glass and left. She looked at the straw-colored liquid doubtfully.

"Can I drink that?" she whispered.

"Vampires seem to like a little bit of wine," Mac said. "I wouldn't drink too much all at once."

She tried it. It tasted odd, but then, she'd only ever drunk ale. Of course, after a few hundred years of nothing to eat or drink, her memory might be off.

"There are humans eating with nonhumans," she said in an undertone. "Is that usual?"

Mac picked a stick of bread out of a napkin-covered basket. "Here it is. Some humans like to be near supernaturals. Some don't. Some think it's, uh, trendy. Kind of a walk on the wild side."

"Wild side? What do they think will happen?"

"Who knows? Most of the supernaturals here just want to get on with their lives."

Constance took another glance around, amazed at the number of nonhumans casually chatting over their meals. She could run away from the Castle. She could find work and make a life for herself.

The possibilities, and perhaps the unfamiliar wine, were making her giddy. Licking her lips, she tasted the perfumed flavor of her lipstick. Mac's gifts had included a tiny pot of bright red gloss. Blood red. Another detail that made her feel wanton and just a little bit dangerous. Had that been Mac's idea?

She smiled at Mac, who was systematically demolishing the bread. "Tell me about this lady friend who helped you find my clothes."

"Holly is a good friend. She enchanted your new clothes so that they would be sure to fit, and then she enchanted my old clothes so that I could still wear them. A practical woman."

"She's a sorceress?"

"A witch." Mac smiled back. "And she's very much in love with a vampire."

"Oh." That made Constance feel much better, both because Holly was spoken for—and also that vampires were loved.

"Say," Mac said, sliding his thumb over the back of her hand. The gesture of gentle possession sent a thrill to her core. "We need to pick which movie to go to. What kind do you want to see?"

Constance felt a wave of confusion. She'd read about movies and knew they were a pleasurable entertainment, but only had a tenuous understanding of what they actually involved. She grabbed at the only title she could remember. "I want to see *Gone with the Wind*."

Mac's face went carefully blank. "I think that one might have left town already. We can rent it later, but let's try for something else tonight."

"Perhaps we should see something you like," she suggested, hoping to appear gracious rather than hopelessly out of touch.

"Hmm, well, there are what they call girl movies and

boy movies. If we went to something I picked, you probably wouldn't like it."

Constance let herself be distracted by one of the servants setting a dish of food alight. "Now why would they burn their food like that? Didn't they leave the meat on the spit long enough?" She turned back to Mac. He looked like he was trying not to laugh, which irritated her. "What do you mean, I wouldn't like your choice? Why wouldn't I like what you like?"

"I could be wrong. I look forward to sitting with you over a long, relaxing evening and finding out. But first, maybe we should try for a romantic comedy."

"Which is what?"

"Something funny with a happy ending."

Constance was mollified. "I think I'd like that."

"See? I know something about these things."

"What's to say I wouldn't like something weighty and serious?"

"You probably would, but then I'd fall asleep. I'm not good with that sort of film."

"Not even to improve your soul?"

"My soul is warped beyond what a movie can fix."

"I believe it. The last book you brought me has things in it my mother wouldn't approve of."

"Do you disapprove?" He gave her a quick grin.

Constance struggled not to smile. "I don't know. I'd have to try them out before I could make up my mind. You're corrupting me, Conall Macmillan."

"I am a demon."

"That's no excuse not to live right."

The servant sailed by, took Mac's food order, and refilled their glasses. It seemed like a good signal to change the subject. Constance asked questions about the food she saw pass by, the clothes of the other patrons, the buildings on the street outside, and anything else that caught her eye. Mac answered each one so patiently she began to feel sorry for him. She worked the subject around to a topic he might find more interesting.

"Did you find anything out from Atreus?" Constance had eventually heard about Mac's rescue of the woman named Ashe, but he hadn't said much more than that.

Mac shook his head, putting one hand over hers again, slowly caressing it with his thumb. The feel of it sent shivers all the way up her shamefully bare arm. "I wasn't sure what was real."

"What did he say?"

Constance leaned closer to the table, careful to keep her shoulders back. The dress, with so little fabric to keep it in place, kept inching toward full disclosure. Mac's gaze slid toward the fall of black silk over her breasts, as if will alone could nudge it aside. She glimpsed the hot, red glitter in his eyes that seemed to surface when Mac was aroused. The demon was stirring just below his skin, bringing an almost scalding heat to his hand.

She tingled with the anticipation of what might come later that night.

"What do you know about the Avatar?" he asked.

"Ah," she said. "I know some of the story."

"Tell me."

Mac's food came, forcing their hands apart. The rich smell steaming off Mac's plate made her vampire stomach queasy. As she sat back, he selected a knife and fork from the vast array spread across the table and began eating. Constance was relieved she didn't have to cope with picking the right silverware—that would surely show how much of a peasant she truly was.

She turned her mind to Mac's question. "There may be truth and lies mixed together."

"Just tell me what you know." The look he gave her came from another side of him—direct, precise, and unrelenting—that had nothing to do with dresses and dates.

She cleared her throat. "The Avatar belonged to the Castle. She was its spirit. She made the wind and the sun and the forests."

"Not the prison for monsters we have now?"

"Yes and no. The version of the story I know is this: Once

upon a time, nine sorcerer kings decided they should be the only ones to have magical powers. So with a mighty spell they made a prison for all the other supernatural beings and called it the Castle. Then the common people began to distrust the sorcerers and no longer wanted them to rule their lands. After a long battle, the sorcerers retreated into the Castle. But now, because it was their new home, they created the Avatar to make sun and wind and forests, and she turned the Castle into a beautiful haven."

Mac cut into his steak. Pink juice pooled around the cut. "So originally it was nice?"

Constance's eyes were drawn to the juice. The bones behind her eye teeth began to hurt, aching to bite. She drank more wine, denying a sudden stab of worry. *He'll be through with the meat soon, and then it will be all right.* "Yes, but the magic of the Avatar failed long ago and the Castle became what you see now."

"Why did it fail?"

"Atreus used his sorcery to turn the Avatar into a living woman. It took hundreds and hundreds of years, but as he did, her power over the Castle faded. All her magic went to flesh and blood, and the Castle gradually became the dungeon you see now."

His fork drooped in his hand. "So you knew this all along? Why didn't you say anything?"

Constance felt the tiniest stab of irritation. "You never asked about it. I had no idea you wanted to know."

But he was already onto the next point. "Atreus said he killed the Avatar. He said she was the mother of his child."

Constance took a quick breath of surprise. "A child? I hadn't heard that. As to killing her—everyone thinks she simply died! Legend has it he kept her in the Summer Room. That's why it's special."

"She lived in the Summer Room? Do you think that's true?"

"I don't know. I only first found it a little while ago. It's all but forgotten."

Mac took a bite, chewed. "I wonder why he killed her. If he did it. Or when."

Nausea bumped at her stomach. "Who knows? Nobody can remember ever seeing her. Or maybe he's making it up. He's mad."

Mac stopped, his fork raised halfway to his mouth. "I'm sorry. This is lousy dinner conversation."

She turned the salt shaker around in her hand, trying not to look at the bloody steak. "Don't apologize. You like solving puzzles. I do, too."

He put his fork down, reached across the table, and squeezed her fingers. His touch was hot, making the skin over her entire body flare with interest. "Thank you."

That made her smile. "I think the reason men and women date is all about anticipation."

His smile was very male. "I'll skip dessert."

"Don't you want the anticipation to last?"

"I'm only human." A confused look came over his face. "Or not."

She grinned. "Come now, love is like a ballad. It has to have plenty of verses."

"Oh, no you don't. I know those old Celtic songs. Everyone always dies horribly at the end, usually at a wedding feast. I'll have no part of those."

Connie pouted. "But the dance tunes always come after."

"Celts. A bunch of manic-depressive maniacs with bagpipes."

"That's unkind."

He cocked an eyebrow. "That's my relations. I'm descended from sheep thieves who backed the wrong king."

Constance looked down. "My family—we just were. We had no land of our own."

"Hardly anybody does anymore."

She met his eyes. They looked soft, and a little amused. "Why not?"

"It's different now. There's lots of ways to make a living

besides farming. Anyone can go to school, men or women. That means you, if you wanted to."

"But Atreus taught me to read and write."

"That's just opening the door. There's an entire world over that threshold."

The statement should have been electrifying, but Constance barely heard it. She was dizzy with wonderment and wine—and something else. The bones behind her teeth ached, jagged stabs of pain where her venom was supposed to be stored. *This doesn't feel right.* Common sense said she should go back to the Castle immediately, but she was damned if she was going to end this evening now. It had barely begun. She raised her eyes to see Mac giving her a curious look.

She used a line she'd read in one of the magazines. "Excuse me, I need to freshen up."

Picking up her tiny black clutch, she made her way toward the ladies' room, careful of her high heels.

Moving helped. So did getting away from the smell of Mac's dinner. There was enough beef on his plate to feed a family for a week. Who knew even a demon could eat that much!

Mac was so different. He wasn't a lord's son or a farmer. He was nothing like the vampire who had tried to Turn her. That one had been an English soldier, or at least someone who wore a soldier's uniform. Lieutenant Clarendon. He'd given her pretty gifts—a silver thimble, a wooden case for her needles—until she'd agreed to meet him by the brook one moonlit night.

Constance found the door with the outline of a woman stenciled on it. She pushed it open.

Looking back, she wondered how long Clarendon had been a vampire himself. He'd been charming, but not like any of the older vampires she'd come across in the Castle. To think she'd been caught by a fledgling. It was all rather embarrassing now.

She set her handbag on the counter and stared at the sink. She wanted to cool herself off with water, but now she was flummoxed. There were traces of water in the sink, but no sign of where it had come from.

Irritability swamped her. She clenched her fists, sharp nails digging into her palms. The pain felt good, like an itch scratched.

Taps. Faucet. She'd seen pictures. Constance grabbed the tap and wrenched it, water gushing in a sudden spray. It splashed her dress.

"Damn!" She wrenched it off just as quickly. She looked back at herself from the mirror, ethereally pale. Her eyes were too dark, her lips too red. *Death.*

The door swung open, another woman walking in. The blonde wore a suit of champagne silk. Long hair piled on top of her head, ringlets falling at her temples. She smelled of iris and thick human blood. Mac's scent had tempted her, but this aroma was almost unbearably delicious.

Constance started to tremble, suddenly very, very hungry. *Oh, no!*

"Are you all right?" the woman asked. "Oh, look, you're all wet."

She grabbed a fluffy hand towel out of the basket on the counter and held it out to Constance. Constance took it, careful not to touch her. "Thank you. I had an accident with the tap," she said softly.

"It'll dry," the woman said cheerily, pulling out a tube of lipstick and leaning into the mirror. She'd been drinking. The lipstick application wasn't going well.

Constance looked down at herself, numbly blotting at the water stains. Strength ebbed from her limbs, leaving a strange rubbery sensation behind. The towel slipped from her fingers, dropping on her toes. Her mind was fading to a white haze, forgetting everything. Her name. Her will. Everything but the imperative to survive.

"Oh, dear. Let me." The woman bent to rescue the towel.

Constance pounced, wrenching the woman's head aside just as she started to rise, towel in hand. It happened so fast, even Constance had trouble following the speed of her own movements. The woman tried to wrench away, but that excited the hunter inside Constance. She snatched her tight with the quick efficiency of a mouser.

Somewhere deep down beneath the white haze, Constance was horrified, but couldn't do a thing about what her body was doing. She licked the skin just beneath the woman's ear, tracing the clean arch of her jaw and down the warm hollow where the pulse beat like the frantic flight of a bird. There was a gagging taste of perfumed lotion, beneath that a burst of hot, salty, succulent human. The taste flirted with Constance's tongue like nothing else—it was better than the wine. Better than cool water on a hot, dusty day. It was life itself, dark and earthy.

An odd, almost painful pressure in her sinuses told Constance her fangs ached to release their venom—but there was nothing to come. No poison waited, ready to give ecstasy. She wasn't a full vampire. Not yet.

The woman whimpered, dread freezing her, making her pliant from sheer terror. She raised a hand to Constance's hair, her fight for freedom now no more than a pleading embrace.

The dance of death.

Constance felt her meal's pulse speed under her lips, quick and fast, titillating the dark hole gnawing in Constance's gut. This one woman wouldn't fill that hole. There would have to be others.

The woman was whimpering. "Please, please, please," over and over, her voice that of a frightened child.

Mother of God, what am I doing?

At some point, they'd sunk to the cold tile, a dizzying pattern of black and white hexagons. Constance closed her eyes. She wanted to throw up, retch, tear herself away, but she clung to her victim. Survival instinct had taken over, her body doing what it had to over her mind's objections.

Her teeth pressed into the woman's neck, denting the skin, but she couldn't find the courage to drive them home. She didn't want to cause pain. Or tear. She wanted to be neat, as if in some crazy way that would make things all right.

The woman was crying. Her hand lay limp against the stark tiles, graceful in defeat.

Constance started to cry, too, every bit as frightened.

I can't stop. I can't do it.

The woman writhed, a sudden buck against Constance's grip. She bit down, a predator gripping its struggling prey. Red splattered the floor.

Holy mother! Blood welled into her mouth, a surprising, hot burst.

Constance shuddered, her body close to a swoon as centuries of denial suddenly ended. She had been starving and had not even known it.

She heard the door open, almost physically felt the intruder's shock. The newcomer's scream sawed through her, giving Constance the impetus to raise her head. She snarled, baring her fangs, jealous of her prey.

"Vampire!" the intruding woman screamed just before she scrambled away.

I've finally done it. I'm the real thing now.

Cold fear—of herself, of the humans who would come after her—drove Constance to her feet.

Chapter 21

Mac saw Connie shoot out of the washroom at warp speed, glasses and flowers flying from the tables as she dashed for the door. "Vampire attack!" someone screamed. "Somebody call an ambulance!"

Oh, shit. Connie was running for her life. She had slipped.

He had broken his promise to make sure she wouldn't get into trouble.

But she'd seemed okay.

Mac was after her in an instant, vaulting over the half wall that blocked his table from a clear path to the exit. There were a couple of others running, too, including one of the werewolf diners. There was always rough justice for a rogue vamp. Mac couldn't let that happen.

Time to cheat. Mac dusted, materializing ahead of Connie. She ran straight into him, knocking them both to the pavement. The light fabric of his dress slacks did nothing to buffer the smack of the gritty road.

"Let me go!" she snarled, her blood-smeared face contorted with pain. "I need to get away!"

She tried to stand, but fell to her hands and knees and curled up, her forehead touching the ruined skirt of her dress.

Mac took her by the shoulders, feeling her body tremble. He couldn't tell if she was sick or in shock, and there was no time to figure it out. One of the werewolves had changed and was bolting ahead of the others, still in his necktie and howling for blood.

Shit! Mac grabbed Connie and dusted.

It was one thing to carry someone out of the Castle. It was another to take a passenger any distance. He made it as far as he could, a churchyard about eight blocks east, and materialized on one of the iron park benches. The cold metal felt good, like a makeshift ice pack. Everything ached as if he'd run a marathon.

Connie was dead weight, her strength utterly gone. She slumped over, resting her head on his knees, skin cold and clammy. Vampires had a lower body temperature, but this felt like she'd been refrigerated. Mac stripped off his jacket and draped it over her, wondering whether she could even feel the cold at this point. Her eyelids flickered open. Even in the darkness, he could see they were clouded.

"Connie," he said, bending to her ear. Her old-fashioned perfume wafted up to him, mixing with the scent of blood and shampoo. She didn't respond. She didn't even blink.

Mac's stomach turned to a cold, hard lump. Something had gone wrong. He'd seen death before. It looked a lot like this. *No, no, no!*

"Connie?"

He had no idea how to help her. Hot, impotent anger flared. He wanted to shake her. He wanted to smack himself for not watching her every second.

There was no emergency room that would deal with a Turning vampire, healthy or sick. He needed another vamp—one he could trust. Mac flipped open his cell phone and dialed Holly's house, praying Caravelli was home.

One thing went right that night. The T-Bird screeched to a halt in front of the church ten minutes later. Mac heard the door slam and Caravelli ran into view. The vampire was muttering something in Italian—a prayer or a curse, Mac couldn't tell.

The vampire paused long enough to take in Mac's altered form, and then bent over Connie. He carefully turned her face so that he could look at her.

"She's unconscious," Mac said.

Caravelli felt her skin, lifted one eyelid, looked at her teeth. "She's barely Turned. Whoever made her knew nothing."

"What does she need?" Mac demanded, cradling her head with one hand. "Whatever it is, I'll get it."

Caravelli looked at him for a long moment. "You realize she's harmed an innocent."

Don't you dare! But Caravelli did dare. It was his job to keep the monsters in line.

Mac swore. "It was my fault. She tried to tell me. I didn't listen and took her out of the Castle, anyway."

"What the hell were you thinking?"

"I didn't know. I didn't understand. I thought I could handle anything that came up."

Caravelli swore again, using words Mac didn't know. But the vampire's tone said it all.

Mac smoothed back her hair. It had fallen out of its pins and was strewn across his lap like swatches of dark silk. His skin was growing hot, the demon inside him suffering as much as the man. "Do something, for God's sake!"

A beat passed. Something in Caravelli's posture softened. "All right. She needs strong blood. Vampire blood. Her first sire wasn't old enough."

"What does that mean?"

"Not enough power to successfully Turn her, for one thing." Caravelli was stripping off his leather jacket. He wore a faded Grateful Dead T-shirt underneath. "Making a vampire isn't easy, but some idiot always thinks he can do it on the sly."

"And if an amateur job goes wrong?"

"If they're both lucky, the victim dies." He nodded at Connie. "From what you said to Holly, the guardsmen took your girl straight to the Castle as soon as she rose. That's what kept her functioning all these years. The magic of the place acted like life support."

"And I put her in danger," Mac said bitterly.

Caravelli made a rude noise. "She should have known better than to date a demon. Sit her up."

Mac did. The vampire pulled a boot knife. Mac tensed.

"Relax. It's for me," Caravelli said with a flicker of a smile. "I get the fun part."

With a grimace, he slashed a six-inch gash on the inside of his left forearm. Sluggish blood welled up, thicker than a human's. He held the wound under Connie's nose. It revived her as quickly as old-fashioned smelling salts.

Caravelli fell to one knee before her, guiding her head to the open vein. "Drink," he said, sounding suspiciously like the cape-swishing villain of a bad movie.

Constance gripped Mac's knee, her long fingernails digging into his flesh. He could see her neck muscles straining, the impulse to drink, and not drink, equally strong.

"Vampires don't taste like humans," Caravelli explained. "We're not normally food for each other."

Mac took her hand, prying it loose so he could hold it. "Go ahead. Do it. It's okay."

She made a noise of disgusted protest, but obeyed. After a moment, she pulled her hand away so that she could grip Caravelli's arm to her lips. He jerked in pain as she bit down.

Mac felt relieved, but unsettled. Bad enough he let her fall into this mess. The fact that he couldn't help her was worse—not even with his blood.

"I called the hospital on the way here," Caravelli said quietly. "The victim was more frightened than injured. I doubt there will be repercussions from the humans."

"Venom?" Mac asked automatically.

"No."

It was the first thing a cop who handles supernatural crimes asked. Presence of venom in the bloodstream was the legal standard for proof of a vampire attack. Caravelli was right. Without that, there wasn't much a victim could do.

"Constance is lucky," the vampire said darkly.

"That won't do her much good if she . . ." Mac trailed off, anger and frustration choking him.

"She'll be all right, but you need to go," said Caravelli, wincing as she lapped and worried at his wound.

Really not a sight Mac had imagined as a first-date memory. "But . . ."

"I'll take her home." Caravelli fixed him with his amber eyes. They flashed in the distant light of a passing car, setting the hairs on Mac's neck on end. "She's not herself right now. She won't be until she sleeps this off and feeds again. There's no point in seeing her like this. She won't thank you for it."

"My place is with her."

"Trust me. I'll make sure she gets what she needs."

Mac knew what he meant. More blood. Human blood—this time from a willing donor.

"Come to our house late tomorrow night. She'll be ready to see you by then."

Mac nodded, feeling awkward. Every cell in his body wanted to keep her for his own, to push Caravelli aside and drag her away. *Yeah, that would be really useful. Grow up, demon boy.*

Caravelli stroked Constance's head with a fatherly gesture. Mac stifled a possessive growl.

"It's all right, Macmillan. She'll be safe with me."

Mac sighed inwardly. *Take a girl out, and she ends up drinking some other guy's blood.* The important thing was that she had the help she needed. This wasn't about his needs.

He still wanted to throw a tantrum. He'd given Constance a dress. Caravelli was giving her life.

Real life makes more life, Atreus had said. *My creations can only hold the limited strength of my sorcery.*

And then, like random lightning, what Connie had said struck him: Atreus had made a woman from the Castle's Avatar, robbing its magic.

Mac had heard Atreus claim to have killed her. The sorcerer also said that the Castle had been crumbling for sixteen years. Atreus had taken in a foundling sixteen years ago.

Holy bat-boy! Sylvius was the Avatar's child. Atreus hadn't killed her—she'd died in childbirth. *My creations can only hold the limited strength of my sorcery.* Once the baby was born, there was no life left for her.

The Castle was failing because Sylvius lived.

What does that mean?

It meant he finally had an insight into the whole insane Castle puzzle. It had taken the sight of Caravelli doing the vampire sire biz—giving some of his Undead life to save Connie—to make the connection. Like it or not, Mac had work to do.

Feeling dismal, Mac got up, touching Connie's shoulder. "I'll see you tomorrow."

Caravelli nodded, but didn't reply. Connie didn't respond at all.

Mac had barely gone a dozen paces before he looked back to see the two vampires huddled together in the small, urban graveyard. The headstones were a wash of grays under the streetlights, graffiti like sprawling spiderwebs across the granite humps.

He turned away, walked a little. He passed one that read: LOVE SUX!

Got that one right.

Chapter 22

October 9, 7:00 p.m.
101.5 FM

"**G**ood evening to all you children of the night out
there in radio land. This is Errata, your hostess
from CSUP, the FM station that *denies* and *defies* the normal in paranormal. Tonight our special guest is Dr. Gaylen
Hooper, Executive Director of Harvest House, a transi-
tional facility for those who have, for one reason or another, moved from one species to another."

"Good evening, Errata."

"Now, Dr. Hooper, there are those who insist that transi-
tioning is impossible and that denying your original form is
at best wishful thinking and at worst an immoral act. How
do you respond to that?"

"You mean those people who say that if you really, really
try hard, you'll suck in those fangs and go back to being a
good little human?"

"Why, Dr. Hooper, don't you buy into the power of positive thinking?"

Mac eyed the big purple and yellow Victorian with a cautious eye. *The last time I was here, the house sucked me out*

like a spider up a vacuum cleaner hose. Then the garden tried to kill me. Of course, I was trying to eat Holly's soul at the time.

He wondered whether the house would notice—or care—that he wasn't a soul eater anymore. He was still a demon.

Mac unfolded himself from his car, an old black two-door Mustang he'd finally gotten back on the road that afternoon. He reached into the backseat, picked up the bouquet of roses and carnations he'd brought, then slammed the door, enjoying its solid sound. He'd missed his car.

He climbed the stairs to the porch and rang the bell. His shoulders hunched, feeling the house watching him.

Caravelli answered. "Come in."

Mac stepped over the threshold. The door closed behind him of its own accord. He had an irrational urge to shoot it.

"It took me a long time to get used to that," Caravelli said.

It was the first time since Mac had gotten back to Fairview that he'd seen Caravelli in decent lighting. For a vampire, he looked pretty healthy these days—more pale than pasty. He also seemed to be doing more breathing than most vamps. *Interesting.*

He'd heard about Holly putting some magical whammy on him, bringing to life the legend of the Chosen that gave a vampire the power to exist on sexual energy rather than blood. *Forced to have sex on a regular basis. Doctor's orders. Lucky bastard.* "How's Connie doing?"

Caravelli waved him into the living room. "She's well. Holly is with her."

"Isn't that risky? For Holly, I mean?"

"Holly has enough magic to control a newly made fledgling. Sit down a moment." He caught Mac's expression. "This won't take long."

Mac complied, setting his flowers on the coffee table. The living room was old-fashioned, with shelves of books reaching the ceiling and dark brass floor lamps with silk shades. "What's up?"

"Lore came to see me. He told me why the hellhounds have been so lax about their duties. I could have broken his neck for not speaking to me sooner, but I understand his motivation."

Mac smirked. "You tore him a new one?"

"Only verbally. Once I ran out of breath, he asked for my help with the council as coolly as if I'd been giving a weather report. He said he also asked you."

"He did. I think we—you—need to convene a council meeting. I'll be there to speak for him."

Caravelli leaned back, stretching out his long legs. "Gathering the leaders is something I would only do in a dire emergency. I wonder if there's an easier way to address this."

"It's not just the hellhounds we have to worry about. The Castle as a whole is failing." Mac told him what he had found out about the Avatar and Sylvius.

"Sylvius," Caravelli mused. "The name fits for a creature born from the natural world of the Castle. The same root word as 'sylvan'—something that comes from the woods."

"An incubus born of a love slave. Sounds like soft porn."

Caravelli snorted. "Sounds perverted. We all want to possess our lovers, but it's quite another thing to actually force one into being and then lock her up."

Mac sat forward. "There's more. I talked to Lore after I left you last night. He's been trying to tell me all about this hellhound prophecy for days. He took me to one of their elders."

"Really? Nobody speaks to them."

"Well, he talked to Lore and Lore talked to me."

"What did he say?"

"They think I have something to do with this prophecy. Mumbo-jumbo aside, here's the facts. There's a ritual to return the blood of the Avatar to the Castle. The guardsmen have somehow put their hands on the instructions."

"What does returning the blood to the Castle involve?"

"Sacrifice." Mac went stone cold as he said it. "Of the Avatar's son."

Caravelli looked stunned. "*What?* Is that what the guardsmen really wanted with Sylvius in the first place?"

"I think that's what Bran and his supporters want. Others simply want a hit of incubus blood. They've been there so long they don't care if the Castle falls down."

"And the prophecy?"

"The Castle made me a demon so that I can put everything back to the way it was before Atreus started messing around."

The vampire's face was growing more and more drawn. "Do you think that's true?"

"It doesn't matter what I think or how I feel. People are going to die if the prison collapses."

"Where does that leave the boy?"

"I know. Kill Sylvius, or let the Castle fall."

Caravelli was silent a moment. "*Merda.*"

Mac grimaced. "I'm not killing the kid."

The vampire lifted a brow. "I'd say that was a given."

"I tried talking him into leaving—I mean, I had to tell him. He had a right to know. But he won't budge. He's afraid if he goes, the Castle goes."

"Is that so bad? How many residents could we rescue?"

"Even if we rescued every last hellhound, thousands of people live in there, and most of them aren't safe to let out."

Caravelli sighed. "Yes, it's time we gathered the council."

Mac felt a sudden pang of doubt. "They never agree on anything. Think a big old group hug will work?"

"We'll find out." Caravelli stood. "I still have Queen Omara's ear, and the fact I have a fledgling—that there is now a Clan Caravelli—will help my standing among the Undead."

Inside Mac, the demon stirred, his skin flaring with heat. "What does being part of your clan mean for Connie?" *She's mine. You can't have her.*

Caravelli gave a smile calculated to turn even a demon's blood to ice. "Everything, but I have no intention of choosing her lovers. She's a woman, not a child. Nevertheless, I'm here to help her, and I'll break your neck if you hurt her. I am her kin now."

The warning hung like smoke in the air. Mac bared his teeth. *In-laws. Great.* "I want to see her. Now."

With a half smile, Caravelli stepped back and made a graceful sweep with his arm. "She's in one of the guest rooms upstairs. Follow me."

He did, his bouquet in hand. They passed through the messy kitchen—Mac remembered once cooking a meal for Holly there—and crossed to the large curved stairway that wound to the upper floors.

Caravelli turned. "You understand she was not a true vampire before."

"Yes." *But I'm not sure what you're getting at.*

"Good." Caravelli started up the oak steps, his feet noiseless on the patterned runner that carpeted the stairs.

They passed the second floor, going all the way up to the third. A stained glass window looked out from the landing, the colors dark against the night sky beyond. They walked down the hall, dark wainscoting emphasizing the gloom. The only light was the faint glow from a couple of wall sconces made to look like candles. Everything in the old house looked straight out of a Victorian novel, down to a landscape painting of what looked to Mac like hairy cows standing in a marsh.

It was a long hallway and most of the heavy paneled doors were shut, adding to the claustrophobic feel. Mac wanted to bolt for bright lights and freedom. "It's kind of dark."

Caravelli gave him an amused glance. "New vampires are particularly sensitive to noise and light. It was more comfortable for her to rest up here, where there's little commotion."

They stopped at the end of the hallway. Alessandro tapped lightly on the last door to the left. After a moment, it opened and Holly stepped out. "Hi."

She had a notebook under her arm. Studying again, Mac supposed. He looked past her, catching a glimpse of more wainscoting and pale flowered wallpaper. There was a bed in the room, covered with a white spread. Connie sat on the edge, her back to the doorway.

"How's it going?" he asked.

"Not bad, I guess." Holly smiled at Mac. "I'm glad you came. The flowers are a nice touch."

"The least I can do."

Holly turned to her lover. "Look, I'm going up to the hospital. They're going to be releasing Ashe tomorrow, and I want to make sure she has everything she needs. She insists on staying at the motel."

Much to everyone's relief, I'll bet. Still, Mac was glad to hear she was recovering.

Caravelli ran the back of his fingers down Holly's arm. "So she's capable of common sense, at least."

Holly made a resigned face and headed for the stairs

Caravelli followed. "If you need me, I'll be in the living room."

"Sure," said Mac. He had flowers, a car, and the vampire dad's permission. For a demon, he felt very teenaged all of a sudden. He walked into the bedroom.

Warm, dry air tickled his throat. The old, ornate radiator must have been cranked on high. The overhead light was off, only a couple of hobnail glass lamps switched on low. Constance turned, and Mac nearly dropped the bouquet. He could just see her profile, the long, dark hair tucked behind one ear, but it was enough to see how much she had changed. She had been pale before, but now the luminous pallor of the Undead showed off her dramatic coloring.

"Hello," he said.

Her beauty reminded Mac of the diamonds of ice that sparkled from the crust of hard, northern snow. *From Snow White to the Snow Queen.* Here was a whole new challenge. He felt his skin growing hot with arousal.

"Mac." She rose, and turned to face him.

She wore a dark sweater and broomstick skirt, probably

Holly's. Mac looked into her eyes. They were still blue, but now they held an unsettling silvery cast. Vampire eyes were like that, flashing silver or gold as the light caught them. The only thing human about her was her expression. It was filled with guilt.

"I'm sorry," she said. "I'm so sorry. I thought I could hold myself back."

Mac handed her the flowers. She cradled them, like one would a baby, bending her head to sniff the blooms. Her hair fell, hiding her face.

"It's all right," he replied. "I'm sorry, too."

She set the flowers aside on the top of an antique dresser. They looked at each other for a long moment, not sure what to say.

"How do you feel?" he asked.

The skin around her eyes contracted. "Hungry. Always hungry. Alessandro says it gets much easier in time."

God, she's so beautiful. His palms were starting to sweat. "First dates are always kind of awkward. If you survive that one, the next is always better."

She gave a slight smile. Her fangs were more pronounced than before, but still slender. Feminine. Lowering her lashes, she tilted her face to the side. Then something in her face changed, a new emotion spreading over her features like a drop of ink bleeding through water.

It was anger.

"You promised you would keep me from hurting someone. You said everything would be all right." Her voice was hoarse, and he heard grief in it.

The words speared him so hard, his chest actually hurt. "I know I did, Connie. I know."

He clenched his fists, wishing guilt was something he could wrestle with, use his huge strength to crush. "I screwed up. I'm so sorry. I didn't understand the risk we were taking. I don't know as much about vampires as I thought I did. And that cost you."

"You were supposed to protect me." She covered her

mouth with her hand, as if to stop herself from saying anything more.

The sight of that gesture was painful, because he understood. Gently, slowly, Mac took her hand in his, moving it away from her face. "Speak out if you want to. I deserve that anger."

She hiccupped, swallowing down unshed tears. Her mouth twitched, fighting to keep from crumpling. "What would you have me do? Swear at you? Tear out your eyes?"

"You have that right."

She turned her face away, obviously embarrassed, but he took her shoulders, turning her body to face his. He lifted her chin until she looked at him. "I'd draw the line at the clawing out the eyes thing, but if it'll help you forgive me, you can do the rest. I'm not your lord and master. Go ahead and kick my ass if it needs it. You're a vamp now. You could make it hurt."

She almost laughed, but it came out in another hiccup. "You really didn't know what would happen?" she asked in a small voice.

"Not like that. I made a mistake. I hope you'll forgive me."

She seemed to deflate, all the anger leaking away.

"Forgive you?" She looked up at him, her silvery blue eyes wild with sorrow. "I wouldn't have blamed you if you'd stayed away. . . . I've become a true monster."

He drew her nearer. Perfectly still, she stayed coiled and tense as he put his hands on her shoulders. "You're mine," he said simply. "As in the woman I adore. I'm not going anywhere, if you'll have me."

As if the weight of his hands was too much, she sank onto the edge of the bed, never taking her eyes from his face. Mac sat down next to her. The old double mattress sagged under his weight.

"I'm cold all the time now," she said, hugging herself. "Worse than before. I feel like I've been back in my grave."

He put his arm around her, holding her close, wrapping her in his demon heat. She burrowed her face against his chest as if she could somehow merge their bodies.

"It's not enough," she said.

He pulled off his sports jacket and folded it around her, the heavy wool engulfing her tiny frame. She shivered in his arms, winding her arms around his neck. "I want to lie with you. I want you, Mac. It's as bad as the hunger."

"Um, no red-blooded man says no, but this isn't our house."

"I don't care," she said, her voice a hoarse whisper. "It's the only thing that's going to make me warm."

Putting words to actions, she shrugged off the jacket and pulled away from him, dragging the long-sleeved sweater over her head. Her hair swished around her shoulders, draping over the lacey mounds of her bra. She still wore the same one Mac had bought for her. That he had wanted so much to see her in last night. *Oh, yeah.*

Forget better judgment. He pulled off his turtleneck and pulled her down on the bed to lie against his chest, cradling her against him. She smelled of fancy soap—something fruity.

For a moment, Connie lay quiet. He let his hands wander up her back, feeling the delicate ridges of her backbone, her ribs, the dip in the small of her back. Her hair fell like a dark cloak around them, silky and private. She kissed his jaw, her soft lips working against the harsh stubble of his chin. Aroused, Mac felt his body temperature spike again, his skin starting to prickle.

"That feels so good," she murmured, rubbing against him like a cat.

Cupping her breasts, he stroked her nipples, watching her eyes flutter closed, her lips part. He raised her perfect pink tips to a hard peak, watching them press against the fabric of her bra. As she hauled in a breath, rearing up, he bent his head to suckle her through the lace, the roughness adding an extra sensation for his tongue.

He tasted her cool skin, buried himself in it, breathed it

in like incense. Her hands raked through his hair, the razor sharpness of her nails alerting every nerve down his spine. Turning, he gave the other breast equal treatment, working until he heard a ragged gasp of pleasure.

Sliding down his body, Connie sought his mouth, drawing in his tongue, teasing his lips with her teeth. *She's changed*, he thought. More than her physical form had altered. Inhibitions had been stripped away, the ability to find and give pleasure brought to the fore.

Of course, that was how a vampire hunted. It ran in the blood Caravelli had fed her, part of the necessary DNA of the species. That was fine with Mac. No complaints on his end. Until she bit him, fangs sinking deep into the heavy muscle of his neck.

The white-hot sensation ripped through his body. He felt his own hot blood guttering in the hollow of his collarbone, the pressure as she bit even deeper, her fangs slicing into flesh.

Shit!

He was about to throw her off when he felt the cold tingle of venom, spreading like an ice cloud through his veins. *Oh, Lord.* The freezing sensation numbed him for a moment, extinguished the pain, then turned to a balmy warmth as it reached his belly.

"You're hot and spicy," she said, her pupils dilated to pools of black. "You make me warm inside."

She licked his chest, dragging her tongue over the swell of muscle, circling his nipple with butterfly flicks of her tongue.

He was lost. Euphoria rose like a tide, sexual desire flooding him with life-and-death urgency. Connie's hands were all over him, his all over her, clothes disappearing, his only objective to bury himself inside her.

Mac was harder than he'd ever been in his life. On fire. He thrust inside her, spearing her flesh as she had his. Her hips rose to meet him, a moan of pleasure escaping her. She was more than ready, slick and welcoming. Her legs hooked around him, holding him tight.

Mac's head swam, the conscious part of his brain buried in animal sensation. The venom drove him, burning through his demon-hot veins like whisky. He pushed harder and harder, plunging and withdrawing, sparing nothing. He was created for only one thing: the here and now. Possession.

Connie came first, the orgasm tearing a throaty cry from her. Her body clenched, pulsing around him, milking him. Her nails shredded his back, writing her claim into his skin. He hissed through his teeth. The feel of her digging in wound through him, a bloody thread piercing his wild desire. The sting of it brought him, a hard, convulsive explosion. Hot and wet, he poured into her, spending himself until he was nothing but a mindless shell.

He collapsed on his side, as exhausted as if his battery pack had suddenly been ripped out. Connie curled against him, hooking a leg over his hip. He was aware of her there, but he was somewhere outside of his body, perhaps a stunned dust mote in the Milky Way.

Wow.

The venom rambled through his body, turning what was left of his mind to boiled spaghetti. Or maybe that was his limbs.

"Mac?" Connie whispered.

Why do women always want to talk after sex?

"Mm?"

He felt her hand, cool and soft, on his cheek. "I didn't take much blood. It's not really food for me. But it was exciting."

This was a conversation he needed to be awake for. He forced his eyes open and took a deep breath. It forced back the venom haze a notch.

"I didn't know demons could be rolled by a vampire bite." He sounded drunk.

"It won't last," she said, her voice thick with apology. "It won't addict you. Alessandro said so."

You were discussing our sex life with him? Great.

"Forgive me."

"Hey, that was pretty fine," he managed a crooked smile. "It's all right?"

"Oh, yeah."

She blinked hard, her eyes filling with pinkish tears. "I can't help myself. Something takes over...."

"Hey. Hey." Mac raised himself on one elbow, drawing her to him. "You couldn't help it. You're just a newbie. Every vampire has to learn control. That's just the way it is."

"I could hurt someone when I bite. I *did* hurt someone, and yet I still want it so much. I didn't think it would be like this. So out of control."

He kissed her, remembering the terror of his own first days with Geneva. The memory made him hug Connie tighter. "Hey, with me, just let yourself go and enjoy it. We're consenting adults, demon and vamp. You can't really hurt me. No harm, no foul."

She wiped her eyes with the back of her hand. "Even if this happened to me unintentionally, I have to be honest—I wanted the power of the Undead. I wanted so much to be able to fight at least some of my own battles. But I had little idea of the price."

"You don't think it's worth it?"

She sank back onto her pillow, looking up at him. "You became a demon. You tell me."

He wanted to sugarcoat the answer, but he stopped himself. She needed the truth. "The first time I Turned, it was awful. This time wasn't so bad. I'm learning to live with it."

"Really?"

"I don't have a choice. I don't know how to go back to being human."

Connie stroked his arm, her fingers running over the curve of his biceps. "What about your people? Your friends? How did they take it?"

Mac hesitated. Another tough question.

"My letters came back unopened."

Connie put her hand to his cheek. "That's sad."

"Their loss. I'm still the same guy."

She was pensive. "Is that really true?"

He captured her hand, kissed her palm. "I've changed, but not as much as they think."

He angled his body to face her, putting all his reassurance into a kiss. Her lips were cool, soft, and sweet, but she seemed suddenly shy. He didn't push.

"What is it?"

"Mac, I . . ." She trailed off, looking away.

He was only half listening, fascinated by the long line of her throat.

"I can see your world is beautiful. There's so much to love in it, but I . . ."

He brought himself back to the conversation. "What?"

She covered her face with her hands. "Too much has changed too fast. I need something I know. I want to go home."

"It's dangerous in the Castle. I'd rather you and Sylvius and, yeah, Viktor, were out here."

"Give us some time."

"Why put yourselves in danger?"

"Oh, Mac, in there I won't feel like a monster. Here, I'm hungry all the time. Starving."

"You'll gain more control."

"But right now it's like a thousand voices shouting in my head, demanding and demanding. I'm not sure where I am inside myself. I feel like a bystander and all these appetites are ruling my soul. I gained strength in some ways, but I'm weaker in others. I bit you. Just now. And I liked it so much."

Mac felt for her, as if his heart spiraled into an abyss. "I know, sweetheart. I've been where you are. You get control by facing your hungers. You can't hide forever."

Her silver-blue eyes were sad. "I know. Please, please understand that after being frozen for so many years, I just need to take all this slowly. Come to me. Come to me often, but give me some time."

Sweetheart, I wish I could.

She squeezed his hand. "I have to do this, Mac. Don't rush me."

She gave him a stubborn look. He loved it, because he could see the steel underneath all her doubts. She was having a rough ride, but she was giving herself what she needed.

Too bad it wasn't in the cards. Mac had wanted to wait, to spare her what he knew, but his options had just run out. "Connie, I need to tell you what I found out about the Castle. And Sylvius."

He leaned over her, wrapping her fingers in his, and told her about Atreus, the Avatar, and the guardsmen's plan to murder her son.

Chapter 23

October 9, 10:00 p.m.
101.5 FM

"**E**arlier this evening, we had special guest Dr. Gaylen Hooper discussing the transition between species. But some supernatural talents are learned—and that's what we're going to talk about now. Please welcome our next guest, John Jameson of the Wizard's Guild. Hello, John."

"Hello, Errata, and a big wizarding hello to the folks at home."

"So, first of all, let's address the first FAQ I see listed on your Web site. What is the difference between a wizard and a sorcerer?"

"Well, first of all, let me say these are equal opportunity talents. Any species can be either a wizard or a sorcerer, although natural ability does play a role."

"How do you mean, John?"

"Some pupils are gifted, just the way some folks naturally take to playing the piano. But back to your original question, Errata. The big difference between wizardry and sorcery is that sorcerers rely on ritual and study. They're all about the big books and summoning demons. Wizards specialize in the mix of magic and technology—y'know, data magic. We've blown open the world of online gaming."

"No summoning demons?"

"Most of us live in apartments. There's the damage deposit to consider."

Mac could have stopped Connie from running back to the Castle. Alessandro could have stopped her. Or so they told themselves. After one look at her face, they both saw there was no point in trying.

Mac had heard that Turning ramped up a person's natural aggression. That was expressing itself in Connie's maternal instinct. Goodbye, milkmaid; hello, mama bear. He approved, even though his inner caveman was feeling a little more cautious.

They took the T-Bird to the Castle, parking in front of the Empire Hotel. Connie was fascinated with the car, and even more fascinated with how fast it could go. Mac could see a small fortune in speeding tickets somewhere in her future. He was going to be keeping a close eye on the keys to his Mustang.

Mac couldn't dust and carry two people with him, so they went through the door in the conventional fashion, the hellhounds looking on curiously but obeying Caravelli's order to let them pass.

After coming and going so many times without a problem, they forgot to be watchful.

"Patrol!" Connie whispered, her head whipping around.

Mac grabbed her shoulders, his gaze following hers. The flash of torchlight on a patch of armor gave the guardsman away.

"Go!" said Caravelli, leaping upward, clinging to the stones of the wall. Spider-swift, he crept upward, vanishing in the murk of darkness above.

Creepy.

Mac dusted, taking Connie with him.

That was too close.

As soon as he materialized in Connie's secret room,

adrenaline surged through Mac. He let Connie go, almost
pushing her away as demon heat bathed his limbs with a
blast of fright and anger. He felt the flush creep up his neck,
hotter than ever before.

The body-heat thing was getting out of control. Maybe
he would have to start carrying one of those little battery-
operated fans. *Bursting into a fireball would definitely be a
showstopper*.

But not this show. Mac was a bit-player in this scene. The
moment he released Connie, she flew across the room to
Sylvius. Viktor got to his feet with a *whuff*.

"You're safe!" she said, falling on to the sofa beside her
son.

"Of course I am." Sylvius stared at Connie, looking at
her curiously. Then nodded slowly. "You've done it. You've
changed. I wondered if you would."

"It was an accident." The words came out sheepishly.

"No, this was meant to be."

Viktor woofed again, this time turning to Mac and snuffling wetly at his jacket. The beast was enormous, as high as
Mac's chest, but something in him reminded him of his old
black lab, although the lab didn't smell as bad. He rubbed
Viktor's ears, anyway, earning a tail wag.

The simple act calmed Mac's demon. He felt his heart
slowing, his skin returning to its usual temperature. The
conversation on the sofa faded into the background.

Mac missed his old dog. As if reading his thoughts, Viktor slurped his face.

I don't miss that part.

There was a knock at the door. "Who is it?" Mac
demanded.

Viktor shuffled to the door, sniffing at the crack.

"Caravelli."

Mac shoulder-checked the beast out of the way and let
the vampire in, drawing back the heavy bolts that secured
the thick door and giving the word that released the wards
Lore had set.

"What the hell is that?" Caravelli asked, glancing at Viktor as he stepped inside. The werebeast was doing some sort of a doggy dance, rising up on his back feet every few steps.

"Viktor! Down!" Mac ordered.

Viktor bounced happily, ignoring him.

Mac gave a two-fingered whistle. Viktor froze. Mac pointed to the floor. Viktor lay down.

"Good boy," Mac said, patting the huge werebeast's head. It felt vaguely ridiculous. There was a person inside there somewhere.

"Now that we have the livestock under control," Caravelli said dryly, "there are some things I need to discuss with Constance since she's going to be away from her sire for the first time."

Viktor looked at the door and whined.

"He wants a walk," Sylvius said. "So do I."

Mac thought about the patrol and weighed the odds of any guardsmen showing up in this corner of the Castle, but Sylvius's expression said he needed to talk. "Come on then," Mac said. "We'll leave them to Vampires 101."

He had no intention of going far. Viktor could probably hold his own or at least run away, but the kid didn't look like a fighter. Plus, Connie would have his head if anything happened to her son.

Sylvius sighed when they closed the door to the room behind them. Viktor loped ahead, shaking a cloud of hair from his ragged coat.

"I can't stay shut up in there forever." Sylvius started walking, his head down. "I need freedom to fly."

"You could always leave. We'll find a place for Viktor. You could talk Connie into going outside the Castle, and then you'd all be safe."

"She won't go without me, will she?"

"No." Mac tried to keep the word neutral, not to lay the guilt on too thick. "This is all she knows. Everyone she loves is here. Including you. Especially you."

"Ah." Sylvius stopped and turned to look at Mac. "I wish I could make it easier instead of harder."

They'd reached the junction with the next corridor, the

limit of how far Mac intended to wander. The torchlight shone behind the incubus, showing the network of fine veins running through the skin of his wings. Mac studied him for a moment, taking in once more the long silver hair and black eyes. Behind all that strangeness was the face of a young man.

He focused on that, wishing for common ground. "If you don't leave, I'm not sure how else to help you."

Mac could make him leave. In fact, if Sylvius, Connie, and Viktor were still in the Castle by the time the council had met, he would be sorely tempted. But he didn't want to force the issue quite yet. He wanted it to be their choice.

Sylvius folded his arms, ducking his head. "If I'm what's left of the Avatar, I can't risk leaving. As I said before, what if I'm the last thing that's keeping the Castle standing? What if I walk out, and it all turns to dust?"

"I don't believe that. It sounds crazy."

"Crazy is Atreus making my mother out of sunbeams and then killing her."

"Your mother died giving birth to you," Mac said gently. "That's not the same thing."

"Guilt has made Atreus go mad. That's as good as a confession."

"Could the decline of the Castle be part of the reason he's sick?"

"No." Anger thickened Sylvius's voice. "Maybe. If it were just that, he'd never have confessed to you." He fell against the wall, turning his face into the stone. There were tears in his voice. "There were others who needed her, not just him. She was the sun and rain. It wasn't right for him to take her for himself. To make me. I shouldn't even exist."

"Bull," Mac said firmly, putting a hand on Sylvius's shoulder. He expected the kid to be upset, but his anguished voice raised the hair on Mac's neck. It wasn't supernatural. It was the pure intensity of a teenager. "And don't think you can restore the Avatar by dying. That's a load of crap."

Sylvius shook his head slowly, his eyes fixed on the flag-stones at his feet. "If I knew it to be a fact, I would cut my own throat and put things back the way they're supposed to be. I'd save the guardsmen the trouble."

Mac saw the dilemma written on Sylvius's face. Stay and risk death. Go and risk the death of everyone here. What the hell was he going to do with the kid? Sixteen was the age of school dances and hockey.

"Mac?"

"Yeah?"

"You'll figure this out, right?"

Constance had always loved the Summer Room.

There was just one problem.

Nothing here dampened her appetites, and now she was suffering, the blood hunger gnawing her from the inside out. She tried to ignore it as irrelevant. Sylvius was protected here. In her sight.

Constance paced, feeling the gauzy swish of Holly's cotton skirt around her calves. She liked the freedom of the modern clothing, but felt sorely underdressed. Her old petticoat had more substance. And warmth. She was freezing cold.

Her son was sprawled on the couch, reading a magazine. Viktor was asleep on his side, filling up the other side of the room. She was the only one suffering from nerves.

For hours, she had talked with Sylvius, turning over the subjects of his birth mother and what that meant. She had understood the overwhelmed expression in Mac's eyes as he kissed her and left with Alessandro to go call the council of Fairview's supernatural leaders. She felt much the same way.

She reached the end of her path and turned again, pacing back in the other direction. Anxiety tingled through her body to the point where she half expected to see sparks shooting from her skin.

Oblivious, Sylvius turned a page. He wasn't worried; he was convinced Mac would take care of everything. He didn't have a mother's imagination.

She was beginning to think Mac was right. They should all just leave the Castle. She would endure the full force of the bloodlust if only Sylvius would be out of danger. If the Castle collapsed as a result of removing the Avatar's son, she would be sorry, but her boy would still be safe. Whether it was right or wrong, he was her priority. She paused to watch her son reading, the perfect picture of sloth. For an illogical instant, she wanted to dump Sylvius off the couch, demand a reaction, and make him worry right along with her. She loved her son, but there were times when she could have throttled him. Some days, that incubus calm was too much.

Let this be over soon. She turned, pacing back the other way, wishing she were less energetic. At this rate, she would never grow tired enough to settle. *Would I have wanted this power if I knew how it felt?* Supernatural strength was an uncomfortable blessing.

Mac said he'd felt the same when he changed. What was it he'd said about Lore? And about Atreus? They'd told him he had a destiny, a mission? *He has a destiny, but Lore told me that if I reached for my power, I risked destroying the good that destiny would bring.*

What did that mean? Were those two halves of the same prophecy? That she would somehow cancel Mac's destiny out?

What kind of a monster am I? Or am I reading too much into Lore's words?

The door blew open with the *crrrrrash* of splintering wood. A charred stink—a smell that mixed magic and gunpowder—brought tears to her eyes. *Guardsmen!*

They'd used a wizard to help them past Lore's wards. Viktor was on his feet in a second, and in the air a second after that. The wizard went down under a mass of snarling fur. Two guardsmen tried to beat the werebeast off, their swords almost useless against Viktor's tough hide.

A spear sailed through the air, landing with a thud in the back of a chair and knocking it to splinters against the stone wall. Glass and books flew as shards of wood spun through the room, a bowl exploding on the floor like a gunshot.

Sylvius flew up toward the ceiling, following the instinct of all winged things to seek safety in height. Constance leaped, landing squarely in front of the guardsmen. She had no plan, just the dead certainty her place was between Sylvius and these men.

"Hide!" Sylvius shouted to Constance, balancing on the top of a bookcase. "Look after yourself. I can fight!"

"So can I!" she retorted. *I have my powers now.* "Where's the wizard who ruined my door?"

The wizard got to his feet and scrabbled from the room, wailing in terror. Viktor bounded after him, barking like this was all a delightful game. There was a wail of anguish a moment later. Viktor liked to play with his dolls.

Connie felt the scream through her bones. One of the guardsmen was Bran. She didn't know the names of the other three, but she recognized their faces. Reynard was nowhere in sight.

"Where's Captain Reynard?" she demanded.

"He's not one of us anymore, Mistress Vampire," said Bran with false politeness. "Captain Reynard was a demon-lover. He refused to use the incubus to save us, much less give us a little pleasure. The guardsmen had enough."

"Mutiny!"

"Call it what you like. I'm in charge now, and we're taking the incubus back."

"Like hell you are!" Sylvius shot back, grabbing a book from a high shelf and hurling it at the guardsmen. It struck one in the side of the head.

"Get him!" Bran commanded.

A red-haired guardsmen carried a heavy recurved bow. In one smooth move, he knocked an arrow and drew it.

"No!" Constance threw herself forward, jumping to dash the thing from his hands. The arrow sang over her head, feathers whirring.

She turned to see the arrow strike Sylvius in the side. He flared with silver light, trying to turn to dust, but the glow flickered and died in an instant.

His wings crumpled, their angle awkward, wrong. He dropped to the floor.

Fury blanked her mind. She grabbed the bowman, hurling him to the floor as if he were no more than a half-empty sack of oats. Her fangs were out, the stink of his fear putting an edge to her hunger, but he wasn't what she wanted. The urge to protect was stronger.

The others were converging on her son. She pushed away from the bowman and ran after them.

Bran was bellowing orders. "Keep him separate from the others, especially the sorcerer. Put Atreus in the corner cell. Keep this one downstairs."

Enraged, Constance grabbed Bran's tattooed arm, spinning him toward her. She swiped with her long, sharp nails, aiming for his eyes, but he jerked away. Long slashes sprang red on his cheek. He backhanded her. She barely staggered back. The look on his face made her give a sharp bark of laughter.

"I'm not a little girl anymore!"

Then he swiped his sword in a beheading blow.

Oh!

The only thing that saved her was diving behind the sofa. She heard the blade chop into it, then Bran cursing when the sword stuck in the old frame. He pulled it away with a splintering of wood.

She was panting, still more angry than afraid. She looked around for something to use as a shield. Someone kicked the sofa, scraping it across the floor. She moved with it, still searching for something to counter the sword.

"Leave her," she heard Bran order. "She's nothing. We got what we came for."

Nothing. The word stung as if Bran had finally gotten a slice of her flesh. She had to act. Get help. Anything but crouch there.

How am I going to defeat four guardsmen? Bran, no less? It didn't matter. She just had to. They couldn't take Sylvius a second time, especially now that Reynard was overthrown. There was no one to keep them in check.

She didn't really know how to fight men with swords. She would have to improvise and hope for the best.

Smoke from the spell clung to the floor, tickling her

nose. She turned her head, looking under the sofa for their feet to see how close the guardsmen were. *Holy Saint Bridget!* One man wore modern lace-up sneakers—traded, no doubt, for one of Lore's captive hounds. She sucked in her breath. It was one thing to be a prison guard. It was quite another to sell your charges for comfortable shoes. *I'll kick his backside clear to Kilkenny.*

She gave up on her hunt for a shield and started working her way forward, crawling on elbows and knees, picking her exit point. She wanted enough room to get to her feet before she had to defend herself.

They moved away, the clank of their armor a soft percussion under the rumble of their voices. She couldn't hear Sylvius. That silence was worse than a cry of pain. *Bloody hell.*

Now that they'd moved, there was more space to maneuver. Crawling from behind the far end of the sofa, she kept low to the ground and out of sight. Frantically, she tried to make a plan. If she whistled for Viktor, would he come? Could she attack Bran from behind? Surprise him with a single swift snap of the neck?

She gathered herself and peered over the arm of the sofa at an empty room.

They were gone.

Sylvius was gone. She was too late. Her throat burned with the urge to scream. *How could this happen? I let them get away!*

She clutched the arm of the sofa like it was the last solid thing in her world. She cursed herself for letting Sylvius stay in the Castle. *I should have made him go. It doesn't matter what he thinks will happen if he leaves this place. To hell with it.*

The doorway gaped like an empty eye socket. The room was a shambles. Her room. The place where she and Mac had made love.

A horrible thought hit her.

She sprang to her feet, half flying to the bed. It was largely untouched, but her heart thumped wildly, frightened into life, until she reached beneath the mattress and found her secret treasure.

The key.

It was safe. She'd not had the courage to use it before. She'd not had the courage to face the world outside the Castle door by herself. She was going to have to do it now.

A plan flowed together in seconds. Mac was meeting with the council. They needed to know what had just happened. She needed to convince them to help. She needed to bring back enough people to defeat the immortal Castle guards.

But that meant she would have to search for Mac on the streets of Fairview, alone with her hunger. The very idea of it filled her with nauseated terror, but fear was something she could overpower. Now she had faced her vampire side. She knew what to expect, and it wouldn't trip her up again. She would be stronger this time.

Brave thoughts didn't stop her hands from shaking. Panic felt like a beast clawing her from the inside, but she squashed it. She was the fiercer beast now. She was a true vampire.

Constance rose, grabbed the stack of magazines Mac had brought her, and shuffled through them until she found the one she wanted. It was filled with news and sporting events and was the one he said he had delivered to his home. She ripped the address label from the cover.

Chapter 24

October 10, 1:00 a.m.
101.5 FM

"This is Oscar Ottwell, your daytime host filling in tonight for the incomparable Errata. We're at 101.5 FM at the beautiful University of Fairview campus. For the next hour I'll be talking communities. I know many of the listeners out there live and work in the area some call Spookytown. Is it a business district, a ghetto, or a neighborhood? Can it be a community with so many different species in so small a space?

"To put it another way, what makes a few square blocks more than a place on a map? The café that remembers you like your tea with lemon? The grandma down the street who lets the kids climb her tree? Or is it the guy down the street who always gives your car a push when the battery goes dead?

"Folks, our lines are open. Call and tell me what makes a neighborhood a community."

October 10, 1:30 a.m.
CSUP boardroom, University of Fairview campus

"That's not the answer!" retorted George de Winter, tossing back his dark mane of overstyled hair. "Fairview is not a homeless shelter. We can't open the door to an unlimited flood of refugee trash who can't even feed themselves."

Mac glared across the scuffed table at the representative for the Clan Albion vampires. The crappy overhead lights in the CSUP boardroom were giving him a demon-sized headache. "Look, dickhead, we can't just wall the Castle up and forget about everyone inside. We have to do something."

"The Castle has survived for who knows how many thousands of years."

"So?"

"Perhaps it's meant to self-destruct. It's a prison filled with the dregs of supernatural civilization."

"Which you don't want in your backyard."

"Of course not. And I don't like your tone."

Am I allowed to stake the stakeholders?

Once upon a time, he'd sat as police liaison on assorted committees and actually enjoyed it—but somewhere between chowing down souls and turning into Mac the Barbarian, he'd lost all patience for idiots. *Fancy that.*

He took a deep breath, refilling his water glass from the pitcher on the table. The others in the room exchanged glances. Mac knew he was there on sufferance, only there because he was Caravelli's guest. *Keep a lid on the sarcasm.*

He tried for a conciliatory tone. "I appreciate your concerns and every effort will be made to minimize the impact on Fairview as a whole."

De Winter gave an eye roll. "I don't see how that's possible. Let the rabble out of the Castle and the humans will quickly find out there's a supernatural prison on their doorstep. Right when we're pushing for equal rights and trying to convince them we're good little law-abiding monsters. Good thinking."

Mac cast a sideways glance at Holly. She was doodling on a legal pad, drawing a bat with a cartoon bubble over its head. The bubble said, "blah, blah, blah." She caught Mac smirking and moved her hand over the drawing to hide it.

"Oh c'mon, George," said Errata, the werecougar radio

host. She was in full kitty Goth regalia, somehow managing to make stretchy faux snakeskin—black, of course—look tasteful. "Sooner or later someone's going to start talking to city hall. Right now they think it's an urban myth, but what are they going to say about us when they find out we're abusing our own people? The council risks a lot more exposure by standing by and pretending this isn't a train wreck."

"And when someone blows the whistle, you'll be right there to break the story," de Winter shot back. "The biggest one since the coming out in Y2K. Forget it. Keep your scoops in the litter box, young lady."

A hostile silence followed. Mac glanced around the table. Most looked like they agreed with the radio host. Others looked worried or about to fall asleep. The room was stuffy, plain, and ugly, one of the light ballasts humming hypnotically overhead.

Holly started to draw a cat eating the bat.

Just enough council members had shown up for a quorum. There were ten present, including Holly, Caravelli, and Errata. The rest were vamps and werewolves. The fey, as usual, hadn't bothered to show. Lore was late, which ticked Mac off. The council meeting had originally been for his benefit.

One of the vamps looked at her watch. Mac had already forgotten her name.

The meeting was going nowhere.

Dr. Perry Baker, university computer prof and the youngest of the wolves, spoke into the sudden quiet. "Look. I agree with Errata. If we know there are people who should leave the Castle, we can't just blow them off. They're our people. They're supernaturals, like us."

"Maybe these are your people," de Winter drawled. "They aren't mine. Not to mention the fact that it's—hello!—a prison, which means bad people are inside. Remember Geneva?"

"De Winter," Caravelli growled. He didn't say anything else, but the other vampire folded his arms and shut up.

"Let me cut to the chase," Mac said. "The hounds have

an extensive information network inside the Castle. Lore told me earlier today that he received word of a group of about forty hellhounds who've escaped from an area that just collapsed. They're working their way toward the door. They're moving slowly because they've got women and children in the pack, and the risk of capture is high."

"Oh," said Errata. "Children."

"So we go get them," said Perry Baker. "Any questions?"

"Is there anyone else we can identify immediately for rescue?" asked Errata.

"Just a moment," said a vampire who had been silent so far. He had been older when he Turned, with the exquisite manners and handsome face of an old-fashioned film star.

Mac turned to Holly, widening his eyes. She scribbled on her notepad, *Big Important Vamp. Beaumont clan. His name is Antoine.*

Everyone turned, as if this guy was worth listening to. He spread his hands a little, an orator's gesture. "We are under the emotional pull of a sad story, and that is making us throw out all our previous policy regarding the Castle. If we begin to rescue people, where do we draw the line?"

"The vampires have opposed every rescue attempt!" Errata objected. "Every time this comes up, Antoine, you block us!"

Antoine leaned forward, eyes flashing. "Mind your tongue, little cat. The wolves have always agreed with us."

"What?" Perry Baker rose from his seat. "All I've ever said is that we'd better know what we're doing before we throw open that door!"

"That's not how I remember it," Errata snarled.

This is going south. "Silence!" Mac shouted, then used his two-finger whistle.

All heads, fangs out and eyes aglow, turned to glower at him. A shudder of demon heat went up his spine.

Mac cleared his throat, forcing himself to calm down. "Antoine is right. We need to be clear about what we're doing. The hellhounds have to be our immediate goal. Because some of the inmates are dangerous, and we don't know for sure which ones those are, we can't just rush in there with big hearts and no brains. It sounds cruel, but I more than anybody know the consequences when someone like Geneva gets loose."

Antoine nodded, his expression relieved.

Errata sat down. The others followed her example. "Okay," she said.

"At the same time," Mac added, "we need to fix the Avatar. In some ways that's the bigger problem."

"I don't really understand this business about the Avatar," said Perry. "How do the guardsmen think they're going to put it back by killing its child?"

Holly pulled a folder out of her backpack and opened it. "I found a passage in a book that talks about the ritual for freeing the spirit from the body. It's called disincorporation."

"Sounds like murder to me," the werecougar replied tightly.

Mac frowned, growing hot with the fierce, dry heat of his demon. *They're talking about Sylvius.* Anger sucked at him, leaving an ashy taste on his tongue. He grabbed his water glass, gulping down the cool liquid. Where he gripped the glass, the condensation on its side fizzled in a puff of steam.

Caravelli gave him a curious look. Mac shrugged. *At least I'm not kidding when I say I'm hot stuff.*

"This ritual is supposed to save the Castle from collapsing?" Antoine asked, sounding subdued.

"That's the theory," Holly answered.

Perry looked confused. "Wouldn't the energy draw have to be huge in order to re-create a spirit form like the Avatar?"

"You mean it would require several deaths?" Mac asked darkly.

"Careful what you say," said Holly quickly. "These spells have a way of listening."

Mac shut his mouth.

"The passage describes a few specific points," Holly said.

"The body is suspended from a large structure. This is going to take time to set up and they'll need a big space to do it in. There's also a body of water nearby, like a lake or a pond, that will be magically set on fire."

Mac scribbled the details on his notepad as Holly spoke. There was only one pond he knew of in the Castle—the place with the dark pool—and that gave him the major creeps. He could see doing a sacrifice there.

De Winter sighed. "Well, I don't see the benefit of involving ourselves in this Avatar business. What's it got to do with Fairview?"

The notepad burst into flame. Mac swore, slapping his hand down on the flames. Caravelli jumped back, throwing his water on the fire before it spread.

All the vampires in the room inched away from Mac. Fire was one of the few things that could hurt them. Mac just sat there, gaping at the drowning flames. *What the frigging hell was that?*

Perry pulled a pen from his pocket and reached across the table, stirring the soggy mess of wet ash until the last cinders were out. "So, have you tried antacids?" He looked over the rims of his wire-framed glasses. "I heard you got over the soul-eating thing, but how long have you been a fire demon?"

"Can we stay on topic?" said de Winter. "Flaming like that is just rude."

Before Mac could struggle through another thought, the boardroom door opened. Lore looked inside, as if uncertain he had the right room.

"Where the hell were you?" Mac demanded.

The hound entered, followed by Connie and Viktor.

Everything else forgotten, Mac jumped to his feet. *Why is she here? She looks scared. Where's the kid?*

She kept one hand on Viktor's head while he sniffed loudly, taking in the scents of the various creatures in the room. Connie looked ragged.

Caravelli tensed. "Constance, what happened? Are you all right?"

"She came to Mac's condo as I was leaving to join you," Lore said. "She has bad news. We have less time than we thought."

"None," Connie said, her voice small but firm. She looked around the room, meeting the glances of everyone in it. "The guardsmen have mutinied against their captain."

Her gaze drifted to meet Mac's. They stood on opposite sides of the room, but the intimacy of her look put them side by side. "They took Atreus, the only sorcerer who had the strength to oppose them."

How the hell did they do that? Mac wondered.

"And they took Sylvius."

Mac caught his breath. *So that's why she's here.*

"The sacrifice boy?" de Winter asked.

She closed her mouth for a moment. Mac caught the quick tremor of her chin. She was fighting back tears. "Yes."

God, she's being brave.

Errata swore. "That's it. We have to get him, and we have to get those hounds."

Everyone started talking at once. Connie slipped across the room to stand beside Mac. Her cold, cold fingers slipped through his, gripping him tight. "I'm so hungry," she whispered. "If Lore hadn't been at your home, I don't know what I would have done."

Mac bent down, whispering in her ear. "But you made it. You found us."

"There were so many people and buildings," she whispered back. "I had no idea your home would be so far away. This city is huge!"

Fairview was actually a medium-sized place, but compared to an eighteenth-century village it would have seemed vast. Mac squeezed her hand.

She ducked her chin, looking dejected. "I thought coming into my power meant I could fight the guardsmen, but they're still too strong. They're soldiers, and I'm not. All I could do was run for help. It doesn't seem like much."

"You did what was necessary," Mac replied. "After centuries out of this world, you mastered your hunger and your fear and journeyed through a completely strange landscape to get the right message to the right people. You're doing just fine."

She looked up, meeting his eyes. She looked sad and tired, but there was a glimmer of pride there, too. "I suppose I am. And I didn't even bite anybody along the way."

Mac squeezed her hand. "Atta girl."

"But I think I might have frightened a few."

Mac didn't want to know.

They turned back to the meeting.

"There is word of a second hellhound pack farther back along the road," Lore was saying. "At least another thirty hounds. Prince Miru-kai's men are in pursuit."

"What about the guardsmen?" Mac asked.

"With panic about the Castle's collapse, word is spreading quickly about the door, and the guardsmen are on alert."

"Damn," said Perry Baker. "We can't mobilize quickly enough. To get enough boots on the ground, we need to contact the loners as well as the packs and prides."

Errata swung her chair around and stood in one smooth motion. "Leave that to me. Radio stations aren't just for talk shows."

October 10, 4:00 a.m.
101.5 FM

"This is Errata Jones at CSUP Radio, 101.5 FM at the University of Fairview. This is a public service announcement and a call for volunteers. Those members of the supernatural community able to provide food and shelter for mothers and children please contact the station at 250-555-2787—that's 250-555-CSUP. Please do so immediately. We need blankets, clothing, and food. Would members of the supernatural community peacekeeping roster or those with medical training please report to the Empire Hotel as soon as possible. Organizers are standing by. Thank you."

*   *   *

The radio called, and people came.

Werecats, hellhounds, vampires, hedge-witches, and even two of the fey. Alessandro said there were familiar faces, but also people no one had ever met before. Lone wolves. A family of bears from a downtown café. The Bakers and the rest of Pack Silvertail, always well organized, were the first on the scene.

The turnout was impressive, given the short notice. They milled in the narrow alley by the Castle door, drinking take-out coffee and huddling in groups. The council members went from one clump to another, relaying their plan. All told, there were about forty fighters. The rest were standing by to deal with refugees and the wounded.

"Just not the numbers to storm the Castle in grand style," said Caravelli regretfully. "Too bad. I always wanted to do something like that."

Mac grunted. "Think Robin Hood—guerrilla warfare."

"Bah. Men in green panty hose."

"Whatever."

"You're in a hot temper."

Mac sighed. "Price of being a fire demon?"

"Do you have a sudden desire to pose for a calendar?"

"Those are fire *fighters*. Y'know. Dalmatians. Funny yellow hats."

"That's just for humans. A bit of soot and all the were-kittens will be begging for you, and only you, to kindle their tender tails."

"I am so not in the mood for vampire humor."

"What would you rather be, the big bad demon or the boy with the spotted dog?"

"I thought you didn't like fire."

"I like watching you squirm."

"Don't start something, crypt boy. I have depths. Hey, does anyone have a gun I could borrow? The sorcerer squished mine."

Lore brought his hounds. With a handful of hounds and Lore's second-in-command, Caravelli was in charge of locating and escorting the closer group of hounds to safety.

This was the simplest part of their plan, because Lore's intelligence placed the group no more than a mile east of the Castle door.

Once they were safe, Caravelli would take charge of securing the path of retreat for the warriors traveling farther into the Castle. While the nearest Castle residents were believed to be at the werecat encampment Mac had seen, there was still a chance of danger from guardsman patrols or a hostile warlord.

Pack Silvertail, along with Lore and the rest of his hounds, were going in search of the group of refugees reported to be farther away. All the other fighters stayed with Holly. She was stationed by the door itself, her magic the last line of defense in the event something nasty tried to leave. It was the most critical position, and she was the only one among them with enough magic to hold the Castle door if everything else went wrong.

Mac, because of his unique demon abilities, was going after the guardsmen's captives, hoping to succeed through stealth. He would go alone.

Or so he thought.

Connie was looking up at him, her silvery blue eyes turning the color of steel.

"But it's dangerous," Mac said, hearing how lame that sounded even as he spoke.

"I'm every bit as much of a monster as you are, Conall Macmillan. You need someone to watch your back. And this is my son we're rescuing. I'm no fine lady to be sitting here and tatting lace while you ride off to war. You need me." She checked the knife at her belt. "I know the Castle better than you do, and speed counts."

She was right, but he was bound by the universal creed of macho heroes. "But . . ."

"Enough." She poked him in the chest. "You're only in charge of me if I say you are. Now I love you, boyo, but you're not thinking clearly. Are you going to take advantage of two and a half centuries of knowledge of this place or are you going to pretend that being a great big demon makes you an expert on things you can't possibly know?"

She loves me. His mind got stuck there.

"Well?" she asked.

"What if you're hurt?"

"I'm a vampire," she said in an exasperated voice. "And what if you're hurt? No one should be on this job alone."

Mac surrendered. *She loves me.*

Perry found Mac a Sig Sauer almost like his old one. He offered to find something for Connie, but she wanted nothing but her belt knife.

"It's what I'm used to. I used to gut chickens, you know," she said, drawing her blade for the thirtieth time to check its edge.

"Handy."

"I had to work for a living."

"And?"

She fixed him with a guarded look, a little uncertain now that she had won the argument to go with him. "Gentlemen generally prefer the embroidering type."

He touched her cheek, momentarily mesmerized by her wintry beauty—all snow and darkness. "Who says I'm a gentleman?"

As a reply, she thrust the knife back in the sheath, managing to make the simple act suggestive. And then she smiled. It wasn't the Mona Lisa smile, but a broad grin.

Oh, yeah.

Mac drew the line at taking Viktor. The last thing he needed was an addled werebeast with obedience issues—and to be honest, Mac had grown too fond of the creature to put him needlessly at risk. Viktor was on a truck bound for Pack Silvertail's rural property. There he could find werebunny rabbits to chase and a very large fenced enclosure suitable for oversized canines.

"Hey. Demon guy."

Mac turned. *Oh, great.* It was Ashe.

Mac took a hard look at Holly's sister. She had a light machine gun slung across her shoulder. She saw him looking at it. "Altered for heavy silver ammunition. I know a guy at Colt."

"Shouldn't you be recuperating?" he asked.

"I'm good."

Mac didn't believe it for a moment. She looked pale and moved like she still hurt.

Ashe looked at Connie. "Hello, again."

"Hello. We never introduced ourselves. My name is Constance." Connie looked Ashe up and down in turn. "Are you Holly's sister?"

"That's right. Ashe Carver."

Connie narrowed her eyes. "Are you here to slay vampires?"

"Not today," said Ashe. "But it sounds like your son's in real trouble. There'll be plenty of action to go around." She patted her weapon.

Mac turned to her. "Y'know, I saved your life. It kinda hurts you're planning to throw it away so soon."

Ashe gave him a lip curl, but it held no rancor. "You never know, Scorch, I might come in handy."

Wonderful. The fire-demon thing's already hot gossip.

"You need a warning label." Mac looked her in the eye. She reminded him of some of the female cops he knew, including his old partner. Solid, for all the kick-ass attitude.

"A warning label. That's the nicest thing anyone's said all week." She turned and walked toward Pack Silvertail's huddle, where the Bakers were assigning teams.

Mac called after her. "Yeah, and it would say 'slow learner.' "

Ashe made a rude gesture.

Connie tilted her head. "She's an unusual woman."

Mac sighed. "Thank God for that."

Chapter 25

Alessandro's group had been the first to move into the Castle. There had been half a dozen guardsmen standing watch inside the door. There were now six guardsmen tied up and in the custody of the bears.

Just before they moved off, he stopped and folded Holly in his arms.

"Be careful," she said.

He held her away, his arms on her shoulders. She was giving him the full force of her lovely green eyes.

"You be careful," he said. Suddenly everything seemed too fragile. He wanted to take everything back and start the night over. A night where there was no Castle, and Holly wouldn't be left behind to battle stray monsters. Maybe they'd have watched a movie.

"Alessandro," she said on an indrawn breath.

"Yes?"

She exhaled, her look confused.

He waited.

"I'm the one with the magic," she said. "Don't take big risks. Don't make me come looking for you."

He could tell she meant it, but that hadn't been what she'd meant to say. They exchanged a look. Her eyes were full of nothing but love, and a trace of fear, and a lot of courage.

"I'll tell you the rest later," she said.

He kissed her again, lightly this time, or he'd never tear himself away. "Take my gun."

"I don't need it."

Yes, she had magic, but he'd made her learn to fire a weapon. He liked insurance.

"Take it, anyway. It'll make me feel better. I'm better with a sword."

Because if she wasn't waiting, what was the point of coming back?

Constance remembered Bran's orders as the guardsmen had captured Sylvius. *Keep him separate from the others, especially the sorcerer. Put Atreus in the corner cell. Keep this one downstairs.*

How could the guardsmen keep control of Atreus? His powers were growing weak, but he could still protect himself. She hadn't had time to think about it before, but now it preyed on her mind. She couldn't think of an answer, and that meant there was a surprise in store.

Not the pleasant kind of surprise, either.

They gambled that Sylvius would still be in his cell, so their destination was the guardsmen's quarters. Constance and Mac had been running for a long time, the terrain rising. As they approached a junction of hallways, Mac threw out an arm, signaling a stop. Constance nearly bumped into him, her shoes skidding on the stone.

"There's someone ahead," Mac mouthed. "I saw movement."

They waited. Then Constance saw it wasn't people.

"My God," Constance breathed.

"There's another one," murmured Mac. "Incredible."

For a moment, the shadows seemed to part. The first was visible only for a moment, a flash of white crossing the corridor ahead. Constance blinked, thinking it was a trick of her eyes. She leaned forward, her body resting against the delicious heat of Mac's broad back. The sensation nearly made her forget everything else.

Then there was another flash of white. This time she got a good look, because it paused.

It was about the size of a deer, its pale coat dappled in light gray. Long, slender legs ended in cloven hooves, a silvery sheen glistening from the long mane and tail. It lifted its head, whuffing, sniffing the air. Nervously, it turned its head.

At the center of its forehead, the spiraling horn shone like mother-of-pearl.

It was so beautiful, Constance wanted to weep. If that was not splendor enough, two more of its kind joined it. Constance blinked, her eyes dry from staring. One of the newcomers touched noses with the first, and the three moved away, passing out of sight.

Mac turned, his eyes alight. He slid his arm around her. "Did you see that?"

"They're from the levels below," said Constance. "If they've been driven this far up the corridors, the lower caverns must be disappearing."

"What else is down there?" Mac asked uneasily.

Constance shook her head. "No one knows for sure."

Alessandro followed Lore's second-in-command through what must have been the worst rat maze in the Castle. These were narrow, cold passageways, some so cramped that Alessandro had to turn sideways to slip through. Torches were rare, and at times there was barely enough light for even his vampire sight to function. However, he wasn't complaining. They had met no guardsmen, and the hounds were perfectly certain of their path.

"How much farther?" he asked.

The lead hound cast a glance over his shoulder. His name was Bevan, a young, solid-looking hound who seemed to be Lore's friend as well as his right hand—or would that be paw?

"Another five minutes," he said, the words colored by the almost Slavic accent the hounds had. At least this one spoke with nonhounds. Many either couldn't or wouldn't.

Alessandro nodded, ducking as the corridor ceiling dipped. He'd already unhooked his broadsword from its hanger and carried it by the scabbard. It had proved a nuisance in the narrow spaces.

There were six hounds following him, six pairs of shuffling feet and six beating hearts. *Hounds are not food*, he told himself, but he could feel the vague tug of hunger, anyway. *Just nerves*. If he stayed long enough, the urge to feed would pass entirely, smothered by the Castle's magic.

Smothered. The word rattled through his head. Claustrophobia tickled between his shoulder blades. *Lore is going to owe me for this*.

Bevan stopped, raising a hand to signal a halt. He raised his head, sniffing. Alessandro did, too, wondering what disturbed their guide. Something unfamiliar struck his senses. It was subtle, no more than a faint metallic tang.

"Run!" Bevan sprang forward, bounding down what was now no more than a hole through the stone.

Alessandro didn't argue. He raced after, vampire speed matching the hellhounds', pace for pace. After a hundred more feet, the passageway widened, allowing for more freedom. He could hear the hounds behind him, one beginning to howl with panic, a strange half-human, half-canine sound. *What's back there?*

And then the tunnel began to tremble, dust falling in gusts as if a giant baker were tossing handfuls of flour. Alessandro heard the clink of stone shifting, the rattle of mortar shaken loose. The roof of the tunnel began to slope upward and he gratefully straightened, lengthening his stride.

The passage opened into a cave, and he took a last bound into the torchlight, hard on Bevan's heels. The cave was filled with hounds, a babble of excited voices. Lore had said there were forty in this group. There had to be at least half that many again, some just babes in arms. Alessandro wheeled, looking behind him. The last of the hounds was leaping out of the passage, arms and legs flying wide.

And then, with a sound like the swish of a sliding door, the tunnel disappeared. He had expected a crash, an avalanche of falling rock. Alessandro gaped for a moment, and turned to Bevan.

"That's how it happens," said the hound. "The outer territories have already gone."

"If we'd still been in there?"

Bevan shrugged.

Forcing his hands to be steady, Alessandro fiddled with his sword, attaching the scabbard back on its hanger. His thoughts felt like rubber balls, frantically bouncing off the insides of his skull. *I hate magic. I really, really hate magic.*

He sucked in a breath and looked around the cave. There was another door. At least they weren't trapped.

Then he took in the hounds. "These are mostly females and children," he said.

"Yes," said Bevan. "The males are dead. Killed by the changelings and goblins."

Alessandro cursed inwardly. Some of the hounds were in their beast form, black dogs with long, pointed snouts and upright ears. They all looked exhausted, especially the children. He had a sudden, vivid memory from his human life, of playing with his own younger siblings. He knew a tired toddler when he saw one.

But there was no time to rest. He looked at their mothers, trying to gauge their condition. All the hounds were ragged, the clothes sewn from coarse, hand-dyed material the weight of old sacking. Their feet were bare. What they did have were bright strings of painted wooden beads—rich, gaudy colors defiant against the Castle's gray-on-gray hues. *Women always find a way to shine.*

He had to believe the beads. These mothers would get their children to safety, if he and the male hounds could secure a path.

Bevan was talking to an older woman, who wore many bright strands around her neck. An elder, and probably a grandmother. She held a little girl on her hip, who peeked at Alessandro with wide, dark eyes. *She's going to break hearts someday.*

The words flew fast in the houndish tongue, with a lot of pointing at the remaining door.

"What does she say?" Alessandro asked Bevan.

"That way leads to the dark pool of water. From there it is possible to find the Castle door."

"Is that way guarded?"

"That is not the problem."

Bevan turned back to the woman, who talked some more.

"What?" Alessandro snapped, apprehension making him impatient. "Are the corridors vanishing?"

"No," said Bevan. He asked another question, got a one-word reply. "They're afraid. There's something out there."

"What?"

"She doesn't know. A creature that spreads darkness. They ran in here before it got too close. And then they were too tired to carry on."

Alessandro pushed past Bevan, storming toward the doorway.

The hound caught his arm. "What are you doing?"

"You and your men stay and keep these people safe."

"What are you going to do?"

"I'm going to find out what that something is."

Connie and Mac raced down the narrow walkway that overlooked the guardsmen's courtyard. Mac stopped, looking over the railing at the benches and empty dormitories below. The fires were burning, but the courtyard was empty.

"Where are the guardsmen?" Connie asked.

"Up to no good," Mac growled. "What are those?"

He pointed to a row of frames that stood in the courtyard. They looked like giant tennis rackets standing on their handles. Some sort of hides were strung in the middle, lashed to the frames as if to stretch them. They were a light brown, with dark rosettes, and whatever creatures they came from had been huge.

"Trolls," Connie said weakly. "Those were trolls. That's Bran's work."

"Do they hunt them?"

"It's punishment. Trolls are slow but they talk. They live in tribes."

Mac's stomach heaved. Did one of those hides belong to the creature he'd seen thrown into a cell? Furious, he flung himself down one of the stairs that zigzagged down to the cells beneath. "Do you see anyone in the cells?"

"Are the caves their cells?" Connie asked, jogging down the stairs after him. "Because there's someone in that one."

"Where?" Mac asked.

"There." She pointed to a cell across the courtyard. "He—I'm pretty sure it's a he—isn't moving."

Mac squinted. She was right. "Good eyesight. That's a guardsman's coat. I'll bet you a quarter that's Reynard."

He turned to Connie. "I need your key."

She gave it to him with a questioning look.

"Let's see if it works on the cell doors. Wait here." Mac dusted across the courtyard, materializing right outside Reynard's cell. The ledge outside the cell door was as wide as a sidewalk, allowing Mac plenty of space to crouch and look inside the bars.

What he saw disgusted him. The cell was tiny, not large enough to lie, or stand, or even sit in comfortably. The captain's usually spotless clothes were torn and blotted with blood.

Perhaps most cruel of all, he was conscious. "My own men did this." Reynard's expression hovered somewhere between a grimace and a rueful smile. "You look shocked, demon."

"I served as a kind of guardsman in my old life. This is shocking."

"They claimed I let you escape."

"Yeah, well, just be glad I got away, because I'm here

now." Mac pressed the gold disk against the lock. It flared with light. The mechanism ground with a shrill squeal, and then a clank. The light winked out. He yanked the door open. It came away in a cloud of stone dust, the raw ends of the bars scraping the rocks.

Reynard moved to crawl out, but his limbs refused to obey.

"Hang on." Mac reached in, grabbing the man's hip and arm and dragging him forward. Reynard collapsed to his hands and knees, his limbs too stiff and weak to stand. Mac steadied him with one hand. The landing at the top of the stairs was small. A false step would take the captain a long, long way down to the courtyard below.

"Where is the incubus now?" Mac demanded.

Reynard shook his head. "Gone. The others took him to the black lake."

Damn. They had guessed wrong, come to the wrong place. "When?"

"Not an hour ago." Reynard grasped the top of the cell door and determinedly got his feet under him.

Mac grabbed the captain's jacket with one hand and hauled him to a standing position. Reynard wobbled dangerously. He hunched, holding one arm across his stomach.

"I'll help you stop them if I can." Reynard said. "Anything to stop Bran."

"Can you walk?"

"Of course. Just give me a moment."

Mac kept one hand on Reynard's shoulder, steadying him. "Do you know where the sorcerer is?"

"Atreus? They took him as well."

Mac glanced across the courtyard to see Connie, leaning on the rail and watching. It was going to be a slog to get Reynard across the courtyard to join her. Or not. "Hold still."

"What?"

They rematerialized on the other side of the courtyard. Reynard grabbed the railing with white knuckles. "God's teeth!"

"Shortcut," Mac said with a grin, but his smile wilted.

He'd been fooled by the guardsman's bravado. Connie grabbed Reynard's arm as he started to slowly collapse. Mac helped her ease him to a sitting position. Connie crouched in front of the captain, then drew back sharply.

She could smell the blood, Mac realized, as he saw her eyes flash silver. Even guardsmen's blood would catch the notice of a fledgling, and they hadn't been in the Castle long enough for her hunger to be entirely subdued.

"How badly are you hurt?" she asked, one hand over her nose and mouth.

Reynard gave a hollow smile. "I simply need to stretch my legs."

He said it as casually as a country gentleman about to take a stroll around his estate. The only trace of strain he showed was a deepening of the lines in his face. He barely let the discomfort reach his eyes, but then he pressed his hand to his stomach. Blood seeped over his fingers, making tiny rivulets over his skin.

"On second thought, perhaps you should leave me," Reynard said.

"If I leave you here, you'll be dead meat," Mac said, frowning down at him. With short, efficient movements, he bent and pulled open the captain's jacket, then tore open the fine cotton shirt beneath. Mac caught his breath. "Sword wound?"

"Bran's ax."

Mac felt his gorge rising for the second time that morning. "Haven't you guys ever heard of rock, paper, scissors?"

Chapter 26

What in Hades?
    The smell was the first thing Alessandro noticed. A stink like melting rubber, cloying to the nose and bitter as it reached the back of the tongue.

He crept down the hall, the dark arch of the stonework growing inky with shadow as he navigated the curve of the corridor. It took him a moment to place what was wrong.

The ever-burning torches were dead. *That can't be good.*

Without light, the stench seemed thicker. Or maybe the smell was simply growing worse. He approached the darkness step by step, using his ears and the feel of the air against his face to navigate. His right sleeve brushed against the stones of the wall, giving him one boundary of the corridor. If he kept the wall within reach, he could reverse his path if needed. The black, lightless space ahead seemed to pulse against his skin. Nerves prickled across his shoulders, down the backs of his arms.

If the torches are extinguished, then the Castle's magic is dead here. Or else there is something so powerful that it has overwhelmed the light.

He froze, reacting to a noise before he realized he'd heard it. The echo of his boots faded to silence. Faint as a whispered oath, something scraped, a long, slow drag over the stones. Statue-still, he listened, waiting. It was a full minute before he heard it again.

Alessandro tried to put an image to what his senses were telling him, but failed. The impenetrable blackness ahead gave no clues. The foul smell gusted on a waft of hot air that felt unpleasantly like an exhaled breath.

Whatever waits ahead is far too close.

He heard another noise, this time behind him. *Trapped!* Alessandro pressed his back to the stone wall, his sword raised. To his right was the unseen menace; to his left was a thin wash of light from where the torches still burned, barely enough for even his predator's eyes. The bend in the corridor obscured whatever lay beyond the curve. He was caught between two unknowns.

Wonderful.

An indistinct shape detached itself from the mottled shadows, sliding like oil into the middle of the corridor. He recognized the silhouette by the size and posture. *Ashe. Is she taking advantage of the confusion to finish her execution job?* He saw her pause, felt her scrutiny.

There was no way he would make this easy for her. He shifted his hands on the sword hilt and waited, letting her come to him. His flexed his knees, his weight ready to lend force to a quick sweep of the blade. It was a technique he'd used time and again as the queen's executioner. A swift blow to separate the head from the body—merciful and final.

At the same time, he heard the scrape from the darkness to his right. Tension crawled up his skin, a live current. The stink clogged the corridor, nearly making him gag.

Ashe ghosted forward. She moved nearly as silently as he did, making it almost accidental that he heard her. Stopping outside the reach of his blade, she reached out, her hand bracing against the wall, her shoulders oddly hunched. *She's still in pain from her battle with the sorcerer.*

"What are you doing here?" he whispered, taking a quick glance toward the darkness.

"There's something down there," she said. "Something big."

"I know. It's blocking the way out."

"The hounds are trapped back there?" she asked.

"They're females and children."

"I know. Kids. Puppies. Whatever."

"What are you doing here, Ashe?"

"I've been scouting for Lore. I came down this way because I thought it would be safer. There're guardsmen galore due west of here. I can't get past."

She took a few steps forward. His sword twitched, and she froze.

"Relax, I'm not here for you, fang-boy." She coughed, trying to stifle the noise. "Sonofabitch, that stinks."

"Get out of here. I'm willing to bet that's some kind of noxious gas, and I don't know what it'll do to living lung tissue."

"What about you?"

"I don't need to breathe."

"That doesn't mean it's not poisonous to you."

As the dragging sound started again, he saw her body curl into itself, a spring coiling for action.

"What the hell is that?" She drifted closer again.

This time, he let her, slowly lowering the sword. It wasn't that he trusted her, but right then there were other threats—and more interesting game for her to hunt. She coughed again, burying her face in the crook of her elbow.

Then, there was light in all that darkness, a flash of orange bleeding to crimson. It was so vivid, Alessandro felt it like a blow. It disappeared, the afterimage burning in his mind.

"Was that fire?" Ashe whispered.

Before he could answer, another glow appeared, dark like smoldering embers. Two smoldering embers, about shoulder height. And then the dragging sound again, like shells or scales hitting the stone floor. Maybe a tail? Claws?

Eyes.

Scales against stone.

Long and low, like a big lizard.

Flame.

Merda! Instincts screamed a warning.

Ashe grabbed his arm in a panicked death-grip. "Oh, fuck!" she croaked, the words robbed of air. She'd drawn the same conclusion.

Dragon.

The collapse of the Castle was bringing the creatures from its deepest levels.

"Run," he said, sounding weirdly calm despite a jitter of panic. "A mortal won't stand a chance in this fight."

He half expected the creature to rush them, but it stayed put, eyes lit with an inconstant, shifting, bloody light. It had to be a good hundred feet away, but he could feel the heat radiating off its body. Dragons lived in fire. Lived with it inside them. He'd heard even their skin burned bare flesh.

"I'm the only backup you've got. Live with it." Ashe released his arm and raised the light machine gun slung across her body. "What do you think? Underbelly?"

Alessandro shrugged. She was right. There was no one else to help, and Ashe Carver was a fighter. "Throat or eyes usually works with anything."

Ashe squared her shoulders. "We'll have those kids out of here by lunchtime."

The dragon's eyes shifted, the scraping sound matching the movement. It was scales making that noise, the swish of its tail on the stone.

It was inching forward. If Alessandro had to guess, he would have said it was curious. He backed away, dragging Ashe with him. This was his first dragon. He wanted a moment to plan.

"We have to separate. Find cover. We're too good a target standing together." Fire loomed large in his mind. Vampires burned all too well, and toast didn't rise to walk the night. "Find a recessed hiding place. Stone shelters from the heat."

"Got it." Ashe pulled away from him and slid into the

shadows, her form melting into the dark on the other side of the corridor.

Alessandro felt grudgingly glad to have her there. *A family that slays together stays together?* He slid back along the corridor until he found the entrance to a side passage where he could let it pass. They weren't going to win by strength, so he wanted to attack from the dragon's blind side, away from its flame.

As it closed in, the creature's outline became visible, lit by the radiance of its eyes. No one Alessandro knew had ever seen one of the great beasts, though legends were plentiful. Unlike the weres or the vampires, dragons were truly wild creatures. They killed, ate, and laid their eggs as they had since the age of their dinosaur cousins. Human settlements were a convenient snack bar. This was the type of creature the Castle had to be meant for—one for which there was no suitable place in the outside world.

The creature's savage beauty struck him first: the delicate bones of the head, the almost feline face surrounded by a flaring fan of skin and bone. The hide was smooth, brick-red with points of cream.

As it came closer, Alessandro could see the short legs were covered in hard, opalescent scales, the claws curved hooks of solid black. It was shorter than a man, but the body was a good twenty feet long.

Just beyond his hiding place, it stopped, round eyes blinking like the flash of rubies, the blast of heat from its flesh like a furnace door opening. Alessandro had willed his lungs to stop, protecting himself from the dragon's breath, but he could hear Ashe coughing convulsively.

The noise was why the beast had stopped. It sniffed, its nostrils flaring to reveal the hot, steaming red of its inner flesh. It looked far too interested in what it smelled. Alessandro had to act fast.

How smart were dragons? Smarter than Holly's cat? He pulled some loose change from his pocket and tossed it as hard as he could down the corridor in front of the creature. The coin landed with a clatter.

It jerked its head around with eerie speed, glowering down the Castle hallway, ready to pounce. Silent as the dead, Alessandro threw a second coin. The dragon took off with a strange side-to-side shuffle, its long body weaving as it ran, the belly scraping over the hard stone floor.

Ashe sprang from her hiding place. Alessandro followed barely a beat later. They raced after it, lagging behind almost at once. For a big creature, the dragon moved like lightning, the lashing, muscular tail ready to crush everything in its wake. Alessandro had to leap more than once to avoid its whip.

It reached the point where the coins had fallen, sniffing the ground like a hound searching for scent. Disappointed, it snorted out a gust of steam and smoke that curled over its head like a question mark. It hunted a moment more, the big head swinging from side to side.

Alessandro felt a glimmer of hope. They were behind the dragon, safe from its flames, and it had stopped. So far everything was going according to Alessandro's hastily sketched plan. The next step was to attack it from both flanks at once.

He communicated the plan with a gesture while they ran. Ashe seemed to understand.

But the dragon started forward again, catching a stray scent. *Not good.* If it reached the end of the corridor, the hellhound families were as good as dead.

Alessandro leaped into the air, using flight to close the gap before the dragon could take aim with its jaws or its fire. He slashed with his sword, trying to catch its throat, but it twisted away. Alessandro dodged, and it snapped the air where he had been a second before.

Ashe fired into the creature's side, making it flinch. The short hail of bullets didn't penetrate its scales, but they must have hurt. The dragon, with a sinuous, writhing movement, turned, jaws open like a trapful of knives. It loosed a blast of flame, fire flowing over the stonework with lascivious tongues.

Ashe!

She hit the ground as the flame roared over her head, the gun clattering as it hit the stone.

Alessandro dropped from the air, his sword driving into the side of the creature's neck in a two-handed thrust. He wanted to aim for a more vulnerable spot, but there had been no time for strategy. Immediately, the flame stopped, scraps of it breaking loose and flying into the air before vanishing to nothing. In its place, a roar ripped the dark passageway, jagged with fury and pain.

A jerk on the sword told Alessandro it was stuck fast. In his desperate attempt to save Ashe, he had pierced the scales, bit into muscle, but had done no real harm. He'd just made it mad. *Merda!*

The dragon convulsed, a shudder passing over its snake-like body down to its thrashing tail. The force of it threw Alessandro off, leaving the sword stuck fast in the beast's neck.

He hit the ground hard, feeling as if his spine connected with his back teeth. A wave of shock short-circuited his muscles. The dragon wheeled, shaking its head against the lopsided weight of the sword. One paw landed on Alessandro's chest, the long, black claws puncturing leather, cloth, and flesh.

Pain of several colors sang through Alessandro's body. He could smell burning flesh and knew it was his own, and felt his dark, sluggish blood sliding down his ribs. He heaved, but the beast was too heavy.

Movement caught his eye. Far to his left, Ashe peeled herself off the floor and rolled to her knees. She was coughing convulsively, barely able to sit up, but she was aiming her weapon.

The dragon looked down at him with the fixed, intense stare of a hunting cat. The tables were turned. After centuries as a predator, Alessandro was at last the prey. Wild denial gave him one last burst of strength, but it was useless.

Gunfire lit up the corridor. A sudden tearing sensation stole Alessandro's wits as the dragon lifted its foot, the claws hooking and shredding as it pushed away. Ashe fell back on her heels, firing again and again, but the tough armor protected the beast.

Alessandro's round of curses matched the gunfire. Anger alone was going to get him off the unforgiving stones and back into the fight. He staggered to his feet, refusing to acknowledge the shifting, crunching feelings in his chest. He was a vampire. He would heal.

Once up, instinct took over. He launched into the air, grabbing the sword again. With the strength of desperation, he tore it out of the dragon's sinewy neck. It hadn't penetrated much past the scales. It had probably felt like a bug bite. The creature roared its annoyance, its mouth stretching wide. The teeth framed its jaws in wicked symmetry, each canine as long as Alessandro's forearm.

He swung for the eyes. The dragon snapped, rearing up as high as the ceiling would allow. Alessandro flew up, but had to dodge as the dragon's tail snaked around. Injured, he wasn't fast enough. It caught him in the side, tossing him against the wall.

The dragon fell back on all four feet, but not before Ashe grabbed the sword from Alessandro. As the dragon opened wide for another blast of flame, Ashe went for the throat. From the inside. Right for the soft flesh above the tongue.

The dragon gnashed down before Ashe's lunge was complete. She jerked aside, barely saving her arm. The sword was not so lucky. The dragon spit it out like a munched-up stir stick, then shook its head like a wet cat.

Ashe raised her automatic again, spreading her feet in a belligerent stance. "Get outta here!" she screamed. "Shoo!"

Shoo?

The automatic spattered bullets right at the dragon's feet, spraying up chips of stone. It inched back, the ruff around its head flattening with distaste. It reared up again, the short front legs pawing the air, and turned its long body away from the annoying stings. Between fits of coughing, Ashe fired again, striking sparks off the stone right where the creature was trying to put its feet.

It hopped and scampered away from them for a dozen yards, its tail slithering in a long, snaking arc behind it. It stopped, back hunched. Only the tip of the tail moved, swishing back and forth in short, irritated jerks.

It's working! Alessandro stared in amazement. Subtlety was accomplishing what brute force could not. He picked himself up again, feeling like a marionette missing his strings.

Even more miraculous was the source of the solution. He wouldn't have expected subtlety from Ashe. She fired again, right at the dragon's heels. With a mighty, frustrated roar, it ran, the waddling, side-to-side gait taking it quickly out of sight.

The torches sputtered and came alive again, almost as if a stagehand had flipped a switch. The dragon had gone far enough away that the magical field surrounding it had dissipated.

"Ugh." Ashe sagged, the automatic hanging loose from its neck strap. Then she coughed again, a wet, wracking sound that told Alessandro she'd inhaled too much of the dragon's fumes. She clutched her ribs like the cough hurt.

Alessandro looked at her, finally noticing her condition. Her long hair was singed away, her jacket blackened from the dragon's flame. It looked like the skin on her hands and one cheek was starting to blister. Her eyes and nose were red and dripping. She was a mess.

"You're injured," he said.

"Could be worse." She shrugged. "You took the brunt of it."

He reached out a hand to touch her shoulder, cautious in case she would revert to killing vampires now that the dragon was gone. He didn't feel like a rematch right then. Or ever.

She didn't flinch at his touch, but she didn't reciprocate, either. "I'm glad we didn't have to kill it. In a weird way, it was kind of pretty."

He couldn't stop a chuckle that was mostly relief. "Ashe Carver, dragon tamer."

She suddenly gave a laugh that was, for once, real. "Wait till I tell that to my daughter. You okay to walk? We still have work to do."

Chapter 27

Reynard should have been dead.

Not that Constance wanted it that way. It was just a fact based on the probable odds—except Mac carried the captain with them, dusting from point to point. Reynard would be saved, no matter what kind of strength Mac had to pull from the marrow of his bones.

Demons were apparently very stubborn.

Constance ran behind the dark, twining cloud that skimmed through the shadows of the Castle. Mac was moving quickly, conserving energy by staying low to the ground.

She quickened her pace, closing the distance between them as the cloud seeped to the ground, splitting into two, and coalescing into the forms of two men. Mac was stopping again, the distances between resting points growing shorter. He was tiring.

Reynard fell back with a groan. Constance winced in sympathy. She remembered when Mac had transported her from the restaurant the other night. Pain had disappeared in dust form, only to come back twice as hard when she became flesh again.

Impatient at the delay, she dropped to one knee beside Reynard, checking the temperature of his skin. He was clammy and cold.

"He's fainted. He needs help," she said. "All the guardsmen heal faster than mortals, but that's not enough to save him."

Mac was sitting with his back to the wall, his knees drawn up. He'd not allowed himself to stop for more than a minute at a time. Eyes closed, he'd propped his head against the stones. He didn't complain. No man of Mac's character would.

She crossed to him, slid down the wall until they were hip to hip. She could feel his heat through their clothes. It was more than just exertion. He was always warm to the touch now, not just when angry or aroused. "It was only a handful of days ago that we sat like this at the Castle door. I told you that you were impossible. I had no idea then that meant you were impossibly brave and good."

"You just wanted me for my blood."

"You just wanted to get under my skirt."

He opened one eye. "Yeah, so what's your point?"

"I'm glad you did." She leaned over, kissed his cheek.

He laughed, kissed her back, then sobered. "How far have we got to go?"

"If we turn south, the passageway will take us to the route we want. If we turn west there, we'll reach the courtyard with the dark pool." Constance looked from Mac to the unconscious guardsman, and then spoke her mind. "How far do we take him? You can't carry him much longer. Not if you want to keep any strength for yourself."

Please forgive me, she said silently to Reynard. *I have to speak up. Mac won't spare himself.*

Mac shook his head. "Reynard's closer to help than he was before. I can take him a little farther. I won't give in yet. Something will turn up."

She opened her mouth to argue, but her emotions tore at her. Pity and fear.

"What's that stink?" Mac said suddenly.

Constance heard a footfall, so faint it might have been no more than the shadow of a sound. She jumped to her feet, listening, her fingers curved into claws. "Who's there?"

"That stink would be eau de dragon." Ashe Carver

swaggered—or perhaps staggered—out of the shadows, her weapon propped casually on her shoulder. She looked terrible—dirty and blistered, like she'd been through a fire. "You wouldn't believe the adventure Caravelli and I had a little while ago."

She stopped, looking down at Reynard. "Who's this?"

"A friend," said Mac.

"I'd hate to see your enemies."

"What happened to you?" Mac asked.

"Not as much as what happened to this dude."

"Captain Reynard needs a surgeon," Constance said.

"Now, there's an understatement." Ashe bent, taking a look at the wounds. "Holy chain saw."

She set her gun down and dropped to one knee, examining the bandage Mac had ripped from Reynard's shirt. "He's bleeding through. How clean was the wound?"

"Not very," said Mac. "His guardsmen locked him in one of their cells."

"Ah, so this is the mutiny guy. I thought the guards' quarters were far to the east of here."

"They are."

"And you've brought him all this way?" Ashe stood and looked at Mac, her brow furrowed with surprise. "Aren't you supposed to be, like, saving the world or something?"

"That's after coffee," Mac returned.

"Whatever." Ashe pulled out a water flask. "Caravelli's gone to fetch his puppy dogs, but they'll be back this way in minutes. I'm just here to chase the dragon away if it comes back."

"Dragon?"

"Long story. Leave your captain with me. Caravelli and I'll take him along when we move the hounds out."

"Are you sure?" Mac said dryly. "There's not much action in watching a man bleed to death."

"Maybe if I'm lucky the dragon will come back. Relax. My husband was a bullfighter. I'm used to pulling medic duty." She knelt, wetting the captain's lips with the water. His eyelids fluttered.

Constance felt a sudden flood of relief, indescribably thankful. The woman had arrived like a knight from a fairy tale. A very strange knight, but Constance wasn't about to argue. She'd take what good luck they could get.

She watched Ashe raise the captain's head, giving him another swallow. "I don't know if you're aware, but we don't need to eat or drink here."

"Uh-huh. Well, aside from the whole blood volume thing, there's the fact that this guy looks like he could use some TLC. We're not all immortal."

Although Reynard was even older than Constance, she let it go. She wasn't going to argue about that, either.

Mac rose. "Then if you've got this covered, we'd better get going."

"Go get 'em, Sparky," said Ashe, standing over the captain like a feral cat guarding her kitten.

Connie and Mac ran until they began seeing guardsmen in the corridors. Mac recognized the area by the fact that the stone of the walls had been polished to a faint sheen. He had approached this place from the other side before, climbing up a staircase slippery with moss.

They ducked into the shadows as a pair of guardsmen passed. They looked Roman, with short red capes and leather armor with plates of dull metal sewn on. He held his breath as they marched by, sandals clumping on the stone.

Both vampires and demons had a talent for hiding in plain sight, but he wondered whether his body heat would eventually give him away. Ever since the council meeting, his core temperature fluctuated between mild curry and extra-strength jalapeño. It wasn't uncomfortable—he wasn't even sweating—but he was conscious of radiating warmth like a bipedal pocket warmer.

The guardsmen passed. Mac and Connie slipped back into the corridor, silently ghosting through it. The hall with the black pond lay just fifty yards ahead. He could just see the outline of steps angling away from either side of the arched entry, leading up to the balconies above. The guardsmen that had passed them turned to the left, mounting the steps and disappearing from view.

The noise level was growing, not the clamor of happy anticipation, but a low murmur of anxious expectancy. It snaked through the dark spaces, brushing Mac's nerves with a cold and flicking tongue. He could almost taste the panic in the voices, sour as bile.

Fear was a powerful motivator. All of this—mutiny and sacrifice—was happening because the guardsmen were afraid of being trapped in a disappearing prison. They thought this was the answer, and Mac was set to rip that last hope from them. *I hate this.*

He felt the same knot in his stomach as he'd felt before kicking down the door of a drug house. A mix of righteous anger and please-don't-shoot-me. He drew his weapon. Connie drew hers, the sound of the blade on the leather sheath raising the hair on his arms.

He inched along the remaining yards to the entrance. Through the doorway, he could see a slice of what lay ahead. He caught a glimpse of the white marble edge of the pool, the stark color warmed by the braziers that lit the cavernous space. Mac's gaze traveled up. When he had seen the space before, the balconies had been empty, but now guardsmen watched from the front rows, filling perhaps a quarter of the space. Had there once been enough guards to fill every seat?

It didn't matter. There were too many of them for a straightforward fight. He looked for cover. There were pillars beside the twin stairways to the balconies. When he got close enough, he eyeballed the pillar on the right. Its angle to the wall made a small but effective hiding place. He pulled Connie into it.

"Stay here," he breathed. "I'm going to take a closer look at what's going on. I'll be right back."

Connie nodded silently, her features lost in the shadows. She gripped his shoulder, pulling him down and brushing his lips with hers. She melted under him, soft and sweet, but with the bite of her teeth against his tongue. *Fierce, dark Connie.* He felt the rush of heat in his blood, licks of fire under his skin.

She drew back quickly, as if his touch had burned her.

He stepped away, his gut gripped by a sudden, contrasting freeze. Those licks of fire hadn't just been inside him. They'd flared along his skin.

Desire burns. Great as a metaphor, but his life would be sheer hell if that started to happen for real. *I'm losing control.*

Reynard had predicted this: *Whatever you touch will be scorched to ashes.*

Dear God, no.

Connie shifted. With a quick flash, her hunter's eyes caught a scrap of light. He caught her arm, pulling her deeper into the shadow before she gave herself away. He felt her flinch under his touch, and he tried to let her go, but she put her hand over his, holding him despite the heat of his flesh.

"Don't let me hurt you," he whispered.

She replied simply by putting her finger against his lips, hushing him. Scorching herself.

Mac's heart broke.

She still clutched him, pressing her comfort into his burning skin. Vampires weren't immune to fire. He could feel it in the tremor of her fingers. *She's in pain.*

"Come back to me," she pleaded. "Promise."

Mac stepped back. *Not if I'm going to hurt you.*

He didn't speak, but somehow she understood. Tears stood in her eyes. Despite his silence, she could sense he was pulling away.

Mac ached. All of him. The feeling was too big to punish just his heart.

He loved her. It was up to him to make her world better, not worse.

Demons destroy. I'm not going to destroy her. Without a word, he faded to dust and went to save Connie's son. *It's the only thing left I can do.*

He materialized in the very back of the balcony that curved above the entrance. From here, he could see that the balconies circled the whole space, forming a small, round theater with a clear view of everything below. No bad seats for the sacrifice.

Guardsmen sat at the front of the balconies, but over to the side Mac noticed a handful of figures standing to the back, half hidden by the darkness. A jolt of anger ran through him. He recognized one of the figures, hawk-nosed, black-haired, garbed in robes heavy with gold embroidery. An exotic figure, like some tribal leader who'd fought Genghis Khan, or the Turks, or Vlad Teppes. It was the half-fey warlord and Atreus's sorcerer rival, Prince Miru-kai.

So that's how Bran pulled this off. The rogue guardsman had help.

But the how didn't matter anymore. What counted was the drama below. Mac looked down.

Although he'd braced himself, momentary shock robbed him of breath. Beside the pool stood a wooden scaffold three times the height of a man. Sylvius hung from one side by his wrists, his white flesh scored by dozens of angry wounds. Beneath him, a wooden bucket collected the blood.

Directly across from him, a cage was suspended from the ceiling. In it was Atreus, captive and forced to witness his son's execution. Silver chains bound him to the bars, the metal robbing him of all magical power. The sorcerer was crumpled in the bottom of the cage, his face clasped behind his hands.

Mac started to shake with anger, his skin searing hot, but he slammed the demon down, forcing his mind to take in every detail, any scrap of information that might be of use. *Think. What do you see?*

Lit by the fire from the four braziers that marked the corners of the space, the scaffold's wood looked dark and stained with age. Wood wasn't plentiful in the Castle. It had probably been saved for use time and again, stored away between atrocities like a macabre Christmas tree.

Half a dozen figures stood around the base of the scaffold, one reading from a grimoire. He looked like a sorcerer, complete with gray beard and staff. The others were guardsmen, including Bran. They were standing in a loose circle around the base of the scaffold, repeating lines from whatever spell the sorcerer was reading. The charred-toast smell of magic hung in the air.

The sorcerer dipped a goblet in the bucket, then raised it to his lips. He drank slowly, letting the blood linger for a moment on his lips before he licked them clean and passed the cup to Bran. The guardsman took it, drank more hastily. Took two swallows instead of one before passing it on. Mac watched Bran's face flush. The guardsman shuddered, breathing deeply, and clenched his fists.

Blood of the incubus, bringing desire and appetite back to these ancient, trapped, frightened men. They were taking a last hit before sacrificing their high to save their Castle from annihilation. If it wasn't all so insane, Mac might have sympathized.

The shackles at Sylvius's wrists looked ordinary, both hands bound together directly above his head. The guardsmen had been cruel. He hung limp and broken, wings dangling like tattered rags, the broken shaft of an arrow still protruding from his side. From what Connie had said, Sylvius had been struck down before he could dust to safety. In too much pain, he had been unable to transform.

Demons—even the incubi—were often thought impossible to kill, but draining their energies did make them vulnerable. Last year, Holly had blasted Geneva's powers away with magic, allowing the master demon's own henchmen to tear out Geneva's throat. Likewise, between the guardsmen's magic-enhanced weapons and his wounds, Sylvius could be slaughtered as easily as a mortal.

Judging from the amount of blood in the bucket, the kid was barely still alive. Mac's demon rose up again, searing with anger. Again, he yanked it back under control.

The first thing was to get Sylvius to safety.

He holstered his weapon. This was going to take more

stealth than firepower. After studying the scaffold a moment, he dusted beneath the square of wooden slats that formed its top surface and re-formed clinging to its underside.

Remaining perfectly still a moment, he waited for a roar of protest from the guardsmen as he materialized. When there was none, Mac concluded he was hidden from the balconies by the top of the scaffold. He still had to worry about the half dozen men on the ground, but he had surprise on his side. Slowly, he slipped his hand into his pocket and slipped out Connie's key. Then he put it in his mouth. *Hope demon spit doesn't mess up the magic.*

The sorcerer chose that moment to gesture to two of the guardsmen participating in the spell. They picked up the bucket with Sylvius's blood and emptied it on the dark water of the marble pool. The blood swirled, feathering the water with the motion of the splash, staining the lip of the pool with pink wavelets. The sorcerer said a word, and the surface of the pool bloomed with flame.

Mac took advantage of the distraction to crawl down the scaffolding, spit out the key, and press it to the lock of Sylvius's shackles. The sudden flare of power jarred the incubus back to consciousness.

"Go!" the youth said, his voice raspy with pain. "You can't save me!"

"If I leave here without you, Connie will kill me," Mac said, wrestling with the lock. "I may as well go for the brass ring."

"Stupid," was all Sylvius could reply.

The shackles released. Using all his strength, Mac caught him in one arm.

"There!" roared Bran. "The demon!"

Gripping the scaffold in one arm and Sylvius in the other, with angry guardsmen all around, Mac had a sudden flashback to King Kong. Then an arrow pierced his thigh. Jolting pain loosened his grip and he fell, Sylvius with him, to the stone floor.

His shoulder took the brunt of the fall. Releasing the

youth, Mac tried to stand, but his left leg was rubber. He drew his gun. Bran kicked him, a smash to the jaw that sent him tumbling over, the gun spinning away.

"You dare to interfere!" Bran roared.

Get over yourself, tattoo boy. Mac braced himself on one knee, his head throbbing. His demon was rising, flaring up with heat. Magic rolled off the burning pool like a fog, swamping his senses. Sylvius's blood was boiling from the water, releasing *something* as it turned to steam. Whether it was the Avatar or not was anybody's guess.

Mac tried to crawl to Sylvius, but Bran kicked him again, sending him sprawling on his back. Miracle of miracles, he landed with the gun only a few feet away.

Guardsmen were pouring down from the balconies, swarming to stop the invader bent on destroying their last hope. Mac groped for the gun, fired, kept firing until it was empty, but there were too many guardsmen coming.

Mac looked up to see another arrow just before it pierced his shoulder. The slither of a drawn sword whispered to his left.

Shit, they're going to kill me. Mac's vision went red with fury.

In a last, desperate move, he surrendered utterly to his demon.

Chapter 28

The instant Mac vanished, Constance grew scared and impatient, the empty, lonely darkness around her closing in like a wall of ice. She was so cold she shuddered, as if her bones had forgotten they had ever held heat—as if she had never been a living woman, just a shadow of hunger. *You'd think all this shaking would keep me warm.*

It wasn't fear for herself that choked her, but for her loved ones. She had to know what was going on. Mac had gone for a quick look around, but she knew very well he meant to leave her in the safety of the shadows. *Well, bollocks to that.* She crept around the pillar and up the staircase to the right, crouching below the level of the solid stone balcony rail to stay out of sight. When she reached the top, she shrank into the corner. The nearest guardsmen were only a stone's throw away, but their attention was firmly on the scene below. She turned her back to them, counting on her dark hair and clothes to melt her into the shadows. Just in case, she held the knife hidden in the folds of her skirt, the handle firm in her chill hand.

She closed her eyes a moment, steadying her courage. Her skin hurt where she had touched Mac, but she already missed his heat. She had seen the loss in his eyes before he left. He clearly didn't understand how she felt.

There was a story of a fairy captive who could only be

freed if his lover embraced him no matter what shape he took—be it bear or wolf or pillar of fire. Just like in the tale, Connie meant to hold on to Mac until he was hers.

Nothing said she couldn't have her prince just because she had pointy teeth. And he would have his milkmaid, even if his touch burned like the forbidden sun. *I'm not letting him go*. She felt tears running down her face, some for Mac, some for herself. Some because she knew she had to face whatever was going on in the courtyard.

She had to do it. She had to look.

Silently, slowly, Constance raised herself up until she could see over the railing. The sight below struck her like a blow from Bran's ax: Atreus, the scaffold, the bucket, and her son. *Oh, God.*

The need to scream was a physical pain, but there were guardsmen too close. One noise, and she would be dead. Or worse—helpless to erase the horrible events she saw. Accidentally, the point of the knife pricked her knee. She rode the sensation, letting it carry her away from the images before her. *What can I do? What can I do?*

"There!" she heard Bran roar. "The demon!"

Then the guardsmen on the balcony were up, scrambling so fast they tipped over the stone bench. It cracked as it fell, but they kept going, down the stairs at a frantic pace. Connie looked over the balcony again, and saw why.

Sylvius was free!

Her heart soared, until she saw an arrow fly, striking Sylvius and Mac to the ground. Then she stood, not caring who saw her.

"Constance!"

She looked up. Atreus was calling to her from the cage. His eyes burned with such anger, she fell back a step.

"Constance, help me!"

He's in a cage, chained with silver. There's nothing he can do to me.

A cry came from the scene below. She lurched to the balcony, nearly toppling over in her haste. The battle was worse. Mac was surrounded.

"Constance!"

The command in Atreus's voice jerked her head up again. Obedience was still a habit.

Habits can be broken.

Atreus grasped the bars, staring at her through the gaps. "I can help them, if you will get me out of here!"

"Why would you help us now? You gave away my child—*your child*!"

He pointed to the ground. "Reynard should have been able to keep him safe!"

"Against all his guardsmen?"

"The past is gone. Sylvius needs help now. Constance, please! Open this cage!"

"I don't trust you."

He jerked the bars in wild frustration. "Can you fight all those men? I can! Get me out! We both love Sylvius. I will protect him!"

It was the one argument she couldn't withstand. She would do anything for Sylvius. For Mac. She looked around wildly. "How can I get up there?"

"Fly! You are a vampire!"

Of course. Fly. I have my powers.

She'd paid dearly enough for them. She remembered the taste of blood in her mouth, and felt a jagged wrench of hunger. *The cost of power is always more than we expect.*

Doubt seized her. She was only newly Turned. *But this is why I wanted these gifts—to protect those I love. Now is the moment when everything I've endured will all make sense.*

She sprang onto the stone railing. It took a moment to find her balance. The top of the rail was barely a handspan wide. Concentrating, she drew in a long breath. Atreus's cage wasn't far—about six feet up and about twenty feet away. Not far at all for someone like Alessandro to leap.

Then she made the mistake of looking down. Sylvius was lying in a bone-white heap. Bran kicked Mac in the face. She gave an involuntary jerk at the sight.

"Bloody hell!" She started to wobble. Her curse echoed in the high cavern.

Atreus cursed. "Look at me; don't look down!"

An arrow shot by, skimming the hem of her skirt. She felt the rush of feathers pass her ankle. She began to lose her balance, slowly, almost gracefully. She fell forward while her arms windmilled backward, her feet trying to mold themselves to the rail through the soles of her shoes.

She slipped, trying to catch herself in empty air. Atreus was kneeling on the floor of his cage, reaching his hand as far as he could through the bars. It was useless. Until he was freed from the silver bonds, he had no power.

But still, he reached out his hand. The gesture was enough to give her courage. In the split second before she plummeted, Constance stretched her arm toward his, wishing she could catch those familiar fingers with her own.

And then she felt herself drawn upward, like a fish on a line.

I'm flying!

"Aaah!" She crashed into the bottom of the cage. It swung wildly, spinning on the chain that suspended it from the ceiling. She grabbed the bars, feet dangling, just as another arrow whistled by.

"Careful, girl!" Atreus roared, trying to steady himself against the violent rocking. "Now get this door open!"

Constance felt like a spider dangling from a broken web. She pulled herself up, doing her best to find a foothold but tilting the cage with her weight. Another arrow pinged against the bars and shattered.

"Make haste!" Atreus demanded.

The lock was old, but she still had to brace herself before even vampire strength could tear open the door. Finally, Constance slid one foot between the bars, grasped the bars of the door, and hauled with all her strength. She had possessed more than human strength before fully Turning, but now she could feel added power. On the other side, Atreus drove his shoulder against the lock.

The door flew off, nearly taking her with it. She let go, sending it spinning to the courtyard below. It landed on someone aiming his sword at Mac. *Good.*

Atreus grabbed her arm and dragged her inside the cage. The space was just large enough for them to crouch side by side. It felt weirdly familiar to be so close to her old master, surrounded by the scent of incense that always clung to him, hearing the rustle of his robes. Constance studied his face. His eyes were clearer than they had been for months. The madness seemed to have retreated like an outgoing tide—but Atreus could be convincing if there was something he wanted. She didn't trust this sudden return of sanity.

"Why are you up here?" Constance asked.

"Bran is in league with Miru-kai."

Constance caught her breath at the name of her master's old enemy.

"They put me here so that I would be forced to watch them murder my boy. And they call me insane. But the jest is on them. Look." Atreus pointed. "Your demon draws the guardsmen away from Sylvius. He is clever."

Mac! "What are you going to do?"

Atreus held up his hands. The silver chains bound his wrists with thick cuffs, then wound around one of the bars of the cage. "I can do nothing chained here like a parrot to his perch. Ah, they tricked me with bowing and fine speeches, and like a fool I listened to their poisoned words."

Constance grabbed the links, meaning to tear them apart.

"You can't do that. They're cast from silver. We'll need the key."

"The key?"

He placed one long finger on her chin. "You took it. You shed your blood on my box. It always tells me who steals my treasures."

Constance met his eyes, shame flooding her body. "I confess I did it, but Mac has the key. He used it to unlock Sylvius's chains."

Atreus let his hand drop. "The key is the only tool in the Castle that can circumvent silver chains. Then the guardsmen have it, I am trapped, and all is lost."

I won't believe that! Gritting her teeth, Constance reached over, grabbed the bar that held the chains, and yanked it from its moorings. "Then we cheat."

Mac surrendered to his demon. He meant to turn to dust.

Instead, he burst into flame.

Bran reeled back, shock blanking his expression. Mac levered himself up, grabbing the sword someone had dropped when the door to Atreus's cage fell from the ceiling. Flames licked down the length of the blade, making it one with Mac's hand.

Then his mind went empty. All his demon was meant for, designed for, was to fight.

He took a step forward, and it became a killing dance. Suddenly, his body was immune to pain, immune to the fatigue of carrying Reynard, to blood loss, to the knowledge that he was one against the entire force of guards.

With a sweep of the sword, Bran was dead, his reactions too slowed by the euphoria of Sylvius's blood to even block Mac's blow. And then the sorcerer leading the ritual. Wherever the sword touched, flames burrowed, their searing, intimate touch making sure no healing followed. Blood puddled where they fell. The others fell back.

Mac followed, and then flames followed as he scythed through his attackers. He was pure demon. He didn't feel joy, revulsion, elation, or pity—just satisfaction, like a thirst finally quenched. It was the pure poetry of combat, violence stripped of excuses. No honor. No grudges. Just the killing act.

Perhaps this was what Reynard had meant when he said Mac's demon would eventually get the upper hand. He *was* fire. Brutal Cleansing. Mac gave the spell to restore the Avatar many deaths to feed on, fulfilling the words that he himself had spoken at the council.

Conscious only of cut and thrust, of the geometry of the sword, Mac moved around and around the pack of guardsmen. It seemed to swell only to have him mow through it again. That was fine with Mac. To the demon, one guard was much like the next.

The smart ones went looking for weapons that could be used from a distance. An arrow nicked him. The two he had already taken were slowing him down. He could feel his own blood beneath his shoes, slippery, treacherous. Though he felt no weakness or pain, his injuries were still taking their toll.

Invincibility, even in a demon, is illusion. There is always a way to die.

The whole place stank of magic from the pond. It was growing thicker by the moment, egging him on, feeding his killing trance. Only his darker side remained, burning to sear away every trace of the guardsmen and their ritual.

Even swallowed up by the demon, Mac tried to protect the one he loved and the ones she loved. Though many fell, Sylvius remained safe, untouched, and secure.

But in the end, there were too many enemies, even for a warrior made of fire. Already wounded, bleeding out, his energy consumed by bright flames, Mac couldn't watch everywhere at once.

Death surprised Mac for the moment it took him to die.

Constance tore the bar from the cage and let it drop, as she had the door, on an advancing guardsman. The links that bound the cuffs together dangled free with a sinuous, snakelike motion.

Atreus stretched out his arms, testing the play of the chain. "Brave, Constance, but it is still not enough."

"What do I need to do?"

"Silver drains my power and defies your strength."

She'd heard that part already. She grabbed his wrist, twisting the cuff around so she could see how it closed. "I have a knife. Maybe I can pick the lock."

"That would take time."

Constance glanced down. Sylvius had crawled away and was hiding beneath the scaffold, away from trampling feet. With a sick lurch, she saw the trail of blood he had left in his wake.

Then she nearly fell out between the gap-toothed bars.

Horror and wonderment hit her like strong liquor, forcing her to grab the cage for support.

Mac had become a creature of fire. A halo of pale flames covered him like a second skin, moving and swirling as he fought. She watched him dodge and thrust, his big, strong body lithe and quick as the blaze itself. *Mac, what have you done?*

"He has become his demon, a perfect killer," Atreus said, answering her silent question.

No. The man I love is still in there. And if he was going to stay in one piece, the battle had to end. Now. There were too many guards for even a demon to fight.

There was no doubt he needed Atreus's help.

Defiantly, Constance slid her thin fingers beneath the rim of the silver cuff, pulling the hinges apart. The edges of the silver cut into her skin, coating the metal with slick blood. Her grip slid.

"This is useless," Atreus snapped. "If these shackles could be so easily bent, no one would bother making silver chains!"

"Let me try!" she snarled back. She resettled her grip, closed her eyes, and threw all the force of her vampire strength behind it. *Please! Please!*

She strained, ducking her head and using her shoulders. The hinge pin snapped, allowing the cuff to bend. Atreus pulled his arm out of her bloodied fingers and ripped at the metal.

"Huh," he said, clearly annoyed she'd proved him wrong. Immediately, he brightened. "This silver can't be pure. Of course you can get the better of it, my girl!" One hand now free, he held out the other, his black eyes bright as stars. "Break the other. Bless you for claiming your vampire blood, Constance, you've saved us."

Now filled with confidence, she had the second cuff off in a moment. Atreus hurled the chains out of the cage, stretching out his arms in triumph. Constance felt the rush of his gathering power. It seemed to swirl around them, whistling through the bars as it gained speed.

Sylvius, Mac, we're coming!

She moved to jump out from where the door had been and launch herself down below, but Atreus caught her sleeve. "Stay one moment," he said, barely turning his head. "It's safer here."

Constance stiffened, something in his words sounding ominous. "What do you mean?"

His attention was fixed on the knot of guardsmen below, Mac burning bright among them. "The guards will never touch my son again."

He rose to one knee, leaning out of the cage. The whoosh of energy grew to a cyclone, rife with a mad, restless energy so like Atreus himself.

Constance had wanted the sorcerer to help. Now she was suddenly terrified. *I used my powers to free him. Did I make a terrible mistake?*

"Stop!" she cried, but the word died in the sudden absence of air.

White lightning filled the cavernous hall, nowhere and everywhere at once. It flicked like the tongue of a serpent, touching pillars, the scaffold, the balcony where Constance had stood. She fell against the bars, flinging her arm over her eyes, praying Atreus could keep it from the metal cage.

Thunder cracked, shaking her through and through, rattling dust from the ceiling. She bit her tongue, the taste of blood confused with the smell of hot stone and the crisp tang of storms.

Atreus stood at the very edge of the cage door, conducting a rising wind as if it were a band of musicians. Blinded by tears from the brightness, Constance barely blinked her vision clear in time to see the lightning gather itself into a bright, throbbing glow, a single ball poised above the battle below. Her eyes sought Mac in the confusion of milling bodies.

All the guardsmen, including Mac, battled directly below the burning globe of energy

"No!" she cried, grabbing at Atreus. "You'll kill them all! You'll kill Mac! You might kill Sylvius."

But her words were lost in the funnel of wind that held

the ball poised on a cushion of air. Anger rushed through her like Mac's red-hot fire. Atreus was laughing. Constance jerked the sorcerer's arm hard, forcing his attention to her. She had only seconds to make him stop.

Atreus wheeled, unable to resist her new strength, and missed his footing. He stepped onto thin air. His mouth opened as if to speak, his eyes holding Constance's in a blank stare of surprise. Another time, he could have saved himself, but all his power was in the storm.

All his power was bent on killing.

She had to stop him. But maybe she already had, deep in her heart. She didn't reach for him, couldn't bring herself to grab his hand.

He had reached out to her, but only so that she could free him to massacre the men below. Enough was enough.

In that instant, Atreus's power speared downward and dragged Atreus with it. He fell like a wind-tossed scrap of paper, drifting, spinning down through the stone cavern to the cruel rock below.

Magic was hanging all around Mac, like fog. Part of him had been aware it had been there all along, growing stronger as he'd been fighting. Now it clogged his mind. Memories from the past few hours flickered, but refused to coalesce. Lightning. Blood. Fire. Pain.

He shook his head to clear it. It helped a little. Enough to notice where he was.

He was sitting in the front row of one of the balconies, looking down at the chaos below. He seemed okay. Unhurt. Even his clothes were clean and unwrinkled.

For some reason that made him afraid.

"Thank you for putting me back,"

He whipped his head around, half jumping to his feet.

A woman was sitting next to him, her legs crossed casually under long skirts made of some gauzy rainbow-colored fabric. Mac's first thoughts were of Renaissance fairies and organic gardening. She looked the tofu type, with one of those ageless faces and long, long straight hair.

She seemed familiar.

He looked harder. There was something about her that was hard to see, as if his eyes kept trying to shift away. He had to force himself to study her face. Black eyes. Hair so pale it looked silver. And then it clicked. She had Sylvius's features.

The Avatar.

"You're back in the Castle," Mac said.

"I am the Castle," she replied. Her voice was husky and low. She folded her hands in her lap. The bangles on her wrists—gold, silver, copper, and metals he couldn't name— jingled as she moved. "You see me as Atreus made me, but in truth I have no physical form."

It made sense. Witches built sentient houses. The Castle was just a big house, conscious in much the same way. The Avatar was its sentience. More complex, more powerful, but the principle was the same.

"Very good," she said, even though he hadn't spoken a word.

"If you're here, is Sylvius all right?"

"He will be fine."

Mac didn't want to look away from the Avatar, but he looked down over the balcony railing, anyway. He wanted to check on Connie, but couldn't find her in the milling crowd below.

"She is unhurt," the Avatar said.

Mac looked up, mildly irritated. He felt a beat behind the conversation.

"You want to know why you were involved in this battle," the Avatar said, making it a statement.

"That would be nice."

"It is a very mortal need. Why is so important to the short-lived. The simple answer is that I needed your strength."

"And the longer and more satisfying answer?"

The Avatar shifted, her bracelets making a clinking sound. "The Castle—I—was failing. Sylvius had just come into his powers and was old enough to release me without suffering harm himself. You were there, and your demon was in a mutable state."

"So it was you who changed me?"

"I took your dormant infection and made it active again. I switched you from a soul eater to a fire demon. Fire demons are much more useful for raising power, and I needed power to complete the spell."

Mac's mood went black. "So the time was right and I was convenient. That's it."

The Avatar gave a half smile. "I knew you were the one the moment you spared Bran's life, right before you met Constance. There is a line you will not cross, one that keeps you from surrendering to darkness. You are someone who has a will to help others. You held on to that despite how the demon changed you. No other demon would risk death to save a teenage incubus from a roomful of guardsmen and sorcerers. Everything you are or ever have been destined you to save me and those who dwell here."

That sounded a lot like the hellhounds' prophecy. Lore had been right. "You mean I was just a pawn of destiny?" he said dryly.

"There is always free will. You could have not saved us. You could have let us all perish."

"But instead I did my bit."

"And I appreciate it," she added.

"Good to know. So you got your spell. Can I go home now?"

She looked perplexed. "Home? You're a wandering spirit."

Mac began to feel sick. "Spirit?"

"You gave your life so that I could be free."

A wave of desperation surged through him. He was dead. He couldn't be dead. He slapped a hand to his chest, but he felt real enough. The bench felt hard and uncomfortable beneath him.

"You feel what you expect to feel," said the Avatar. "Just as you see me because your mind needs an image to talk to."

Mac licked his lips. Or thought he did. Whatever. "You

said Sylvius is all right. How come he got to live and I
didn't?"

"Sylvius was two beings in one. Me, and his father's son.
There's only one of you."

Mac looked over the railing again, trying to catch a
glimpse of the kid. He caught sight of Connie instead. She
was leaning on Caravelli, starting to sob. *She's found out.*
She knows I'm gone. That should be me holding her.

"But you can't." The Avatar sounded vaguely perplexed,
as if he were being slow. She didn't look so relaxed now.

Mac swiveled to face her. "Look, you turned me into a
monster. A killing machine. I did terrible things to fulfill
your spell. Soul-destroying things."

"That's true." She didn't sound very worried about it.

"You owe me for that. You turned me into a murderous
monster."

She leaned forward, not exactly angry but definitely intense. "Yes, as part of the spell to restore me, you killed
a great many guardsmen. You paid for those deaths with
your own life. Isn't that atonement enough? And wasn't it
in a good cause?"

Mac didn't say anything more. *How do I argue with a*
pile of stone?

The Avatar put a hand on his knee. It felt cold, heavier
than a woman's hand should have been. "Very well. You
died in my service. I acknowledge my debt to you. What
would you have me do? Do you wish to return to your
human life?"

Mac lifted his head.

"Can you do that?" Mac heard the hope in his voice.
Hope for everything he'd lost—his job, his family, his
friends. He could see himself back at his desk, dirty coffee
cup and files and more work than was humanly possible to
accomplish stacked before him. It looked like heaven.

And there was more. He could keep October morn-
ings. The smell of coffee. Dogs. Going for a run in the rain.
He wouldn't have to die, a wisp of nothing fading into the
dark.

The Avatar gave an apologetic smile. "It is difficult to remove a demon symbiont from its host. It is harder still to keep that infection from returning. I would have to set safeguards in place to limit your contact with the supernatural world. If you were human again, my doors would be closed to you. You would find the supernatural community outside your reach."

On first hearing, it sounded like a small price to pay. Mac looked out over the cavernous gloom, the small figures below lit by the fire from the lake. It was a macabre scene, like something from a medieval painting of hell.

Then he felt the Castle's words like lights going out in his heart, one by one. No supernatural community meant no Holly. No Caravelli, or Lore, or Sylvius. He could have his old life, but it would be without those friends who had been there for him, demon or not. Worst and most terrible: No Connie. He would be doomed to live without her love.

Mac felt his limbs growing cold. Was that death, or just sadness?

"Does a human life not please you?" asked the Avatar.

"Is there a door number two? One where I get to be a white hat?"

She sat back, turning the bracelets around and around her wrists. The long, pale hair fell over her face, and she was silent for so long Mac thought she had lost interest in him.

Mac slouched against the balcony rail, looking out over the cavern. When the Avatar spoke, he jumped. His thoughts had wandered away—down to Connie, and Holly, and all those who had fought beside him that day.

"Then would you serve me?" she asked. "You were a guardsman in your old life."

"I dunno. Doesn't sound like your guards are all that happy."

"They fell into despair because I was gone. In truth, it was my absence that killed them. Not your sword or Atreus's mad spell of fire."

Mac turned to face her. She sat, looking up at him. Her expression was earnest.

"I want to make amends." She lifted a hand, and let it fall with a jingle. "The few guards that remain are good men, but they're lost. They need someone to lead them. Someone stronger than they are, like a demon."

Mac's heart sank. "Demons destroy. We've been down that road already."

"I'll make you the demon with the badge that helps people."

"That makes no sense." He could feel despair seeping into him, cold and gray.

"Yes, it does. It was as a demon that you looked after Constance, and loved her, and gave her the strength to grow into her own power. She's her own woman now, servant to no one. You rescued her son, twice. You carried Reynard to safety. You put the events in motion that saved Lore's people. You have high ideals, and the demon gave you the physical strength to live up to your own standards. The creatures of the Castle need human compassion, but in a form that matches their own."

"I surrendered to the fire demon. I slaughtered your men because I couldn't control it. Why would those guardsmen who are left follow me?"

"They will know you by how you lead them. You know how such men work far better than I do. You're one of them."

"I think they'll complain if I burn them to crispy critters."

"I will give you mastery over your demon nature. It is something you would have developed in time, anyway. It takes practice to harness your powers. Isn't that what you told Constance?"

"Then I get some control on the heat thing?"

"Of course."

Mac rallied, his spirits rising despite himself. "And none of this no-eating crap. I keep my appetites, thank you very much. In fact, you should have more repression-free zones like the Summer Room. It's healthier that way for everybody. Maybe if people get to let off steam now and again, they'll stop hunting the incubi like truffles."

The Avatar blinked, looking taken aback. "That would be up to you."

Mac froze. "Up to me?"

She waved a hand, taking in the entire cavern. "I must regenerate rivers and forests, a sky and stars. That's a lot to look after." She shrugged. "I'll have to leave a lot of the smaller details up to you."

"You actually need me," said Mac, surprise bubbling through him.

The Avatar nodded. "Yes, Conall Macmillan. And this time I'm asking your permission. Will you help me become the beautiful place I once was? Will you look after my people?"

Mac thought about Reynard and the guards, the warlords and the smugglers, and all the downtrodden of the Castle. It was more than an army of social service agencies could ever hope to clean up, and he was proposing to do it on his own.

"Hell, yes." And then he laughed.

Cleaning up the street was exactly the kind of work that got Mac up in the morning. Besides, he wouldn't be on his own. He had friends, and there were folks in Fairview who cared about what happened behind the Castle door. They'd proved that today.

Most of all, there was Connie. If ever there was a girl worth being resurrected for, she was the one.

"I'll do it."

The Avatar smiled, and it was like the sunrise. "Good."

"Just a few more things before we shake hands...."

The Castle laughed, sounding very much like a lovely woman. "Of course there are. But just remember that the only thing that matters is the joy that gives you life."

Chapter 29

Suddenly, Mac was standing in front of the Empire Hotel. From the looks of things, it was early evening, the street still full of cars and people. *What am I doing here?* It was an interesting choice of locations for his resurrection. He guessed the Castle had some fine-tuning issues, but whatever. For a newly restored Avatar, he supposed it could be worse.

What do I know? He was grateful to be alive, too grateful to even think about the alternatives—death, or eternity as a ghost. *Crap.* That was one mental road he refused to go down. Not until he had time for a proper mental breakdown.

Which was never.

Leaning against the wall, he looked around. People were walking by, talking on cell phones, holding hands, absorbed in their evening plans. Car radios. Conversations. The bleed of jazz from inside the pub. Fairview was noisy.

Mac had missed that. The Castle was so damned quiet. Lore had said something about hooking up TV and radio reception. He was going to have to talk to him about that.

Mac jogged around the corner to the alley. It was jammed with people. It looked like the word of the hellhound exodus had spread and every supernatural citizen in Fairview had shown up to gawk. Quite a few seemed to actually be helping. He recognized the waiter—what was his name? Joe?—from the pub. He was passing out coffee and pastries to the volunteers.

Mac slipped through the crowd to see what was happening at the door. Ashe Carver was sitting on the ground, Reynard's head in her lap. *Good. They made it out okay.*

She had one hand on Reynard's forehead, lightly resting there. It looked like they had both received medical care—probably from a fey healer or a witch. Reynard was zonked out, but his injuries looked far better than they should have.

Still, in Mac's book, Reynard should have been in a hospital, but that was impossible. Guardsmen could leave the Castle for only hours at a time—just long enough to retrieve an escaped inmate. So, after several hundred years of dedicated service, the captain was lying in a dirty alley instead of a proper ward.

No wonder the guards went rogue.

Things were going to change. Mac started a mental list.

He paused to get details from Ashe, but then Caravelli burst out the door, his sword—oddly crumpled—in one hand and a hellhound child in his other arm. "Goddamned dragon!"

Mac couldn't suppress a snicker. The kid ruined the whole Prince of Darkness image.

"What happened?" said Ashe, craning her neck to look up at him.

"It came back. It took one look at the fire pond and did a belly flop right in the middle."

"It killed itself?" Ashe said, her voice going up an octave.

He passed off the child to one of the hound women. The little girl must have been lost, because they looked very, very happy to see her.

"No, the dragon likes it." Caravelli made a dramatic face. "It's wallowing in it like a big, fire-breathing pig, rolling around in sheer bliss. Nobody can get through there.

We've had to detour the second group of hounds through the balconies."

"Leave it there for now," said Mac.

It was clear the vampire, on some level, was enjoying himself. The hellhounds were looking at him like he was the Second Coming.

"We'll leave the dragon there for now," Caravelli said, still looking directly at Ashe. "We've got it surrounded in case it tries to move."

"How are we going to get it back where it belongs?" she asked.

"Caravelli?" Mac said.

The vampire ignored him. "It looks like the tunnels that vanished are opening up again. Maybe by tomorrow we can convince it to go home."

This is weird. "Caravelli?" Mac waved his hand in front of the vampire's face. No reaction. Then he waved his hand *through* Caravelli.

Outrage slammed through him. *I'm still a ghost!* This was a disaster. Mac looked frantically around. *Okay, everybody here is supernatural. Surely somebody is psychic.* He didn't see Holly anywhere.

And he hadn't seen Constance. He turned around again, looking everywhere for her small, dark form. Lore was sitting with Sylvius on some overturned crates, one hand around his friend's shoulders. Mac ran over to them. "Hey, can you see me?" He snapped his fingers under the hellhound's nose. "Yo, Fido!"

Nothing.

Mac stopped, caught short by the stricken set of Sylvius's body. He was curled over, his head nearly on his knees. The first thing he noticed was that the kid wasn't hurt anymore. No blood. No wounds. Even his color was good.

"You'll be okay," Lore said. "I have faith. So should you."

Mac nearly missed Sylvius's answer, it was so quiet. "But Macmillan died! So many did. And what's going to happen to me now?"

"You'll do what you must."

Which was true, but clearly not what Sylvius wanted to hear.

"I'm not who I was. The Avatar took back the part of me that was her." Sylvius raised his head. "What's left?"

With a shock of surprise, Mac understood. Sylvius was a young man. No wings. With the silver hair and black eyes, he was striking to look at, but he was human—or humanish—like his father.

What was a teenage ex-love god going to do when he finally discovered the twenty-first century? If ever there was a need for adult supervision, this was it.

Mac spun on his heel, hurrying into the Castle. He had to fix this invisibility problem pronto—but first he had to see with his own eyes that Constance was all right.

When the worst was over— and that had gone on and on, with battle and injury and death—Constance went back to the Summer Room. She needed solitude, if just for a minute or two.

I should be with Sylvius. He needed her. But they'd grieved together for hours. She had nothing left. If she could only gather her strength and fumble the pieces of her heart together—then, maybe, she could help someone else.

The Summer Room was just as she had left it, violated and broken. It had become her home—the home she had ached and longed for—and it was destroyed. *Like everything else.* Crying felt useless. She'd already sobbed until her ribs ached. There had been so much to cry about—but weeping did no good. It changed nothing.

Atreus had finally found respite from his madness. Someday she would find the energy to wonder whether his madness was guilt at what he had done to the Avatar, or if his love for the Avatar had been the result of insanity. Right now, all that mattered was that he had destroyed, and destroyed, until he finally destroyed himself.

She had been, in the drama of the great Atreus of Muria,

what they called collateral damage. After two and a half centuries of service, her master had destroyed her world without a thought for her happiness. And not just hers. If she had let him go at the end, it was only to stop the carnage yet to come.

She was done with masters.

Her servant's tale was so small, it could be written on a handkerchief.

A man had loved her. He had loved her despite her human weakness and her vampire strength, her innocence and her bloodlust. He'd kept coming back despite the fact that she asked him to lay down his life for a child not his own.

And then he died, and left her.

Mac was dead.

It was her fault.

Events had followed, one after the other, like a string of beads, and it all led back to her. Lore had warned her about wanting her vampire powers, but she had fallen prey to temptation. The first time she had really used those powers, she had released Atreus. He had killed Mac.

And she was left empty of all but a stunned, silent grief.

She fell onto the sofa, trying not to see the splintered wound left by Bran's sword. She could feel the shards of wood under her hand, digging through the cotton of Holly's skirt. Constance put her hands over her face, hiding from the candlelight. Bran might have broken all the furniture, but the magic candles still burned on, their length never altering one bit.

All the wrong things seemed to go on forever.

Cold air wafted through the room. With the door caved in, there was nothing to stop the unpredictable Castle breezes. Connie shivered, mourning Mac's heat. Mourning Mac.

The cold came again, more acute now. She shuddered, somehow finding enough will to get up and drape one of the tapestries across the door.

Connie?

She started, looking around. She had heard Mac's voice, but there was no one, nothing in the room but her. *Grief is driving me mad.*

"Connie!"

Astonishing. Mac's voice was coming from the candlestick next to the hearth.

Constance sighed. Well, all right. Everyone else in the Castle seemed to have lost their minds—Viktor and Atreus, for instance. Now it was her turn. She sat back down on the sofa.

"Connie."

She gasped, shrinking back. That had come from right in front of her face!

The light flickered, all the candles guttering. Slowly, slowly, Mac emerged into view, leaning over the sofa to stare down at her.

"I can see right through you," she whispered.

"So my mother always said."

His voice caressed her, a wave of tiny shocks that brought her feelings back to life. After such sudden loss, her relief was beyond description.

And then he was gone. "Mac?" She was clearly losing her mind.

A cold breeze stirred the room, making her shiver. Then she felt his lips, soft and hard at once, familiar and warm. Not burning now, but still filled with all the heat of a man reunited with his mate.

And he was there again, bending down to hold her, a filmy shadow of himself. Constance held very still, seeking only with her mouth, connecting again and again. She drank him in, closing her eyes, tasting his smoky, spicy flavor. Eyes shut, she could imagine him fully there, his big, hot body curling around her, cherishing her, giving her back the life she had lost. Forgetting that, no, he was only madness, or a ghost, or a memory, she reached up with one hand to cup his cheek. First her fingers touched only warmth, a tingle that somehow resolved into the rough, whiskered angle of his jaw.

She let her eyes flicker open. "Mac?"

His hand was on her arm, solid, warm, and heavy. His dark eyes were laughing, as if he were playing the most wonderful joke. "The Avatar said the only thing that matters is the joy that gives me life. Who knew she meant it literally?"

Constance felt her mouth drift open. He was laughing. A sudden hot wave of emotion erupted. "What do you think you're doing to me?" She jumped to her feet, nearly bumping his chin. "Do you think this is a jest?"

He fell back a step, his eyes round and wide at her temper. For a moment, she saw the boy he must have been. He opened and closed his mouth, obviously groping for something to say. "I came back from the dead for you, sweetheart."

Constance burst into tears. "You could have told me you were going to do that!"

"Oh, it was just a setback," he said, taking her in his arms. "I would have called, but y'know, reception sucks in here."

"What the bloody hell are you talking about?" she muttered into his chest, absolutely dizzy with the wonderful, warm feel of him. He wasn't too hot. Just toasty-right, warming her through and through.

He hugged her. "It's a long story, but I'll be here to tell it."

She sniffed. "You died and it was my fault."

He chuckled, looking over the top of her head. "How do you figure that?"

She pushed him away. "I set Atreus free. And then he killed you. And then he fell."

He sobered. "It wasn't your fault that he was crazy, and letting him go might well have saved us all. I think his magic thunderbolt gave a helluva boost to the Avatar's spell, plus it did stop the battle."

Constance put her hand to his cheek. "How are you here? I saw . . ."

"I made a deal with the Castle. I'm part of it now. I gained a lot of control over my powers, and I, uh . . ." He paused. "I got a job here. I mean, I can come and go, but this is it for me. I'm home."

"Like the guardsmen?"

"No, I'm better off than they are by a long shot."

"A job?"

Mac shrugged. "Kind of part-cop, part-gamekeeper, part-troubleshooter. The Avatar needs a go-to guy to keep the place running. Someone to do the day-to-day work."

"And you don't mind?"

"Strange as this sounds, I think it might be my dream job."

She lowered her head, her hands still wrapped in the thick fabric of his sweater. "Was that the only reason you came back?"

She could hear the smile in his words. "Why do you think? I love you. Besides, you brought me back to life with a kiss. After something like that, a guy's gotta stick around."

Constance looked up into his face, touching his cheek, his arm, his hair, convincing herself he was there. He didn't move, just let her reassure her senses, a trace of demon red in his dark, laughing eyes.

Finally, he reached down, scooping her up in his arms.

"I noticed something about being dead," he announced, striding across the room.

"What?"

"It made me want to make sure I'm alive. Good thing the bed's still in one piece."

She grabbed his arm as he set her on the bed. "How can you? There's a dragon. There are still hounds trying to find the door, and guardsmen and . . . nobody knows you're here!"

He shed his jacket, crawling onto the soft bed at the same time. "Y'know, with the new job and all, I think this might be the last peace and quiet I get for a while."

"Hmm." Constance reached up, linking her arms around his neck. "And so I get a part of you before the rest of the Castle gets their chance?"

"Sweetheart, all my parts are yours." He gave her a long, lingering kiss that left her aching in all the right places.

"I love you, Mac."

"Good." He slid his hand under her sweater, finding the soft mound of her breast. He squeezed it gently, bringing a groan to her throat. "Because I'm going to need you with me for a long, long time."

She reached up, running her fingers down his strong neck, down to the hollow of his throat. "I'm here. Always."

"Good." With a single, liquid movement, he pulled off his sweater, the muscles of his stomach and chest bunching as he moved.

"Saints above," Constance breathed.

Mac stopped, letting the sweater fall. "It's nothing you haven't seen before."

"Yes, it is."

He looked down, frowning. "What the hell?"

Constance sat up, her fingers hesitating as she touched the sworls of blue that covered his skin. "The Castle has marked you."

His only response was a hiss of breath. "Well, it said it would find a way to deal with the heat."

The designs that marked his skin were different from the guardsmen's tattoos. More elaborate, more striking. He was covered in flames, twined like the intricate designs of the Celtic heritage he shared with Constance. She touched her tongue to the knot work, tracing its line around his nipple, her fangs skimming over the tender nub. He shuddered, rising to his knees. She moved with him, undulating against his hard, broad body.

"Too many clothes," he rasped.

She popped the catch of her bra, letting it slide from her shoulders with a shrug. The look on his face made her smile.

It might have been a slightly evil smile. He hurriedly began unbuttoning his jeans.

Mac was a masterwork. The tattoos flowed thickly over his skin, parting like waves around his manhood. Constance traced them down his arms and legs, making each one her own with tongue and teeth. She explored each complex line down to the arches of his feet, the broad bones of his wrists, where each flame finally wound back on itself, lost in its own maze.

There were surprises in the design, touches of red and green and yellow, little treasures to discover. The pattern roamed over his strong calves, up the backs of his thighs, and over the mounds of his hard, muscular buttocks. Then it spread out, fanning from his waist over the expanse of his shoulders.

They took their time, shedding what was left of their clothes slowly, enjoying the luxury of the soft bed admidst the chaos of the room. Constance thought of an island or a magic carpet or a ship, safe and warm and theirs.

She mapped him utterly, finding the secrets of each knot and circle, and then he rolled her over, impatient for conquest. He pinned her wrists.

"I want it all," he murmured. "I want all of you."

His mouth was on her breasts, demanding, pulling, laving her to swollen, aching peaks. She hooked her legs around him, feeling his heat against the tender skin of her thighs. She wanted that heat inside, driving her to a scorching, explosive release. Making her feel alive.

She needed it. Now.

But he claimed her a piece at a time, her lips, her eyes, her shoulders, her navel, ensuring each surrender before the final assault. She squirmed, breaking beneath her desire, her fangs aching for his flesh, but he wouldn't let her bite.

When Mac finally did take her, he filled everything, demanded everything. She could keep nothing back against the urgent, pushing thrusts. Waves of contractions gripped her, drawing him deeper, breaking her apart until she spun away into nothing.

He finally let go with a roar.

And then she used her teeth, mounting him and lapping up the elixir of his spicy blood like an exotic treat. When the venom hit him, the cycle began—deliciously—again.

Mac made her vampire powers absolutely worth the price.

*   *   *

"We aren't ever going to grow old," said Mac much later, "and neither is this."

"Mmm," Connie murmured, thinking he looked especially good in blue, and rolled over, indulging in a long, feline stretch.

She caught her breath and stared from one side of the room to the other. The Summer Room was now a suite. The bed had shared space with a sitting area when she and Mac had begun their reunion. Now it was in a separate room, with two mahogany chests of drawers and a large mirrored wardrobe. She could see the sofa and chairs beyond, now sword-thrust free.

He looked up. "Ah, I ordered a few things when I was chatting with the Avatar."

Constance rolled off the bed, staggering a little as her legs remembered how to walk. "How did it do this?"

"Hey, if it can make whole caverns disappear, it can add a kitchen."

"Kitchen?"

"I like to cook." He opened the wardrobe and pulled out a fluffy white robe. "Put this on. You'll find some other clothes, too. Just some basics, until you can go shopping."

Constance took the robe, her mind spinning. "You thought to ask for all this?"

He shrugged. "I'm not a complete barbarian. I know how to pick out wall coverings."

The statement went oddly with the tattoos.

Never mind. She pulled on the robe, luxuriating in its plush feel, and walked silently into the sitting room. Much was as she remembered from before. The door was fixed, of course. The books and the carpet were the same. Her piles of magazines, and the candles. Lamps now, as well.

Mac followed her. He'd pulled on his jeans, but left his chest bare. He folded his arms, his feet planted apart, watching her admire their home.

Constance looked again, and again, her curiosity carrying her from room to room and back again. There was too much new to see all at once. A kitchen with cupboards and dishes and knives and forks and . . .

"That's a fridge," Mac said. "Apparently electricity is possible here, if you think to ask."

. . . and a beautiful dining area with eight chairs around a huge table and something he called a buffet but looked like a Welsh dresser to her. More dishes.

A bathroom with a large, white tub.

"And a Jacuzzi. I always wanted one of those. I mean, why not?"

And more rooms running off a hallway to the left. She couldn't even take those in yet.

A lot of it looked modern—Mac's idea of what a home should look like. It looked like the houses in her magazines, which made it all right with her. *She* was the mistress of this wonderful home. Constance Moore. The milkmaid.

She had a sudden urge to start dancing.

She kissed Mac until her head spun.

"I suppose I should go talk to the others. Let them know I'm back," he said, sounding a little regretful.

By then her attention was captivated by a curious, flat thing dominating the sitting room wall. Was it a dark mirror? A strange painting? She understood that art was very different now—not that she knew a thing about it in the first place, but still, this was odd. . . .

She looked at Mac, puzzled by the amusement in his eyes.

A quick grin. "Flat-screen TV."

Chapter 30

Holly got into the T-Bird, leaning her head against the seat. "Take me home, James. I want a bath."

Alessandro felt the same way. He'd lost track of when he'd last slept. They'd gotten all the hounds out at last. Holly had insisted on staying until every last one was housed for at least the next few days. The Empire Hotel had taken quite a few at no charge. Of course, most of the place was badly in need of repair, so it wasn't like they were losing income from paying guests. Good tax deduction there somewhere, he guessed.

Holly was eating one of the pastries the waiter from the Empire's pub had brought over, probably stale by now. "Y'know, this guy, Joe," she said around a mouthful. "He said he was Viktor's brother."

"The big weremutt?"

"Yeah, Constance obviously knew him. I thought she'd go into hysterics, she was so happy to see him."

"Hmm." Alessandro examined the parking ticket he'd just plucked out from under the windshield wiper. "Do you think city hall would take battling dragons as an excuse to waive a fine?"

"Ha-ha." Holly took another bite. "Joe—Josef—has quite the story. After what those two brothers have been through, I can see why the one decided to go doggie and not come back."

"Hmm." Alessandro shoved the ticket onto the dash, not interested in another story until he had had a good day's sleep. They'd been about to leave about an hour ago and then—surprise—the hero of the hour had strolled out of the Castle door looking like he'd eaten a canary, Constance on his arm.

After that, everyone wanted to call it a wrap. The adventure was over, for now. What could top Mac's death and resurrection? *Show-off.* Not that Alessandro wasn't happy to see him alive. He was growing fond of Mac in a strange way.

His mind jumped tracks, too tired to hold on to a thought. He glanced at Holly. "Did your sister talk to you? She was looking for you before she left for the night."

Holly barely managed to swallow before she yawned. "Yeah. We're having lunch tomorrow before she goes back to Spain to see Eden. She seems really happy about that. Hey, you two seemed to be getting along all of a sudden."

He wasn't going to jinx it by agreeing. "Good thing she's leaving in time so you can write your exams in peace."

Holly made a strangled noise. "Exams. Hellhounds. Family stuff. Everything always happens at once."

"Hmm."

They drove in silence for a few minutes.

"Holly." Alessandro gripped the steering wheel a little harder.

"Yeah?" She was still leaning against the seat, just rolling her head to look at him. The napkin from the pastry was crumpled tightly in her hand, the ends tucked carefully together. She knew crumbs in the car drove him crazy.

"Do you regret . . ." He trailed off, then made himself finish the sentence. "Ashe being here made me think—do you regret not having a family?"

Their house—her house—was coming into view.

"What makes you say that?"

Why do women always answer a question with a question? He pulled into the driveway and turned off the motor.

"Just wondered."

"It was something Ashe said, wasn't it?"

"No. We fought a dragon together. There wasn't exactly time to chat." He stared out the windshield, feeling caught. *Why did I bring this up?*

"She said I should come clean, so I figured she'd been talking."

"What do you mean by 'come clean'?"

He gave up staring and turned to look at her. Wind rustled in the hawthorn trees, the sound muffled by the car.

"Alessandro, I'm pregnant."

The bottom fell out of his world, sheared off by the short statement. "Oh."

"I didn't want to say anything to you until I was sure."

"Oh." It seemed the only sound he was capable of making. *Whose is it?*

He took a breath, feeling the slow, slow thud of his heart. Who knew words could hurt so much?

Why am I still existing?

She blinked. "You don't get it, do you?"

"I know how women get pregnant, Holly." The snarl in his voice scared him. Pure vampire. He got out of the car, his only thought to walk away.

She scrambled out her side. "It's yours. I know why you would wonder, but it is, I swear."

He froze, every muscle going still. "How?"

"You're my Chosen. That makes you, um, different in more ways than we expected." She gave a faint, apologetic smile. "I hope you don't mind. I wasn't really expecting it, either. It's not like we were, um, taking precautions."

Alessandro began to walk around the car toward her, giving himself the half dozen steps to process the information. Irrelevant thoughts flew through his head. There was rain in the wind. He'd left the upstairs light on. The cat would be hungry. His brain was ducking the issue.

I'm going to be a father?

Six centuries of existence, and he hadn't seen that one coming. Trust Holly to come up with the impossible. He stopped in front of her, looking down into her eyes. She looked so uncertain, it broke his heart.

She was still only a young woman. Vulnerable. She worked so hard, and now she was adding a family to her already-full plate. *I'll be there for you.*

"That's the best news I've ever had," he said, and meant it.

She took his hands, gripping them hard. "Thank you."

He raised her fingers to his lips. Grateful, but confused. He cleared his throat. "I don't know what . . ." *I don't know what to do.*

She smiled, heartbreakingly happy. "I'm just guessing, but it's probably going to be a witch like me. I mean, your DNA is still basically human, right?"

That made a nicer picture than a baby with fangs and a pint-sized sword. Still, that wasn't what he'd meant to ask. *What kind of a father will I make?*

She reached up, kissing him, giving herself entirely.

He kept his question to himself. He would be the best father in the world.

Because that's what her eyes told him he would be.

October 17, 11:00 p.m.
101.5 FM

"This is Errata at CSUP at the University of Fairview with a quick public service notice. Are you interested in an exciting career in law enforcement with a difference? Are you stimulated by the opportunity to work with a variety of nonhuman species in a challenging teamwork environment? If so, please apply with resume addressed to Conall Macmillan, care of the Empire Hotel."

Mac had guessed right about the new job. It kept him busier than a vampire at a blood drive, and he loved it.

He sat at the kitchen table doodling on his notepad—making lists, crossing things out. Troll fences. New mattresses for the guardsmen. Grow lights for the garden some of the kobolds wanted. And signage—everything needed signs in this place!

And that was just the caretaker stuff.

There were also problems like Miru-kai. The Prince had vanished the moment the battle had begun. There had been very few sightings of him since. That didn't mean they'd heard the last of old M.K. Top-notch villains didn't give up that easily.

Before Mac tackled the warlords—so far he'd counted eight that amounted to any real threat—he had to rebuild his forces. He was trying to recruit new guardsmen—with plenty of improvements to their conditions of employment—and find ways to help the old ones. There were discipline issues, policy and procedures, and that whole intangible element of institutional culture. It was a lot to fix, but he had to start somewhere. He'd start with the fence.

Connie sat across from him, reading *Wuthering Heights* for the third time. Novels had become her new passion, second only to a celebrity dance show she'd discovered on TV. And shopping. Now that she had some control over her hunger, she loved trips to Spookytown's boutiques with Holly. But every time she went out and no matter what else Connie bought, she came back with more books. He loved watching her discover all the possibilities the world held.

Mac didn't get the attraction of the literary brood fests like *Wuthering*, but whatever. He'd put up with her blow-by-blow analysis of Heathcliff and Cathy if she forgave him for introducing Sylvius to the joys of the outside world. Strictly supervised, of course.

It was almost working.

Most recently, Mac had bought Sylvius and Lore tickets to Sedona to see his old friends there. He was hoping Sylvius would stay for a while. He knew the New Agers wouldn't lead a first-time human too far astray. Besides, they'd always wanted an angel. Sylvius had lost his wings, but he was still a better candidate than Mac.

He hoped the kid liked tofu.

"Mac," Connie said, breaking his concentration.

He looked up from his list. "Yeah?"

"How do you feel about throwing a dinner party? It's something I've wanted to do for a long time. We could invite Holly and Alessandro and Reynard and that nice young werewolf Perry Baker and, well, whoever else you'd like."

"We can do that." That meant he'd be doing the cooking, but that had always been a hobby of his, so that was okay.

She reached across the table, touching his hand. "Thanks."

"Happy to oblige." Mac smiled, turning back to his list. She went back to her book.

"Not sure what to do about you vamps, though," he said. "It always feels weird with half the guests not eating."

She blushed faintly. She was still shy about the whole feeding issue. A few times a week she had to head into Fairview for a proper meal. All neatly arranged, of course, by her protective sire. "For us, it's the company that matters."

"More for the rest of us, I guess."

She looked over the top of her book, one eyebrow raised. "Are you going to work all night?"

He put down his pencil. "I'm done."

"What are you working on?"

"Just some wishful thinking."

"What about?"

He waved dismissively at the page. "Just goofing around."

"Let me see." Vampire-quick, she snatched the notepad to her side of the table and set Emily Brontë aside. "What is this?"

He chuckled. "Well, there're so many rules in a place like this, it would be a lot easier if they could be boiled down into a few simple principles. Short and sweet."

She giggled, a girlish sound he liked. "Oh, this is good. One: Don't frighten the humans. Two: Don't annoy the dragon. Three: Don't annoy Mac. Are you sure you don't want to put the last one on top?"

"Am I that hard to live with?"

She leaned over the table, bracing herself on her elbows. He glanced down a moment, well aware of the drape of her V-necked shirt. *Oh, yeah.*

"There should be a number four," she said, giving him that Mona Lisa smile.

He leaned forward, meeting her lips. "What's that?"

"Come to bed when I say so."

"Are you sure that one shouldn't be on top?"

"We can take turns being on top."

He felt the smile in her kiss, the laugh trembling on her tongue, and he knew who really ruled the Castle—or at least who really ruled him.

Oh, Snow White, you've come a long way.

Read on for a sneak peek of
Sharon Ashwood's next Dark Forgotten novel,

UNCHAINED

Coming from Signet Eclipse in July 2010

Reynard fell to his knees in the dirt beside Ashe. He put a hand on her shoulder—a hot, firm touch. "Are you hurt?"

"Get down!" she barked, dragging him to the ground by the collar of his fancy coat.

The next shot missed his head by a whisker.

She could smell his sweat, the dirt, and the tang of crushed plants. She'd landed in a herbaceous border, destroying the gardeners' careful work. A mound of thyme was bleeding spice into the night air.

She could hear the clock tower of the main building chiming eleven. She should have been home watching the late news, not chasing monsters around a botanical garden tourist trap. Wait, they'd bagged the monster. So why was someone still shooting at them?

Reynard gripped her arm. "Are you hurt?" he repeated.

"No." She turned to look at him, careful not to raise her head too far. "How about you?"

"No."

They lay still for a moment, breathing, listening to the dark spring night.

"Anyone trying to kill you these days?" she asked.

"Not outside the Castle."

His eyes glittered. It might have been humor. She couldn't quite tell. He was too closed, too different, like a map with no street names or landmarks. Just a lot of really nice geography.

Ashe swallowed hard, willing her jackhammer pulse to slow down. "Then the shooter must be after me."

"A common occurrence?"

"Not since I moved to Fairview." *Shit. Shit.* This was all supposed to be in the past. She had relocated, given up life on the road, scaled down the hunting to almost nothing—just the odd case. She'd let the word go out that she was retired. Sure, there'd always be some unhappy campers—friends and relatives of the supernatural monsters she'd exterminated—but even they'd grown quiet.

Quiet enough that Ashe had taken the risk of sending for her daughter.

Shit.

Ashe crawled backward, a slithering motion that brought her to the shadow of a thick bush. She rose into a crouch, molding her body to the shape of the greenery, hiding in the dense leaves. She guessed at the angle the bullets had traveled. That put the shooter high up the tall column of rock that formed the lookout in the center of the sunken garden. She knew there was a nearly vertical staircase that led up to the platform at the top, but it wasn't lit at night. All she could see was the dark spire of stone that blotted out the stars.

Reynard moved around to her left, noiseless as a phantom. Wisps of dark hair framed his face. His neck cloth had come untied. Ashe couldn't help notice that messy looked good on him.

He rested on one knee, raising the long musket. "Stay down," he said quietly. "I'll take care of this."

A sour burn of impatience caught in Ashe's throat. "There's no way to make the shot at this distance."

"No?"

"It's dark."

"I live in a dungeon. I've adapted to the dark." He

sighted down the long barrel as confidently as if it had one of the supercalifragilistic nightscopes Ashe had seen in the latest mercenary's mag.

They were wasting time. Firing would give away their position. They'd be better off sneaking up on the sniper. "That thing has a range of two feet. A crooked two feet."

He sighed lightly and cranked back the hammer. It was at that moment she saw it had a real, honest-to-Goddess flint secured in the jaws of the mechanism. This thing relied on sparks and naked gunpowder. They'd be lucky if it didn't blow up.

"They won't be expecting us to return fire," he said evenly.

"Because it's not possible! I have a real gun, and I can't make that shot."

Thoroughly ignoring her, Reynard pulled the trigger, jerking as the musket recoiled. It banged like a giant cap gun and smelled like a chemistry lab gone wrong. Ashe opened her mouth to protest and got a mouthful of foul-tasting smoke.

And there was a distant, sharp cry of pain. Reynard had hit his mark.

"That's not possible!" She realized she sounded annoyed.

He made a noise that was almost a laugh. "Just a touch of a spell. I thought witches were open to magic."

"I'm not a witch anymore."

He gave her a look, grabbed the musket, and slipped into the darkness. Swearing, Ashe ran to catch up. The entrance to the staircase was on the other side of the tall spire of rock, forcing them to circle its base. The colored lights that illuminated the flower beds dwindled, then stopped as soon as they left the footpath. Ashe tripped, nearly going down on one knee before she bumped into Reynard.

He steadied her, and she could feel the remnants of magic in his touch. She'd broken her own magic with an unwise spell when she was still a teenager, but that didn't mean she couldn't feel power.

She was picking up far more than the few traces cling-ing to Reynard's long, strong fingers. Right now she felt power spilling over her like sand in a windstorm, stinging in a thousand tiny bites. Whoever—whatever—had been shooting at them was hurt, and not human.

She thought again about her daughter, and knew fear.

Reynard took a step forward. Ashe grabbed his arm. "You had only one shot in your musket. I should go first."

He pulled what looked like a very modern Smith & Wesson—it was hard to tell in the dark—from a holster hidden at the small of his back. "I could reload. I also carry a backup. As Mac is so fond of saying, shit happens."

The obscenity sounded wrong coming from him. Of course, every assumption she'd made about him so far that night had been off base. Not a good thing when they were supposed to be covering each other's backs.

Reynard started up the stairs, showing just how good his night vision was. Ashe brought up the rear. There was an iron railing to her right, but that was her gun hand, so she left it alone. Her skin crawled, not just with power but with vertigo. Normally she didn't mind heights, but all that changed when she couldn't see where she was putting her feet. She felt for the steps and counted each one. Good to know how many steps she'd climbed in case she had to reverse course in a hurry. Thinking you were at the bot-tom of the pitch-dark stairs when you weren't could be a problem.

More plants and bushes grew on the rock spire. Leaves brushed her face like slick, green fingers. She fought not to jump, stumble, and finish the night with a broken leg.

They reached the landing, where the stairs took a sharp turn. Overhead was a wash of stars, thick and bright be-cause the gardens were outside the city. Above the canopy of trees, the moon gave a thin wash of light. Ashe saw Rey-nard hold up his left hand, then point. His right hand was curled around his weapon. Ashe grasped her own gun with both hands, reassured by its cold, heavy weight.

They went up the last dozen stairs. At the top was a

kidney-shaped platform surrounded by an iron railing. It was like another small garden. The flower bed, maple tree, and bench would have made for a lovely resting place in daylight. At night, it was eerie.

Reynard turned right and swept his gun downward to point at the fallen shooter. Ashe aimed at the figure sprawled facedown on the ground. He was twisted as if an effort to duck had spun him around.

Vampire. Now that she was close, Ashe could almost taste his essence. His energy was pouring needles of power over her like the skitter of insect feet on her skin. She glided to the left of the figure, Reynard to the right, until they stood on opposite sides of their quarry.

What happened next depended entirely on the vamp. Why had he shot at her? She wanted an explanation. She'd be happy to keep him alive—vibrantly undead?—at least long enough to question him. Longer if he played nice. Then again, he'd tried to kill her already. If he attacked, there'd be no messing around.

The vamp was male, medium height, dressed in jeans. A scatter of weapons and a tripod were strewn around him. She smelled blood, but saw only a shining stain on the back of his jacket. It was too dark for color. He was motionless, but still she kicked his rifle out of reach. It was a sniper's piece—night scope and all the fancy fixings.

"Weapon says he means business," she said softly.

"It seems your enemies put forward their best efforts," Reynard replied.

"I'm so flattered." Ashe took another quick inventory of the vamp. Short leather boots. The glint of a fancy watch. Dark hair, collar length. "Y'know, at first I wondered why someone would shoot from a place with only one escape route."

As she spoke, she shifted the Colt to her left hand and reached into the pocket that ran up the outside of her right thigh. Familiarity, certainty, washed through her. Slaying wasn't her happy place, but it was one she knew inside and out.

Ashe pulled out a long, straight, sharp stake. "Then it came to me. Vamps can fly. And then I thought of another thing. I was called out here on an emergency. How did an assassin know where I'd be? Somebody's been doing some planning, and I'm going to want names."

The vampire struck. The speed was breathtaking; he lifted himself from a facedown sprawl to a frontal attack in less than a second—but she'd been expecting that. Ashe felt the thing's body pound into the stake, using its own momentum to drive the weapon home. All she had to do was brace her feet against all that brute force and lean into it.

The vamp flailed its arms, trying to change direction and pull away, trying to slash and bite and escape all at once. She'd judged the vamp's height fairly well, but the stake had entered just below its heart. Ashe felt her feet skid on the stone beneath her, sliding far too close to the iron railing and the sheer drop beyond.

Reynard yelled, grabbing the vamp from behind. In a flash of moonlight, she could see the vampire's face—features twisted in pain and anger. Reynard was managing to pin its arms, something no human should have been able to do. That seemed to scare the monster even more than the stake.

Ashe twisted her weapon, driving upward. The vampire gasped. She stopped a hairsbreadth from skewering him, praying Reynard's strength would hold. She was taking a risk, pausing like this, but a chance at information was worth it.

"Why were you shooting at me?" she demanded.

It bared fangs, giving a rattling hiss.

"Scary, but I've seen better," she said.

Reynard did something that made the vampire wince. "Answer."

"Abomination!" it snarled, and gave one last lunge at her.

Last being the operative term. Ashe slammed the stake upward just before his fangs could reach her flesh.

The vampire was suddenly deadweight. Reynard let the body drop, wood still protruding from its chest.

"Shit." Ashe looked down at the vampire. She knew she

would feel plenty later—anger, triumph, regret, pity, self-justification—but at the moment she was blank. She'd done what she had to do. Once the adrenaline wore off, the rest could engulf her.

The vampire had called her an abomination. She had opened her mouth to comment on how strange that was, coming from a bloodsucking monster, but closed her mouth again. It was weird enough that she didn't want to even think about it. Besides, there were other, more pressing questions—such as why the vamp had chosen to die rather than talk.

It could be vengeance. It could be something else. Whatever it was, it was personal. That thought made her queasy.

"Are you all right?" Reynard asked.

"Yeah," Ashe said, keeping her voice light, impersonal. "He went down easily enough."

Reynard sat down on the bench, head bowed. Ashe looked away. He didn't look happy, but skewering the enemy wasn't a cheery kind of thing. But then again, you didn't get into this kind of work to talk about your feelings.

Ashe turned to lean on the railing. Below was the garden, bathed in starlight. A much better view than the vampire. The body had already started to shrivel. In about twenty minutes, it would be a pile of dust. It was as if time caught up with vamps, grinding them to nothing. Once he was gone, they would search his possessions for clues.

Above, the stars glittered like sequins on a torch singer's evening gown. Below, the gardens glowed like a fairy kingdom. It seemed distant and surreal, a pretty mirage she could look at but not touch. She was made from a different element—something dark and dangerous.

At some point along the way, when her parents died, or when her husband died, or maybe when she'd bagged her first monster, she'd let herself slide into the darkness. Now that her daughter was home, she had to snap out of it. Kids needed a bright, shiny world. Eden needed something besides a monster-slaying action figure for a mom. Too bad Ashe didn't know how to be anything else.

She would try. Goddess knew she would try. She would try to see the beauty in the world and look away from the shadows.

She heard Reynard shift on the bench behind her.

"You should come see the view," she said.

"No, thank you." His voice was quiet. The dark made it oddly intimate.

"Why not?"

He was silent for a few heartbeats. "I have to go back to the Castle."

"So?" She turned, leaning against the rail to face him.

He raised his head, but didn't meet her eyes. "Whatever I see out here will make me restless, and I don't have a choice about going back. It's best I see as little as possible."

There was so much regret in the words, it bruised her. Regret—that she knew. She could almost taste it like coppery blood on her tongue, sharp and familiar.

Now, finally, there was something about him that she understood.

And, Goddess help her, she suddenly wanted to fix it.